CHASING
THE DIME

MICHAEL CONNELLY

CHASING THE DIME

ORION

First published in Great Britain in 2002 by Orion,
an imprint of the Orion Publishing Group Ltd.

Copyright © Hieronymus, Inc. 2002

Published by arrangement with
Little, Brown and Company (Inc.),
New York, NY, USA

A CIP catalogue record for this book is
available from the British Library.

ISBN 0 75282 141 5 (hardback)
0 75285 590 5 (trade paperback)

Printed in Great Britain by
Clays Ltd, St Ives plc

The Orion Publishing Group Ltd
Orion House
5 Upper Saint Martin's Lane
London, WC2H 9EA

This is for Holly Wilkinson

CHASING
THE DIME

1

The voice on the phone was a whisper. It had a forceful, almost desperate quality to it.

Henry Pierce told the caller he had the wrong number. But the voice became insistent.

"Where is Lilly?" the man asked.

"I don't know," Pierce said. "I don't know anything about her."

"This is her number. It's on the site."

"No, you have the wrong number. There is no one named Lilly here. And I don't know anything about any site. Okay?"

The caller hung up without responding. Then Pierce hung up, annoyed. He had plugged in the new phone only fifteen minutes earlier and already he had gotten two calls for someone named Lilly.

He put the phone down on the floor and looked around the almost empty apartment. All he had was the black leather couch he sat on, the six boxes of clothes in the bedroom and the new phone. And now the phone was going to be a problem.

Nicole had kept everything — the furniture, the books, the CDs and the house on Amalfi Drive. She didn't keep it, actually: he had given it all to her. The price of his guilt for letting things slip away. The new apartment was nice. It was high luxury and security, a premier address in Santa Monica. But he was going to miss the house on Amalfi. And the woman who was still living in it.

He looked down at the phone on the beige carpet, wondering if he should call Nicole and let her know he had moved from the hotel to the apartment and had the new number. But then he shook his head. He had already sent her the e-mail with all the new information. To call her would be breaking the rules she had set and he had promised to follow on their last night together.

3

The phone rang. He leaned down and checked the caller ID screen this time. The call was coming from the Casa Del Mar again. It was the same guy. Pierce thought about letting it ring through to the message service that came with the new phone number, but then he picked up the phone and clicked the talk button.

"Look, man, I don't know what the problem is. You have the wrong number. There is nobody here named —"

The caller hung up without saying a word.

Pierce reached over to his backpack and pulled out the yellow pad on which his assistant had written down the voice mail instructions. Monica Purl had set up the phone service for him, as he had been too busy in the lab all week preparing for the following week's presentation. And because that was what personal assistants were for.

He tried to read the notes in the dying light of the day. The sun had just slipped beneath the Pacific and he had no lamps yet for the new apartment's living room. Most new places had sunken lights in the ceiling. Not this one. The apartments were newly renovated, with new kitchens and windows, but the building was old. And slab ceilings without internal wiring could not be renovated in a cost-effective way. Pierce didn't think about that when he rented the place. The bottom line was he needed lamps.

He quickly read through instructions on using the phone's caller ID and caller directory features. He saw that Monica had set him up with something called the convenience package — caller ID, caller directory, call waiting, call forwarding, call everything. And she noted on the page that she had already sent the new number out to his A-level e-mail list. There were almost eighty people on this list. People who he would want to be able to reach him at any time, almost all of them business associates or business associates he also considered friends.

Pierce pressed the talk button again and called the number Monica had listed for setting up and accessing his voice mail program. He then followed the instructions provided by an electronic voice for creating a pass code number. He decided on 92102 — the day Nicole had told him that their three-year relationship was over.

He decided not to record a personal greeting. He would rather hide behind the disembodied electronic voice that announced the number and instructed the caller to leave a message. It was impersonal, but it was an impersonal world out there. He didn't have time to make everything personal.

When he was finished setting up the program a new electronic voice told him he had nine messages. Pierce was surprised by the number — his phone had not been put into service until that morning — but immediately hopeful that maybe one was from Nicole. Maybe several. He suddenly envisioned himself returning all the furniture Monica had ordered for him online. He saw himself carrying the cardboard boxes of his clothes back inside the house on Amalfi Drive.

But none of the messages were from Nicole. None of them were from Pierce's associates or associates/friends, either. Only one was for him — a "welcome to the system" message delivered by the now familiar electronic voice.

The next eight messages were all for Lilly, no last name mentioned. The same woman he had already fielded three calls for. All the messages were from men. Most of them gave hotel names and numbers to call back. A few gave cell numbers or what they said was a private office line. A few mentioned getting her number off the net or the site, without being more specific.

Pierce erased each message after listening to it. He then turned the page on his notebook and wrote down the name Lilly. He underlined it while he thought about things. Lilly — whoever she was — had apparently stopped using the number. It had been dropped back into circulation by the phone company and then reassigned to him. Judging by the all-male caller list, the number of calls from hotels and the tone of trepidation and anticipation in the voices he had listened to, Pierce guessed that Lilly might be a prostitute. Or an escort, if there was a difference. He felt a little thrill of curiosity and intrigue go through him. Like he knew some secret he wasn't supposed to know. Like when he called up the security cameras on his screen at work and surreptitiously watched what was going on in the hallways and common areas of the office.

He wondered how long the phone number would have been out of use before it was reassigned to him. The number of calls to the line in one day indicated that the phone number was still out there — probably on the website mentioned in a few of the messages — and people still believed it was Lilly's valid number.

"Wrong number," he said out loud, though he rarely spoke to himself when he wasn't looking at a computer screen or engaged in an experiment in the lab.

He flipped the page back and looked at the information Monica had written down for him. She had included the phone company's customer service number. He could and should call to get the number changed. He also knew it would be an annoying inconvenience to have to resend and receive e-mail notifications correcting the number.

Something else made him hesitate about changing the number. He was intrigued. He admitted it to himself. Who was Lilly? Where was she? Why did she give up the telephone number but leave it on the website? There was a flaw in the logic flow there, and maybe that was what gripped him. How did she maintain her business if the website delivered the wrong number to the client base? The answer was that she didn't. She couldn't. Something was wrong and Pierce wanted to know what and why.

It was Friday evening. He decided to let things stand until Monday. He would call about changing the number then.

Pierce got up from the couch and walked through the empty living room to the master bedroom, where the six cardboard boxes of his clothing were lined against one wall and a sleeping bag was unrolled alongside another. Before moving into the apartment and needing it, he hadn't used the sleeping bag in almost three years — since a trip to Yosemite with Nicole. Back when he had time to do things, before the chase began, before his life became about only one thing.

He went onto the balcony and stared out at the cold blue ocean. He was twelve floors up. The view stretched from Venice on the south side to the ridge of the mountains sliding into the sea off Malibu to the north. The sun was gone but there were violent slashes of orange and purple still in the sky. This high up, the sea breeze was cold and bracing. He put his hands in the pockets of his pants. The fingers of his left hand closed around a coin and he brought it out. A dime. Another reminder of what his life had become.

The neon lights on the Ferris wheel on the Santa Monica Pier were on and flashing a repetitive pattern. It made him remember a time two years earlier when the company had rented the pier's entire amusement park for a private party celebrating the approval of the company's first batch of patents on molecular memory architecture. No tickets, no lines, no getting off a ride if you were having fun. He and Nicole had stayed in one of the open yellow gondolas of the Ferris wheel for at least a half hour. It had been cold that night, too, and they huddled against each other. They'd watched the sun go down. Now he couldn't look at the pier or even a sunset without thinking about her.

In acknowledging this about himself, he realized he had rented an apartment with views of the very things that would remind him of Nicole. There was a subliminal pathology there that he didn't want to explore.

He put the dime on his thumbnail and flipped it into the air. He watched it disappear into the darkness. There was a park below, a strip of green between the building and the beach. He had already noticed that homeless people snuck in at night and slept in sleeping bags under the trees. Maybe one of them would find the fallen dime.

The phone rang. He went back into the living room and saw the tiny LED screen glowing in the darkness. He picked up the phone and read the screen. The call was coming from the Century Plaza Hotel. He thought about it for two more rings and then answered without saying hello.

"Are you calling for Lilly?" he asked.

A long moment of silence went by but Pierce knew someone was there. He could hear television sounds in the background.

"Hello? Is this call for Lilly?"

Finally a man's voice answered.

"Yes, is she there?"

"She's not here at the moment. Can I ask how you got this number?"

"From the site."

"What site?"

The caller hung up. Pierce held the phone to his ear for a moment and then clicked it off. He walked across the room to return the phone to its cradle when it rang again. Pierce hit the talk button without looking at the caller ID display.

"You've got the wrong number," he said.

"Wait, Einstein, is that you?"

Pierce smiled. It wasn't a wrong number. He recognized the voice of Cody Zeller, one of the A-list recipients of his new number. Zeller often called him Einstein, one of the college nicknames Pierce still endured. Zeller was a friend first and a business associate second. He was a computer security consultant who had designed numerous systems for Pierce over the years as his company grew and moved to larger and larger spaces.

"Sorry, Code," Pierce said. "I thought you were somebody else. This new number is getting a lot of calls for somebody else."

"New number, new place, does this mean you're free, white and single again?"

"I guess so."

"Man, what happened with Nicki?"

"I don't know. I don't want to talk about it."

He knew talking about it with friends would add a permanency to the end of their relationship.

"I'll tell you what happened," Zeller said. "Too much time in the lab and not enough between the sheets. I warned you about that, man."

Zeller laughed. He'd always had a way of looking at a situation or set of facts and cutting away the bullshit. And his laughter told Pierce he was not overly sympathetic to his plight. Zeller was unmarried and Pierce could never remember him in a long-term relationship. As far back as college he promised Pierce and their friends he would never practice monogamy in his lifetime. He also knew the woman in question. In his capacity as a security expert he also handled online backgrounding of employment applicants and investors for Pierce. In that role he worked closely at times with Nicole James, the company's intelligence officer. Make that former intelligence officer.

"Yeah, I know," Pierce said, though he didn't want to talk about this with Zeller. "I should've listened."

"Well, maybe this means you'll be able to take your spoon out of retirement and meet me out at Zuma one of these mornings."

Zeller lived in Malibu and surfed every morning. It had been nearly ten years since Pierce had been a regular on the waves with him. In fact, he had not even taken his board with him when he moved out of the house on Amalfi. It was up on the rafters in the garage.

"I don't know, Code. I've still got the project, you know. I don't think my time is going to change much just because she —"

"That's right, she was only your fiancée, not the project."

"I don't mean it like that. I just don't think I'm —"

"What about tonight? I'll come down. We'll hit the town like the old days. Put on your black jeans, baby."

Zeller laughed in encouragement. Pierce didn't. There had never been old days like that. Pierce had never been a player. He was blue jeans, not black jeans. He'd always preferred to spend the night in the lab looking into a scanning tunneling microscope than pursuing sex in a club with an engine fueled by alcohol.

"I think I'm going to pass, man. I've got a lot of stuff to do and I need to go back to the lab tonight."

"Hank, man, you've got to give the molecules a rest. One night out. Come on, it will straighten you out, shake up your own molecules for once. You can tell me all about what happened with you and Nicki, and I'll pretend to feel sorry for you. I promise."

Zeller was the only one on the planet who called him Hank, a name Pierce hated. But Pierce was smart enough to know that telling Zeller to stop was out of the question, because it would prompt his friend to use the name at all times.

"Call me next time, all right?"

Zeller reluctantly backed off and Pierce promised to keep the next weekend open for a night out. He made no promises about surfing. They hung up and Pierce put the phone in its cradle. He picked up his backpack and headed for the apartment door.

2

Pierce used his scramble card to enter the garage attached to Amedeo Technologies and parked his 540 in his assigned space. The entrance to the building came open as he approached, the approval coming from the night man at the dais behind the double glass doors.

"Thanks, Rudolpho," Pierce said as he went by.

He used his electronic key to take the elevator to the third floor, where the administrative offices were located. He looked up at the camera in the corner and nodded, though he doubted Rudolpho was watching him. It was all being digitized and recorded for later. If ever needed.

In the third-floor hallway he worked the combo lock on his office door and went in.

"Lights," he said as he went behind his desk.

The overhead lights came on. He turned on his computer and entered the passwords after it booted up. He plugged in the phone line so he could quickly check his e-mail messages before going to work. It was 8 P.M. He liked working at night, having the lab to himself.

For security reasons he never left the computer on or attached to a phone line when he wasn't working on it. For the same reason he carried no cell phone, pager or personal digital assistant. Though he had one, he rarely carried a laptop computer, either. Pierce was paranoid by nature — just a gene splice away from schizophrenia, according to Nicole — but also a cautious and practical researcher. He knew that every time he plugged an outside line into his computer or opened a cellular transmission, it was as dangerous as sticking a needle into his arm or having sex with a stranger. You never knew what you might be bringing into the pipeline. For some people, that was probably part of the thrill of sex. But it wasn't part of the thrill of chasing the dime.

He had several messages but only three that he decided to read this night. The first was from Nicole and he opened it immediately, again with a hope in his heart that made him uncomfortable because it verged on being maudlin.

But the message was not what he was looking for. It was short, to the point and so professional that it was devoid of any reference to their ill-fated romance. Just a former employee's last sign-off before moving on to bigger and better things — in career and romance.

Hewlett,

I'm out of here.

Everything's in the files. (by the way, the Bronson deal finally hit the media — SJMN got it first. nothing new but you might want to check it out.)

Thanks for everything and good luck.

Nic

Pierce stared at the message for a long time. He noted that it had been sent at 4:55 P.M., just a few hours earlier. There was no sense in replying, because her e-mail address would have been wiped from the system at 5 P.M. when she turned in her scramble card. She was gone and there seemed to be nothing so permanent as being wiped from the system.

She had called him Hewlett and he wondered about that for a long moment. In the past she had used the name as an endearment. A secret name only a lover would use. It was based on his initials — HP, as in Hewlett-Packard, the huge computer manufacturer that these days was one of the Goliaths to Pierce's David. She always said it with a sweet smile in her voice. Only she could get away with nicknaming him with a competitor's name. But her using it in this final message, what did it mean? Was she smiling sweetly when she wrote this? Smiling sadly? Was she faltering, changing her mind about them? Was there still a chance, a hope of reconciliation?

Pierce had never been able to judge the motives of Nicole James.

He couldn't now. He put his hands back on the keyboard and saved the message, moving it to a file where he kept all her e-mails, going back the entire three years of their relationship. The history of their time together — good and bad, moving from co-workers to lovers — could be read in the messages. Almost a thousand messages from her. He knew keeping them was obsessive but it was a routine for him. He also had files for e-mail storage in regard to a number of his business relationships. The file for Nicole had started out that way, but then they moved from business associates to what he thought would be partners in life.

He scrolled through the e-mail list in the Nicole James file, reading the captions in the subject lines the way a man might look through photos of an old girlfriend. He outright smiled at a few of them. Nicole was always the master of the witty or sarcastic subject line. Later — by necessity, he knew — she mastered the cutting line and then the hurtful line. One line caught his eye during the scroll — "Where do you live?" — and he opened the message. It had been sent four months before and was as good a clue as any as to what would become of them. In his mind this message represented the start of the descent for them — the point of no return.

> I was just wondering where you live because I haven't seen you at Amalfi in four nights.
>
> Obviously this is not working, Henry. We need to talk but you are never home to talk. Do I have to come to that lab to talk about us? That would certainly be sad.

He remembered going home to talk to her after that one, resulting in their first breakup. He spent four days in a hotel, living out of a suitcase, lobbying her by phone, e-mail and flowers before being invited to return to Amalfi Drive. A genuine effort on his part followed. He came home every night by eight for at least a week, it seemed, before he started to slip and his lab shifts began lasting into the small hours again.

Pierce closed the message and then the file. Someday he planned to print out the whole scroll of messages and read it like a novel. He knew it would be the very common, very unoriginal story of how a man's obsession led him to lose the thing that was most important to him. If it were a novel, he would call it *Chasing the Dime*.

He went back to the current e-mail list and the next message he read was from his partner Charlie Condon. It was just an end-of-the-week reminder about the presentation scheduled for the next week, as if Pierce needed to be reminded. The subject line read "RE: Proteus" and was a return on a message Pierce had sent Charlie a few days before.

It's all set with God. He's coming in Wednesday for a ten o'clock Thursday. The harpoon is sharpened and ready. Be there or be square.

CC

Pierce didn't bother replying. It was a given that he would be there. A lot was riding on it. No, everything was riding on it. The God referred to in the message was Maurice Goddard. He was a New Yorker, an ET investor Charlie was hoping would be their whale. He was coming in to look at the Proteus project before making his final decision. They were giving him a first look at Proteus, hoping it would be the closer on the deal. The following Monday they would file for patent protection on Proteus and begin seeking other investors if Goddard didn't come on board.

The last message he read was from Clyde Vernon, head of Amedeo security. Pierce figured he could guess what it said before he opened it, and he wasn't wrong.

Trying to reach you. We need to talk about Nicole James. Please call me ASAP.

Clyde Vernon

Pierce knew Vernon wanted to know how much Nicole knew and the circumstances of her abrupt departure. Vernon wanted to know what action he would need to take.

Pierce smirked at the security man's inclusion of his full name. He then decided not to waste time on the other e-mails and turned off the computer, careful to unplug the phone line as well. He left the office and went down the hallway, past the wall of fame, to Nicole's office. Her former office.

Pierce had the override combination for all doors on the third floor. He used it now to open the door and step into the office.

"Lights," he said.

But the overhead lights did not respond. The office's audio receptor was still registered to Nicole's voice. That would likely be changed on Monday. Pierce went to the wall switch and turned on the lights.

The top of the desk was clear. She had said she'd be gone by Friday at five and she had made good on the promise, probably sending him that e-mail as her last official act at Amedeo Technologies.

Pierce walked around the desk and sat down in her chair. He could still pick up a scent of her perfume — a whisper of lilac. He opened the top drawer. It was empty except for a paper clip. She was gone. That was for sure. He checked the three other drawers and they were all empty except for a small box he found in the bottom drawer. He took it out and opened it. It was half full of business cards. He took one out and looked at it.

Nicole R. James
Director of Competitive Intelligence
Public Information Officer

Amedeo Technologies
Santa Monica, California

After a while he put the card back in the box, and the box back in the drawer. He got up and went to the row of file cabinets against the wall opposite the desk.

She'd insisted on hard copies of all intelligence files. There were four double-drawer cabinets. Pierce took out his keys and used one to unlock a drawer labeled BRONSON. He opened the drawer and took out the blue file — under Nicole's filing system the most current file on any competitor was blue. He opened the file and glanced through the printouts and a photocopy of a news clipping from the business section of the *San Jose Mercury News*. He'd seen everything before except for the clipping.

14

It was a short story about one of his chief competitors in the private sector getting an infusion of cash. It was dated two days earlier. He had heard about the deal in general already — through Nicole. Word traveled fast in the emerging-technologies world. A lot faster than through the news media. But the story was a confirmation of everything he'd already heard — and then some.

Bronson Tech Gets Boost from Japan

By Raul Puig

Santa Cruz–based Bronson Technologies has agreed to a partnership with Japan's Tagawa Corporation that will provide funding for the firm's molecular electronics project, the parties announced Wednesday.

Under terms of the agreement Tagawa will provide $16 million in research funds over the next four years. In return Tagawa will hold a 20 percent interest in Bronson.

Elliot Bronson, president of the six-year-old company, said the money will help put his company into the lead in the vaunted race to develop the first practical molecular computer. Bronson and a host of private companies, universities and governmental agencies are engaged in a race to develop molecular-based random access memory (RAM) and link it to integrated circuitry. Though practical application of molecular computing is still seen by some as at least a decade away, it is believed by its proponents that it will revolutionize the world of electronics. It is also seen as a potential threat to the multibillion-dollar silicon-based computer industry.

The potential value and application of molecular computing is seen as limitless and, therefore, the race to develop it is heated. Molecular computer chips will be infinitely more powerful and smaller than the silicon-based chips that currently support the electronics field.

"From diagnostic computers that can be dropped into the

bloodstream to the creation of 'smart streets' with microscopic computers contained in the asphalt, molecular computers will change this world," Bronson said Tuesday. "And this company is going to be there to help change it."

Among Bronson's chief competitors in the private sector are Amedeo Technologies of Los Angeles and Midas Molecular in Raleigh, N.C. Also, Hewlett-Packard has partnered with scientists at the University of California, Los Angeles. And more than a dozen other universities and private firms are putting significant funding into research into nanotechnology and molecular RAM. The Defense Advanced Research Projects Agency is partially or wholly funding many of these programs.

A handful of companies have chosen to seek private backing instead of relying on the government or universities. Bronson explained that the decision makes the company more nimble, able to move quickly with projects and experimentation without having to seek government or university approval.

"The government and these big universities are like battleships," Bronson said. "Once they get moving in the right direction, then watch out. But it takes them a long while to make the turns and get pointed the right way. This field is too competitive and changes too rapidly for that. It's better to be a speed boat at the moment."

Non-reliance on government or university funding also means less sharing of the wealth as patents in the area become more valuable in years to come.

Several significant advances in the development of molecular computing have occurred in the last five years, with Amedeo Tech seemingly leading the way.

Amedeo is the oldest company in the race. Henry Pierce, 34, the chemist who founded the company a year after leaving Stanford, has been granted numerous patents in the areas of molecular circuitry and the creation of molecular memory and logic gates — the basic component of computing.

Bronson said he hopes to now level the playing field with the funding from Tagawa.

"I think it will be a long and interesting race but we're going to be there at the finish line," he said. "With this deal, I guarantee it."

The move to a significant source of financial support — a "whale" in the parlance of the emerging-technologies investment arena — is becoming favored by the smaller companies. Bronson's move follows Midas Molecular, which secured $16 million in funding from a Canadian investor earlier this year.

"There is no two ways about it, you need the money to be competitive," Bronson said. "The basic tools of this science are expensive. To outfit a lab costs more than a million before you even get to the research."

Amedeo's Pierce did not return calls but sources in the industry indicated his company is also seeking a significant investor.

"Everybody is out hunting whales," said Daniel F. Daly, a partner in Daly & Mills, a Florida-based investment firm that has monitored the emergence of nanotechnology. "Money from the hundred-thousand-dollar investor gets eaten up too quickly, so everybody's into one-stop shopping — finding the one investor who will see a project all the way through."

Pierce closed the file, the newspaper clip inside it. Little in the story was new to him but he was intrigued by the first quote from Bronson mentioning molecular diagnostics. He wondered if Bronson was toeing the industry line, talking up the sexier side of the science, or whether he knew something about Proteus. Was he talking directly to Pierce? Using the newspaper and his newfound Japanese money to throw down the gauntlet?

If he was, then he had a shock coming soon. Pierce put the file back in its place in the drawer.

"You sold out too cheap, Elliot," he said as he closed it.

As he left the office he turned off the lights by hand.

Outside in the hallway, Pierce momentarily scanned what they called the wall of fame. Framed articles on Amedeo and Pierce and the patents and the research covered the wall for twenty feet. During business hours, when employees were about in the offices, he never stopped to look at these. It was only in private moments that he glimpsed the wall of fame and felt a sense of pride. It was a scoreboard of sorts. Most of the articles came from science journals, and the language was impenetrable to the layman. But a few times the company and its work poked through into the general media. Pierce stopped before the piece that privately made him the most proud. It was a *Fortune* magazine cover nearly five years old. It showed a photograph of him — in his ponytail days — holding a plastic model of the simple molecular circuit he had just received a patent for. The caption to the right side of his smile asked, "The Most Important Patent of the Next Millennium?"

Then in small type beneath it added, "He thinks so. Twenty-nine-year-old wunderkind Henry Pierce holds the molecular switch that could be the key to a new era in computing and electronics."

The moment was only five years old but it filled Pierce with a sense of nostalgia as he looked at the framed magazine cover. The embarrassing label of wunderkind notwithstanding, Pierce's life changed when that magazine hit the newsstands. The chase started in earnest after that. The investors came to him, rather than the other way around. The competitors came. Charlie Condon came. Even Jay Leno's people came calling about the longhaired surfer chemist and his molecules. The best moment of all that Pierce remembered was when he wrote the check that paid off the scanning electron microscope.

The pressure came then, too. The pressure to perform, to make the next stride. And then the next. Given the choice, he wouldn't go back. Not a chance. But Pierce liked to remember the moment for all that he didn't know then. There was nothing wrong with that.

3

The lab elevator descended so slowly that there was no physical indication it was even moving. The lights above the door were the only way to know for sure. It was designed that way, to eliminate as many vibrations as possible. Vibrations were the enemy. They skewed readings and measurements in the lab.

The door slowly opened on the basement level and Pierce stepped out. He used his scramble card to enter the first door of the mantrap and then, once inside the small passageway, punched in the October combination on the second door. He opened it and entered the lab.

The lab was actually a suite of several smaller labs clustered around the main room, or day room, as they called it. The suite was completely windowless. Its walls were lined on the inside with insulation containing copper shavings that knocked down electronic noise from the outside. On the surface of these walls the decorations were few, largely limited to a series of framed prints from the Dr. Seuss book *Horton Hears a Who!*

The secondary labs included the chemlab to the left. This was a "clean room" where the chemical solutions of molecular switches were made and refrigerated. There was also an incubator for the Proteus project which they called the cell farm.

Opposite the chemlab was the wire lab, or the furnace room, as most of the lab rats called it, and next to it was the imaging lab, which housed the electron microscope. All the way to the rear of the day room was the laser lab. This room was sheathed in copper for added protection against intruding electronic noise.

The lab suite appeared empty, the computers off and the probe stations unmanned, but Pierce picked up the familiar smell of cooking carbon. He checked the sign-in log and saw that Grooms had signed in but had not yet signed out. He walked over to the wire lab and looked through the little glass door. He didn't see anyone. He opened the door and stepped in, immediately being hit with the heat and the smell. The vacuum oven was operating, a new batch of carbon wires being made. Pierce assumed Grooms had started the batch and then left the lab to take a break or get something to eat. It was understandable. The smell of cooking carbon was intolerable.

He left the wire lab and closed the door. He went to a computer next to one of the probe stations and typed in the passwords. He pulled up the data on the switch tests he knew Grooms had been planning to conduct after Pierce had gone home early to set up his phone. According to the computer log, Grooms had run two thousand tests on a new group of twenty switches. The chemically synthesized switches were basic on/off gates that one day could — or would — be used to build computer circuitry.

Pierce leaned back in the computer seat. He noticed a half full cup of coffee on the counter next to the monitor. He knew it was Larraby's because it was black. Everybody else in the lab used cream but the immunologist assigned to the Proteus project.

As Pierce thought about whether to continue with the gateway confirmation tests or to go into the imaging lab and pull up Larraby's latest work on Proteus, his eyes drifted up toward the wall behind the computers. Scotch-taped to the wall was a dime. Grooms had put it up a couple years earlier. A joke, yes, but a solid reminder of their goal. Sometimes it seemed to be mocking them. Roosevelt turning the side of his face, looking the other way, ignoring them.

It wasn't until that moment that Pierce realized he wasn't going to be able to work this night. He had spent so many nights working in the confines of the lab suite that it had cost him Nicole. That and other things. Now that she was gone, he was free to work without hesitation or guilt and he suddenly realized he couldn't do it. If he ever spoke to her again, he would tell her this. Maybe it would mean he was changing. Maybe it would mean something to her.

Behind him there was a sudden loud banging sound and Pierce jumped in his seat. Turning around and expecting to see Grooms returning, he saw Clyde Vernon come through the mantrap instead. Vernon was a wide and husky man with just a fringe of hair around the outer edges of his head. He had a naturally ruddy complexion that always gave him a look of consternation. In his mid-fifties, Vernon was by far the oldest person working at the company. After him Charlie Condon was probably the oldest at forty.

This time the look of consternation Vernon carried was real.

"Hey, Clyde, you scared me," Pierce said.

"I didn't mean to."

"We do a lot of sensitive readings in here. Banging the door open like that could ruin an experiment. Luckily, I was just reviewing experiments, not conducting any."

"I'm sorry, Dr. Pierce."

"Don't call me that, Clyde. Call me Henry. So let me guess, you put out a 'be on the look out for' on me, and Rudolpho called it in when I came through. And that made you come all the way in from home. I hope you don't live too far away, Clyde."

Vernon ignored Pierce's fine deductive work.

"We need to talk," he said instead. "Did you get my message?"

They were in the early stages of getting to know each other. Vernon might be the oldest person working at Amedeo, but he was also the newest. Pierce had already noticed that Vernon had difficulty calling him by name. He thought maybe it was an age thing. Pierce was the president of the company but at least twenty years younger than Vernon, who had come to the company a few months earlier after putting in twenty-five years with the FBI. Vernon probably thought it would be improper to address Pierce by his first name, and the gulf in age and real-life experience made it difficult to call him Mr. Pierce. Dr. Pierce seemed a bit easier for him, even though it was based on academic degrees not medical ones. His real plan seemed to be to never address him by any name if possible. To the point it was noticeable, especially in e-mail and telephone conversations.

"I just got your e-mail about fifteen minutes ago," Pierce said. "I was out of the office. I was probably going to call you when I got finished here. You want to talk about Nicole?"

"Yes. What happened?"

Pierce shrugged his shoulders in a helpless gesture.

"What happened is that she left. She quit her job and she, uh, quit me. I guess you could say she quit me first."

"When did this happen?"

"Hard to tell, Clyde. It was happening for a while. Like slow motion. But it all sort of hit the fan a couple weeks ago. She agreed to stay until today. Today was her last day. I know when we brought you in here you warned me about fishing off the company dock. I think that's what you called it. I guess you were right."

Vernon took a step closer to Pierce.

"Why wasn't I told about this?" he protested. "I should've been told."

Pierce could see the color moving higher on Vernon's cheeks. He was angry and trying to control it. It wasn't about Nicole so much as his need to solidify his position in the company. After all, he didn't leave the bureau after so many years to be kept in the dark by some punk scientist boss who probably smoked pot on the weekends.

"Look, I know you should have been told but because there were some personal issues involved I just . . . I didn't really want to talk about it. And to tell you the truth, I probably wasn't going to call you tonight, because I still don't want to talk about it."

"Well, we need to talk about it. She was the intelligence officer of this company. She shouldn't have been allowed to just waltz out the door at the end of the day."

"All the files are still there. I checked, even though I didn't need to. Nicki would never do anything like you are suggesting."

"I am not suggesting any impropriety. I am just trying to be thorough and cautious about this. That's all. Did she take another job that you know of?"

"Not as of the last time we spoke. But she signed a no-compete contract when we hired her. We don't have to worry about that, Clyde."

"So you think. What were the financial arrangements of the separation?"

"Why is that your business?"

"Because a person in need of finances is vulnerable. It's my business to know if a former or current employee with intimate knowledge of the project is vulnerable."

Pierce was beginning to get annoyed with Vernon's rapid questioning and condescending demeanor, even though it was the same demeanor he treated the security man with on a daily basis.

"First of all, her knowledge of the project was limited. She gathered intelligence on the competitors, not on us. To do that, she had to have a sense of what we're doing in here. But I don't think she was in a position to know exactly what we're doing or where we are in any of the projects. Just like you don't, Clyde. It is safer that way.

"And second, I'll answer your next question before you ask it. No, I never told her on a personal level the details of what we are doing. It never came up. In fact, I don't even think she cared. She treated the job like a job, and that probably was the main problem with us. I didn't treat it as a job. I treated it like it was my life. Now, anything else, Clyde? I want to get some work done."

He hoped camouflaging the one lie in verbiage and indignation would get it by Vernon.

"When did Charlie Condon know about this?" Vernon asked.

Condon was the company's chief financial officer, but more important, he was the man who had hired Vernon.

"We told him yesterday," Pierce said. "Together. I heard she'd made an appointment to talk to him last before she left today. If Charlie didn't tell you, there is nothing I can do about that. I guess he didn't see it as necessary, either."

That was a shot, reminding Vernon that he had been left out of the loop by his own sponsor. But the former FBI man shook it off with a quick frown and moved on.

"You didn't answer before. Did she receive a severance?"

"Of course. Yes. Six months' pay, two years' medical and life insurance. She's also selling the house and keeping all proceeds. Satisfied? I hardly think she's vulnerable. She should clear more than a hundred grand on that house alone."

Vernon seemed to calm a bit. Knowing that Charlie Condon had been in the loop eased things for him. Pierce knew Vernon viewed Charlie as being the practical business side of the company while Pierce was the more ephemeral talent side. And somehow Pierce's being on the talent side lowered Vernon's respect for him. Charlie was different. He was all business. If he had signed off on Nicole James's departure, then it was going to be okay.

But then again, if Vernon was satisfied, he wasn't going to say so to Pierce.

"I am sorry if you don't like the questions," he said. "But it's my job and my duty to maintain the security of this firm and its projects. There are many people and companies whose investment must be safeguarded."

He was alluding to the reason he was there. Charlie Condon had hired him as a showpiece. Vernon was there to placate potential investors who needed to know that the company's projects were safe and secure and, therefore, that their investments would be safe and secure. Vernon's pedigree was impressive and more vitally important to the company than the actual security work he performed.

When Maurice Goddard had made his first trip out from New York to be shown around the place and receive the initial presentation, he had also been introduced to Vernon and had spent twenty minutes talking about plant security and personnel with him.

Pierce now looked at Clyde Vernon and felt like screaming at him, letting him know how close they were to running out of significant funding and how inconsequential he was in the scheme of things.

But he held his tongue.

"I understand your concerns perfectly, Clyde. But I don't think you have to worry about Nicole. Everything is cool."

Vernon nodded and finally conceded, perhaps sensing the growing tension behind Pierce's eyes.

"I think you're probably right."

"Thank you."

"Now, you said you were selling the house."

"I said she's selling it."

"Yes. Have you moved yet? Do you have a number where you can be reached?"

Pierce hesitated. Vernon had not been on the A-list of people who had gotten his new number and address. Respect was a two-way street. While Pierce viewed Vernon as capable, he also knew what had gotten the man the job was his FBI pedigree. Of his twenty-five years in the bureau, Vernon had spent half in the L.A. field office on white collar crime and corporate espionage investigations.

But Pierce viewed Vernon largely as a poseur. He was always on the move, charging down hallways and banging through doors like a man on a mission. But the bottom line was that there wasn't a whole lot to the mission of providing project security to a firm that employed thirty-three people, only ten of which could get through the mantrap and inside the lab, where all the secrets were kept.

"I've got a new phone number but I don't remember it," Pierce said. "I'll get it to you as soon as I can."

"What about the address?"

"It's over in the Sands on the beach. Apartment twelve oh one."

Vernon took out a little notebook and wrote down the information. He looked just like a cop from an old movie, his big hands crowding the small notebook as he scribbled. *Why do they always have such small notebooks?* It was a question Cody Zeller had once posited after they'd seen a cop flick together.

"I'm going to get back to work now, Clyde. After all, all those investors are counting on us, right?"

Vernon looked up from his notebook, one eyebrow raised as he tried to gauge whether Pierce was being sarcastic.

"Right," he said. "Then I'll let you get back to it."

But after the security man had retreated through the mantrap, Pierce again realized he could not get back to it. An inertia had set in. For the first time in three years he was unencumbered by interests outside the lab and free to do the work. But for the first time in three years he didn't want to.

He shut down the computer and got up. He followed Vernon's wake through the mantrap.

4

When he got back to his office Pierce turned the lights on by hand. The voice-recognition switch was bullshit and he knew it. Something installed simply to impress the potential investors Charlie Condon walked through the place every few weeks. It was a gimmick. Just like all the cameras and Vernon. But Charlie said it was all necessary. It symbolized the cutting-edge nature of what they did. He said it helped investors envision the company's projects and importance. It made them feel good about writing a check.

But the result was that the offices sometimes seemed to Pierce to be as soulless as they were high-tech. He had started the company in a low-rent warehouse in Westchester, having to take readings on experiments in between takeoffs and landings at LAX. He had no employees. Now he had so many he needed an employee relations officer. He drove a fender-dented Volkswagen Beetle then — the old kind. And now he drove a BMW. There was no doubt, he and Amedeo had certainly come a long way. But with increasing frequency he would drift off to memories of that warehouse lab beneath the flight pattern of runway 17. His friend Cody Zeller, always looking for a movie reference, had once told him that "runway 17" would be his "Rosebud," the last words whispered from his dying lips. Other similarities to *Citizen Kane* notwithstanding, Pierce thought there was a possibility Zeller might be right about that.

Pierce sat down at his desk and thought about calling Zeller and telling him he'd changed his mind about going out. He also thought about calling the house to see if Nicole wanted to talk. But he knew he couldn't do that. It was her move to make and he had to wait her out — even if it never happened.

He took the pad out of his backpack and called the number for accessing his home voice mail by remote location. He tapped in the

26

password and was told electronically that he had one new message. He played it and heard the nervous voice of a man he didn't know.

"Uh, yes, hello, my name is Frank. I'm at the Peninsula. Room six twelve. So give me a call when you can. I got your number from the website and I wanted to see if you're available tonight. I know it's late but I thought I'd try. Anyway, it's Frank Behmer, room six twelve at the Peninsula. Hope to hear from you soon."

Pierce erased the message but once more felt the weird magic of secretly being inside somebody's hidden world. He thought for a few moments and then called Information to get the number for the Peninsula in Beverly Hills. Frank Behmer had been so nervous while leaving the message that he hadn't included the callback number.

He called the hotel and asked for Behmer in room 612. The call was picked up after five rings.

"Hello?"

"Mr. Behmer?"

"Yes?"

"Hi. Did you call for Lilly?"

Behmer hesitated before answering.

"Who is this?"

Pierce didn't hesitate. He had been anticipating the question.

"My name is Hank. I handle Lilly's calls. She's kind of busy at the moment but I'm trying to reach her for you. To set it up for you."

"Yes, I tried the cell number but she didn't call back."

"The cell number?"

"The one on the site."

"Oh, I see. You know, she is listed on several sites. Do you mind my asking which one you got her numbers from? We're trying to figure out which one is most effective, if you know what I mean."

"I saw it on the L.A. Darlings site."

"Oh, L.A. Darlings. Right. That's one of our better sites."

"That's really her on there, right? In the picture?"

"Uh, yes, sir, that's really her."

"Beautiful."

"Yes. Okay, well, like I said, I'll get her to call you as soon as I get ahold of her. Shouldn't take too long. But if you don't hear from either me or Lilly within an hour, then it's not going to happen."

"Really?"

Disappointment tumbled off his voice.

"She's very busy, Mr. Behmer. But I'll try my best. Good night."

"Well, tell her I'm just in town on business for a few days and I'd treat her real nice, if you know what I mean."

Now there was a slight note of pleading in his voice. It made Pierce feel guilty about the subterfuge. He felt that he suddenly knew too much about Behmer and his life.

"I know what you mean," he said. "Good-bye."

"Good-bye."

Pierce hung up. He tried to put his misgivings aside. He didn't know what he was doing or why, but something was pulling him down a pathway. He rebooted his computer and jacked in the phone line. He then went online and tried a variation of web configurations until he hit on www.la-darlings.com and was connected to a site.

The first page was text. It was a warning/waiver form explaining that there was explicit adult fare waiting on the website. By clicking the ENTER button, the visitor was acknowledging that he or she was over eighteen years old and was not offended by nudity or adult content. Without reading all the fine print, Pierce clicked on the ENTER button and the screen changed to the site's home page. Running along the left border was a photo of a naked woman holding a towel in front of herself and a raised finger in front of her lips in a don't-tell-anyone pose. The site titling was in a large purple font.

L.A. Darlings

A free directory of adult entertainment and services

Beneath was a row of red tabs labeled with the available services, ranging from escorts categorized by race and hair color to massage and fetish experts of all genders and sexual orientation. There was even a tab for hiring actual porno stars for private sessions. Pierce knew there were countless sites like these all over the Internet. It was likely that every Internet provider in every city and town had at least one of these sites — the equivalent of an online bordello — sitting in its chips. He had never taken the time to explore one, though he knew that Charlie Condon had once used such a site to hire an escort for a potential investor. It was a decision he regretted and never repeated — the investor was drink-drugged and robbed by the escort before any sex act even took place. Needless to say, he did not invest in Amedeo Technologies.

Pierce clicked on the BLONDE ESCORTS tab for no reason other than it was a place to start looking for Lilly. The page opened in two halves. On the left side of the page was a scrolling panel of thumbnail photos of the blonde escorts with their first names appearing under each picture. When he clicked on one of the thumbnails, the escort's page would then open on the right — the photo enlarged for easier and better viewing.

Pierce scrolled down the panel, looking at the names. There were nearly forty different escorts, but none was named Lilly. He closed it out and went to the brunettes section next. Halfway through the thumbnails he came to an escort with the name Tiger Lilly under her picture. He clicked on the photo and her page appeared on the right. He checked the phone number — it wasn't the same as his.

He closed the page and went back to the thumbnails panel. Further down he came to another escort named simply Lilly. He clicked her page open and checked the number. It was a match. He had found the Lilly whose phone number he now had.

The photo on the ad was of a woman in her mid-twenties. She had dark shoulder-length hair and brown eyes, a deep tan. She was kneeling on a bed with brass railings and was naked beneath a black fishnet negligee. The curves of her breasts were clearly visible. The tan lines of her crotch were seen also. Her eyes looked directly into the camera. Her full lips formed what Pierce thought was meant to be an inviting pout.

If the photo had not been altered and if it was really Lilly, then she was beautiful. Just as Frank Behmer had said. Pure fantasy, an escort dream. Pierce understood why his phone had been ringing constantly since he had plugged it in. The wealth of competition on this website and all the others on the net didn't matter. A man scrolling through the photos — shopping for a woman, as it were — would be hard-pressed to go past this one without picking up the phone.

There was a blue ribbon posted below the photo. Pierce moved the cursor to it and a pop-up caption said "photo verified by staff," meaning the model in the photo was actually the woman who had placed the ad. In other words, you got what you saw if you arranged to meet the escort. Supposedly.

"Photo verifier," Pierce said. "That's not a bad job."

His eyes moved to the ad copy below the photo and he scrolled down as he read it.

Special Desires

Hello, Gentlemen. My name is Lilly and I'm the most soothing, pleasing and down-to-earth escort on the whole Westside. I'm 23 yoa, 34-25-34 (all natural), 5-1 and 105 lbs. and don't smoke. I'm part Spanish and part Italian and all American! So if you're looking for the time of your life, then give me a call and come visit me at my safe and secure townhouse near the beach. I never rush and satisfaction is guaranteed! All special desires considered. And if you want to double your pleasure, visit my girlfriend Robin's page in the Blonde Escorts section. We work together as a team — on you or ourselves! I love my work and love to work. So call me!

Incall only. VIPs only.

Below the ad was the phone number now assigned to Pierce's apartment, as well as a cell phone number.

Pierce picked up the phone and called the cell number. He got her voice mail.

"Hi, it's Lilly. Leave your name and number and I'll call you right back. I don't return calls to pay phones. And if you're in a hotel, remember to leave your full name or they won't put my call through. Thanks. I hope to see you real soon. Bye-bye."

Pierce had made the call before he was sure of what he wanted to say. The beep sounded and he started talking.

"Uh, yes, Lilly, my name is Henry. I sort of have a problem because I have your old phone number. What I mean is, the phone company gave it to me — it's in my apartment and . . . I don't know . . . I'd like to talk to you about it."

He blurted out the number and hung up.

"Shit!"

He knew he had sounded like an idiot. He wasn't even sure why he was calling her. If she had given up the number, there was nothing she could do about it now to help him except get it off the website. And that thought raised the primary question: Why was the number still on her site?

He looked at her photo on the screen again. He studied it. Lilly was stunningly beautiful and he felt a heaviness at his center, the growing hunger of lust. Finally, a single thought pushed through: *What am I doing?*

It was a good and valid question. He knew what he needed to do was pull the plug on the computer, get a new number on Monday and then concentrate on the work and forget about all of this.

But he couldn't. He went back to the keyboard and closed Lilly's page and went back to the home page. He then opened the Blonde Escorts panel again and scrolled down until he found a thumbnail photo with the name Robin beneath it.

He opened the page. The woman named Robin was blonde as advertised. She lay naked on her back on a bed. Red rose petals were piled on her stomach and strategically used to partially cover her breasts and crotch. She had a red lipstick smile. There was a blue ribbon beneath the picture, indicating that the photo had been verified. He scanned down to the ad copy.

American Beauty

Hello, Gentlemen. My name is Robin and I'm the girl you have been dreaming about. I'm a true blonde and blue-eyed all-American girl. I'm 24 yoa, 38-30-36 and almost six feet tall. I don't smoke but I love champagne. I can come to you or you can come to me. It doesn't matter because I never rush you. Absolutely positive GFE. And if you want to double your pleasure, visit my girlfriend Lilly's page in the brunettes section. We work together as a team — on you or on ourselves! So give me a call. Satisfaction guaranteed!

VIPs only please.

There was a phone number and a pager number at the bottom of the ad. Without thinking too much about it, Pierce wrote them down in his notebook. He then moved back up to the photo. Robin was attractive but not in the aching sort of way that Lilly was. Robin had sharp lines to her mouth and eyes and a colder look. She was more in line with what Pierce had always thought he would find on one of these sites. Lilly wasn't.

Pierce reread the ad and was left wondering what "absolutely positive GFE" meant. He had no clue. He then realized that the ad copy on both pages — Robin's and Lilly's — had likely been written by the same person. Repetitive phrases and structure indicated this. He also noticed as he looked at the photo that the same brass bed was in both photos. He pulled down his Internet directory and quickly switched back to Lilly's web page to confirm.

The bed was the same. He didn't know what this meant other than perhaps another confirmation that the two women worked together.

The main difference he picked up from the copy was that Lilly only entertained clients at her apartment. Robin worked it either way, going to a client or allowing him to come to her. Again, he didn't know if this meant anything in the world in which they lived and worked.

He leaned back in his chair, looking at the computer screen and wondering what to do next. He looked at his watch. It was almost eleven.

Abruptly he leaned forward and picked up the phone. Checking his notes, he called the number from Robin's page. He lost his nerve and was about to hang up after four rings when a woman answered in a sleepy, smoky voice.

"Uh, Robin?"

"Yes."

"I'm sorry, did I wake you?"

"No, I'm awake. Who's this?"

"Um, my name's Hank. I, uh, saw your page on L.A. Darlings. Am I calling too late?"

"No, you're fine. What's Amedeo Techno?"

He realized she had caller ID. A shock of fear went through him.

Fear of scandal, of people like Vernon knowing something secret about him.

"Actually, it's Amedeo Technologies. Your readout must not show the whole name."

"Is that where you work?"

"Yes."

"Are you Mr. Amedeo?"

Pierce smiled.

"No, there is no Mr. Amedeo. Not anymore."

"Really? Too bad. What happened to him?"

"Amedeo was Amedeo Avogadro. He was a chemist who about two hundred years ago was the first to tell the difference between molecules and atoms. It was an important distinction but he wasn't taken seriously for about fifty years, until after he was dead. He was just a man ahead of his time. The company was named after him."

"What do you do there? Play around with atoms and molecules?"

He heard her yawn.

"Sort of. I'm a chemist, too. We're building a computer out of molecules."

He yawned.

"Really? Cool."

Pierce smiled again. She sounded neither impressed nor interested.

"Anyway, the reason I'm calling is that I see that you work with Lilly. The brunette escort?"

"I did."

"You mean not anymore?"

"No, not anymore."

"What happened? I've been trying to call her and —"

"I'm not talking about Lilly with you. I don't even know you."

Her voice had changed. It had taken on a sharper edge. Pierce instinctively knew he could lose her if he didn't play it right.

"Okay, sorry. I was just asking because I liked her."

"You'd been with her?"

"Yeah. A couple times. She seemed like a nice girl and I was wondering where she went. That's all. She suggested the last time that maybe all three of us could get together next time. Do you think you could get a message to her?"

"No. She's long gone and whatever happened to her . . . just happened. That's all."

"What do you mean? What exactly happened?"

"You know, mister, you're really creeping me out, asking all of these questions. And the thing is, I don't have to talk to you. So why don't you just spend the night with your own molecules."

She hung up.

Pierce sat there with the phone still to his ear. He was tempted to call back but instinctively knew it would be fruitless attempting to get anything out of Robin. He had spoiled it with the way he had handled it.

He finally hung up and thought about what he had gathered. He looked at the photo of Lilly still on his computer screen. He thought about Robin's cryptic comment about something having happened to her.

"What happened to you?"

He moved the screen back to the home page and clicked on a tab marked ADVERTISE WITH US. It led to a page with instructions for placing ads on the site. It could be done through the net by submitting a credit card number, ad copy and a digital photograph. But in order to receive the blue ribbon signaling a verified photo on the ad, the advertiser had to submit all the materials in person so that she could be confirmed as the woman in the photograph. The site's brick-and-mortar location was on Sunset Boulevard in Hollywood. This was apparently what Lilly and Robin had done. The page listed the office's hours as Monday through Saturday, nine to five during the week and ten to three on Saturdays.

Pierce wrote the address and hours down on his notepad. He was about to disconnect from the site when he decided to call up Lilly's page once again. He printed out a color copy of her photo on the DeskJet. He then shut down the computer and disconnected the phone line. Again a voice inside told him he had gone as far with this as he could go. As he should go. It was time to change his phone number and forget about it.

But another voice — a louder voice from the past — told him something else.

"Lights," he said.

The office dropped into darkness. Pierce didn't move. He liked the darkness. He always did his best thinking in the dark.

5

The stairway was dark and the boy was scared. He looked back to the street and saw the waiting car. His stepfather saw the hesitation and put his hand out the car window. He waved the boy forward, waved him in. The boy turned back and looked up into the darkness. He turned on the flashlight and started up.

He kept the light down on the steps, not wanting to announce he was coming up by lighting the room at the top. Halfway there one of the stairs creaked loudly under his foot. He stood frozen still. He could hear his own heartbeat banging in his chest. He thought about Isabelle and the fear she probably carried in her own chest every day and night after night. He drew his resolve from this and started up again.

Three steps from the top he cut the light off and waited for his eyes to adjust. In a few moments he thought he could see a dim light from the room up ahead of him. It was candlelight licking at the ceiling and walls. He pushed himself against the side wall and took the last three steps up.

The room was large and crowded. He could see the makeshift beds lined against the two long walls. Still figures, like heaps of rummage sale clothes, slept on each. At the end of the room a single candle burned and a girl, a few years older and dirtier, heated a bottle cap over the flame. The boy studied her face in the uneven light. He could see that it wasn't Isabelle.

He started moving down the center of the room, between the sleeping bags and the newspaper pallets. From side to side he looked, searching for the familiar face. It was dark but he could tell. He'd know her when he saw her.

He got to the end, by the girl with the bottle cap. And Isabelle wasn't there.

"Who are you looking for?" asked the girl.

36

She was drawing back the plunger on the hypodermic, sucking the brown-black liquid through a cigarette butt filter from the bottle cap. In the murky light the boy could see the needle scarring on her neck.

"Just somebody," he said.

She looked away from her work and up to his face, surprised by his voice. She saw the young face in the camouflage of oversized and dirty clothes.

"You're a young one," she said. "You better get out of here before the houseman comes back."

The boy knew what she meant. All the squats in Hollywood had somebody in charge. The houseman. He exacted a fee in money or drugs or flesh.

"He finds you, he'll bust your cherry ass and put you out on —"

She suddenly stopped and blew out the candle, leaving him in the dark. He turned back to the door and the stairs, and all his fears seized up in him like a fist closing on a flower. A silhouette of a man stood at the top of the steps. A big man. Wild hair. The houseman. The boy involuntarily took a step back and tripped over someone's leg. He fell, the flashlight clattering on the floor next to him and going out.

The man in the doorway moved and started coming at him.

"Hanky boy!" the man yelled. "Come here, Hank!"

6

Pierce awoke at dawn, the sun rescuing him from the dream of running from a man whose face he could not see. He had no curtains in the apartment yet and the light streamed through the windows and burned through his eyelids. He crawled out of the sleeping bag, looked at the photo of Lilly he had left on the floor and went into the shower. When he was finished he had to dry off with two T-shirts he'd dug out of one of the clothing boxes. He'd forgotten to buy towels.

He walked over to Main Street to get coffee, a citrus smoothie and the newspaper. He read and drank slowly, almost feeling guilty about it. Most Saturdays he was in the lab by dawn.

When he was finished with the paper it was almost nine. He walked back to the Sands and got into his car, but he didn't go to the lab as usual.

Fifteen minutes before ten o'clock Pierce got to the Hollywood address he had written down for L.A. Darlings. The location was a multi-level office complex that looked as legitimate as a McDonald's. L.A. Darlings was located in Suite 310. On the glazed glass door the largest lettering read ENTREPRENEURIAL CONCEPTS UNLIMITED. Beneath this was a listing in smaller letters of ten different websites, including L.A. Darlings, that apparently fell under the Entrepreneurial Concepts umbrella. Pierce could tell by the titling of the site addresses that they were all sexually oriented and part of the Internet's dark universe of adult entertainment.

The door was locked but Pierce was a few minutes early. He decided to use the time by taking a walk and thinking about what he was going to say and how he was going to play this.

"Here, I'll open it."

He turned as a woman approached the door with a key. She was about twenty-five and had crazy blonde hair that seemed to point in all directions. She wore cutoff jeans and sandals and a short shirt that exposed her pierced navel. She had looped over her shoulder a purse that looked big enough to hold a pack of cigarettes but not the matches. And she looked as though ten o'clock was definitely too early for her.

"You're early," she said.

"I know," Pierce said. "I came from the Westside and I thought there'd be more traffic."

He followed her in. There was a waiting area with a raised reception counter in front of a partition that guarded an entrance to a rear hallway. To the right and unguarded was a closed door with the word PRIVATE on it. Pierce watched as the woman walked behind the counter and threw her purse into a drawer.

"You'll have to wait a couple minutes until I get set up. I'm the only one here today."

"Slow on Saturdays?"

"Most of the time."

"Well, who is watching the machines if you're the only one here?"

"Oh, well, there's always somebody back there. I just meant I'm by myself up front today."

She slid into a chair behind the counter. The silver ring protruding from her stomach caught Pierce's eye and reminded him of Nicole. She had worked at Amedeo for more than a year before he happened upon her in a coffee shop on Main Street on a Sunday afternoon. She had just come from a workout and was dressed in gray sweatpants and a sports bra, exposing a gold ring piercing her navel. It was like discovering a secret about someone of longtime acquaintance. She had always been a beautifully attractive woman in his eyes but everything changed after that moment in the coffee shop. Nicole became erotic to him and he went after her, wanting to check for hidden tattoos and to know all of her secrets.

Pierce wandered around the confines of the waiting room while the woman behind the counter did whatever it was she had to do to get set up. He heard a computer start booting up and some drawers opening and closing. He noticed on one wall an arrangement of logos of various websites operated through Entrepreneurial Concepts. He saw L.A. Darlings and several others. Most of them were pornography sites, where a $19.95-a-month subscription bought access to thousands of downloadable photos of your favorite sex acts and fetishes. It was all presented on the wall in complete, unashamed legitimacy. The PinkMink.com banner could have been the same as an advertisement for acne ointment.

Next to the wall of banners was the door marked PRIVATE. Pierce glanced back at the woman behind the counter and saw that she was preoccupied with something on her computer screen. He turned back and tried the doorknob. It was unlocked and he opened the door. It led to an unlit hallway with three sets of double doors spaced twenty feet apart on the left side.

"Um, excuse me," the woman said from behind him. "You can't go in there."

Signs hanging on thin chains from the ceiling in front of the doors marked them as studio A, studio B and studio C.

Pierce backed out and closed the door. He returned to the counter. He saw that she was now wearing a pin with her name on it.

"I thought it was the rest rooms. What is that back there?"

"Those are the photo studios. We don't have public facilities here. They're down in the building's lobby."

"I can wait."

"What can I do for you?"

He leaned his elbows on the counter.

"I've sort of got a problem, Wendy. One of the advertisers with a page on L.A. Darlings dot com has my phone number. Calls that should be going to her are going to me instead. And I think if I were to show up at somebody's hotel room door, there'd be some disappointment involved."

He smiled but she apparently didn't appreciate his attempt at humor.

"A misprint?" she said. "I can fix that."

"It's not exactly a misprint."

He told his story of getting a new phone number, only to learn that it was the same line on the web page ad for the woman named Lilly.

She was sitting behind the counter. She looked up at him with suspicious eyes.

40

"If you just got the number, why don't you just get another?"

"Because I didn't realize I had this problem and I already had change-of-address cards with the number on it printed and mailed out. It would be very expensive and time-consuming to do that all over again with a new number. I'm sure if you told me how to contact this woman, she'd agree to alter her page. I mean, she's not getting any business off it if all her calls are going to me anyway, right?"

Wendy shook her head like his explanation and reasoning were beyond her.

"All right, let me see something."

She turned to the computer and went to the L.A. Darlings site and into the Brunette escorts list. She clicked on the picture of Lilly and then scrolled down to the phone number.

"You're saying this is your number, not hers, but it used to be hers."

"Exactly."

"Then if she changed her number, why wouldn't she change it with us, too?"

"I don't know. That's why I'm here. Would you have another way of contacting her?"

"Not that I can give you. Our client information is confidential."

Pierce nodded. He had expected that.

"That's fine. But can you see if there is another contact number and then you could call her and tell her about this problem?"

"What about this cell number?"

"I tried it. It takes voice mail. I've left three messages for her explaining all of this but she hasn't called back. I don't think she's getting the messages."

Wendy scrolled up and looked at the photo of Lilly.

"She's hot," she said. "I bet you're getting a lot of calls."

"I've only had the phone a day and it's driving me nuts."

Wendy pushed her chair back and stood up.

"I'm going to check something. I'll be right back."

She went around the partition behind the counter and disappeared into the back hallway, the slapping sound of her sandals receding as she went. Pierce waited a moment and then leaned over the counter and scanned all surfaces. His guess was that Wendy was not the only one who worked at the counter. It was probably a job shared by two or three minimum-wage employees. Employees who might need help remembering passwords to the system.

He looked for Post-its on the computer and the back of the counter's facade but saw nothing. He reached down and lifted the blotter but there was nothing under it but a dollar bill. He dug his finger around in a dish of paper clips but found nothing. He reached further across the counter to see if there was a pencil drawer. There wasn't.

Just as he thought of something, he heard the sound of her sandals. She was coming back. He quickly reached into his pocket, found a dollar and then reached back over the counter. He lifted the blotter, put down the dollar and grabbed the one that was there. He put it in his pocket without looking at it. His hand was still there when she came around the partition, holding a thin file, and sat down.

"Well, I figured out one part of the problem," she said.

"What's that?"

"This girl stopped paying her bill."

"When was that?"

"In June she paid up through August. Then she didn't pay for September."

"Then why's her page still on the site?"

"Because sometimes it takes a while to clean out the deadbeats. Especially when they look like this chick."

She gestured to the computer screen with the file and then put it down on the counter.

"I wouldn't be surprised if Mr. Wentz wanted to keep her on there even though she didn't pay. Guys see girls like that on the site and they'll keep coming back."

Pierce nodded.

"And the number of hits on the site is how they determine the rates for the ads, right?"

"You got it."

Pierce looked at the screen. In a way, Lilly was still working. If not for herself, then for Entrepreneurial Concepts Unlimited. He looked back at Wendy.

"Is Mr. Wentz back there? I'd like to speak to him."

"No, it's Saturday. You'd be lucky even to catch him here during the week, but I've never seen him on a Saturday."

"Well, what can be done about this? My phone's ringing off the hook."

"Well, I can take notes and then maybe on Monday somebody could —"

"Look, Wendy, I don't want to wait until Monday. I have a problem now. If Mr. Wentz isn't here, then go get the guy baby-sitting the servers. There has to be somebody who can go into the server and take her page down. It's a simple process."

"There's one guy back there but I don't think he's authorized to do anything. Besides, he was sort of asleep when I looked in there."

Pierce leaned over the counter and put a forceful tone into his voice.

"Lilly — I mean, Wendy, listen to me. I insist that you go back there and wake him up and bring him out here. You have to understand something here. You are in a legally precarious position. I have informed you that your website has my phone number on it. Because of this error I am repeatedly receiving phone calls of what I consider to be an offensive and embarrassing nature. So much so that I was here at your place of business this morning before you even opened. I want this fixed. If you put it off until Monday, then I am going to sue you, this company, Mr. Wentz and anybody else I can find associated with this place. Do you understand?"

"You can't sue me. I just work here."

"Wendy, you can sue anybody you want to in this world."

She stood up, an angry look in her eyes, and pirouetted around the partition without a word. Pierce didn't care if she was angry. What he cared about was that she had left the file on the counter. As soon as the sound of her sandals was gone he bent over and flipped open the file. There was a copy of the photo of Lilly, along with a printout of her ad copy and an advertiser's information form. This was what Pierce wanted. He felt a surge of adrenaline zing through him as he read the sheet and tried to commit everything to memory.

Her name was Lilly Quinlan. Her contact number was the same cell phone number she had put on her web page. On the address line she had put a Santa Monica address and apartment number.

Pierce quickly read it silently three times and then put everything back in the file just as he heard the sandals and another pair of shoes approaching from the other side of the partition.

7

The first thing Pierce did when he got back to the car was grab a pen from the ashtray and write Lilly Quinlan's address on an old valet parking stub. After that he pulled the dollar bill out of his pocket and examined it. It had been face down under the blotter. He now studied it and found the words *Arbadac Arba* written across George Washington's forehead on the front of the bill.

"Abra Cadabra," he said, reading each word backwards.

He thought there was a good chance that the words were a user name and password for entering the Entrepreneurial Concepts computer system. While he was pleased with the moves he'd made in getting the words, he was unsure how useful they would be now that he had gotten Lilly Quinlan's name and address out of the hard-copy file.

He started the car and headed back toward Santa Monica. The address of Lilly's apartment was on Wilshire Boulevard near the Third Street Promenade. As he got close and started reading the numbers on the buildings, he realized that there were no apartment complexes in the vicinity of the address she had written on the advertiser's information sheet. When he finally pulled up in front of the business with the matching address on the door, he saw that it was a private mail drop, a business called All American Mail. The apartment number Lilly Quinlan had written on the info sheet was actually a box number. Pierce parked at the curb out front but wasn't sure what he could do. It appeared that he was at a dead end. He thought for a few minutes about a plan of action and then got out.

Pierce walked into the business and immediately went into the alcove where the mailboxes were. He was hoping the individual doors would have glass in them so he could look into Lilly Quinlan's and see if there was any mail. But the boxes all had aluminum doors with no glass. She had listed her address as apartment 333 on the info sheet. He located box 333 and just stared at it for a moment, as if it might give him some sort of answer. It didn't.

Pierce eventually left the alcove and went to the counter. A young man with a swath of pimples on each cheek and a name tag that said *Curt* asked how he could help him.

"This is sort of weird," Pierce said. "I need a mailbox but I want a specific number. It sort of goes with the name of my business. It's called Three Cubed Productions."

The kid seemed confused.

"So what number do you want?"

"Three three three. I saw you have a box with that number. Is it available?"

It was the best Pierce could come up with while sitting in the car. Curt reached under the counter and came back up with a blue binder, which he opened to pages listing boxes by number and their availability. His finger drew down a column of numbers and stopped.

"Oh, this one."

Pierce tried to read what was on the page but it was upside down and too far away.

"What?"

"Well, it's occupied at the moment but it might not be for long."

"What's that mean?"

"It means there's a person in that box, but she didn't pay this month's rent. So she's in the grace period. If she shows up and pays, she keeps the box. If she doesn't show up by the end of the month, then she's out and you're in — if you can wait that long."

Pierce put a concerned look on his face.

"That's kind of long. I wanted to get this set up. Do you know if there's a number or an address for this person? You know, to contact her and ask if she still wants the box."

"I've sent out two late notices and put one in the box. We usually don't call."

Pierce became excited but didn't show it. What Curt had said meant that there was another address for Lilly Quinlan. This excitement was immediately tempered by the fact that he had no idea how to get it from the young man who had it.

"Well, is there a number? If you could call this woman right now and find something out, I'd be willing to rent the box right now. And I'd pay for a year up front."

"Well, I'll have to look it up. It will take me a minute."

"Take your time. I'd rather get all of this done now than have to come back."

Curt went to a desk that was against the wall behind the counter and sat down. He opened a file drawer and took out a thick hanging file. He was still too far away for Pierce to be able to read any of the documents he was going through. Curt ran his finger down one page and then held it on a spot. With his other hand he picked up the phone on the desk but was interrupted before making the call by a customer who had entered the shop.

"I need to send a fax to New York," she said.

Curt got up and went to the counter. From underneath he pulled out a fax cover sheet and told the woman to fill it out. He returned to the desk. He put his finger back on the document and lifted the phone.

"Am I going to be charged for faxing this cover sheet?"

It was the other customer.

"No, ma'am. Only the documents you need to fax."

He said it like he had said it only a million times before.

Finally, he punched in a number on the phone. Pierce tried to watch his finger and get the number but it was too fast. Curt waited a long time before finally speaking into the phone.

"This is a message for Lilly Quinlan. Could you please call us at All American Mail. Rent on your box is overdue and we'll be re-renting it if we do not hear from you. My name is Curt. Thank you very much."

He gave the number and hung up, then came toward Pierce at the counter. The woman with the fax shook it at him.

"I'm in a big hurry," she said.

"I'll be right with you, ma'am," Curt said.

He looked at Pierce and shook his head.

"I got her machine. There's really nothing that I can do until either I hear from her or the end of the month comes and I don't. That's the policy."

"I understand. Thanks for trying."

Curt started running his finger down the columns in the binder again.

"You want to leave a number where I can reach you if I hear from her?"

"I'll just check with you tomorrow."

Pierce took a business card off a plastic rack on the counter and headed toward the door. Curt called after him.

"What about twenty-seven?"

Pierce turned back.

"What?"

"Twenty-seven. Isn't that what three cubed is?"

Pierce slowly nodded. Curt was smarter than he looked.

"I've got that box open if you want it."

"I'll think about it."

He waved and returned to the door. Behind him he heard the woman telling Curt that he shouldn't make paying customers wait.

In the car Pierce put the business card in his shirt pocket and checked his watch. It was almost noon. He had to get back to his apartment to meet Monica Purl, his assistant. She'd agreed to wait at his apartment for the shipment of furniture he had ordered. The delivery window was noon until four and Pierce had decided Friday morning that he'd rather pay someone else to wait while he used the time in the lab preparing the next week's presentation for Goddard. Now he doubted he was going to go to the lab, but he would still use Monica to wait for the delivery. He also now had another plan for her as well.

When he got to the Sands he found her waiting in the lobby. The security officer on the door would not let her go up to the twelfth floor without approval of the resident she was going to visit.

"Sorry about that," Pierce said. "Were you waiting long?"

She was carrying a stack of magazines for reading while she waited for the delivery.

"Just a few minutes," Monica said.

They went into the elevator alcove and had to wait. Monica Purl was a tall, thin blonde with the kind of skin that was so pale that just touching it might leave a mark. She was about twenty-five and had been with the company since she was twenty. She had been

Pierce's personal assistant for only six months, getting the promotion from Charlie Condon for her five years of service. In that time Pierce had learned that the aura of fragility her build and coloring projected was false. Monica was organized and opinionated and got things done.

The elevator opened and they got on. Pierce hit the twelve button and they started to ascend, the elevator moving quickly.

"You sure you want to be in this place when the big one hits?" Monica asked.

"This building was engineered to take an eight point oh," he replied. "I checked before I rented. I trust the science."

"Because you're a scientist?"

"I guess."

"But do you trust the builders who carry out the science?"

It was a good point. He didn't have anything to say to that. The door slid open on twelve and they walked down the hall to his apartment.

"Where am I going to tell them to put everything?" Monica asked. "Do you have like a design plan or a layout in mind?"

"Not really. Just tell them to put stuff where you think it will look good. I also need you to do a favor for me before I leave."

He opened the door.

"What kind of favor?" Monica said suspiciously.

Pierce realized that she thought he might be making a move on her. Now that he and Nicole were no more. He had a theory that all attractive women thought that all men were out to make a move on them. He almost laughed but didn't.

"Just a phone call. I'll write it down."

In the living room he picked up the phone. There was a broken dial tone and when he checked messages there was only one and it was for Lilly. But it was not from Curt at All American Mail. It was just another potential client checking on her availability. He erased the message and tried to figure it out, finally deciding that Lilly had put down her cell phone number on the mailbox application forms. Curt had called her cell phone.

It wouldn't change his plan.

He brought the phone to the couch and sat down and wrote the name Lilly Quinlan on a fresh page of his notebook. He then pulled the business card out of his pocket.

"I want you to call this number and say you are Lilly Quinlan. Ask for Curt and tell him you got his message. Tell him his call was the first you'd heard about your payment being overdue and ask him why they didn't send you a notice in the mail. Okay?"

"Why — what is this for?"

"I can't explain it all to you but it's important."

"I don't know if I want to impersonate somebody. It's not —"

"What you are doing is totally harmless. It's what hackers call social engineering. What Curt is going to tell you is that he did send you a notice. Then you say, 'Oh, really? What address did you send it to?' When he gives you the address write it down. That's what I need. The address. As soon as you get it you can get off the call. Just tell him you'll come by as soon as you can to pay, and hang up. I just need that address."

She looked at him in a way she had never looked at him before during the six months she had worked directly for him.

"Come on, Monica, it's no big deal. It's not harming anyone. And it might actually be helping someone. In fact, I think it will."

He put the notebook and pen on her lap.

"Are you ready? I'll dial the number."

"Dr. Pierce, this doesn't seem —"

"Don't call me Dr. Pierce. You never call me Dr. Pierce."

"Then Henry. I don't want to do this. Not without knowing what I am doing."

"All right then, I'll tell you. You know the new phone number you got me?"

She nodded.

"Well, it belonged previously to a woman who has disappeared, or something has happened to her. I'm getting her calls and I'm trying to figure out what happened to her. You see? And this call I want you to make might get me an address where she lives. That's all I want. I want to go there and see if she's okay. Nothing else. Now, will you make the call?"

She shook her head as if warding off too much information. Her face looked as if Pierce had just told her he'd been taken aboard a spaceship and sodomized by an alien.

"This is crazy. How did you ever get caught up in this? Did you

50

know this woman? How do you know she disappeared?"

"No, I don't know her. It was purely random. Because I got the wrong number. But now I know enough to know I have to find out what happened or make sure she's okay. Will you please do this for me, Monica?"

"Why don't you just change your number?"

"I will. First thing Monday I want you to change it."

"And meantime, just call the police."

"I don't have enough information yet to call the police. What would I tell them? They'll think I'm a nut."

"And they might be right."

"Look, will you do this or not?"

She nodded in resignation.

"If it will make you happy and it will keep my job."

"Whoa. Wait a minute. I'm not threatening you about your job. If you don't want to do it, fine, I'll get somebody else. It's got nothing to do with your job. Are we clear on that?"

"Yes, clear. But don't worry, I'll do it. Let's just get it over with."

He went over the call with her once more and then dialed the number of All American Mail and handed the phone to Monica. She asked for Curt and then pulled off the call as planned, with only a few moments of bad acting and confusion. Pierce watched as she wrote down an address on the notepad. He was ecstatic but didn't show it. When she hung up she handed him the pad and the phone.

Pierce checked the address — it was in Venice — then tore the page off the pad, folded it and put it in his pocket.

"Curt seemed like a nice guy," Monica said. "I feel bad about lying to him."

"You could always go visit him and ask him out for a date. I've seen him. Believe me, one date with you would make him happy the rest of his life."

"You've seen him? Were you the one he was talking about? He said a guy was in there and wanted my mailbox. I mean, Lilly Quinlan's mailbox."

"Yeah, that was me. That's how I —"

The phone rang and he answered it. But the caller hung up. Pierce looked at the caller ID directory. The call had come from the Ritz-Carlton in the Marina.

"Look," he said, "you need to leave the phone plugged in so when the furniture comes, security can call up here for approval to let them up. But meantime, you're probably going to get a lot of calls for Lilly. Since you're a woman, they're going to think you're her. So you might want to say something right off like 'This isn't Lilly, you've got the wrong number.' Something like that. Other-wise —"

"Well, maybe I should pretend I'm her so I can get more information for you."

"No, you don't want to do that."

He opened his backpack and pulled out the printout of the photo from Lilly's web page.

"That's Lilly. I don't think you want to pretend you're her with these callers."

"Oh my God!" Monica exclaimed as she looked at the photo. "Is she like a prostitute or something?"

"I think so."

"Then what are you doing trying to find this prostitute when you should be —"

She stopped abruptly. Pierce looked at her and waited for her to finish. She didn't.

"What?" he said. "I should be what?"

"Nothing. It's not my business."

"Did you talk with Nicki about her and me?"

"No. Look, it's nothing. I don't know what I was going to say. I just think it's strange that you're running around trying to find out if this prostitute is all right. It's weird."

Pierce sat back down on the couch. He knew she was lying about Nicole. They had gotten close and used to go to lunch together all the times Pierce couldn't get out of the lab — which was almost every day. Why would it end now that Nicki was gone? They were probably still talking every day, exchanging stories about him.

He also knew that she was right about what he was doing. But he was too far down the road and around the bend. His life and career had been built on following his curiosity. In his last year at Stanford he sat in on a lecture about the next generation of microchips. The professor spoke of nanochips so small that the supercomputers of the day could and would be built to the size of a dime. Pierce

52

became hooked and had been pursuing his curiosity — chasing the dime — ever since.

"I'm just going to go over to Venice," he told Monica. "I'm just going to check things out and leave it at that."

"You promise?"

"Yes. You can call me at the lab after the furniture gets here and you're leaving."

He stood up and slung his backpack over his shoulder.

"If you talk to Nicki, don't mention anything about this, okay?"

"Sure, Henry. I won't."

He knew he couldn't count on that but it would have to do for the moment. He headed to the apartment door and left. As he went down the hall to the elevator he thought about what Monica had said and considered the difference between private investigation and private obsession. Somewhere there was a line between them. But he wasn't sure where it was.

8

There was something wrong about the address, something that didn't fit. But Pierce couldn't place it. He worried over it as he drove into Venice but it didn't open up to him. It was like something hidden behind a shower curtain. It was blurred but it was there.

The address Lilly Quinlan had given as a contact address to All American Mail was a bungalow on Altair Place, a block off the stretch of stylish antiques stores and restaurants on Abbot Kinney Boulevard. It was a small white house with gray trim that somehow made Pierce think of a seagull. There was a fat royal palm squatting in the front yard. Pierce parked across the street and for several minutes sat in his car, studying the house for signs of recent life.

The yard and ornamentation were neatly trimmed. But if it was a rental, that could have been taken care of by a landlord. There was no car in the driveway or in the open garage in back and no newspapers piling up near the curb. Nothing seemed outwardly amiss.

Pierce finally decided on the direct approach. He got out of the BMW, crossed the street and followed the walkway to the front door. There was a button for a doorbell. He pushed it and heard an innocuous chime sound from somewhere inside. He waited.

Nothing.

He pushed the bell again, then knocked on the door.

He waited.

And nothing.

He looked around. The Venetian blinds behind the front windows were closed. He turned and nonchalantly surveyed the homes across the street while he reached a hand behind his back and tried the doorknob. It was locked.

54

Not wanting the day's journey to end without his getting some piece of new information or revelation, he stepped away from the door and walked over to the driveway, which went down the left side of the house to a single stand-alone garage in the rear yard. A huge Monterey pine that dwarfed the house was buckling the driveway with its roots. They were headed for the house and Pierce guessed that in another five years there would be structural damage and the question would be whether to save the tree or the house.

The garage door was open. It was made of wood that had been bowed by time and its own weight. It looked like it was permanently fixed in the open position. The garage was empty except for a collection of paint cans lined against the rear wall.

To the right of the garage was a postage-stamp-sized yard that offered privacy because of a tall hedge that ran along the borders. Two lounge chairs sat in the grass. There was a birdbath with no water in it. Pierce looked at the lounge chairs and thought about the tan lines he had seen on Lilly's body in the web page photo.

After hesitating for a moment in the yard, Pierce went to the rear door and knocked again. The door had a window cut into its upper half. Without waiting to see if someone answered, he cupped his hands against the glass and looked in. It was the kitchen. It appeared neat and clean. There was nothing on the small table pushed against the wall to the left. A newspaper was neatly folded on one of the two chairs.

On the counter next to the toaster was a large bowl filled with dark shapes that Pierce realized were rotten pieces of fruit.

Now he had something. Something that didn't fit, something that showed something wasn't right. He knocked sharply on the door's window, even though he knew no one was inside who could answer. He turned and looked around the yard for something to maybe break the window with. He instinctively grabbed the knob and turned it while he was pivoting.

The door was unlocked.

Pierce wheeled back around. The knob still in his hand, he pushed and the door opened six inches. He waited for an alarm to sound but his intrusion was greeted with only silence. And almost immediately he could smell the sickly sweet stench of the rotten fruit. Or maybe, he thought, it was something else. He took his hand off the knob and pushed the door open wider, leaned in and yelled.

"Lilly? Lilly, it's me, Henry."

He didn't know if he was doing it for the neighbors' sake or his own but he yelled her name two more times, expecting and getting no results. Before entering, he turned around and sat down on the stoop. He considered the decision, whether to go in or not. He thought about Monica's reaction earlier to what he was doing and what she had said: Just call the cops.

Now was the moment to do that. Something was wrong here and he certainly had something to call about. But the truth was he wasn't ready to give this away. Not yet. Whatever it was, it was his still and he wanted to pursue it. His motivations, he knew, were not only in regard to Lilly Quinlan. They reached further and were entwined with the past. He knew he was trying to trade the present for the past, to do now what he hadn't been able to do back then.

He got up off the back step and opened the door fully. He stepped into the kitchen and closed the door behind him.

There was the low sound of music coming from somewhere in the house. Pierce stood still and scanned the kitchen again and found nothing wrong except for the fruit in the bowl. He opened the refrigerator and saw a carton of orange juice and a plastic bottle of low fat milk. The milk had an August 18 use-by date. The juice's was August 16. It had been well over a month since the contents of each had expired.

Pierce went to the table and slid back the chair. On it was the *Los Angeles Times* edition from August 1.

There was a hallway running off the left side of the kitchen to the front of the house. As Pierce moved into the hall he saw the pile of mail building below the slot in the front door. But before he got to the front of the house he explored the three doorways that broke up the hallway. One was to a bathroom, where he found every horizontal surface crowded with perfumes and female beauty aids, all of it waiting under a fine layer of dust. He chose a small green bottle and opened it. He raised it to his nose and smelled the scent of lilac perfume. It was the same stuff Nicole used; he had recognized the bottle. After a moment he closed and returned the bottle to its place and then stepped back into the hallway.

The other two doors led to bedrooms. One appeared to be the master bedroom. Both closets in this room were open and jammed with clothing on wood hangers. The music was coming from an alarm clock radio located on a night table on the right side. He checked both tables for a phone and possibly an answering machine, but there was none.

The other bedroom appeared to be used as a workout location. There was no bed. There was a stair machine and a rowing machine on a grass mat, a small television in front of them. Pierce opened the only closet and found more clothing on hangers. He was about to close it when he realized something. These clothes were different. Almost two feet of hanger space was devoted to small things — negligees and leotards. He saw something familiar and reached in for the hanger. It was the black fishnet negligee she had posed in for the website photo.

This reminded him of something. He put the hanger back in its place and went back into the other bedroom. It was the wrong bed. Not the brass railings of the photo. In that moment he realized what was wrong, what had bothered him about the Venice address. Her ad copy. Lilly had said she met clients at a clean and safe town-house on the Westside. This was no townhouse and that was the wrong bed. It meant there was still another address connected to Lilly Quinlan that he still had to find.

Pierce froze when he heard a noise from the front of the house. He realized as an amateur break-in artist he had made a mistake. He should have quickly scanned the whole house to make sure it was empty instead of starting at the back and moving slowly toward the front.

He waited but there was no other sound. It had been a singular banging sound followed by what sounded like something being rolled across the wood floor. He slowly moved toward the door of the bed-room and then looked down the hall. Just the pile of mail on the floor at the front door.

He stepped to the side of the hallway, where he felt the wood was probably less likely to creak, and made his way slowly to the front of the house. The hallway opened to a living room on the left and a dining room on the right. There was no one in either room. He saw nothing that would explain the sound he had heard.

The living room was kept neat. It was filled with Craftsman-style furniture that was in keeping with the house. What wasn't was the double rack of high-end electronics below the plasma television hanging on the wall. Lilly Quinlan had a home entertainment station that had probably run her twenty-five grand — a tweakhead's wet dream. It seemed out of character with everything else he had seen so far.

Pierce stepped over to the door and squatted by the pile of mail. He started looking through it. Most of it was junk mail addressed to "current resident." There were two envelopes from All American Mail — the late notices. There were credit card bills and bank statements. There was a large envelope from the University of Southern California. He looked specifically for letters — bills — from the phone company and found none. He thought this was odd but quickly assumed her phone bills might have been sent to the box at All American Mail. He put one of the bank statements and a Visa bill into the back pocket of his jeans without a second thought — the first being that he was compounding the crime of breaking and entering with a federal mail theft rap. He decided not to pursue thoughts on this and got up.

In the dining room he found a rolltop desk against the rear wall. He turned a chair from the table to the desk, opened it and sat down. He quickly went through the drawers and determined that this was her bill paying station. There were checkbooks, stamps and pens in the center drawer. The drawers going down either side of the desk were filled with envelopes from credit card companies and utilities and other bills. He found a stack of envelopes from Entrepreneurial Concepts Unlimited, though these had been addressed to the mail drop. On each envelope Lilly had written the date the bill was paid. Again noticeably missing was a stack of old phone bills. Even if she did not receive the bills by mail at this address, it did appear she paid her bills at this desk. But there were no receipts, no envelopes with the date of payment written on them.

Pierce didn't have time to dwell on it or to go through all the bills. He wasn't sure what he would find in them that might help him determine what had happened to Lilly Quinlan anyway. He went back to the center drawer and quickly went through the registers of the checkbooks. There had been no activity in either account since the end of July. Going back quickly through one of the books, he found record of payment to the telephone company ending in June. So she did pay the phone bill with the account he held in his hand and very likely at the desk where he sat. But he could find no other record of the billing in the drawers. He couldn't even find a phone.

Feeling hurried by the situation, he gave up on the contradiction and closed the drawer. He reached to the handle to pull the rolltop down when he saw a small book pushed far into one of the storage slots at the top of the desk. He reached in for it and found it to be a small personal phone book. He used his thumb to buzz through the pages and saw that it was filled with hand-written entries. Without another thought, he shoved the book into his back pocket along with the mail he had decided to take.

He rolled the top down, stood up and took a last survey of the two front rooms, looking for a phone and not finding one. Almost immediately he saw a shadow move behind the closed blinds of the living room window. Someone was going to the front door.

A blade of sheer panic sliced through Pierce. He didn't know whether to hide or run down the hallway and out the back door. Instead, he couldn't do anything. He stood there, unable to move his feet as he heard a footstep on the tiled stoop outside the front door.

A metallic clack made him jump. Then a small stack of mail was pushed through the slot in the door and fell to the floor on top of the other mail. Pierce closed his eyes.

"Jesus!" he whispered as he let out his breath and tried to relax.

The shadow crossed the living room blinds again, going the other way. And then it was gone.

Pierce stepped over and looked at the latest influx of mail. A few more bills but mostly junk mail. He used his foot to push the envelopes around to make sure and then he saw a small envelope addressed by hand. He bent down to pick it up. In the upper left corner of the envelope it said *V. Quinlan* but there was no return address to go with it. The postmark was partially smeared and he could only make out the letters *pa, Fla*. He turned the envelope over and checked the seal. He would have to tear the envelope to open it.

Something about opening this obviously personal piece of mail seemed more intrusive and criminal to him than anything else he had done so far. But his hesitation didn't last long. He used a fingernail to pry open the envelope and pulled out a small piece of folded paper. It was a letter dated four days earlier.

Lilly,

I am worried sick about you. If you get this, please just call me to let me know you are okay. Please, honey? Since you have stopped calling me I haven't been able to think right. I am very worried about you and that job of yours. Things around here were never really the best and I know I didn't do everything right. But I don't think that you shouldn't tell me if you are all right. Please call me if and when you get this.

Love,
Mom

He read it twice and then refolded the page and returned it to the envelope. More than anything else in the apartment, including the rotten fruit, the letter stabbed Pierce with a sense of doom. He didn't think the letter from V. Quinlan would ever be answered by a phone call or otherwise.

He closed the envelope as best as he could and quickly buried it in the pile of mail on the floor. The intrusion of the mail carrier had served to instill in him a sense of the risk he was running by being in the house. He'd had enough. He quickly turned and headed back down the hallway to the kitchen.

He went through the back door and closed it but left it unlocked. As nonchalantly as an amateur criminal can be, he walked around the corner of the house and down the driveway toward the street.

Halfway down the side of the house he heard a loud bang from up on the roof and then a large pinecone rolled off the eave and landed in front of him. As Pierce stepped over it he realized what had made the startling noise while he had been in the house. He nodded as he put it together. At least he had solved one mystery.

9

Lights."

Pierce swung around behind his desk and sat down. From his backpack he pulled out the things he had taken from Lilly Quinlan's house. He had a Visa bill and a bank statement and the phone book.

He started paging through the phone book first. There were several listings for men by first name or first name with a following initial only. These numbers ran the gamut of area codes. Many local but still more from area codes outside of Los Angeles. There were also several listings for local hotels and restaurants, as well as a Lexus dealer in Hollywood. He saw a listing for Robin and another listing for ECU, which he knew was Entrepreneurial Concepts Unlimited.

Under the heading "Dallas" there were several numbers for hotels, restaurants and male first names listed. The same was true of a heading for Las Vegas.

He found a listing for Vivian Quinlan with an 813 area code phone number and an address in Tampa, Florida. That solved the mystery of the smeared postmark on the letter. Near the end of the book he found an entry for someone listed as Wainwright that included a phone number and an address in Venice that Pierce knew was not far from the home on Altair.

He flipped back to the Q listings and used his desk phone to call the number for Vivian Quinlan. A woman answered the phone in two rings. Her voice sounded like a broom sweeping a sidewalk.

"Hello?"

"Mrs. Quinlan?"

"Yes?"

"Uh, hi, I'm calling from Los Angeles. My name's Henry Pierce and —"

"Is this about Lilly?"

Her voice had an immediate, desperate tone to it.

"Yes. I'm trying to locate her and I was wondering if you could help me."

"Oh, thank God! Are you police?"

"Uh, no, ma'am, I'm not."

"I don't care. Someone finally cares."

"Well, I'm just trying to find her, Mrs. Quinlan. Have you heard from her lately?"

"Not in more than seven weeks and that just isn't like her. She always checked in. I'm very worried."

"Have you contacted the police?"

"Yes, I called and talked to the Missing Persons people. They weren't interested because she's an adult and because of what she does for a living."

"What does she do for a living, Mrs. Quinlan?"

There was a hesitation.

"I thought you said you knew her."

"I'm just an acquaintance."

"She works as a gentleman's escort."

"I see."

"No sex or anything. She told me she goes to dinner with men in tuxedos mostly."

Pierce let that go by as a mother's denial of the obvious. It was something he had seen before in his own family.

"What did the police say to you about her?"

"Just that she probably went off with one of these fellows and that I'd probably hear from her soon."

"When was that?"

"A month ago. You see, Lilly calls me every Saturday afternoon. When two weeks went by with no phone calls I called the police. They didn't call me back. After the third week I called again and talked to Missing Persons. They didn't even take a report or anything, just told me to keep waiting. They don't care."

For some reason a vision bled into his mind and distracted him. It was the night he had come home from Stanford. His mother was waiting for him in the kitchen, the lights off. Just waiting there in the dark to tell him the news about his sister, Isabelle.

When Lilly Quinlan's mother spoke, it was his own mother.

"I called in a private detective but he's been no help. He can't find her neither."

The content of what she was saying finally brought him out of it.

"Mrs. Quinlan, is Lilly's father there? Can I talk to him?"

"No, he's long gone. She never knew him. He hasn't been here in about twelve years — ever since the day I caught him with her."

"Is he in prison?"

"No, he's just gone."

Pierce didn't know what to say.

"When did Lilly come out to L.A.?"

"About three years ago. She first went to a flight attendant school out in Dallas but never did that job. Then she moved to L.A. I wish she'd become a flight attendant. I told her that in the escort business even if you don't have sex with those men, people will still think that you did."

Pierce nodded. He supposed that it was sound motherly advice. He pictured a heavyset woman with big hair and a cigarette in the corner of her mouth. Between that and her father, no wonder Lilly went about as far as she could get from Tampa. He was surprised it was only three years ago that she left.

"Where did you hire a private detective, there in Tampa or out here in L.A.?"

"Out there. Not much use to hire one here."

"How did you hire one out here?"

"The policeman in Missing Persons sent me a list. I picked from there."

"Did you come out here to look for her, Mrs. Quinlan?"

"I'm not in good health. Doctor says I've got emphysema and I've got my oxygen that I'm hooked up to. There wasn't much I could do comin' out there."

Pierce reconstructed his vision of her. The cigarette was gone and the oxygen tube replaced it. The big hair remained. He thought about what else he could ask or what information he might be able to get from the woman.

"Lilly told me she was sending you money."

It was a guess. It seemed to go with the whole mother-daughter relationship.

"Yes, and if you find her, tell her I'm getting real short about now. I'm real low. I had to give a lot of what I had to Mr. Glass."

"Who is Mr. Glass?"

"He's the private detective I hired. But I don't hear from him anymore. Now that I can't pay him anymore."

"Can you give me his full name and a number for him?"

"I have to look it up."

She put down the phone and it was two minutes before she came back and gave him the number and address for the private investigator. His full name was Philip Glass. His office was in Culver City.

"Mrs. Quinlan, are there any other contacts you have for Lilly out here? Any friends or anything like that?"

"No, she never gave me any numbers or told me about any friends. Except she once mentioned this girl Robin who she worked with sometimes. Robin was from New Orleans and they had stuff in common, she told me."

"Did she say what?"

"I think they both had the same kind of trouble with men in their family when they were young. That's what I expect she meant."

"I understand."

Pierce was trying to think like a detective. Vivian Quinlan seemed like an important piece of the puzzle, yet he could not think of anything else to ask her. She was three thousand miles away and was obviously kept literally and figuratively distant from her daughter's world. He looked down at the phone book on the desk in front of him and finally came up with something to ask.

"Does the name Wainwright mean anything to you, Mrs. Quinlan? Did Lilly or Mr. Glass ever mention that name?"

"Um, no. Mr. Glass didn't mention any names. Who is it?"

"I don't know. It's just someone she knew, I guess."

That was it. He had nothing else.

"Okay, Mrs. Quinlan, I'm going to keep trying to find her and I'll tell her to call you when I do."

"I'd appreciate that and make sure you tell her about the money, that I'm getting real low."

"Right. I will."

He hung up and thought for a few moments about what he

knew. Probably too much about Lilly. It made him feel depressed and sad. He hoped one of her clients did take her away with a promise of riches and luxury. Maybe she was in Hawaii somewhere or in a rich man's penthouse in Paris.

But he doubted it.

"Guys in tuxedos," he said out loud.

"What?"

He looked up. Charlie Condon was standing in the door. Pierce had left it open.

"Oh, nothing. Just talking to myself. What are you doing here?"

He realized that Lilly Quinlan's phone book and the mail were spread in front of him. He nonchalantly picked up the daily planner he kept on the desk, looked at it like he was checking a date and then put it down on top of the envelopes with her name on them.

"I called your new number and got Monica. She said you were supposed to be here while she waited for furniture to be delivered. But nobody answered in the lab or in your office, so I came by."

He leaned against the door frame. Charlie was a handsome man with what seemed like a perpetual tan. He had worked as a model in New York for a few years before getting bored and going back to school for a master's in finance. They had been introduced by an investment banker who knew Condon was skilled at taking under-financed emerging-technology firms and matching them with investors. Pierce had joined with him because he'd promised to do it with Amedeo Technologies without Pierce having to sacrifice his controlling interest to investors. In return, Charlie would hold 10 percent of the company, a stake that could ultimately be worth hundreds of millions — if they won the race and went public with a stock offering.

"I missed your calls," Pierce said. "I just got here, actually. Stopped to get something to eat first."

Charlie nodded.

"I thought you'd be in the lab."

Meaning, why aren't you in the lab? There is work to be done. We're in a race. We've got a presentation to a whale to make. You can't chase the dime from your office.

"Yeah, don't worry, I'll get there. I just have some mail to go through. You came all the way in to check on me?"

"Not really. But we only have until Thursday to get our shit together for Maurice. I wanted to make sure everything was all right."

Pierce knew they were placing too much importance on Maurice Goddard. Even Charlie's e-mail reference to the investor as God was a subliminal indication of this. It was true that Thursday's dog and pony show would be the dog and pony show of all time, but Pierce had growing concern about Condon's reliance on this deal. They were seeking an investor willing to commit at least $6 million a year over three or four years, minimum. Goddard, according to the due diligence conducted by Nicole James and Cody Zeller, was worth $250 million, thanks to his getting in early on a few investments like Microsoft. It was clear that Goddard had the money. But if he didn't come across with a significant funding plan after Thursday's presentation, then there had to be another investor out there. It would be Condon's job to go out and find him.

"Don't worry," Pierce said. "We'll be ready. Is Jacob coming in for it?"

"He'll be here."

Jacob Kaz was the company's patent attorney. They had fifty-eight patents already granted or applied for and Kaz was going to file nine more the Monday after the presentation to Goddard. Patents were the key to the race. Control the patents and you are in on the ground floor and will eventually control the market. The nine new patent applications were the first to come out of the Proteus project. They would send a shock wave through the nanoworld. Pierce almost smiled at the thought of it. And Condon seemed to read his thoughts.

"Did you look at the patents yet?" he asked.

Pierce reached down into the kneehole beneath his desk and knocked his fist on the top of the steel safe bolted there to the floor. The patent drafts were in there. Pierce had to sign off on them before they were filed but it was very dry reading, and he'd been distracted by other things even before Lilly Quinlan came up.

"Right here. I'm planning to get to them today or come back in tomorrow."

It would be against company policy for Pierce to take the applications home to review.

Condon nodded his approval.

"Great. So, everything else okay? You doin' all right?"

"You mean with Nicki and everything?"

Charlie nodded.

"Yeah, I'm cool. I'm trying to keep my mind on other things."

"Like the lab, I hope."

Pierce leaned back in his chair, spread his hands and smiled. He wondered how much Monica had told him when he had called the apartment.

"I'm here."

"Well, good."

"By the way, Nicole left a new clip in the Bronson file on the Tagawa deal. It's hit the media."

"Anything?"

"Nothing we didn't know already. Elliot said something about biologicals. Very general, but you never know. Maybe he's gotten wind of Proteus."

As he said it Pierce looked past Condon at the framed one-sheet poster on his office wall next to the door. It was the poster from the 1966 movie *Fantastic Voyage*. It showed the white submarine *Proteus* descending through a multicolor sea of bodily fluids. It was an original poster. He had gotten it from Cody Zeller, who had obtained it through an online Hollywood memorabilia auction.

"Elliot just likes to talk," Condon said. "I don't know how he could know anything about Proteus. But after the patent is granted he'll know about it. And he'll be shitting bricks. And Tagawa will know they backed the wrong horse."

"Yeah, I hope so."

They had flirted with Tagawa earlier in the year. But the Japanese company wanted too large a piece of the company for the money, and negotiations broke down early. Though Proteus was mentioned in the early meetings, the Tagawa representatives were never fully briefed and never got near the lab. Now Pierce had to concern himself with exactly how much about the project was mentioned, because it stood to reason that the information was passed on to Tagawa's new partner, Elliot Bronson.

"Let me know if you need anything and I'll get it done," Condon said.

It brought Pierce out of his thoughts.

"Thanks, Charlie. You going back home now?"

"Probably. Melissa and I are going to Jar tonight for dinner. You want to go? I could call and make it for three."

"Nah, that's okay. But thanks. I've got the furniture coming in today and I'll probably work on getting my place set up."

Charlie nodded and then hesitated for a moment before asking the next question.

"You going to change your phone number?"

"Yeah, I think I have to. First thing Monday. Monica told you, huh?"

"A little bit. She said you got some prostitute's old number and guys are calling all the time."

"She's an escort, not a prostitute."

"Oh, I didn't know there was a big difference."

Pierce couldn't believe he had jumped to defend a woman he didn't even know. He felt his face getting red.

"There probably isn't. Anyway, when I see you Monday I'll probably give you a new number, okay? I want to get done here so I can get in the lab and do something today."

"Okay, man, I'll see you Monday."

Condon left then, and after Pierce was sure he was down the hall he got up and closed his door. He wondered how much more Monica had told him, whether she was spreading alarm about his activities. He thought about calling her but decided to wait until later, to talk about it with her in person.

He went back to Lilly's phone book, leafing through it once again. Almost to the end he came across a listing he hadn't noticed before. It simply said USC and had a number. Pierce thought about the envelope he had seen in her house. He picked up the phone and called the number. He got a recording for the admissions office of the University of Southern California. The office was closed on weekends.

Pierce hung up. He wondered if Lilly had been in the process of applying to USC when she disappeared. Maybe she had been trying to get out of the escort business. Maybe it was the reason she had disappeared.

He put the phone book aside and opened the Visa statement. It showed zero purchases on the card for the month of August and notice for an overdue payment on a $354.26 balance. The payment had been due by August 10.

The bank statement from Washington Savings & Loan was next. It was a combined statement showing balances in checking and savings accounts. Lilly Quinlan had not made a deposit in the month of August but had not been short of funds. She had $9,240 in checking and $54,542 in savings. It wasn't enough for four years at USC but it would have been a start if Lilly was changing her direction.

Pierce looked through the statement and the collection of posted checks the bank had returned to her. He noticed one to a Vivian Quinlan for $2,000 and assumed that was the monthly installment on maternal upkeep. Another check, this one for $4,000, was made out to James Wainwright and on the memo line Lilly had written, "Rent."

He tapped the check lightly against his chin as he thought about what this meant. It seemed to him that $4,000 was an excessively high monthly rent for the bungalow on Altair. He wondered if she had paid for more than one month with the check.

He put the check back in the stack and finished looking through the bank records. Nothing else hooked his interest and he put the checks and the statement back in the envelope.

The third-floor copy room was a short walk down the hall from Pierce's office. Along with a copier and a fax machine, the small room contained a power shredder. Pierce entered the room, opened up his backpack and fed the pieces of Lilly Quinlan's opened mail into the shredder, the whine of the machine seemingly loud enough to draw the attention of security. But no one came. He felt a sense of guilt drop over him. He didn't know anything about federal mail theft laws but was sure he had probably just compounded the first offense of stealing the mail by now destroying it.

When he was finished he stuck his head out into the hall and checked to make sure he was still alone on the floor. He then returned and opened one of the storage cabinets where stacks of packages containing copier paper were stored. From his backpack he removed Lilly Quinlan's phone book and then reached into the cabinet with it, dropping it behind one of the stacks of paper. He believed it could go as long as a month there without being discovered.

Once finished with hiding and destroying the evidence of his crime, Pierce took the lab elevator down to the basement and passed through the mantrap into the suite. He checked the sign-in log and saw that Grooms had been in that morning as well as Larraby and a few of the lower-tier lab rats. They had all come and gone. He picked up the pen and was about to sign in when he thought better of it and put the pen back down.

At the computer console Pierce entered the three passwords in correct order for a Saturday and logged in. He called up the testing protocols for the Proteus project. He started to read the summary of the most recent testing of cellular energy conversion rates, which had been conducted by Larraby that morning.

But then he stopped. Once again he could not do it. He could not concentrate on the work. He was consumed by other thoughts, and he knew from past experience — the Proteus project being an example — that he must run out the clock on the thing that consumed him if he was to ever return to the work.

He shut down the computer and left the lab. Back up in his office he took his notebook out of his backpack and called the number he had for the private investigator, Philip Glass. As he expected for a Saturday afternoon, he got a machine and left a message.

"Mr. Glass, my name is Henry Pierce. I would like to talk to you as soon as possible about Lilly Quinlan. I got your name and number from her mother. I hope to talk to you soon. You can call me back at any time."

He left both his apartment number and the direct line to his office and hung up. He realized that Glass might recognize the apartment number as having once belonged to Lilly Quinlan.

He drummed his fingers on the edge of his desk. He tried to figure out the next step. He decided he was going up the coast to see Cody Zeller. But first he called his apartment number and Monica answered in a gruff voice.

"What?"

"It's me, Henry. My stuff get there yet?"

"They just got here. Finally. They're bringing in the bed first. Look, you can't blame me if you don't like where I tell them to put stuff."

"Tell me something. Are you having them put the bed in the bedroom?"

"Of course."

"Then I'm sure I'll like it just fine. What are you so short about?"

"It's just this goddamn phone. Every fifteen minutes some creep calls for Lilly. I'll tell you one thing: wherever she is, she must be rich."

Pierce had a growing feeling that wherever she was, money didn't matter. But he didn't say that.

"The calls are still coming in? They told me they'd get her page off the website by three o'clock."

"Well, I got a call about five minutes ago. Before I could say I wasn't Lilly the guy asked if I'd do a prostate massage, whatever that is. I hung up on him. It's totally gross."

Pierce smiled. He didn't know what it was, either. But he tried to keep the humor out of his voice.

"I'm sorry. Hopefully they won't take long getting it all up there and you can leave as soon as they are finished."

"Thank God."

"I need to go to Malibu, or else I'd come back now."

"Malibu? What's in Malibu?"

Pierce regretted mentioning it. He had forgotten about her earlier interest and disapproval of what he was doing.

"Don't worry, nothing to do with Lilly Quinlan," he lied. "I'm going to see Cody Zeller about something."

He knew it was weak but it would have to do for now. They hung up and Pierce started putting his notebook back in his backpack.

"Lights," he said.

10

The drive north on the Pacific Coast Highway was slow but nice. The highway skirted the ocean, and the sun hung low in the sky over Pierce's left shoulder. It was warm but he had the windows down and the sunroof open. He couldn't remember the last time he had taken a drive like this. Maybe it was the time he and Nicole had ducked out of Amedeo for a long lunch and driven up to Geoffrey's, the restaurant overlooking the Pacific and favored by Malibu's movie set.

When he got into the first stretch of the beach town and his view of the coast was stolen by the houses crowding the ocean's edge, he slowed down and watched for Zeller's house. He didn't have the address offhand and had to recognize the house, which he hadn't seen in more than a year. The houses on this stretch were jammed side to side and all looked the same. No lawns, built right to the curb, flat as shoe boxes.

He was saved by the sight of Zeller's black-on-black Jaguar XKR, which was parked out in front of his house's closed garage. Zeller had long ago illegally converted his garage into a workroom and had to pay garage rent to a neighbor to protect his $90,000 car. The car's being outside meant Zeller had either just gotten home or was about to head out. Pierce was just in time. He pulled a U-turn and parked behind the Jag, careful not to bump the car Zeller treated like a baby sister.

The front door of the house was opened before he reached it — either Zeller had seen him on one of the cameras mounted under the roof's eave or Pierce had tripped a motion sensor. Zeller was the only person Pierce knew who rivaled him in paranoia. It was probably what had bonded them at Stanford. He remembered that when they were freshmen Zeller had an often spoken theory that

President Reagan had lapsed into a coma after the assassination attempt in the first year of his presidency and had been replaced by a double who was a puppet of the far right. The theory was good for laughs but he was serious about it.

"Dr. Strangelove, I presume," Zeller said.

"Mein führer, I can walk," Pierce replied.

It had been their standard greeting since Stanford when they saw the movie together at a Kubrick retrospective in San Francisco.

They gave each other a handshake invented by the loose group of friends they belonged to in college. They called themselves the Doomsters, after the Ross MacDonald novel. The handshake consisted of fingers hooked together like train car couplings and then three quick squeezes like gripping a rubber ball at a blood bank — the Doomsters had sold plasma on a regular basis while in college in order to buy beer, marijuana and computer software.

Pierce hadn't seen Zeller in a few months and his hair hadn't been cut since then. Sun-bleached and unkempt, it was loosely tied at the back of his neck. He wore a Zuma Jay T-shirt, baggies and leather sandals. His skin was the copper color of smoggy sunsets. Of all the Doomsters he always had the look the others had aspired to. Now it was wearing a little long in the tooth. At thirty-five he was beginning to look like an aging surfer who couldn't let it go, which made him all the more endearing to Pierce. In many ways Pierce felt like a sellout. He admired Zeller for the path he had cut through life.

"Check him out, Dr. Strange himself out in the Big Bad 'Bu. Man, you don't have your wets with you and I don't see any board, so to what do I owe this unexpected pleasure?"

He beckoned Pierce inside and they walked into a large loft-style home that was divided in half, with living quarters to the right and working quarters to the left. Beyond these distinct areas was a wall of floor-to-ceiling glass that opened to the deck and the ocean just beyond. The steady pounding of the ocean's waves was the heartbeat of the house. Zeller had once informed Pierce that it was impossible to sleep in the house without earplugs and a pillow over one's head.

"Just thought I'd take a ride out and check on things here."

They moved across the beech flooring toward the view. In a

73

house like this it was an automatic reflex. You gravitated to the view, to the blue-black water of the Pacific. Pierce saw a light misting out on the horizon but not a single boat. As they got close to the glass he could look down through the deck railing and see the swells rolling in. A small company of surfers in multicolor wets sat on their boards and waited for the right moment. Pierce felt an internal tug. It had been a long time since he'd been out there. He'd always found the waiting on the swells, the camaraderie of the group, to be more fulfilling than the actual ride in on the wave.

"Those are my boys out there," Zeller said.

"They look like Malibu High teenagers."

"They are. And so am I."

Pierce nodded. Feel young, stay young — a common Malibu life ethic.

"I keep forgetting about how nice you got it out here, Code."

"For a college dropout, I can't complain. Beats selling one's purity of essence for twenty-five bucks a bag."

He was talking about plasma. Pierce turned away from the view. In the living area there were matching gray couches and a coffee table in front of a freestanding fireplace with an industrial, concrete finish. Behind this was the kitchen. To the left was the bedroom area.

"Beer, dude? I've got Pacifica and Saint Mike."

"Yeah, sure. Either one."

While Zeller went to the kitchen Pierce moved toward the work area. A large floor-to-ceiling rack of electronics acted to knock down the exterior light and partition off the area where Zeller made his living. There were two desks and another bank of shelves containing code books and software and system manuals. He stepped through the plastic curtain that used to be where the door to the garage was. He took a step down and was in a climate-controlled computer room. There were two complete computer bays on either side of the room, each equipped with multiple screens. Each system seemed to be at work. Slowly unspooling data trails moved across each screen. Digital inchworms crawling through whatever was Zeller's project at the moment. The walls of the room were covered in black foam padding to dampen exterior noise. The room was dimly lit by mini-spots. There was an unseen stereo playing an old Guns N' Roses disc that Pierce had not heard in more than ten years.

Affixed to the padding of the rear wall was a procession of stickers depicting company logos and trademark names. Most were household words, companies pervasive in daily life. There were many more stickers on the wall than the last time Pierce visited. He knew that Zeller put up a logo every time he conducted a successful intrusion into that company's computer services system. They were the notches on his belt.

Zeller earned $500 an hour as a white-hat hacker. He was the best of the best. He worked as an independent, usually hired by one of the Big Six accounting firms to conduct penetration tests on its clients. In a way it was a racket. The system that Zeller could not defeat was rare. And after each successful penetration his employer usually turned around and got a fat digital security contract from the client, with a nice bonus going to Zeller. He had once told Pierce that digital security was the fastest growth area in the corporate accounting industry. He was constantly fielding high-price offers to come on board full-time with one or another of the big firms, but he always demurred, saying he liked working for himself. Privately, he told Pierce that it was also because working for himself allowed him to eschew the random drug testing of the corporate world.

Zeller came into the clean room with two brown bottles of San Miguel. They double-clicked bottles before drinking. Another tradition. It tasted good to Pierce, smooth and cold. Bottle in hand, he pointed to a red and white square affixed to the wall. It was the most recognized corporate symbol in the world.

"That one's new, isn't it?"

"Yeah, I just got that one. Took the job out of Atlanta. You know how they got some secret formula for making the drink? They were —"

"Yeah, cocaine."

"That's the urban myth. Anyway, they wanted to see how well the formula was protected. I went in from total scratch. Took me about seven hours and then I e-mailed the formula to the CEO. He didn't know we were doing a penetration test — it was handled by people below him. I was told he almost had a goddamn coronary.

He had visions of the formula going out across the net, falling into the hands of the Pepsi and Dr Pepper people, I guess."

Pierce smiled.

"Cool. You working on something right now? It looks busy."

He indicated the screens with his bottle.

"No, not really. I'm just doing a little trolling. Looking for somebody I know is out there hiding."

"Who?"

Zeller looked at him and smiled.

"If I told you that, I'd have to kill you."

It was business. Zeller was saying that part of what he sold was discretion. They were friends who went back to good times and one seriously bad time — at least for Pierce — in college. But business was business.

"I understand," Pierce said. "And I don't want to intrude, so let me get to it. Are you too busy to take on something else?"

"When would I need to start?"

"Uh, yesterday would be nice."

"A quickie. I like quickies. And I like working for Amedeo Tech."

"Not for the company. For me. But I'll pay you."

"I like that better. What do you need?"

"I need to run some people and some businesses, see what comes up."

Zeller nodded thoughtfully.

"Heavy people?"

"I don't really know but I'd use all precautions. It involves the adult entertainment field, you could say."

Now Zeller smiled broadly, his burned skin crinkling around the eyes.

"Oh, baby, don't tell me you bumped your dick into something."

"No, nothing like that."

"Then what?"

"Let's sit down. And you'd better bring something to take notes with."

In the living room Pierce gave him all the information he had on Lilly Quinlan without explanation about where it was coming from. He also asked Zeller to find what he could on Entrepreneurial Concepts Unlimited and Wentz, the man who operated it.

"You got a first name?"

"No. Just Wentz. Can't be too many in the field, I would guess."

"Full scans?"

"Whatever you can get."

"Stay inside the lines?"

Pierce hesitated. Zeller kept his eyes level on him. He was asking if Pierce wanted him to stay within the bounds of the law. Pierce knew from experience that there was much more out there to be found if Zeller crossed the lines and went into systems he was not authorized to enter. And he knew Zeller was an expert at crossing them. The Doomsters were formed when they were college sophomores. Computer hacking was just coming into vogue for their generation and the members of the group, largely under the direction of Zeller, did more than hold their own. They mostly committed pranks, their best being the time they hacked into the local telephone company's 411 information bank and changed the number for the Domino's Pizza closest to campus to the home number of the dean of the Computer Sciences Department.

But their best moment was also their worst. All six of the Doomsters were busted by the police and later suspended. On the criminal side everybody got probation with the charges to be expunged after six months without further trouble. Each boy also had to complete 160 hours of community service. On the school side they were all suspended for one semester. Pierce went back after serving both the suspension and the probation. Under the magnifying glass of police and school administrators, he switched from computer sciences to a chemistry curriculum and never looked back.

Zeller never looked back, either. He didn't go back to Stanford. He was scooped up by a computer security firm and given a nice salary. Like a gifted athlete who leaves school early for the pros, he could not go back to school once he sampled the joys of having money and doing what he loved for a living.

"Tell you what," Pierce finally answered. "Get whatever you can get. In fact, on Entrepreneurial Concepts, I think some variation of *abra cadabra* might help you get in. Try it backwards first."

"Thanks for the head start. When do you need this?"

"Like I said, yesterday will be fine."

"Right, a quickie. You sure you didn't stick your dick into something nasty?"

"Not that I know of."

"Nicole know about this?"

"Nope, there's no reason. Nicole's gone, remember?"

"Right, right. This the reason why?"

"You don't give up, do you? No, it's got nothing to do with her."

Pierce finished his beer. He didn't want to hang around, because he wanted Zeller to get to work on the assignment he was giving him. But Zeller seemed in no hurry to start.

"Want another beer, commander?"

"Nah, I'm gonna pass. I've gotta get back to my apartment. I have my assistant baby-sitting the furniture movers. Besides, you're going to get on this thing, aren't you?"

"Oh, yeah, man. Right away."

He gestured toward his work area.

"Right now all my machines are booked. But I'll get on it tonight. I'll call you by tomorrow night."

"All right, Code. Thanks."

He got up. They pumped each other's hand. Blood brothers. Doomsters again.

11

By the time Pierce got to his apartment the movers were gone but Monica was still there. She'd had them arrange the furnishings in a way that was acceptable. It didn't really take advantage of the view from the floor-to-ceiling windows that ran along one side of the living room and dining room, but Pierce didn't care all that much. He knew he'd be spending little time in the apartment anyway.

"It looks nice," he said. "Thanks."

"You're welcome. I hope you like everything. I was just about to leave."

"Why did you stay?"

She held up her stack of magazines in two hands.

"I wanted to finish a magazine I was reading."

Pierce wasn't sure why that necessitated her staying at the apartment but he let it go.

"Listen, there's one thing I want to ask you before you leave. Come sit down for a second."

Monica looked put out by the request. She probably envisioned another phone call impersonating Lilly Quinlan. Nevertheless, she sat down on one of the leather club chairs she'd ordered to go with his couch.

"Okay, what is it?"

Pierce sat on the couch.

"What is your job title at Amedeo Technologies?"

"What do you mean? You know what it is."

"I want to see if *you* know what it is."

"Personal assistant to the president. Why?"

"Because I want to make sure you remember that it is *personal* assistant, not just assistant."

She blinked and looked at his face for a long moment before responding.

"All right, Henry, what's wrong?"

"What's wrong is that I don't appreciate your telling Charlie Condon all about my phone number problems and what I'm trying to do about it."

She straightened her back and looked aghast but it was a bad act.

"I didn't."

"That's not what he said. And if you didn't tell him, how did he know everything after he talked to you?"

"Look, okay, all I told him was that you'd gotten this prostitute's old number and you were getting all kinds of calls. I had to tell him something because when he called I didn't recognize his voice and he didn't recognize mine and he said, 'Who's this?' and I kind of snapped at him because I thought he was, you know, calling for Lilly."

"Uh-huh."

"And I couldn't make up a lie on the spot. I'm not that good, like some people. Lying, social engineering, whatever you call it. So I told him the truth."

Pierce almost mentioned that she was pretty good at lying about not telling Charlie at the start of the conversation but he decided not to inflame the situation.

"And that's all you told him, that I had gotten this woman's phone number? You left it at that? You didn't tell him about how you got her address for me and I went to her house?"

"No, I didn't. What's the big deal anyway? You guys are partners, I thought."

She stood up.

"Can I please go?"

"Monica, sit down here for one more second."

He pointed to the chair and she reluctantly sat back down.

"The big deal is that loose lips sink ships, you understand that?"

She shrugged her shoulders and wouldn't look at him. She looked down at the stack of magazines in her lap. On the cover of the top one was a photo of Clint Eastwood.

"My actions reflect on the company," Pierce said. "Especially right now. Even what I do in private. If what I do is misrepresented or blown out of proportion, it could seriously hurt the company. Right now our company makes zero money, Monica, and we rely on investors to support the research, to pay the rent and the salaries, everything. If investors think we're shaky, then we've got a big problem. If things about me — true or false — get to the wrong people, we could have trouble."

"I didn't know Charlie was the wrong people," she said in a sulking voice.

"He's not. He's the right people. That's why I don't mind what you said to him. But what I will mind is if you tell anybody else about what I am doing or what's going on with me. Anyone, Monica. Inside or outside the company."

He hoped she understood he was talking about Nicole and anybody else she encountered in her daily life.

"I won't. I won't tell a soul. And please don't ask me to get involved in your personal life again. I don't want to baby-sit deliveries or do anything outside of the company again."

"Fine. I won't ask you to. It was my mistake because I didn't think this would be a problem and you told me you could use the overtime."

"I can use the overtime but I don't like all of these complications."

Pierce waited a moment, watching her the whole time.

"Monica, do you even know what we do at Amedeo? I mean, do you know what the project is all about?"

She shrugged.

"Sort of. I know it's about molecular computing. I've read some of the stories on the wall of fame. But the stories are very . . . scientific and everything's so secret that I never wanted to ask questions. I just try to do my job."

"The project isn't secret. The processes we're inventing are. There's a difference."

He leaned forward and tried to think of the best way to explain it to her without making it confusing or treading into protected areas. He decided to use a tack that Charlie Condon often used with potential investors who might be confused by the science. It was an explanation Charlie had come up with after talking about the project in general once with Cody Zeller. Cody loved movies. And so did Pierce, though he rarely had time to see them in theaters anymore.

"Did you ever see the movie *Pulp Fiction*?"

Monica narrowed her eyes and nodded suspiciously.

"Yes, but what does it —"

"Remember, it's a movie about all these gangsters crossing paths and shooting people and shooting drugs, but at the heart of everything is this briefcase. And they never show what's in the briefcase but everybody sure wants it. And when somebody opens it you can't see what's in it but whatever it is glows like gold. You see that glow. And it's mesmerizing for whoever looks into the briefcase."

"I remember."

"Well, that's what we're after at Amedeo. We're after this thing that glows like gold but nobody can see it. We're after it — and a whole bunch of other people are after it — because we all believe it will change the world."

He waited a moment and she just looked at him, uncomprehending.

"Right now, everywhere in the world, microprocessing chips are made of silicon. It's the standard, right?"

She shrugged again.

"Whatever."

"What we are trying to do at Amedeo, and what they are trying to do at Bronson Tech and Midas Molecular and the dozens of other companies and universities and governments around the world we are competing with, is create a new generation of computer chips made of molecules. Build an entire computer's circuitry with only organic molecules. A computer that will one day come out of a vat of chemicals, that will assemble itself from the right recipe being put in that vat. We're talking about a computer without silicon or magnetic particles. Tremendously less expensive to build and astronomically more powerful — in which just a teaspoon of molecules could hold more memory than the biggest computer going today."

She waited to make sure he was done.

"Wow," she said in an unconvincing tone.

Pierce smiled at her stubbornness. He knew he had probably sounded too much like a salesman. Like Charlie Condon, to be precise. He decided to try again.

"Do you know what computer memory actually is, Monica?"

"Well, yeah, I guess."

He could tell by her face that she was just covering. Most people in this day and age took things like computers for granted and without explanation.

"I mean how it works," he said to her. "It's just ones and zeros in sequence. Every piece of data, every number, every letter, has a specific sequence of ones and zeros. You string the sequences together and you have a word or a number and so on. Forty, fifty years ago it took a computer the size of this room to store basic arithmetic. And now we're down to a silicon chip."

He held his thumb and finger up, just a half inch apart. Then he squeezed them together.

"But we can go smaller," he said. "A lot smaller."

She nodded but he couldn't tell if she saw the light or was just nodding.

"Molecules," she said.

He nodded.

"That's right, Monica. And believe me, whoever gets there first is going to change this world. It is conceivable that we could build a whole computer that is smaller than a silicon chip. Take a computer that fills a room now and make it the size of a dime. That's our goal. That's why in the lab we call it 'chasing the dime.' I'm sure you've heard the saying around the office."

She shook her head.

"But why would someone want a computer the size of a dime? They couldn't even read it."

Pierce started laughing but then cut it off. He knew he had to keep this woman quiet and on his side. He shouldn't insult her.

"That's just an example. It's a possibility. The point is, the computing and memory power of this type of technology are limitless. You're right, nobody needs or wants a computer the size of a dime. But think what this advancement would mean for a PalmPilot or a laptop computer. What if you didn't need to carry any of those? What if your computer was in the button of your shirt or the frame of your eyeglasses? What if in your office your desktop wasn't on your desk but in the paint on the walls of your office? What if you talked to the walls and they talked back?"

She shook her head and he could tell she still could not comprehend the possibilities and their applications. She could not break free of the world she currently knew and understood and accepted. He reached into his back pocket and took out his wallet. He removed his American Express card and held it up to her.

"What if this card was a computer? What if it contained a memory chip so powerful that it could record every purchase ever made on this account along with the date, time and location of the purchase? I'm talking about for the lifetime of its user, Monica. A bottomless well of memory in this thin piece of plastic."

Monica shrugged.

"That would be cool, I guess."

"We're less than five years away. We have molecular RAM right now. Random access memory. And we're perfecting logic gates. Working circuits. We put them together — logic and memory — and you have integrated circuitry, Monica."

It still excited him to speak of the possibilities. He slid the credit card back into his wallet and pocketed it. He never took his eyes off her and could tell he still wasn't making a dent. He decided to stop trying to impress her and get to the point.

"Monica, the thing is, we're not alone. It is highly competitive out there. There are a lot of private companies out there just like Amedeo Technologies. A lot of them are bigger and with a lot more money. There's also DARPA, there's UCLA and other universities, there's —"

"What is DARPA?"

"Defense Advanced Research Projects Agency. The government. The agency that keeps its eye on all emerging technologies. It's backing several separate projects in our field. When I started the company I consciously chose not to have the government be my boss. But the point is, most of our competitors are well funded and dug in. We're not. And so to keep going, we need the funding stream to keep flowing. We can't do anything that stops that flow, or we drop out of the race and there is no Amedeo Technologies. Okay?"

"Okay."

"It would be one thing if this was a car dealership or a business like that. But I happen to think we have a shot at changing the world here. The team I've assembled down in that lab is second to none. We have the —"

"I said okay. But if all this is so important, maybe you ought to think about what you're doing. I just talked about it. You're the one who is out there going to her house and doing things underhanded."

Anger flared up inside of him and he waited a moment to let it subside.

"Look, I was curious about this and just wanted to make sure the woman was all right. If that is being underhanded, then okay, I was underhanded. But now I'm done with it. On Monday I want you to get my number changed and hopefully that will be the end of it."

"Good. Can I go now?"

Pierce nodded. He gave up.

"Yes, you can go. Thanks for waiting for the furniture. I hope you have a good weekend, what's left of it, and I'll see you on Monday."

He didn't look at her when he said it or when she got up from the chair. She left without another word to him and he remained angry. He decided that once things blew over he would get another personal assistant and Monica could go back to the general pool of assistants at the company.

Pierce sat on the couch for a while but was drawn out of his thinking reverie by the phone. It was another caller for Lilly.

"You're too late," he said. "She quit the business and went to USC."

Then he hung up.

After a while he picked up the phone again and called Information in Venice for the number of James Wainwright. A man answered his next call and Pierce got up and walked to the windows as he spoke.

"I'm looking for Lilly Quinlan's landlord," he said. "For the house over on Altair in Venice."

"That would be me."

"My name's Pierce. I'm trying to locate Lilly and want to know if you've had any contact with her in the last month or so?"

"Well, first of all, I don't think I know you, Mr. Pierce, and I don't answer questions about my tenants with strangers unless they state their business and convince me I should do otherwise."

"Fair enough, Mr. Wainwright. I'd be happy to come see you in person if you'd prefer. I'm a friend of the family. Lilly's mother, Vivian, is worried about her daughter because she hasn't heard from her in eight weeks. She asked me to do some checking around. I can give you Vivian's number in Florida if you want to call and check on me."

It was a risk but Pierce thought it was one worth taking to convince Wainwright to talk. It wasn't too far from the truth, anyway. It was social engineering. Turn the truth just a little bit and make it work for you.

"I have her mother's number on her application. I don't need to call, because I don't have anything that will help you. Lilly Quinlan's paid up through the end of the month. I don't have occasion to see or talk to her unless she has a problem. I have not spoken to or seen her in a couple months, at least."

"The end of the month? Are you sure?"

Pierce knew that that didn't jibe with the check records he had examined.

"That's right."

"How did she pay her last rent, check or cash?"

"That's none of your business."

"Mr. Wainwright, it is my business. Lilly is missing and her mother has asked me to look for her."

"So you say."

"Call her."

"I don't have time to call her. I maintain thirty-two apartments and houses. You think I have —"

"Look, is there somebody who takes care of the lawn that I could talk to?"

"You're already talking to him."

"So you haven't seen her when you've been over there?"

"Come to think of it, a lot of times she'd come out and say hello when I was there cutting the lawn or working the sprinklers. Or she'd bring me out a Pepsi or a lemonade. One time she gave me a cold beer. But she hasn't been there the last few times I've been there. Her car was gone. I didn't think anything of it. People have lives, you know."

"What kind of car was it?"

"Gold Lexus. I don't know the model but I know it was a Lexus.

Nice car. She took good care of it, too."

Pierce couldn't think of anything else to ask. Wainwright wasn't much of a help.

"Mr. Wainwright, will you check the application and then call her mother? I need you to call me back about this."

"Are the police involved? Is there a missing-persons report?"

"Her mother's been talking to the police but she doesn't think they're doing much. That's why she asked me. Do you have something to write with?"

"Sure do."

Pierce hesitated, realizing that if he gave his home number, Wainwright might recognize it as the same number he had for Lilly. He gave him the direct line to his office at Amedeo instead. He then thanked him and hung up.

He sat there looking at the phone, reviewing the call repeatedly and coming to the same conclusion each time. Wainwright was being evasive. He either knew something or was hiding something, or both.

He opened his backpack and got out the notebook in which he had written down the number for Robin, Lilly's escort partner.

This time when he called he tried to deepen his voice when she answered. His hope was that she would not recognize him from the night before.

"I was wondering if we could get together tonight."

"Well, I'm open, baby. Have we ever dated? You sound familiar."

"Uh, no. Not before."

"Whacha got in mind?"

"Um, maybe dinner and then go to your place. I don't know."

"Well, honey, I get four hundred an hour. Most guys want to skip the dinner and just come see me. Or I go see them."

"Then I can just come to you."

"Okay, fine. What's your name?"

He knew she had caller ID, so he couldn't lie.

"Henry Pierce."

"And what time were you thinking about?"

He looked at his watch. It was six o'clock.

"How about seven?"

It would give him time to come up with a plan and to get to a cash machine. He knew he had some cash, but not enough. He had a card that could get him $400 maximum on a withdrawal.

"An early-bird special," she said. "That's fine with me. Except there ain't a special rate."

"That's okay. Where do I go?"

"Got a pencil?"

"Right here."

"I'm sure you have a hard pencil."

She laughed and then gave him an address of a Smooth Moves shop on Lincoln in Marina del Rey. She told him to go into the shop and get a strawberry blitz and then call her from the pay phone out front at five minutes before seven. When he asked her why she did it this way she said, "Precautions. I wanna get a look at you before I bring you on up. And I like those little strawberry thingees anyway. That's like bringing me flowers, sugar. Have 'em put some energy powder in it for me, would you? I get a sneaky idea that I'm gonna need it with you."

She laughed again but it sounded too practiced and hollow to Pierce. It gave him a bad feeling. He said he would get the smoothie and make the call and thanked her, and that was the end of it. As he cradled the phone he felt a wave of trepidation sweep through him. He thought about the speech he had given Monica and how she had correctly turned it right back at him.

"You idiot," he said to himself.

12

At the appointed time Pierce picked up a pay phone outside of Smooth Moves and called Robin's number. Turning his back to the phone, he saw that across Lincoln was a large apartment complex called the Marina Executive Towers. Only the building didn't really qualify as a tower or towers. It was short and wide — three stories of apartments over a garage. The complex covered half a city block and its length was broken up by color gradations. Its exterior was painted three different pastels — pink, blue, yellow — as it worked its way down the street. A banner hanging off the roofline announced short-term executive rentals and free maid service. Pierce realized it was a perfect place for a prostitute to carry out her business. The place was probably so large and the turnover of renters so high that a steady procession of different men coming in and out would not be noticeable or curious to other residents.

Robin picked up after three rings.

"It's Henry. I called —"

"Hey, baby. Let me get a look at you here."

Without trying to be too obvious about it, he scanned the windows of the apartment building across the street, looking for someone looking back at him. He didn't see anybody or any curtain movement but he noticed that the windows of several apartments had mirrored glass. He wondered if there was more than one woman like Robin working in the building.

"I see you got my smoothie," she said. "You get that energy powder?"

"Yes. They call it a booster rocket. That what you wanted?"

"That's it. Okay, you look all right to me. You're not a cop, are you?"

"No, I'm not."

"You sure?"

"Yes."

"Then say it. I'm taping this."

"I am not a police officer, okay?"

"All right, come on up then. Go across the street to the apartment building and at the main door push apartment two oh three. I'll see you soon."

"Okay."

He hung up and crossed the street and followed her instructions. At the door, the button marked 203 had the name Bird after it. *As in robin,* Pierce thought. When he pushed the button, the door lock was buzzed without any further inquiry from Robin over the intercom. Inside, he couldn't find the stairs, so he took the elevator the one flight up. Robin's apartment was two doors from the elevator.

She opened the door before he got a chance to knock. There was a peephole and she apparently had been watching. She took the smoothie from his hand and invited him in.

The place was sparsely furnished and seemed devoid of any personal object. There was just a couch, a chair, a coffee table and a standing lamp. A museum print was framed on the wall. It looked medieval: two angels leading the newly deceased toward the light at the end of a tunnel.

As Pierce stepped in he could see that the glass doors to the balcony had the mirrored film on them. They looked almost directly across to the Smooth Moves shop.

"I could see you but you couldn't see me," Robin said from behind him. "I could see you looking."

He turned to her.

"I was just curious about the setup. You know, how you work this."

"Well, now you know. Come sit down."

She moved to a couch and gestured for him to sit next to her. He did. He tried to look around. The place reminded Pierce of a hotel room but he guessed atmosphere wasn't what was important for the business usually conducted within the apartment. He felt her hand take his jaw and turn his face to hers.

"You like what you see?" she asked.

He was pretty sure she was the woman in the photo on the web page. It was hard to be certain because he had not studied it as long and as often as the photo of Lilly. She was barefoot and wore a light blue tank top T-shirt and a pair of red corduroy shorts cut so high that a bathing suit might have been more modest. She was braless and her breasts were huge, most likely the result of implants. Nipples the size of Girl Scout cookies were clearly outlined on the T-shirt. Her blonde hair was parted in the middle and cascaded down the sides of her face in ringlets. She wore no makeup that he could see.

"Yes, I do," he answered.

"People tell me I have a Meg Ryan thing going."

Pierce nodded, although he didn't see it. The movie star was older but a lot softer on the eyes.

"Did you bring me something?"

At first he thought she was talking about the smoothie but then he remembered the money.

"Yeah, I've got it here."

He leaned back on the couch to reach into his pocket. He had the four hundred ready in its own thick fold of twenties fresh from the cash machine. This was the part he had rehearsed. He didn't mind losing the four hundred but he didn't want to give it to her and then be kicked out when he revealed the true reason he was there.

He pulled the money out so she could see it and know it was close and hers for the taking.

"First time, baby?"

"Excuse me?"

"With an escort. First time?"

"How do you know that?"

"Because you're supposed to put that in an envelope for me. Like a gift. It is a gift, isn't it? You're not paying me to do anything."

"Yes, right. A gift."

"Thank you."

"Is that what the G in GFE stands for? Gift?"

She smiled.

"You really are new at this, aren't you? *Girlfriend,* sweetie. Absolutely positive girlfriend experience. It means you get whatever you want, like with your girlfriend before she became your wife."

"I'm not married."

"Doesn't matter."

She reached for the money as she said it but Pierce pulled his hand back.

"Uh, before I give you this . . . gift, I have to tell you something."

All the warning lights on her face fired at once.

"Don't worry, I'm not a cop."

"Then what, you don't want to use a rubber? Forget it, that's rule number one."

"No, it's not that. In fact, I don't really want to have sex with you. You're very attractive but all I want is some information."

Her posture became sharper as she seemed to grow taller, even while sitting down.

"What the fuck are you talking about?"

"I have to find Lilly Quinlan. You can help me."

"Who is Lilly Quinlan?"

"Come on, you name her on your web page. Double your pleasure? You know who I'm talking about."

"You're the guy from last night. You called last night."

He nodded.

"Then get the fuck out of here."

She quickly stood up and walked toward the door.

"Robin, don't open that door. If you don't talk to me, then you'll talk to the cops. That's my next move."

She turned around.

"The cops won't give a shit."

But she didn't open the door. She just stood there, angry and waiting, one hand on the knob.

"Maybe not now but they'll care if I go to them."

"Why, who are you?"

"I have some juice," he lied. "That's all you have to know. If I go to them, they'll come to you. They won't be as nice as me . . . and they won't pay you four hundred dollars for your time."

He put the money down on the couch where she had been sitting. He watched her eyes go to it.

"Just information, that's all I want. It goes no further than me."

He waited and after a long moment of silence she came back over to the couch and grabbed the money. She somehow found space for it in her tiny shorts. She folded her arms and remained standing.

"What information? I hardly knew her."

"You know something. You talk about her in the past tense."

"I don't know anything. All I know is that she's gone. She just . . . disappeared."

"When was that?"

"More than a month ago. Suddenly she was just gone."

"Why do you still have her name on your page if she's been gone that long?"

"You saw her picture. She brings in customers. Sometimes they settle for just me."

"Okay, how do you know her disappearance was so sudden? Maybe she just packed up and left."

"I know because one minute we were talking on the phone and the next minute she didn't show up, that's why."

"Show up for what?"

"We had a gig. A double. She set it up and called me. She told me the time and then she didn't show up. I was there and then the client showed up and he wasn't happy. First of all, there was no place to park and then she wasn't there and I had to scramble around to get another girl to come back over here to my place — and there are no other girls like Lilly, and he really wanted Lilly. It was a fucking fiasco, that's what it was."

"Where was this?"

"Her place. Her gig pad. She didn't work anywhere else. No outcall. Not even to here. I always had to go to her. Even if they were my clients wanting the double, we had to go to her pad, or it didn't happen."

"Did you have a key to her place?"

"No. Look, you've gotten your four hundred's worth. It would have been easier just to fuck and forget you. That's it."

Pierce angrily reached into his pocket and pulled out the rest of his cash. It was $230. He'd counted it in the car. He held it out to her.

"Then take this, because I'm not done. Something happened to her and I'm going to find out what."

She grabbed the money and it disappeared without her counting it.

"Why do you care?"

93

"Maybe because nobody else does. Now if you didn't have a key to her place, how do you know she didn't show up that night?"

"Because I knocked for fifteen fucking minutes and then me and the guy waited for another twenty. I'm telling you, she wasn't in there."

"Do you know if she had something set up before the gig with you?"

Robin thought for a little bit before answering.

"She said she had something to do but I don't know if she was with a client. Because I wanted to do it earlier but she said she was busy with something at the time I wanted. So we set the time she wanted, and so she should have been there but wasn't."

Pierce tried to imagine what questions a cop would ask her but couldn't guess how the police would approach this. He thought about it as if it were a problem at work, with his usual rigorous approach to problem solving and theory building.

"So before she was to meet with you she had to do something," he said. "That something could have been meeting a client. And since you say she worked nowhere else but the apartment, she had to have met this client at the apartment. Nowhere else, right?"

"Right."

"So when you got there and knocked on the door, she could've been inside with or without this other client but just not answering."

"I guess so, but she should've been done by then and she would have answered. It was all set up. So maybe it wasn't a client."

"Or maybe she was not allowed to answer. Maybe she couldn't answer."

This seemed to give Robin pause, as though she realized how close she might have come to whatever fate befell Lilly.

"Where is this place? Her apartment."

"It's over in Venice. Off Speedway."

"What's the exact address?"

"I don't remember. I just know how to get there."

Pierce nodded. He thought about what else he needed to ask her. He had the feeling he had one shot with her. No second chances.

"How'd you two get together for these, uh, gigs?"

"We linked on the website. If people wanted us both, they'd ask

94

and we'd set it up if we were both available."

"I mean, how did you two meet in order to have the link? How did you meet in the first place?"

"We met at a shoot and sort of hit it off. It went from there."

"A shoot? What do you mean?"

"Modeling. It was a girl-girl scene and we met at the studio."

"You mean, for a magazine?"

"No, a website."

Pierce thought of the doorway he had opened at Entrepreneurial Concepts.

"Was it for one of the websites Entrepreneurial Concepts operates?"

"Look, it doesn't matter what —"

"What was the name of the site?"

"It was called something like fetish castle dot something or other. I don't know. I don't have a computer. What does it matter?"

"Where was the shoot, at Entrepreneurial Concepts?"

"Yeah. At the studios."

"So you got the job through L.A. Darlings and Mr. Wentz, right?"

He saw her eyes flare at the mention of the name but she didn't respond.

"What's his first name?"

"I'm not talking to you about him. You can't tell him you got any information from me, you understand?"

He thought he now saw a flash of fear in her eyes.

"I told you, everything you tell me here is private. I promise you that. What's his name?"

"Look, he's got connections and people who work for him who are very mean. *He's* mean. I don't want to talk about him."

"Just tell me his name and I'll leave it at that, okay?"

"It's Billy. Billy Wentz. Most people call him Billy Wince because he hurts people, okay?"

"Thank you."

He stood up and looked around the apartment. He walked over to the corner of the living room and looked into a hallway that he guessed led to the bedroom. He was surprised to learn there were two bedrooms with a bathroom in between.

"Why do you have two bedrooms?"

"I share the place with another girl. We each have our own."

"From the website?"

"Yes."

"What's her name?"

"Cleo."

"Billy Wentz put you with her, too."

"No. Grady did."

"Who is Grady?"

"He works with Billy. He really runs the place."

"So why don't you do doubles with Cleo? It'd be more convenient."

"I probably will. But I told you, I was getting a lot of business
with Lilly. There aren't many girls that look like her."

Pierce nodded.

"You don't live here, do you?"

"No. I work here."

"Where do you live?"

"I'm not telling you that."

"You keep any clothes here?"

"What do you mean?"

"You have any clothes besides those? And where are your
shoes?"

He gestured to what she was wearing.

"Yes, I changed when I got here. I don't go out like this."

"Good. Change back and let's go."

"What are you talking about? Where?"

"I want you to show me where Lilly's place is. Or was."

"Uh-uh, man. You got your information, that's it."

Pierce looked at his watch.

"Look, you said four hundred an hour. I've been here twenty
minutes, tops. That means I get forty more minutes, or you give me
two-thirds of my cash back."

"That's not how it works."

"That's how it works today."

She stared at him angrily for a long moment and then walked
silently past him toward the bedroom to change. Pierce walked
over to the balcony doors and looked out across Lincoln.

He saw a man standing at the pay phone in front of Smooth Moves, holding a smoothie and looking up at the windows of the building Pierce was in. Another smoothie, another client. He wondered how many women were working in the building. Did they all work for Wentz? Did he own the place? Maybe he even had a piece of the smoothie shop.

He turned around to ask Robin about Wentz and from the angle he was at was able to look down the hallway and through the open bedroom door. Robin was naked and pulling a tight pair of faded blue jeans up over her hips. Her perfectly tanned breasts hung down heavily as she bent over in the process.

When she straightened up to pull the zipper closed over her flat stomach and the small triangle of golden hair below, she looked directly at him through the door. She didn't flinch. Instead, there was a defiant look on her face. She reached over to the bed and picked up a white T-shirt, which she pulled over her head without making any move to turn or hide her nakedness from him.

She came out of the bedroom and slipped her feet into a pair of sandals she pulled from under the coffee table.

"Did you enjoy that?" she asked.

"Yes. I did. I guess I don't have to tell you, you have a beautiful body."

She walked past him and into the kitchenette. She opened a cabinet over the sink and took out a small black purse.

"Let's go. You've got thirty-five minutes."

She went to the front door, opened it and stepped out into the hallway. He followed.

"You want your smoothie?"

It was sitting untouched on the breakfast bar.

"No, I hate smoothies. Too fattening. My vice is pizza. Next time bring me a pizza."

"Then why'd you ask for the smoothie?"

"It was just a way of checking you out, seeing what you would do for me."

And establishing some control, Pierce thought but didn't say. Control that didn't always last long once the money was paid and the clothes were off.

Pierce stepped into the hallway and looked back into the place where Robin made her living. He felt an uneasiness. A sadness even. He thought about her web page. What was an absolutely positive girlfriend experience and how could it come out of a place like that?

He closed the door, made sure it was locked, and then followed Robin to the elevator.

13

Pierce drove and Robin directed. It was a short trip from the Marina to Speedway in Venice. He tried to make the best use of his time on the way over. But he knew Robin was reluctant to talk.

"So, you're not an independent, are you?"

"What are you talking about?"

"You work for Wentz — the guy who runs the website. He's what I guess you'd call a digital pimp. He sets you girls up in that place, runs your web page. How much does he get? I saw on the site he charges four hundred a month to run your picture but I have a feeling he gets a lot more than that. Guy like that, he probably owns the apartment building and the smoothie shop."

She didn't say anything.

"He gets a share of that first four hundred I gave you, doesn't he?"

"Look, I'm not talking to you about him. You'll get me killed, too. When we get to her place, that's it. We're done. I'll take a cab."

"Too?"

She was silent.

"What do you know about what happened to Lilly?"

"Nothing."

"Then why did you say 'too' just then?"

"Look, man, if you knew what was smart for you, you'd leave this thing alone, *too*. Go back to the square world, where it's nice and safe. You don't know these people or what they can do."

"I have an idea."

"Yeah? How would you have any fucking idea?"

"I had a sister once. . . ."

"And?"

"And you could say she was in your line of work."

He looked away from the road to Robin. She kept her eyes

99

straight ahead.

"One morning a school bus driver up on Mulholland spotted her body down past the guardrail. I was away at Stanford at the time."

He looked back at the road.

"It's a funny thing about this city," he continued after a while. "She was lying out there in the open like that, naked . . . and the cops said they could tell by the . . . evidence that she had been there at least a couple days. And I always wondered how many people saw her, you know? Saw her and didn't do anything about it. Didn't call anybody. This city can be pretty cold sometimes."

"Any city can."

He glanced back at her. He could see the distress in her eyes, like she was looking at a chapter from her own life. A possible final chapter.

"Did they ever catch the guy?" she asked.

"Eventually. But not until after he killed four more."

She shook her head.

"What are you doing here, Henry? That story has got nothing to do with any of this."

"I don't know what I'm doing. I'm just . . . following something."

"Good way to get yourself hurt."

"Look, nobody's going to know you talked to me. Just tell me, what did you hear about Lilly?"

Silence.

"She wanted to get out, didn't she? She made enough money, she was going to go to school. She wanted to get out of the life."

"Everybody wants to get out. You think we enjoy it?"

Pierce felt ashamed of the way he was pushing her. The way he had used her hadn't been too different from the rest of her paying customers.

"I'm sorry," he said.

"No, you're not. You're just like the others. You want something and you're desperate for it. Only I can give you the other thing a lot easier than I can give you what you want."

He was silent.

"Turn left up here and go down to the end. There's only one parking space for her unit. She used to leave it open for the client."

He turned off Speedway as instructed and was in an alley behind rows of small apartments on either side. They looked like four-to-six-unit buildings with three-foot-wide walking alleys in between. It was crowded. It was the kind of neighborhood where one barking dog could set everybody on edge.

When he got to the last building, Robin said, "Somebody took it."

She pointed to a car parked in a spot below a stairway to an apartment door.

"That's the place up there."

"Is that her car?"

"No, she had a Lexus."

Right. He remembered what Wainwright had said. The car in the space was a Volvo wagon. Pierce backed up and squeezed his BMW between two rows of trash cans. It wasn't a legal space but cars could still get past in the alley and he wasn't expecting to be there long.

"You'll have to climb over and get out this side."

"Great. Thanks."

They got out, Pierce holding the door as Robin climbed over the seats. As soon as she was out she started heading back down the alley toward Speedway.

"Wait," Pierce said. "This way."

"No, I'm finished. I'm walking back to Speedway and catching a cab."

Pierce could have argued with her about it but decided to let her go.

"Look, thanks for your help. If I find her, I'll let you know."

"Who, Lilly or your sister?"

That gave him pause for a moment. From those you least expect it comes insight.

"You going to be all right?" he called after her.

She suddenly stopped, turned and strode back to him, the anger flaring in her eyes again.

"Look, don't pretend you care about me, okay? That phony shit is more disgusting than the men who want to come on my face. At least they're honest about it."

She turned and walked off again down the alley. Pierce watched her for a few moments to see if she'd look back at him but she didn't. She kept on going, pulling a cell phone out of her purse so she could call a cab.

He walked around the Volvo and noticed that blankets in the back were used to cover the tops of two cardboard boxes and other bulky items he couldn't see. He climbed the stairs to Lilly's apartment. When he got there he saw that the door was ajar. He leaned over the railing and looked up the alley but Robin was almost to Speedway and too far to call to.

He turned back to the door and leaned his head in close to the jamb but he didn't hear anything. With one finger he pushed the door, remaining on the porch as it swung inward. As it opened he could see a sparsely furnished living room with a stairway going up the far wall to a loft. Under the loft was a small kitchen with a pass-through window to the living room. Through the pass-through he could see the torso of a man, moving about and putting liquor bottles into a box on the counter.

Pierce leaned forward and looked in without actually entering the apartment. He saw three cardboard boxes on the floor of the living room but there seemed to be no one else in the apartment except the man in the kitchen. The man appeared to be clearing things out and boxing them all up.

Pierce reached over and knocked on the door and called out, "Lilly?"

The man in the kitchen was startled and almost dropped a bottle of gin he was holding. He then carefully put the bottle on the counter.

"She's not here anymore," he called from the kitchen. "She's moved."

But he stayed in the kitchen, motionless. Pierce thought that was odd, as if he didn't want his face seen.

"Then who are you?"

"I'm the landlord and I'm busy. You'll have to come back."

Pierce started putting it together. He stepped into the apartment and moved toward the kitchen. When he got to the doorway he saw a man with long gray hair pulled back into a ponytail. He wore a dirty white T-shirt and dirtier white shorts. He was deeply tanned.

"Why would I come back if she moved away?"

It startled him again.

"What I mean is, you can't come in here. She's gone and I'm working."

"What's your name?"

"My name doesn't matter. Please leave now."

"You're Wainwright, aren't you?"

The man looked up at Pierce. The acknowledgment was in his eyes.

"Who are you?"

"I'm Pierce. I talked to you today. I was the one who told you she was gone."

"Oh. Well, you were right, she's long gone."

"The money she paid you was for both places. The four grand. You didn't tell me that."

"You didn't ask."

"Do you own this building, Mr. Wainwright?"

"I'm not answering your questions, thank you."

"Or does Billy Wentz own it and you just manage it for him?"

Again, the acknowledgment flickered in the eyes and then went out.

"Okay, leave now. Get out of here."

Pierce shook his head.

"I'm not leaving yet. If you want to call the cops, go ahead. See what they think about your clearing her stuff out even though you told me she was paid up through the month. Maybe we look under the blankets in the back of your car, too. I'm betting we'd find a plasma TV that used to hang on the wall of the house she rented over on Altair. You probably went by there first, right?"

"She abandoned the place," Wainwright said testily. "You should have seen the kitchen in there."

"I'm sure it must've been just awful. So awful, I guess, you decided to clear the place out and maybe even double-dip on the rent, huh? Housing in Venice is tight. You already got a new tenant lined up? Let me guess, another L.A. darling?"

"Look, you don't try to tell me my business."

"I wouldn't dream of it."

"What do you want?"

"To look around. To look at the things you're taking."

"Then hurry up, because as soon as I'm done in here I'm leaving. And I'm locking the door whether you're still here or not."

Pierce stepped toward him, entering the kitchen and dropping his gaze down into the box on the counter. It was full of liquor bottles and odd glassware, nothing important. He pulled up one of the brown bottles and saw that it was sixteen-year-old scotch. Good stuff. He dropped the bottle back into the box.

"Hey, easy!" Wainwright protested.

"So, does Billy know you're clearing the place out?"

"I don't know any Billy."

"So you got the house over on Altair and this place. What other properties are under the wing of Wainwright Properties?"

Wainwright folded his arms and leaned back against the counter. He wasn't talking and Pierce suddenly had the urge to take one of the bottles out of the box and smash it across his face.

"How about the Marina Executive Towers? That one of yours?"

Wainwright reached into one of the front pockets of his pants and took out a package of Camels. He shook out a cigarette and then returned the pack to his pocket. He turned on one of the stove's gas burners and lit the cigarette off the flame, then reached into the box and rooted around in the glassware until he found what he was looking for. He came out with a glass ashtray that he put on the counter and dipped his cigarette into.

Pierce noticed the ashtray had printing on it. He leaned forward slightly to read it.

STOLEN FROM NAT'S DAY OF THE LOCUST BAR

HOLLYWOOD, CA

Pierce had heard of the place. It was a dive that was so low, it was high. It was favored by the black-clad Hollywood night creepers. It was also close to the offices of Entrepreneurial Concepts Unlimited. Was it a clue? He had no idea.

"I'm going to take that look around now," he said to Wainwright.

"Yeah, you do that. Be quick."

While he listened to Wainwright clinking glasses and jarring bottles as he packed the box, Pierce went into the living room and crouched in front of the boxes that had already been packed. One contained dishware and other kitchen items. The other two contained things from the loft. Bedroom things. There was a basket of assorted condoms. There were several pairs of high-heel shoes. There were leather straps and whips, a full leather head mask with zippers positioned at the eyes and mouth. On her L. A. Darlings page Lilly did not advertise sadomasochistic services. Pierce wondered if this meant there was another website out there, something darker and with a whole new set of elements to consider in her disappearance.

The last box he checked was full of bras and sheer underwear and negligees and miniskirts on hangers. It was clothing similar to what Pierce had seen in one of the closets of the house on Altair. For a moment he wondered what Wainwright planned to do with the boxes. Sell everything in a bizarre yard sale? Or was he simply going to hold it while he re-rented the apartment and house?

Satisfied with his inventory of the boxes, Pierce decided to check out the loft. As he got up, his eyes came upon the door and he noticed the dead bolt. It was a double-key lock. A key was necessary to open or close the lock from both sides. He now understood Wainwright's threat to lock the door whether Pierce was done with his search or not. If you did not have a key, you could be locked in as well as locked out. Pierce wondered what this meant. Did Lilly lock her clients inside the apartment with her? Perhaps it was a way of ensuring payment for services rendered. Maybe it meant nothing at all.

He moved to the staircase and headed up to the loft. On the landing at the top there was a small window that looked out across the rooftop across the alley to the far edge of the beach and the Pacific. Pierce looked down into the alley and saw his car. His eyes tracked down the alley to Speedway. He caught a glimpse of Robin under a streetlight as she got into a green and yellow cab, closing the door as it took off.

He turned from the window to the loft. It was no more than two hundred square feet on the upper level, including the space of a small bath with a shower. The air up there smelled of an unpleasant mixture of heavy incense and something else that Pierce could not readily place. It was like the spoiled air in a refrigerator that has

105

been turned off. It was there but was overpowered by the incense that held to the room like a ghost.

On the open floor there was a king-size bed with no headboard. It took up most of the available space, leaving room for one small side table and a reading light. On the table was an incense burner that was a Kama Sutra sculpture of a fat man and a thin woman coupling in a rear-entry position. A long ash from a burned down incense stick lapped over the sculpture's bowl and onto the table. Pierce was surprised Wainwright had not taken the piece. He was taking everything else, it seemed.

The bedspread was a light blue and the carpet beige. He went to a small closet and slid open the door. It was empty, the contents now in one of the boxes below.

Pierce looked at the bed. It looked to have been carefully made, the spread tucked tightly under the mattress. But there were no pillows, which he thought was strange. He thought maybe it was one of the rules of the escort business. Robin had said the number one rule was no unprotected sex. Maybe number two was no pillows — too easy to smother you with.

He got down on the carpet and looked underneath the box spring. There was nothing but dust.

But then he saw a dark spot in the beige carpeting. Curious, he straightened up and pushed the bed against the far wall to uncover the spot. One of the wheels was jammed and he had a difficult time, the bed sliding and bumping on the carpet.

Whatever had spilled or dripped on the carpet was dry. It was a brownish black color and Pierce didn't want to touch it, because he thought it might be blood. He also understood now that it was the source of the odor underlying the smell of incense in the room. He got up and pushed the bed back over the spot.

"What the hell are you doing up there?" Wainwright called up.

Pierce didn't answer. He was consumed with the purpose at hand. He took hold of one corner of the bedspread and pulled it up, revealing the mattress below. No mattress cover or top sheet. No blanket.

He started pulling off the bedspread. He wanted to see the mattress. Sheets and blankets could easily be taken from an apartment and thrown away. Even pillows could be discarded. But a king-size mattress was another matter.

As he pulled the bedspread he questioned the instincts he was blindly following. He didn't understand how he knew what he seemingly knew. But as the bedspread slipped off the mattress, Pierce felt like his intestines had collapsed inside. The center of the mattress was black with something that had congealed and dried and was the color of death. It could only be blood.

"Jesus Christ!" Wainwright said.

He had come up the steps to see what the dragging sounds were all about. He was standing behind Pierce.

"Is that what I think it is?"

Pierce didn't answer. He didn't know what to say. Yesterday he plugged in a new phone. Little more than twenty-four hours later it had led to this ghastly discovery.

"Wrong number," he said.

"What?" Wainwright asked. "What are you saying?"

"Never mind. Is there a phone here?"

"No, not that I know of."

"You have a cell phone?"

"In the car."

"Go get it."

14

Pierce looked up when Detective Renner walked in. He tried to keep his anger in check, knowing that the cooler he played this, the faster he would get out and get home. Still, over two hours in an eight-by-eight room with nothing but a five-day-old sports page to read had left him with little patience. He had already given a statement twice. Once to the patrol cops who responded to Wainwright's call, and then to Renner and his partner when they had arrived on the scene. One of the patrol cops had then taken him to the Pacific Division station and locked him in the interview room.

Renner had a file in his hand. He sat down at the table across from Pierce and opened it. Pierce could see some sort of police form with handwriting in all the boxes. Renner stared at the form for an inordinate amount of time and then cleared his throat. He looked like a cop who'd been around more crime scenes than most. Early fifties and still solid, he reminded Pierce of Clyde Vernon in his taciturn way.

"You're thirty-four years old?"

"Yes."

"Your address is Twenty-eight hundred Ocean Way, apartment twelve oh one."

"Yes."

This time exasperation crept into his voice. Renner's eyes came up momentarily to his and then went back to the form.

"But that is not the address on your driver's license."

"No, I just moved. Ocean is where I live now. Amalfi Drive is where I used to live. Look, it's after midnight. Did you really keep me sitting in here all this time so you could ask me these obvious questions? I already gave you my statement. What else do you want?"

Renner leaned back and looked sternly at Pierce.

"No, Mr. Pierce, I kept you here because we needed to conduct a thorough investigation of what appears to be a crime scene. I am sure you don't begrudge us that."

"I don't begrudge that. I do begrudge being kept in here like a suspect. I tried that door. It was locked. I knocked and nobody came."

"I'm sorry about that. There was no one in the detective bureau. It's the middle of the night. But the patrol officer should not have locked the door, because you are not under arrest. If you want to make a personnel complaint against him or me, I'll go get you the necessary forms to fill out."

"I don't want to make a complaint, okay? No forms. Can we just get on with this so I can get out of here? Is it her blood?"

"What blood?"

"On the bed."

"How do you know it is blood?"

"I'm assuming. What else could it be?"

"You tell me."

"What? What is that supposed to mean?"

"It was a question."

"Wait a minute, you just said I was not a suspect."

"I said you are not under arrest."

"So you're saying I am not under arrest but I *am* a suspect in this?"

"I am not saying anything, Mr. Pierce. I am simply asking questions, trying to figure out what happened in that apartment and what is happening now."

Pierce pulled back his growing anger. He didn't say anything. Renner referred to his form and spoke without looking up.

"Now in the statement you gave earlier, you say that your new telephone number on Ocean Way belonged at one time to the woman whose apartment you went to this evening."

"Exactly. That's why I was there. To find out if something happened to her."

"Do you know this woman, Lilly Quinlan?"

"No, never met her before."

"Never?"

"Never in my life."

"Then why did you do this? Go to her apartment, go to the trouble. Why didn't you just change your number? Why did you care?"

"I'll tell you, for the last two hours I've been asking myself the same thing. I mean, you try to check on somebody and maybe do something good and what do you get? Locked in a room for two hours by the cops."

Renner didn't say anything. He let Pierce rant.

"What does it matter why I cared or whether or not I had a reason to do what I did? Shouldn't *you* care about what happened to her? Why are you asking *me* the questions? Why isn't Billy Wentz sitting in this room instead of me? I told you about him."

"We'll deal with Billy Wentz, Mr. Pierce. Don't worry. But right now I am talking to you."

Renner was then quiet a moment while he scratched his forehead with two fingers.

"Tell me again how you knew about that apartment in the first place."

Pierce's earlier statements had been replete with shadings of the truth designed to cover any illegalities he had committed. But the story he had told about finding the apartment had been a complete lie designed to keep Robin out of the investigation. He had made good on his promise not to reveal her as a source of information. Of everything that he had said over the last four hours, it was the only thing he felt good about.

"As soon as I plugged in my phone I started getting calls from men who wanted Lilly. A few of them were former clients who wanted to see her again. I tried to engage these men in conversation, to see what I could find out about her. One man today told me about the apartment and where it was. So I went over."

"I see, and what was this former client's name?"

"I don't know. He didn't give it."

"You have caller ID on your new phone?"

"Yes, but he was calling from a hotel. All it said was that it was coming from the Ritz-Carlton. There are a lot of rooms there. I guess he was in one of them."

Renner nodded.

"And Mr. Wainwright said you called him earlier today to ask about Miss Quinlan and another property she rented from him."

"Yes. A house on Altair. She lived there and worked in the apartment off Speedway. The apartment was where she met her clients. Once I told him she was missing, he went and cleared out her property."

"Had you ever been to that apartment before?"

"No. Never. I told you that."

"How about the house on Altair? Have you been there?"

Pierce chose his words like he was choosing his steps through a minefield.

"I went there and nobody answered the door. That's why I called Wainwright."

He hoped Renner wouldn't notice the change in his voice. The detective was asking far more questions than during the initial statement. Pierce knew he was on treacherous ground. The less he said, the better chance he had of getting through unscathed.

"I'm trying to get the chain of events correct," Renner said. "You told us you went to this place ECU in Hollywood first. You get the name Lilly Quinlan and address for a mail drop in Santa Monica. You go there and use this thing you call social engagement to —"

"Engineering. Social engineering."

"Whatever. You *engineer* the address to the house out of the guy at the mail drop, right? You go to the house first, then you call Wainwright, and then you run into him at the apartment. Do I have all of this straight?"

"Yes."

"Now you have said in both your statements so far tonight that you knocked and found no one home and so you left. That true?"

"Yes, true."

"Between the time you knocked and found no one home and when you left the premises, did you go into the house on Altair, Mr. Pierce?"

There it was. The question. It required a yes or a no. It required a true answer or a lie which could easily be found out. He had to assume he had left fingerprints in the house. He remembered specifically the knobs on the rolltop desk. The mail he had looked through.

He had given them the Altair address more than two hours ago. For all he knew, they had already been there and already had his fingerprints. The whole question might be a trap set to snare him.

"The door was unlocked," Pierce said. "I went in to make sure she wasn't in there. Needing help or something."

Renner was leaning slightly forward across the table. His eyes came up to Pierce's and held. Pierce could see the line of white below his green irises.

"You were inside that house?"

"That's right."

"Why didn't you tell us that before?"

"I don't know. I didn't think it was necessary. I was trying to be brief. I didn't want to take up anyone's time, I guess."

"Well, thanks for thinking of us. Which door was unlocked?"

Pierce hesitated but knew he had to answer.

"The back."

He said it like a criminal in court pleading guilty. His head was down, his voice low.

"Excuse me?"

"The back door."

"Is it your custom to go in the back door of the home of a perfect stranger?"

"No, but that was the door that was unlocked. The front wasn't. I told you, I wanted to see if something was wrong."

"That's right. You wanted to be a rescuer. A hero."

"It's not that. I just —"

"What did you find in the house?"

"Not a lot. Spoiled food, a giant pile of mail. I could tell she hadn't been there in a long while."

"Did you take anything?"

"No."

He said it without hesitation, without blinking.

"What did you touch?"

Pierce shrugged.

"I don't know. Some of the mail. There's a desk. I opened some drawers."

"Were you expecting to find Miss Quinlan in a desk drawer?"

112

"No. I just . . ."

He didn't finish. He reminded himself that he was walking on a ledge. He had to keep his answers as short as possible.

Renner changed his posture, leaning back in his seat now, and changed questioning tacks as well.

"Tell me something," he said. "How did you know to call Wainwright?"

"Because he's the landlord."

"Yes, but how did you know that?"

Pierce froze. He knew he could not give an answer that referred in any way to the phone book or mail he had taken from the house. He thought of the phone book hidden behind the stacks of paper in the office's copy room. For the first time he felt a cold sweat forming along his scalp.

"Um, I think . . . no, yeah, it was written down somewhere on the desk in her house. Like a note."

"You mean like a note that was out in the open?"

"Yeah, I think so. I . . ."

Again he stopped himself before he gave Renner something else with which the detective could club him. Pierce lowered his eyes to the table. He was being walked into a trap and had to figure a way out. Making up the note was a mistake. But now he could not backtrack.

"Mr. Pierce, I just came from that house over on Altair and I looked all through that desk. I didn't see any note."

Pierce nodded like he agreed, even though he had just said the opposite.

"You know what it was, it was my own note I was picturing. I wrote it after I talked to Vivian. She was the one who told me about Wainwright."

"Vivian? Who is Vivian?"

"Lilly's mother. In Tampa, Florida. When she asked me to look for Lilly she gave me some names and contacts. I just remembered, that's where I got Wainwright's name."

Renner's eyebrows peaked halfway up his forehead as he registered his surprise again.

"This is all new information, Mr. Pierce. You are now saying that Lilly Quinlan's mother asked you to look for her daughter?"

"Yes. She said the cops weren't doing anything. She asked me to do what I could."

Pierce felt good. The answer was true, or at least truer than most of the things he was saying. He thought he might be able to survive this.

"And her mother in Tampa had the name of her daughter's landlord?"

"Well, I think she got a bunch of names and contacts from a private detective she had previously hired to look for Lilly."

"A private detective."

Renner looked down at the statement in front of him as if it had personally let him down for not including mention of the private investigator.

"Do you have his name?"

"Philip Glass. I have his number written down in a notebook that is in my car. Take me back to the apartment — my car's there — and I can get it for you."

"Thank you, but I happen to know Mr. Glass and how to reach him. Have you talked to him?"

"No. I left a message and didn't hear back. But from what Vivian told me, he hadn't had much success in finding Lilly. I wasn't expecting much. I never knew if he was good or just ripping her off, you know?"

It was an opportunity for Renner to tell him what he knew about Glass but the detective didn't take it.

"What about Vivian?" he asked instead.

"I have her number in the car, too. I'll give you everything I've got as soon as I can get out of here."

"No, I mean what about Vivian in Florida? How did you know to contact her there?"

Pierce coughed. It was like he had been kicked in the gut. Renner had trapped him again. The phone book again. He could not mention it. His respect for the taciturn detective was rising at the same time he felt his mind sagging under the weight of his own lies and obfuscation. He now saw only one way out.

15

Pierce had to give her name. His own lies had left him no other way out. He told himself that Renner would eventually get to her on his own anyway. Lilly Quinlan's site was linked to hers. The connection was inevitable. At least by giving Robin's name now, he might be able to control things. Tell them just enough to get out of there, then he would call her and warn her.

"A girl named Robin," he said.

Renner shook his head once in an almost unnoticeable way.

"Well, well, another new name," he said. "Why doesn't that surprise me, Mr. Pierce? Tell me now, who is Robin?"

"On Lilly Quinlan's web page she mentions the availability of another girl she works with. It says, 'Double your pleasure.' The other girl's name is Robin. There is a link from Lilly's page to Robin's page. They work together. I went to the page and called Robin's number. She couldn't help me very much. She said she thought Lilly might have gone home to Tampa, where her mother lived. So later on I called Information in Tampa and got phone numbers for people named Quinlan. Eventually, that led me to contacting Vivian."

Renner nodded.

"Must've been a lot of names. Good Irish name like Quinlan's not too rare."

"Yes, there were."

"And Vivian being at the end of the alphabet. You must've called information in Tampa quite a few times."

"Yes."

"What's the area code for Tampa, by the way?"

"It's eight one three."

Pierce felt good about finally being able to answer a question without having to lie and worry about how it would fit with other lies he had told. But then he saw Renner reach into the pocket of his leather bomber jacket and pull out a cell phone. He opened it and punched in the number for 813 information.

Pierce realized he would be caught directly in a lie if Vivian Quinlan's phone number was unlisted.

"What are you doing? It's after three in the morning in Tampa. You'll scare her to death if you —"

Renner held up a hand to silence him and then spoke into the phone.

"Residential listing for Tampa. The name is Vivian Quinlan."

Renner then waited and Pierce watched his face for reaction. As the seconds passed it felt as though his stomach were being twisted into a double helix formation.

"Okay, thank you," Renner said.

He closed the phone and returned it to his pocket. He glanced at Pierce for a moment, then withdrew a pen from his shirt pocket and wrote a phone number down on the outside of the file. Pierce could read the number upside down. He recognized it as the number he had gotten out of Lilly Quinlan's phone book.

He exhaled, almost too loudly. He had caught a break.

"I think you are right," Renner said. "I think I will check with her at a more reasonable hour."

"Yes, that might be better."

"As I think I told you earlier, we don't have Internet access here in the squad, so I haven't seen this website you've mentioned. As soon as I get home I'll check it out. But you say the site is linked to this other woman, Robin."

"Exactly. They worked together."

"And you called Robin when you couldn't get ahold of Lilly."

"Right again."

"And you talked on the phone and she told you Lilly went off to Tampa to see momma."

"She said she didn't know. She thought she might have gone there."

"Did you know Robin previous to this telephone call?"

"No, never."

"I'm going to take a shot in the dark here, Mr. Pierce, and say I'm

116

betting Robin is a pay-for-play girl. A prostitute. So what you are telling me is that a woman engaged in this sort of business gets a call from a perfect stranger and ends up telling this stranger where she thinks her missing partner in crime went. It just sort of comes out, I guess, huh?"

Pierce almost groaned. Renner would not let it go. He was relentlessly picking at the frayed ends of his statement, threatening to unravel the whole thing. Pierce just wanted to get out, to leave. And he now realized that he needed to say or do anything that would accomplish that. He no longer cared about consequences down the road. He just needed to get out. If he could get to Robin before Renner, then hopefully he could make it work.

"Well . . . I guess I sort of was able to convince her that, you know, I really wanted to find her and make sure everything was all right. Maybe she was worried about her, too."

"And this was over the telephone?"

"Yes, the telephone."

"I see. Okay, well, we'll be checking all of this with Robin."

"Yes, check with her. Can I —"

"And you'd be willing to take a polygraph test, wouldn't you?"

"What?"

"A polygraph. It wouldn't take long. We'd just shoot downtown and get it taken care of."

"Tonight? Right now?"

"Probably not. I don't think I could get anybody out of bed to give it to you. But we could do it tomorrow morning, first thing."

"Fine. Set it up for tomorrow. Can I go now?"

"We're almost there, Mr. Pierce."

His eyes dropped to the statement again. *Surely,* Pierce thought, *we have covered everything on the form. What is left?*

"I don't understand. What else is there to talk about?"

Renner's eyes came to Pierce's without any movement of his head or face.

"Well, your name came up a couple of times on the computer. I thought maybe we'd talk about that."

Pierce felt his face flush with heat. And anger. The long ago arrest was supposed to have been erased from his record. *Expunged* was the legal term. He had completed the probation and did the 160

117

hours of public service. That was a long time ago. How did Renner know?

"You're talking about the thing up in Palo Alto?" he asked. "I was never officially charged. It was diverted. I was suspended from school for a semester. I did public service and probation. That was it."

"Arrested on suspicion of impersonating a police officer."

"It was almost fifteen years ago. I was in college."

"But you see what I'm looking at here. Impersonating an officer then. Running around like some kind of detective now. Maybe you've got a hero complex, Mr. Pierce."

"No, this is totally different. What that was back then was I was on the phone, trying to get some information. Social engineering — I was soshing out a number. I acted like I was a campus cop so I could get a phone number. That was it. I don't have a hero complex, whatever that is."

"A phone number for who?"

"A professor. I wanted his home number and it was unlisted. It was nothing."

"The report says you and your friends used the number to persecute the professor. To pull an elaborate prank on him. Five other students were arrested."

"It was harmless but they had to make an example of us. It was when hacking was just getting big. We were all suspended and got probation and community service but the punishment was more severe than the crime. What we did was harmless. It was minor."

"I'm sorry but I don't consider impersonating a police officer to be either harmless or minor."

Pierce was about to protest further but held his tongue. He knew he would not convince Renner. He waited for the next question and after a moment the detective continued.

"Says in the records you did your community service in a DOJ lab in Sacramento. Were you thinking of becoming a cop then or something?"

"It was after I changed my major to chemistry. I just worked in the blood lab. I did typing and matching, basic work. It was far from cop work."

"But it must have been interesting, huh? Dealing with cops, putting together the evidence for important cases. Interesting enough for you to stay on after you did your hours."

"I stayed because they offered me a job and Stanford is expensive. And they didn't give me the important cases. Mostly the cases came to me in FedEx boxes. I did the work and shipped it all back. No big deal. In fact, it was kind of boring."

Renner moved on without transition.

"Your arrest for impersonating an officer also came a year after your name came up on a crime report down here. It's on the computer."

Pierce started to shake his head.

"No. I've never been arrested for anything down here. Just that time up at Stanford."

"I didn't say you were arrested. I said your name's on a crime report. Everything's on computer now. You're a hacker, you know that. You throw in a name and sometimes it's amazing what comes out."

"I am not a hacker. I don't know the first thing about it anymore. And whatever crime report you are talking about, it must be a different Henry Pierce. I don't remem—"

"I don't think so. Kester Avenue in Sherman Oaks? Did you have a sister named Isabelle Pierce?"

Pierce froze. He was amazed that Renner had made the connection.

"The victim of a homicide, May nineteen eighty-eight."

All Pierce could do was nod. It was like a secret was being told, or a bandage ripped off an open wound.

"Believed to have been the victim of a killer known as the Doll-maker, later identified as Norman Church. Case closed with the death of Church, September nine, nineteen ninety."

Case closed, Pierce thought. As if Isabelle were simply a file that could be closed, put in a drawer and forgotten. As if a murder could ever really be solved.

He came out of his thoughts and looked at Renner.

"Yes, my sister. What about it? What's it got to do with this?"

Renner hesitated and then slowly his weary face split into a small smile.

"I suppose it has everything and nothing to do with it."

"That doesn't make sense."

"Sure it does. She was older than you, wasn't she?"

"A few years."

"She was a runaway. You used to go look for her, didn't you? Says so on the computer, so it must be right, right? At night. With your dad. He'd —"

"Stepfather."

"Stepfather, then. He'd send you into the abandoned buildings to look because you were a kid and the kids in those squats didn't run from another kid. That's what the report says. Says you never found her. Nobody did, until it was too late."

Pierce folded his arms and leaned across the table.

"Look, is there a point to this? Because I would really like to get out of here, if you don't mind."

"The point is, you went searching for a lost girl once before, Mr. Pierce. Makes me wonder if you're not trying to make up for something with this girl Lilly. You know what I mean?"

"No," Pierce said in a voice that sounded very small, even to himself.

Renner nodded.

"Okay, Mr. Pierce, you can go. For now. But let me say for the record that I don't believe for a moment you've told me the whole truth here. It's my job to know when people are lying and I think you're lying or leaving things out, or both. But, you know, I don't feel too bad about it, because things like that catch up with a person. I may move slow, Mr. Pierce. Sure, I kept you waiting in here too long. A fine, upstanding citizen like you. But that's because I am thorough and I'm pretty good at what I do. I'll have the whole picture pretty soon. I guarantee it. And if I find out you crossed any lines in that picture, it's going to be my pleasure, if you know what I mean."

Renner stood up.

"I'll be in touch about that polygraph. And if I were you, I might want to think about going back to that nice new apartment on Ocean Way and staying there and staying away from this, Mr. Pierce."

Pierce stood up and walked awkwardly around the table and Renner to the door. He thought of something before leaving.

"Where's my car?"

"Your car? I guess it's wherever you left it. Go to the front desk. They'll call a cab for you."

"Thanks a lot."

"Good night, Mr. Pierce. I'll be in touch."

As he walked through the deserted squad room to the hallway that led to the front desk and the exit, Pierce checked his watch. It was twelve-thirty. He knew he had to get to Robin before Renner did but her number was in the backpack in his car.

And as he approached the front counter he realized he had no money for a cab. He had given every dollar he had on him to Robin. He hesitated for a moment.

"Can I help you, sir?"

It was the cop behind the counter. Pierce realized he was staring at him.

"No, I'm fine."

He turned and walked out of the police station. On Venice Boulevard he started jogging west toward the beach.

16

As Pierce went down the alley to his car he saw that Lilly Quinlan's apartment was still a nest of police activity. Several cars were clogging the alley and a mobile light had been set up to spray the front of the apartment with illumination.

He noticed Renner standing out front, conversing with his partner, a detective whose name Pierce did not remember. It meant Renner had probably driven right by Pierce on his way back to the crime scene and had not noticed him or had intentionally decided not to offer him a ride. Pierce chose the second possibility. A cop on the street, even at night, would notice a man jogging in full dress. Renner had purposely gone by him.

Standing — or maybe hiding — next to his car while he cooled down from the jog over, Pierce watched for a few minutes and soon Renner and his partner went back inside the apartment. Pierce finally used the keyless remote to unlock the door of the BMW.

He slipped into the car and gently closed the door. He fumbled with the key, trying to find the ignition, and realized the ceiling light was off. He thought it must have burned out because it was set to go on when the door was open. He reached up and tapped the button anyway and nothing happened. He tapped it again and the light came on.

He sat there looking up at the light for a long moment and considering this. He knew the light had a three-setting cycle controlled by pushing the button on the ceiling next to it. The first position was the convenience setting, engaging the light when the door was open. Once the door was closed the light would fade out after about fifteen seconds or the ignition of the car, whichever came first. The second position turned on the light full-time, even if the door was closed. The third position turned the light off with no automatic convenience response.

Pierce knew he always kept the light set on the first position so the interior would be lit when he opened the door. That had not occurred when he had gotten into the car. The light had to have been in the third position of the cycle. He had then pushed the button once — to position one — and the light did not come on, because the door had already been closed. He had pushed it a second time and the light came on in position two.

Opening and closing the door, he went through the cycle until he had confirmed his theory. His conclusion was that someone had been in his car and changed the light setting.

Suddenly panicked by this realization, he reached between the two front seats to the backseat floor. His hand found his backpack. He pulled it forward and made a quick check of its contents. His notebooks were still there. Nothing seemed to be missing.

He opened the glove box and that too seemed undisturbed. Yet he was sure someone had been inside the car.

He knew the most expensive thing in the car was probably the leather backpack itself, yet it had not been taken. This led him to conclude that the car had been searched but not burglarized. That explained why it had been relocked. A car burglar probably wouldn't have bothered to disguise what had happened.

Pierce looked up at the lit doorway of the apartment and knew what had happened. Renner. The police. They had searched his car. He was sure of it.

He considered this and decided there were two possibilities as to how it had happened and how the mistake that led to his tip-off had occurred. The first was that the searcher opened the door — probably with a professional "slim jim" window channel device — and then hit the light button twice to extinguish the light so as not to be seen in the car.

The second possibility was that the searcher entered the car and closed the door, the overhead light going out on its timer delay. The searcher would have then pushed the overhead button to turn the light back on. When the search was completed he would have then pushed the button again to turn the light off, leaving it in the cycle position Pierce had found it.

His guess was that it was the latter possibility. Not that it mattered. He thought about Renner inside the apartment. He knew then why the detective had not given him a ride. He had wanted to search the car. He beat Pierce back to the scene and searched his car.

The search would have been illegal without his permission but Pierce actually felt the opposite of angry about it. He knew there was nothing in the car that incriminated him in the Lilly Quinlan disappearance or any other crime. He thought about Renner and the disappointment he probably felt when the car turned up clean.

"Fuck you, asshole," he said out loud.

Just as he was about to finally key the engine he saw the mattress being removed from the apartment. Two people he assumed were crime scene specialists gingerly carried the bulky piece vertically through the door and down the stairs to a van marked LAPD SCIENTIFIC INVESTIGATION DIVISION.

The mattress had been wrapped in thick plastic that was opaque like a shower curtain. The wide and dark blotch at its center clearly showed through. The sight of it being held up in the harsh light immediately depressed Pierce. It was as if they were holding up a billboard that advertised that he had been too late to do anything for Lilly Quinlan.

The mattress was too big and wide to fit in the van. The people from the Scientific Investigation Division hoisted it up onto a rack on top of the vehicle and then secured it with rope. Pierce guessed that the plastic wrapping would secure the integrity of whatever evidence would come from it.

When he looked away from the van he noticed that Renner was standing in the doorway of the apartment, looking at him. Pierce held his stare for a long moment and then started the car. Because of all the official cars clogging the alley, he had to back all the way down to Speedway before being able to turn around and head home.

At his apartment ten minutes later he lifted the phone and immediately got the broken dial tone indicating he had messages. Before checking them he hit the redial button because he knew the last call he had made had been to Robin. The call went to voice mail without a ring, indicating she had turned off the phone or was on a call.

"Listen, Robin, it's me, Henry Pierce. I know you were angry with me but please listen to what I have to say right now. After you left I found the door to Lilly's apartment open. The landlord was in there clearing the place out. We found what looked like blood on the bed and we had to call the cops. I pretty much kept you —"

The beep sounded and he was cut off. He hit redial again, wondering why she had set such a short message window on her phone service. He got a busy signal.

"Damn it!"

He started over and got the busy signal again. Frustrated, he walked out through the bedroom to the balcony. The sea breeze was strong and biting. The Ferris wheel lights were still on, though the amusement park had closed at midnight. He pushed redial again and held the phone to his ear. This time it rang and after one ring was picked up by the real Robin. Her voice was sleepy.

"Robin?"

"Yeah, Henry?"

"Yes, don't hang up. I was just leaving you a message. I —"

"I know. I was just listening to it. Did you get mine?"

"What, a message? No. I just got home. I've been with the cops all night. Listen, I know you're mad at me but, like I was trying to say on the message, the cops are going to be calling you. I kept you out of it. I didn't say you brought me there or anything else. But when they asked me how I knew Lilly was from Tampa and her mother was there, I told them you told me. It was the only way out. For me, I admit, but I didn't think it would be a problem for you. I mean, your pages are linked. They would have gotten around to talking to you anyway."

"It's okay."

He was silent for a moment, surprised by her reaction.

"I told them I convinced you I wanted to find Lilly to make sure she was okay and that you believed me and that's why you told me things about her."

"You know, you did convince me. That's why I called and left a message. Good thing I have caller ID and had your number. I wanted to tell you I was sorry about what I said in that alley. That was very uncool."

"Don't worry about it."

"Thanks."

They were both silent for a moment.

"Look," Pierce said. "The mattress in that place . . . There was a lot of blood. I don't know what happened to Lilly but if she was trying to get out of the business to go to school . . . I know you're afraid of Billy Wentz but you should be more than that, Robin. Whatever you do, be careful."

She didn't say anything.

"You have to get away from him and that business. But, listen to me, when you do, don't tell a soul about it. Just disappear without them knowing you're leaving. I think that might have been the mistake Lilly made. She might've told him or told somebody that took it back to him."

"And you think he did this? She made him money. Why would he —"

"I don't know. I don't know what to think. It could've been the person she was with before she was supposed to meet you. It could've been a lot of things. I saw things in that apartment, whips and masks and things. Who knows what happened to her. But it could have been Wentz sending out the message: Nobody leaves. All I'm saying is that it's a dangerous world you work in, Robin. You should get out of it and you should be damn careful about it when you do."

She was silent and he knew he wasn't telling her anything she didn't already know. Then he thought he heard her crying but he wasn't sure.

"Are you all right?"

"Yes," she said. "It's just that it's not so easy, you know. Quitting. Getting out and going back to the square. I mean, what else do I do? I make a lot of money doing this. More than I'll ever make anywhere else. What should I do, work at a McDonald's? I probably couldn't even get a job there. What do I put on the application, that I've been whoring for the last two years?"

It wasn't the conversation Pierce thought he was going to get into with her. He walked inside from the balcony and back into the living room. He had two new chairs but took his usual spot on the old couch.

"Robin? I don't even know your last name."

"LaPorte. And my name isn't Robin, either."

"What is it?"

"It's Lucy."

"Well, I like that better. Lucy LaPorte. Yeah, I like that. It's got a good sound."

"I have to give everything else to these men. I decided I'd keep my name."

She seemed to have stopped crying.

"Well . . . Lucy, if I can call you that. You keep my number. When you're ready to walk away from that life, you call me and I'll do everything I can to help you do it. Money, job, an apartment, whatever you need, just call me and you've got it. I'll do what I can."

"It's because of your sister that you'd do it, isn't it?"

Pierce thought about this before answering.

"I don't know. Probably."

"I don't care. Thank you, Henry."

"Okay, Lucy. I think I'm going to crash now. It's been a long day and I'm tired. I'm sorry I woke you up."

"Don't worry about it. And don't worry about the cops. I'll handle them."

"Thanks. Good night."

He ended the call and then checked his voice mail for messages. He had five. Or rather, Lilly had three and he had two. He erased Lilly's as soon as he determined they were not for him. His first message was from Charlie.

"Just wanted to see how it went in the lab today and to ask if you'd had a chance to review the patent apps yet. If you see any problems, we should know first thing Monday so we have time to fix —"

He erased the message. His plan was to review the patent applications in the morning. He'd call Charlie back after that.

He listened to the entire message from Lucy LaPorte.

"Hey, it's Robin. Look, I just wanted to say I'm sorry about what I said to you at the end. I've just been mad at the whole fucking world lately. But the truth is I can tell you care about Lilly and want to make sure she's okay. Maybe I acted the way I did because I wish there was somebody in the world that cared that way about me. So, anyway, that's it. Give me a call sometime if you want. We can just hang out. And next time I won't make you buy a smoothie. Bye."

For some reason he saved the message and clicked off. He thought maybe he'd want to listen to it again. He bumped the phone against his chin for a few minutes while he thought about Lucy. There was an underlying sweetness about her that pushed through her harsh mouth and the reality of what she did in order to make her way in the world. He thought about what she had said to him about using the name Robin and keeping the name Lucy for herself.

I have to give everything else to these men. I decided I'd keep my name.

He remembered the police detective sitting in the living room, talking to his mother and stepfather. His father was there, too. He told them that Isabelle had been using another name on the street and with the men she went with to get money. He remembered that the detective said that she used the name Angel.

Pierce knew that Renner had him pegged. What had happened so long ago was always close below the surface. It had bubbled up over the top when the mystery of Lilly Quinlan presented itself. In his desire to find Lilly, to maybe save her, he was finding and saving his own lost sister.

Pierce thought it was an amazing and horrible world out there. What people did to one another but mostly to themselves. He thought maybe this was the reason he shut himself away in the lab for so many hours each day. He shut himself away from the world, from knowing or thinking about bad things. In the lab everything was clear and simple. Quantifiable. Scientific theory was tested and either proved or disproved. No gray areas. No shadows.

He suddenly felt an overwhelming urge to talk to Nicole, to tell her that in the last two days he had learned something he hadn't known before. Something that was hard to put into words but still palpable in his chest. He wanted to tell her that he no longer was going to chase the dime, that as far as he was concerned, it could chase him.

He clicked on the phone and dialed her number. His old number. Amalfi Drive. She picked up the phone after three rings. Her voice was alert but he could tell she had been asleep.

128

"Nicole, it's me."

"Henry . . . what?"

"I know it's late but I —"

"No . . . we talked about this. You told me you weren't going to do this."

"I know. But I want to talk to you."

"Have you been drinking?"

"No. I just want to tell you something."

"It's the middle of the night. You can't do this."

"Just this one time. I need to tell you something. Let me come over and —"

"No, Henry, no. I was sound asleep. If you want to talk, call me tomorrow. Good-bye now."

She hung up. He felt his face grow hot with embarrassment. He had just done something that before this night he was sure he would never have done, that he couldn't even imagine himself doing.

He groaned loudly and stood up and went to the windows. Out past the pier to the north he could make out the necklace of lights that marked the Pacific Coast Highway. The mountains rising above it were dark shapes barely discernible below the night sky. He could hear the ocean better than he could see it. The horizon was lost somewhere out there in the darkness.

He felt depressed and tired. His mind drifted from Nicole back to thoughts about Lucy and what he now knew appeared to have been Lilly's fate. As he looked out into the night he promised himself that he would not forget what he had said to Lucy. When she decided she wanted out and was ready to make the move, he would be there, if for no other reason than for himself. Who knows, he thought, it could end up being the best thing he ever did with his life.

Just as he looked at it, the lights of the Ferris wheel went out. He took that as a cue and went back inside the apartment. On the couch he picked up the phone and dialed his voice mail. He listened to the message from Lucy one more time, then went to bed. He had no sheets or blankets or pillows yet. He pulled the sleeping bag up onto the new mattress and climbed inside. He then realized he hadn't eaten anything all day. It was the first time he remembered that ever having happened during a day spent outside the lab. He fell asleep as he was mentally composing a list of things to do when he woke up in the morning.

Soon he was dreaming of a dark hallway with open doors on each side. As he moved down the hallway he would look through each doorway. Each room he looked into was like a hotel room with a bed and a bureau and a TV. And each room was occupied. Mostly by people he didn't recognize and who did not notice him looking. There were couples who were arguing, fucking and crying. Through one doorway he recognized his own parents. His mother and father, not his stepfather, though they were at an age that came after they were divorced. They were getting dressed to go out to a cocktail party.

Pierce moved on down the hallway and in another room saw Detective Renner. He was by himself and was pacing alongside the bed. The sheets and covers were off the bed and there was a large bloodstain on the mattress.

Pierce moved on and in another room Lilly Quinlan was on the bed, as still as a mannequin. The room was dark. She was naked and her eyes were on the television. Though Pierce could not see the screen from his angle of view, the blue glow it threw on Lilly's face made her look dead. He took a step into the room to check on her and she looked up at him. She smiled and he smiled and he turned to close the door, only to find there was no door to the room. When he looked back to her for an explanation, the bed was empty and only the television was on.

17

At exactly noon on Sunday the phone woke up Pierce. A man said, "Is it too early to speak to Lilly?"

Pierce said, "No, actually it's too late."

He hung up and looked at his watch. He thought about the dream he'd had and set to work interpreting it, but then groaned as the first memory of the rest of the night poked into his thoughts. The call he'd made to Nicole in the middle of the night. He climbed out of the sleeping bag and off the bed to take a long, hot shower while he thought about whether to call her again to apologize. But even the stinging hot water couldn't wash away the embarrassment he felt. He decided it would be best not to call her or try to explain himself. He'd try to forget what he had done.

By the time he was dressed his stomach was loudly demanding food but there was nothing in the kitchen, he had no money and his ATM card was tapped out until Monday. He knew he could go to a restaurant or a grocery store and use a credit card but that would take too long. He had come out of the embarrassment of the Nicole call and the baptism of the shower with a desire to put the Lilly Quinlan episode behind him and let the police handle it. He had to get back to work. And he knew that any delay in getting to Amedeo might undermine his resolve.

By one o'clock he was entering the offices. He nodded to the security man behind the front dais but did not address him by name. He was one of Clyde Vernon's new hires and had always acted coolly toward Pierce, who was happy to return the favor.

Pierce kept a coffee mug full of spare change on his desk. Before beginning any work, he dropped his backpack on the desk, grabbed the mug and took the stairs down to the second floor, where snack and soda machines were located in the lunchroom. He almost emptied the mug buying two Cokes, two bags of chips and a package of Oreos. He then checked the lunchroom refrigerator to see if anybody had left anything edible behind but there was nothing to steal. As a rule the janitorial crew emptied the refrigerator out every Friday night.

One bag of chips was empty by the time he got back to the office. Pierce tore into the other and popped one of the Cokes open after sliding behind the desk. He removed the new batch of patent applications from the safe below his desk. Jacob Kaz was an excellent patent attorney but he always needed the scientists to back-read the introductions and summaries of the legal applications. Pierce always had the final sign-off on the patents.

So far, the patents Pierce and Amedeo Technologies had applied for and received over the past six years revolved around protecting proprietary designs of complex biological architectures. The key to the future of nanotechnology was creating the nanostructures that would hold and carry it. This was where Pierce had long ago chosen for Amedeo Tech to make its stand in the arena of molecular computing.

In the lab Pierce and the other members of his team designed and built a wide variety of daisy chains of molecular switches that were delicately strung together to create logic gates, the basic threshold of computing. Most of the patents Pierce and Amedeo held were in this area or the adjunct area of moleculary RAM. A small number of other patents centered on the development of bridging molecules, the latticework of sturdy carbon tubes that would one day connect the hundreds of thousands of nanoswitches that together would make a computer as small as a dime and as powerful as a digital Mack truck.

Before beginning his review of the new group of patents, Pierce leaned back in his chair and looked up at the wall behind his computer monitor. Hanging on the wall was a caricature drawing of Pierce holding up a microscope, his ponytail flying and his eyes wide as if he had just made a fantastic discovery. The caption above it said "Henry Hears a Who!"

Nicole had given it to him. She'd had an artist on the pier draw it after Pierce had told her the story of his favorite childhood memory, his father reading and telling stories to him and his sister. Before his parents split. Before his father moved to Portland and started a whole new family. Before things started to go wrong for Isabelle.

His favorite book at the time had been Dr. Seuss's *Horton Hears a Who!* It was the story of an elephant who discovers a whole world existing on a speck of dust. A nanoworld long before there was any thought of nanoworlds. Pierce still knew many of the lines from the book by heart. And he thought of them often in the course of his work.

In the story Horton is outcast by a jungle society that doesn't believe his discovery. He is most persecuted by the monkeys — known as the Wickersham gang — but ultimately saves the tiny world on the speck of dust from the monkeys and proves its existence to the rest of society.

Pierce opened the Oreos and ate two of the cookies whole, hoping the sugar charge would help him focus.

He began reviewing the applications with excitement and anticipation. This batch would move Amedeo into a new arena and the science to a new level. Pierce knew it would flat-out rock the world of nanotechnology. And he smiled as he thought about the reaction his competitors would have when their intelligence officers copied the non-proprietary pages of the applications for them or when they read about the Proteus formula in the science journals.

The application package was for protecting a formula for cellular energy conversion. In the layman's terms used in the summary of the first application in the package, Amedeo was seeking patent protection for a "power supply system" that would energize the biological robots that would one day patrol the bloodstreams of human beings and destroy pathogens threatening their hosts.

They called the formula Proteus in a nod to the movie *Fantastic Voyage.* In the 1966 film a medical team is placed in a submarine called the *Proteus,* then miniaturized with a shrink ray and injected into a man's body to search for and destroy an inoperable blood clot in the brain.

The film was science fiction and it was likely that shrink rays would always remain the purview of the imagination. But the idea of attacking pathogens in the body with biological or cellular

133

robots, not too distant in imagination from the *Proteus,* was on the far horizon of scientific fact.

Since the inception of nanotechnology the potential medical applications had always been the sexiest side of the science. More intriguing than a quantum leap in computing power was the potential for curing cancer, AIDS, any and all diseases. The possibility of patrolling devices in the body that could encounter, identify and eliminate pathogens through chemical reaction was the Holy Grail of the science.

The bottleneck, however — the thing that kept this side of the science theoretical while rafts of researchers pursued molecular RAM and integrated circuits — was the question of a power supply. How to move these molecular submarines through the blood with a power source that was natural and compatible with the body's immune system.

Pierce, along with Larraby, his immunology researcher, had discovered a rudimentary yet highly reliable formula. Using the host's own cells — in this case, Pierce's were harvested and then replicated for research in an incubator — the two researchers developed a combination of proteins that would bind with the cell and draw an electrical stimulus from it. That meant power to drive the nanodevice could come from within and therefore be compatible with the body's immune system.

The Proteus formula was simple and that was its beauty and value. Pierce imagined all forward nanoresearch in the field being based upon this one discovery. Experimentation, and other discoveries and inventions leading to practical use, formerly seen as two decades or longer out on the horizon might now be half again as close to reality.

The discovery, made just three months earlier while Pierce was in the midst of his difficulties with Nicole, was the single most exciting moment of his life.

"Our buildings, to you, would seem terribly small," Pierce whispered as he finished his review of the patents. "But to us, who aren't big, they are wonderfully tall."

The words of Dr. Seuss.

Pierce was pleased with the package. As usual, Kaz had done an excellent job of blending science-speak and layman's language in the top sheets of each patent. The meat of each application, how-ever, contained the science and the diagrammed segments of the formula. These pages were written by Pierce and Larraby and had been reviewed by both researchers repeatedly.

The application package was good to go, in Pierce's opinion. He was excited. He knew floating such a patent application package into the nanoworld would bring a flood of publicity and a subse-quent rise in investor interest. The plan was to show the discovery to Maurice Goddard first and lock down his investment, then sub-mit the applications. If all went well, Goddard would realize he had a short lead and a short window of opportunity and would make a preemptive strike, signing up as the company's main funding source.

Pierce and Charlie Condon had carefully choreographed it. Goddard would be shown the discovery. He would be allowed to check it out for himself in the tunneling electron microscope. He would then have twenty-four hours to make his decision. Pierce wanted a minimum of $18 million over three years. Enough to charge forward faster and further than any competitor. And he was offering 10 percent of the company in exchange.

Pierce wrote a congratulatory note to Jacob Kaz on a yellow Post-it and attached it to the cover sheet of the Proteus application package. He then locked it back in the safe. He'd have it sent by secure transport to Kaz's office in Century City in the morning. No faxes, no e-mails. Pierce might even drive it over himself.

He leaned back, threw another Oreo into his mouth and checked his watch. It was two o'clock. An hour had gone by since he had been in the office but it had seemed like only ten minutes. It felt good to have the feeling again, the vibe. He decided to capitalize on it and move into the lab to do some real work. He grabbed the rest of the cookies and got up.

"Lights."

Pierce was in the hallway pulling the door closed on the dark-ened office when the phone rang. It was the distinctive double ring of his private line. Pierce pushed the door back open.

"Lights."

Few people had his direct office number but one of them was Nicole. Pierce quickly moved around the desk and looked down at the caller ID screen on the phone. It said *private caller* and he knew it wasn't Nicole, because her cell phone and the line from the house on Amalfi were uncloaked. Pierce hesitated but then remembered that Cody Zeller had the number. He picked up the phone.

"Mr. Pierce?"

It wasn't Cody Zeller.

"Yes?"

"It's Philip Glass. You called me yesterday?"

The private investigator. Pierce had forgotten.

"Oh. Yes, yes. Thanks for calling back."

"I didn't get the message until today. What can I do for you?"

"I want to talk to you about Lilly Quinlan. She's missing. Her mother hired you a few weeks ago. From Florida."

"Yes, but I am no longer employed on that one."

Pierce remained standing behind his desk. He put his hand on top of the computer monitor as he spoke.

"I understand that. But I was wondering if I could talk to you about it. I have Vivian Quinlan's permission. You can check with her if you want. You still have her number?"

It took a long while for Glass to respond, so long that Pierce thought he may have quietly hung up.

"Mr. Glass?"

"Yes, I'm here. I'm just thinking. Can you tell me what your interest is in all of this?"

"Well, I want to find her."

This was met with more silence and Pierce started to understand that he was dealing from a position of weakness. Something was going on with Glass, and Pierce was at a disadvantage for not knowing it. He decided to press his case. He wanted the meeting.

"I'm a friend of the family," he lied. "Vivian asked me to see what I could find out."

"Have you talked to the LAPD?"

Pierce hesitated. Instinctively he knew that Glass's cooperation might be riding on his answer. He thought about the events of the night before and wondered if they could already be known by Glass. Renner had said he knew Glass and he most likely planned to call him. It was Sunday afternoon. Maybe the police detective was waiting until Monday, since Glass seemed to be on the periphery of the case.

"No," he lied again. "My understanding from Vivian was that the LAPD wasn't interested in this."

"Who are you, Mr. Pierce?"

"What? I don't under—"

"Who do you work for?"

"No one. Myself, actually."

"You're a PI?"

"What's that?"

"Come on."

"I mean it. I don't under— oh, private investigator. No, I'm not a PI. Like I said, I'm a friend."

"What do you do for a living?"

"I'm a researcher. I'm a chemist. I don't see what this has to do with —"

"I can see you today. But not at my office. I'm not going in today."

"Okay, then where? When?"

"One hour from now. Do you know a place in Santa Monica called Cathode Ray's?"

"On Eighteenth, right? I'll be there. How will we know each other?"

"Do you have a hat or something distinctive to wear?"

Pierce leaned down and opened an unlocked desk drawer. He pulled out a baseball cap with blue stitched letters over the brim.

"I'll be wearing a gray baseball cap. It says MOLES in blue stitching above the brim."

"Moles? As in the small burrowing animal?"

Pierce almost laughed.

"As in molecules. The Fighting Moles was the name of our softball team. Back when we had one. My company sponsored it. It was a long time ago."

"I'll see you at Cathode Ray's. Please come alone. If I feel you are not alone or it looks like a setup, you won't see me."

"A setup? What are you —"

Glass hung up and Pierce was listening to dead space.

He put down the phone and put on the hat. He considered the

strange questions the private detective had asked and thought about what he had said at the end of the conversation and how he had said it. Pierce realized it was almost as if he had been scared of something.

18

Cathode Ray's was a hangout for the tech generation — usually everybody in the place had a laptop or a PDA on the table next to their double latte. The place was open twenty-four hours a day and provided power and high-speed phone jacks at every table. Connections to local Internet service providers only. It was close to Santa Monica College and the film production and fledgling software districts of the Westside, and it had no corporate affiliations. These combined to make it a popular place with the plugged-in set.

Pierce had been there on many prior occasions, yet he thought it an odd choice by Glass for the meeting. Glass sounded like an older man over the phone, his voice gravelly and tired. If that was the case, then he would stand out in a place like Cathode Ray's. Considering the paranoia that had come over the phone line from him, it seemed strange for him to have picked the coffee shop for the meeting.

At three o'clock Pierce entered Cathode Ray's and took a quick scan around the place for an older man. No one stood out. No one looked at him. He got in line for coffee.

Before leaving the office, he had dumped what change remained in his desk mug into his pocket. He counted it out while waiting and concluded that he had just enough for a basic coffee, medium size, with a little left over for the tip jar.

After hitting the cup with heavy doses of cream and sugar, he moved out to the patio area and selected an empty table in the corner. He sipped his coffee slowly but it was still twenty minutes before he was approached by a short man in black jeans and a black T-shirt. He had a clean-shaven face and dark, hard eyes that were deeply set. He was much younger than Pierce had guessed, maybe late thirties at the most. He had no coffee, he had come straight to the table.

"Mr. Pierce?"

Pierce offered his hand.

"Mr. Glass?"

Glass pulled out the other chair and sat down. He leaned across the table.

"If you don't mind, I'd like to see your ID," he said.

Pierce put his cup down and started digging in his pocket for his wallet.

"Probably a good idea," he said. "Mind if I look at yours?"

After both men had convinced themselves they were sitting with the right party, Pierce leaned back and studied Glass. He seemed to Pierce to be a large man stuck in a small man's body. He exuded intensity. It was as if his skin were stretched too tight over his whole body.

"Do you want to get a coffee before we start to talk?"

"No, I don't use caffeine."

That seemed to figure.

"Then I guess we should get to it. What's with all the spook stuff?"

"Excuse me?"

"You know, the 'make sure you're alone' and 'what do you do for a living' stuff. It all seems to be a little strange."

Before speaking, Glass nodded as if he agreed.

"What do you know about Lilly Quinlan?"

"I know what she was doing for a living, if that's what you mean."

"And what was that?"

"She was an escort. She advertised through the Internet. I'm pretty sure she worked for a guy named Billy Wentz. He's sort of a digital pimp. He runs the website where she kept a page. I think he set her up in other things — porno sites, stuff like that. I think she was involved in the S and M scene as well."

The mention of Wentz seemed to bring a new intensity to Glass's face. He folded his arms on the table and leaned forward.

"Have you spoken to Mr. Wentz yourself?"

Pierce shook his head.

"No, but I tried to. I went to Entrepreneurial Concepts yesterday — that's his umbrella company. I asked to see him but he wasn't there. Why do I feel like I am telling you things you already know? Look, I want to ask questions here, not answer them."

"There is little I can tell you. I specialize in missing-persons investigations. I was recommended to Vivian Quinlan by someone I know in the LAPD's Missing Persons Unit. It went from there. She paid me for a week's work. I didn't find Lilly or much else about her disappearance."

Pierce considered this for a long moment. He was an amateur and he had found out quite a bit in less than forty-eight hours. He doubted that Glass was as inept as he was presenting himself to be.

"You did know about the website, right? L.A. Darlings?"

"Yes. I was told she was working as an escort and it was pretty easy to find her. L.A. Darlings is one of the more popular sites, you could say."

"Did you find her house? Did you talk to her landlord?"

"No and no."

"What about Lucy LaPorte?"

"Who?"

"She uses the name Robin on the website. Her page is linked to Lilly's."

"Oh, yes, Robin. Yes, I spoke to her on the phone. It was very brief. She was not cooperative."

Pierce was suspicious of whether Glass had really called. It seemed to him Lucy would have mentioned that an investigator had already inquired about Lilly. He planned to check with her about the supposed call.

"How long ago was that? The call to Robin."

Glass shrugged.

"Three weeks. It was at the beginning of my week of work. She was one of the first I called."

"Did you go see her?"

"No, other things came up. And at the end of the week Mrs. Quinlan was not willing to pay me for further work on the case. That was it for me."

"What other things came up?"

Glass didn't respond.

"You talked to Wentz, didn't you?"

141

Glass looked down at his folded arms but didn't reply.

"What did he tell you?"

Glass cleared his throat.

"Listen to me very carefully, Mr. Pierce. You want to stay clear of Billy Wentz."

"Why?"

"Because he is a dangerous man. Because you are moving in an area that you know nothing about. You could get very seriously hurt if you are not careful."

"Is that what happened to you. Did you get hurt?"

"We are not talking about me. We are talking about you."

A man with an iced latte sat down at the table nearest them. Glass looked over and studied him with paranoid eyes. The man took a PalmPilot out of his pocket and opened it. He slid out the stylus and went to work on the device. He paid no mind to Glass or Pierce.

"I want to know what happened when you went to see Wentz," Pierce said.

Glass unfolded his arms and rubbed his hands together.

"Do you know . . ."

He stopped and didn't go on. Pierce had to prompt him.

"Know what?"

"Do you know that so far the only place in which the Internet is significantly profitable is in the adult entertainment sectors?"

"I've heard that. What does —"

"Ten *bill*ion dollars a year is made off the electronic sex trade in this country. A lot of it is over the net. It's big business, with ties to top-flight corporate America. It's everywhere, available on every computer, on every TV. Turn on the TV and order hard-core porn courtesy of AT and T. Go online and order a woman like Lilly Quinlan to your door."

Glass's voice took on a fervor that reminded Pierce of a priest in a pulpit.

"Do you know that Wentz sells franchises across the country? I inquired. Fifty thousand dollars a city. There is now a New York Darlings and a Vegas Darlings. Miami, Seattle, Denver and on and on. Linked to these sites he has porn sites for every imaginable sexual persuasion and fetish. He —"

"I know all of that," Pierce broke in. "But what I am interested in is Lilly Quinlan. What does all of that have to do with what happened to her?"

"I don't know," Glass said. "But what I am trying to tell you is that there is too much money at stake here. Stay away from Billy Wentz."

Pierce leaned back and looked at Glass.

"He got to you, didn't he? What did he do, threaten you?"

Glass shook his head. He wasn't going to go there.

"Forget about me. I came here today to try to help you. To warn you about how close you are to the fire. Stay away from Wentz. I can't stress that enough. *Stay away.*"

Pierce could see in his eyes the sincerity of the warning. And the fear. Pierce had no doubt that Wentz had in some way gotten to Glass and scared him off the Quinlan case.

"Okay," he said. "I'll keep clear."

19

Pierce toyed with the idea of going back to the lab after his coffee with Philip Glass but ultimately admitted to himself that the conversation with the private detective had stunted the motivation he had felt only an hour before. Instead, he went to the Lucky Market on Ocean Park Boulevard and filled a shopping cart with food and other basics he would need in the new apartment. He paid with a credit card and loaded the numerous bags into the trunk of his BMW. It wasn't until he was in his parking space in the garage at the Sands that he realized that he would have to make at least three trips up and down the elevator to get all of his purchases into the apartment. He had seen other tenants with small pushcarts, ferrying laundry or groceries up or down the elevator. Now he realized they had the right idea.

On the first trip he took the new plastic laundry basket he had bought and filled it with six bags of groceries, including all of the perishables he wanted to get up and into the apartment refrigerator first.

As he came into the elevator alcove two men were standing by the door that led to the individual storage rooms that came with each apartment. Pierce was reminded that he needed to get a padlock for his storage room and to get the boxes of old records and keepsakes Nicole was still holding for him in the garage at the house on Amalfi. His surfboard, too.

At the elevator one of the men pushed the call button. Pierce exchanged nods with them and guessed that they might be a gay couple. One man was in his forties with a small build and a spreading waist. He wore pointed-toe boots that gave him two extra inches in the heel. The other man was much younger, taller and harder, yet he seemed to defer in body language to his older partner.

When the elevator door opened they allowed Pierce to step on first and then the smaller man asked him what floor he wanted. After the door closed he noticed that the man did not push another button after pressing twelve for him.

"You guys live on twelve?" he asked. "I just moved in a few days ago."

"Visitors," said the smaller one.

Pierce nodded. He turned his attention to the flashing numbers above the door. Maybe it was being so soon after the warning from Glass or the way the smaller man kept stealing glances at the reflection of Pierce in the chrome trim on the door, but as the elevator rose and the numbers got higher, so did his anxiety. He remembered how they had been standing near the storage room door and approached the elevator only when he did. As if they had been waiting there for some reason.

Or for some person.

The elevator finally reached twelve and the door slid open. The men stepped to the side to allow Pierce to step out first. With both hands holding the laundry basket, Pierce nodded forward.

"You guys go ahead," he said. "Can you punch the first floor for me? I forgot to get the mail."

"There is no mail on Sundays," the smaller man said.

"No, I mean yesterday's. I forgot to get it."

Nobody moved. The three of them stood there looking at one another until the door started to close and the big man reached out and hit the bumper with a hard forearm. The door shuddered and slowly reopened, as if recovering from a sucker punch. And finally the smaller one spoke.

"Fuck the mail, Henry. You're getting off here. Am I right, Six-Eight?"

Without answering, the man obviously named because of his longitudinal dimensions moved in and grabbed Pierce by the upper arms. He pivoted and hurled Pierce through the open door into the twelfth-floor hallway. His momentum took him across the hall and crashing into a closed door marked ELECTRICAL. Pierce felt his breath blast out of his lungs and the laundry basket slipped from his grasp, landing with a loud thud on the floor.

"Easy now, easy. Keys, Six-Eight."

145

Pierce's breath had still not returned. The one named Six-Eight moved toward him and with one hand pressed him back against the door. He slapped Pierce's pants pockets with the other. When he felt the keys he dove his big hand into the pocket and pulled out the key ring. He handed it to the other man.

"Okay."

With the smaller man leading the way — and knowing the way — Pierce was pushed down the hall toward his apartment. When he got his breath back he started to say something but the bigger man's hand came around from behind and covered his face and his words. The small one held up a finger without looking back.

"Not yet, Bright Boy. Let's get inside so we don't disturb the neighbors more than we have to. You just moved in, after all. You don't want to make a bad impression."

The smaller one walked with his head down, apparently studying the keys on the ring.

"A Beemer," he said.

Pierce knew the keyless remote to his car carried the BMW insignia on it.

"I like Beemers. It's the full package; you got power and luxury and a real solid feel. You can't beat that in a car — or a woman."

He looked back at Pierce and smiled with a raised eyebrow. They got to the door and the smaller man opened it with the second key he tried. Six-Eight pushed Pierce into the apartment and shoved him down onto the couch. He then stepped away and the other man took a position in front of Pierce. He noticed the phone on the arm of the couch and picked it up. Pierce watched him play with the buttons and go through the caller ID directory.

"Been busy here, Henry," he said as he scrolled the list. "Philip Glass . . ."

He looked back at Six-Eight, who had stationed himself near the apartment's front hallway, his massive arms folded across his chest. The small man crinkled his eyes in a question.

"Isn't that the guy we had a discussion with a few weeks back?"

Six-Eight nodded. Pierce realized that Glass must have called the apartment before reaching him at Amedeo.

The small man went back to the phone readout and soon his eyes lit on another familiar listing.

146

"Oh, so now Robin's calling *you*. That's wonderful."

But Pierce could tell by the man's voice that it wasn't wonderful, that it was going to be anything but wonderful for Lucy LaPorte.

"It's nothing," Pierce said. "She just left a message. I can play it for you if you want. I kept it."

"You falling in love with her, are you?"

"No."

The smaller guy turned and gave a false smile to Six-Eight. Then suddenly he moved his arm in a quick overhand motion and hit Pierce with the phone on the bridge of his nose, delivering a blow with the full power of the sweeping arc.

Pierce saw a flash of red and black blast across his vision and a searing pain screamed through his head. He couldn't tell if his eyes were closed or he'd gone blind. He instinctively rocked backwards on the couch and turned away from the blow in case another was coming. He vaguely heard the man in front of him yelling but what he was saying wasn't registering. Then strong, large hands clamped around his upper arms again and he was pulled upright and completely off the couch.

He could feel himself being hoisted over Six-Eight's shoulders and then carried. He felt his mouth filling with blood and he struggled to open his eyes but still couldn't do it. He heard the rolling sound of the balcony's sliding door, then the cool air from the ocean touching his skin.

"Wha . . . ," he managed to say.

Suddenly the hard shoulder that had been in his gut was gone and he started a headfirst free fall. His muscles tightened and his mouth opened to emit the final furious sound of his life. Then, at last, he felt the huge hands grab his ankles and hold. His head and shoulders slammed hard against the rough concrete of the textured exterior of the building.

But at least he was no longer falling.

A few seconds went by. Pierce brought his hands to his face and touched his nose and eyes. His nose was split vertically and horizontally and was bleeding profusely. He managed to wipe his eyes and open them partially. Twelve stories below he could see the green lawn of the beachside park. There were people on blankets down there, most of them homeless. He saw his blood falling in thick

147

drops into the trees directly below. He heard a voice from above him.

"Hello down there. Can you hear me?"

Pierce said nothing and then the hands that held his ankles shook violently, bouncing him off the outside wall again.

"Do I have your attention?"

Pierce spit a mouthful of blood onto the exterior wall and said, "Yes, I hear you."

"Good. I suppose by now you know who I am."

"I think so."

"Good. No need to mention names then. I just wanted to make sure we're at a point of knowledge and understanding here."

"What do you want?"

It was hard to talk upside down. Blood was pooling in the back of his throat and on the roof of his mouth.

"What do I want? Well, I first wanted to get a look at you. A guy spends his time sniffing your asshole for two days, you want to see what he looks like, right? There's that. And then I wanted to give you a message. Six-Eight."

Pierce was suddenly hoisted up. Still upside down, his face had come up to the open bars of the balcony railing. Through the bars he saw that the talker had stooped down so that they were face-to-face, the bars between them.

"What I wanted to say was that not only did you get the wrong number, you got the wrong world, partner. And you got about thirty seconds to decide whether you want to go back to where you came from or you want to go on to the next world. You understand what I am saying to you?"

Pierce nodded and started to cough.

"I . . . unnerstan . . . I'm . . . I'm done."

"You're damn right you're done. I ought to have my man drop your stupid ass right here and now. But I don't need the heat, so I'm not going to do that. But I have to tell you, Bright Boy, if I catch you sneaking and sniffing around again, you're gonna get dropped. Okay?"

Pierce nodded. The man Pierce was pretty sure was Billy Wentz then reached a hand between the bars and roughly patted Pierce's cheek.

"Be good now."

He stood up and gave a signal to Six-Eight. Pierce was pulled over the balcony and dropped on the balcony's floor. He broke the fall with his hands and then pushed his way into the corner. He looked up at his two attackers.

"You got a nice view here," said the smaller man. "What do you pay?"

Pierce looked out at the ocean. He spit a wad of thick blood onto the floor.

"Three thousand."

"Jesus Christ! I can get three fucking places for that."

Now just straddling the edge of consciousness, Pierce wondered how Wentz had intended the word *fucking* to be interpreted. Was he talking about places for fucking or was he just routinely cursing? He tried to shake off the clouds that were encroaching. It occurred to him then that the threat to himself aside, it was important to try to protect Lucy LaPorte.

He spit more blood onto the balcony floor.

"What about Lucy? What are you going to do?"

"Lucy? Who the fuck is Lucy?"

"I mean, Robin."

"Oh, our little Robin. You know, that's a good question, Henry. 'Cause Robin's a good earner. I have to be prudent. I have to calm myself when it comes to her. Rest assured that whatever we do, we won't leave marks and she'll be back, good as new, in two, three weeks at the most."

Pierce scrabbled his legs on the concrete in an effort to get up but he was too disoriented and weak.

"Leave her alone," he said as forcefully as he could. "I used her and she didn't even know it."

Wentz's dark eyes seemed to take on a new light. Pierce saw anger work its way into them. He saw Wentz put one hand on the top of the balcony railing as if to brace himself.

"Leave her alone, he says."

He shook his head again as if to ward off some encroaching power.

"Please," Pierce said. "She didn't do anything. It was me. Just leave her alone."

The small man looked back at Six-Eight and smiled, then shook his head.

"Do you believe this? Telling me like that?"

He turned back toward Pierce, took one step toward him and then swiftly brought his other foot up into a vicious kick. Pierce was expecting it and was able to use his forearm to deflect most of the power but the pointed toe of the boot struck him on the right side of the rib cage. It felt like it took at least two ribs with it.

Pierce slid down into the corner and tried to cover up, expecting more and trying to control the burning pain spreading across his chest. Instead, Wentz leaned down over him. He yelled at Pierce, spittle raining down on him with the words.

"Don't you fucking dare try to tell me how to run my business. Don't you fucking dare!"

He straightened up and dusted off his hands.

"And one other thing. You tell anybody about our little discussion here today and there will be consequences. Dire consequences. For you. For Robin. For the people you love. Do you understand what I'm telling you?"

Pierce weakly nodded.

"Let me hear you say it."

"I understand the consequences."

"Good. Then let's go, Six-Eight."

And Pierce was left alone, gulping for breath and clarity, trying to stay in the light when he sensed darkness closing in all around.

20

Pierce grabbed a T-shirt out of a box in the bedroom and held it to his face, trying to stop the bleeding. He straightened up and went into the bathroom and saw himself in the mirror. His face was already ballooning and turning color. The swelling of his nose was crowding his vision and widening the wounds on his nose and around his left eye. Most of the bleeding seemed to be internal, a steady stream of thick blood going down the back of his throat. He knew he had to get to a hospital but he had to warn Lucy LaPorte first.

He found the phone on the living room floor. He tried to go to the caller ID directory but the screen remained blank. He tried the on button but couldn't get a dial tone. The phone was broken — either by the impact with his face or when Wentz had thrown it to the floor.

Holding the shirt to his face, involuntary tears streaming out of his eyes, Pierce looked about the apartment for the box holding the earthquake kit he had ordered delivered with the furniture. Monica had showed him a listing of the kit's inventory before ordering it. He knew it contained a first aid kit, flashlights and batteries, two gallons of water, numerous freeze-dried food items and other supplies. It also contained a basic phone that did not use electric current. It simply needed to be jacked into the wall for it to work.

He found the box in the bedroom closet and dripped blood all over it as he desperately used both hands to rip it open. He lost his balance and almost fell over. He realized he was fading. The loss of blood, the depletion of adrenaline. He finally found the phone and took it to the wall jack next to the bed. He got a dial tone. Now all he needed was Robin's number.

He had it written in a notebook but that was in his backpack down in his car. He didn't think he could make it down there without passing out on the way. He wasn't even sure where his keys

151

were. The last he remembered, they had been in the hands of Billy Wentz.

Leaning against the wall, he first called Information for Venice and tried the name Lucy LaPorte, asking the operator to check under various spellings. But there was no number, unlisted or otherwise.

He then slid down the wall to the floor next to the bed. He began to panic. He had to get to her but couldn't — he thought of something and called the lab. But there was no answer. Sundays were sacrosanct with the lab rats. They worked long hours and usually six days a week. But rarely on Sunday. He tried Charlie Condon's office and home but got machines at both numbers.

He thought about Cody Zeller but knew he never answered his phone. The only way to reach him was by page and then he would be at the mercy of waiting for a callback.

He knew what he had to do. He punched in the number and waited. After four rings Nicole answered.

"It's me. I need your help. Can you go to —"

"Who is this?"

"Me, Henry."

"It doesn't sound like you. What are you —"

"Nicki!" he shouted. "Listen to me. This is an emergency and I need your help. We can talk about everything after. I can explain after."

"Okay," she said in a tone that indicated she wasn't convinced. "What is the emergency?"

"You still have your computer hooked up?"

"Yes, I don't even have a sign on the house yet. I'm not —"

"Okay, good. Go to your computer. Hurry, go!"

He knew she had a DSL line — he had always been paranoid about it. But now it would get them to the site faster.

When she got to the computer she switched to a headset she kept at the desk.

"Okay, I need you to go to a website. It's L.A. dash darlings dot com."

"Are you kidding me? Is this some —"

"Just do it! Or somebody might die!"

"Okay, okay. L.A. dash darlings . . ."

He waited.

"Okay, I'm there."

He tried to visualize the website on her screen.

"Okay, double click the Escorts folder and go to Blondes."

He waited.

"You got it?"

"I'm going as fast as — okay, now what?"

"Scroll through the thumbnails. Click on the one named Robin."

Again he waited. He realized his breathing was loud, a low whistle coming out of his throat.

"Okay, I've got Robin. Those tits have gotta be fake."

"Just give me the number."

She read off the number and Pierce recognized it. It was the right Robin.

"I'll call you back."

He pressed the plunger on the phone, held it for three seconds, and then let go, getting a new dial tone. He called the number for Robin. He was getting light-headed. What was left of his vision was starting to blur around the edges. After five rings his call went to voice mail.

"Goddamnit!"

He didn't know what to do. He couldn't send the police to her. He didn't even know where her real home was. The message signal beeped after her greeting. As he spoke, his tongue started to feel too big for his mouth.

"Lucy, it's me. It's Henry. Wentz came here. He messed me up and I think he's going to see you next. If you get this message, get out of there. Right now! Just get the hell out of there and call me when you get somewhere safe."

He added his number to the message and hung up.

He held the bloody shirt back up to his face and leaned against the wall. The flow of adrenaline and endorphins that had flooded his system during the attack from Wentz was ebbing and the deep throb of pain was settling in like winter. It was penetrating his whole body. It seemed as though every muscle and joint ached. His face felt like a neon sign pulsing with rhythmic bursts of searing fire. He didn't feel like moving anymore. He just wanted to pass out and wake up when he was healed and everything was better.

Without moving anything but his arm, he raised the phone off its cradle again and brought it up so he could see the keypad. He thumbed the redial button and waited. The call rang through to Lucy's voice mail again. He wanted to curse out loud but now it would hurt his face to move his mouth. He blindly felt around for the phone cradle and hung up the phone.

It rang while his hand was still on it and he raised it back to his ear.

" 'Lo?"

"It's Nicki. Can you talk? Is everything all right?"

"No."

"Should I call back?"

"No, I me ehry'ing's nah all ri."

"What's wrong? Why are you talking funny? Why did you need the number of *that* woman?"

Despite his pain and fear and everything else, he found himself angry at the way she said "that woman."

"Lohn story and I cah . . . I . . ."

He felt himself fading out but as he started to roll off the wall to the floor, the angle of his body sent jabbing pain through his chest and he groaned from somewhere deep inside.

"Henry! Are you hurt! Henry! Can you hear me?"

Pierce slid his hips down along the rug until he could lie flat on his back. Somehow an instinctive warning came through. He knew he might drown in his own blood if he stayed in his current position. Thoughts of rock stars drowning in their own vomit passed through his mind. He had dropped the phone and it was on the carpet next to his head. In his right ear he could hear the tinny sound of a far-off voice calling his name. He thought he recognized the voice and it made him smile. He thought of Jimi Hendrix drowning in his own puke and decided he'd rather drown in his own blood. He tried to sing, his voice a wet whisper.

" 'Suze me why I iss the sy . . ."

He couldn't make *k* sounds for some reason. That was strange. But soon it didn't matter. The small voice in his right ear drifted off and soon there was a loud blaring sound in the darkness. And soon even that was gone and there was only darkness all around him. And he liked the darkness.

21

A woman Pierce had never seen before was running her fingers through his hair. She seemed strangely detached and perfunctory for so intimate an action. The woman then leaned in closer to him and he thought she was going to kiss him. But she put her hand on his forehead. She then lifted some sort of tool, a light, and shined it in one eye and then the other. He then heard a man's voice.

"Ribs," he said. "Three and four. We might have a puncture."

"We put a mask over this nose and he'll probably hit the roof," the woman said.

"I'll give him something."

Now Pierce saw the man. He moved into view when he raised a hypodermic needle in a gloved hand and squeezed a little spray into the air. Next he felt the jab in his arm and pretty soon warmth and understanding flowed through his body, tickling across his chest. He smiled and almost laughed. Warmth and understanding in a needle. The wonders of chemistry. He had made the right choice.

"Extra straps," the woman said. "We're going vertical."

Whatever that meant. Pierce's eyes were closing. The last thing he saw before escaping into the warmth was a policeman standing over him.

"He going to make it?" he asked.

Pierce didn't hear the answer.

The next time he regained consciousness he was standing. But not really. He opened his eyes and they were all there, crowded close to him. The woman with the light and the man with the needle. And the cop. And Nicole was there, too. She was looking up at him with tears in her dark green eyes. Even so, she was beautiful to him, her skin brown and smooth, her hair pulled back in a ponytail, the blonde highlights shining.

The elevator started to drop and Pierce suddenly thought he might throw up. He tried to get out a warning but couldn't move his jaw. It was like he was tied tightly to the wall. He started to - struggle but couldn't move. He couldn't even move his head.

His eyes met Nicole's. She reached up and put her hand on his cheek. "Hold on, Hewlett," she said. "You're going to be all right."

He noticed how much taller than her he was. He didn't used to be. There was a pinging sound that seemed to echo in his head. Then the elevator door slid open. The man and woman came to either side of him and walked him out. Only he wasn't walking, and he finally realized what "going vertical" meant.

Once they were out he was lowered and rolled through the lobby. A lot of faces watched as he passed by. The doorman whose name he didn't know looked down at him somberly as he was rolled through the door. He was lifted into an ambulance. He wasn't feeling any pain but he had difficulty breathing. It was more labor-intensive than usual.

After a while he noticed that Nicole was sitting next to him. It looked like she was outright crying now.

He found that in the horizontal position he could move a little bit. He tried to speak but his voice sounded like a muffled echo. The woman, the paramedic, then leaned into his field of vision, looking down at him.

"Don't speak," she said. "You've got a mask on."

No kidding, he thought. *Everybody's got a mask on.* He tried again, this time speaking as loudly as he could. Again it was muffled.

The paramedic leaned in again and lifted the breathing mask.

"Hurry. What is it? You can't take this off."

He looked past her arm at Nicole.

"Gaw Lucy. Geh 'er ow a dare."

The mask was put back in place. Nicole leaned close to him and spoke.

"Lucy? Who is Lucy, Henry?"

"I me . . ."

The mask was lifted.

"Rahvin. Gaw 'er."

Nicole nodded. She got it. The mask was put back over his mouth and nose.

156

"Okay, I will. As soon as we get to the hospital. I brought the number with me."

"No, now!" he yelled through the mask.

He watched as Nicole opened her purse and took out a cell phone and a small spiral pad. She punched in a number she read from the pad and waited with the phone to her ear. She then reached out with the phone to his ear and he could hear Lucy's voice. It was voice mail. He groaned and tried to shake his head but couldn't.

"Easy," the paramedic said. "Easy now. Once we get to the ER we'll take off the straps."

He closed his eyes. He wanted to go back to the warmth and the darkness. The understanding. Where nobody asked him why. Especially himself.

Pretty soon he was there.

Clarity came and went over the next two hours as he was taken into the ER, examined by a doctor with a Caesar haircut, treated and then admitted to the hospital. His head finally cleared and he woke up in a white hospital room, startled from sleep by the staccato cough from somebody on the other side of the plastic curtain that was used as a room divider. He looked around and saw Nicole sitting on a chair, her cell phone to her ear. Her hair was loose now and fell around her shoulders. The phone's antenna poked up through its silken smoothness. He watched her until she closed the phone without a word.

"Ni'i," he said in a hoarse voice. "Thas . . ."

It was still hard to make the *k* sound without pain. She stood up and went to his side.

"Henry. You —"

The cough sounded from the other side of the curtain.

"They're working on getting you a private room," she whispered. "Your med plan pays for it."

"Where am I?"

"St. John's. Henry, what happened? The police got there before I did. They said all these people on the beach called on their cell phones and said two guys were hanging somebody over the balcony. You, Henry. There's blood on the outside wall."

Pierce looked at her through swollen eyes. The swelling of the bridge of his nose and the gauze on the wound split his vision in half. He remembered what Wentz said right before he left.

"I dohn remember. Wha else did dey say?"

"That's it. They started knocking on doors in the building and when they got to yours it was wide open. You were in the bedroom. I got there when they were taking you out. A detective was here. He wants to talk to you."

"I don't remember anything."

He said it with as much force as he could. It was getting easier to talk. All he had to do was practice.

"Henry, what kind of trouble are you in?"

"I don't know."

"Who is Robin? And Lucy? Who are they?"

He suddenly remembered he needed to warn her.

"How long have I been here?"

"A couple hours."

"Gi' me your phone. I've got to phone her."

"I've been calling that number every ten minutes. I was just calling when you woke up. I keep getting voice mail."

He closed his eyes. He wondered if she had gotten his message and gotten out of there and away from Wentz.

"Le' me see your phone anyway."

"Let me do it. You probably shouldn't be moving around too much. Who do you want to call?"

He gave her the number for his voice mail and then the pass code number. She didn't seem to attach any significance to it.

"You've got eight messages."

"Any that are for Lilly just erase. Don't listen."

That was all of them except for one message which Nicole said he should listen to. She turned up the phone and held it out so he could listen when she replayed it. It was Cody Zeller's voice.

"Hey, Einstein, I've got some stuff for you on that thing you asked about. So give me a buzz and we'll talk. Later, dude."

Pierce erased the message and handed back the phone.

"Was that Cody?" Nicole asked.

"Yes."

"I thought so. Why does he still call you that? It's so high school."

" 'ollege, actually."

It hurt to say "college" but not as badly as he thought it would.

"What was he talking about?"

"Nothing. He was doing some online stuff for me."

He almost started telling her about it and everything else. But before he could put the words together a man in a lab coat came through the door. He had a clipboard. He was in his late fifties with silver hair and a matching beard.

"This is Dr. Hansen," Nicole said.

"How are you feeling?" the doctor asked.

He leaned over the bed and used his hand on Pierce's jaw to turn his face slightly.

"Only hurts when I breathe. Or talk. Or when somebody does that."

Hansen let go of his jaw. He used a penlight to study Pierce's pupils.

"Well, you've got some pretty substantial injuries here. You have a grade-two concussion and six stitches in your scalp."

Pierce hadn't even remembered that injury. It must have come when he hit the outside wall of the building.

"The concussion is the cause of the loginess you may be feeling and any headache discomfort. Let's see, what else? You have a pulmonary contusion, a deep shoulder contusion; you've got two fractured ribs and, of course, the broken nose. The lacerations on your nose and surrounding your eye are going to require plastic surgery to properly close without permanent scarring. I can get somebody in here tonight to do that, depending on the swelling, or if you have a personal surgeon, then you can contact him."

Pierce shook his head. He knew there were many people in this town who kept personal plastic surgeons on call. But he wasn't one of them.

"Whoever you can get . . ."

"Henry," Nicole said. "This is your face you're talking about. I think you should get the best possible surgeon you can."

"I think I can get you a very good one," Hansen said. "Let me make some calls and see what I come up with."

"Thank you."

He said the words pretty clearly. It seemed as though his speech facility was quickly adapting to the new physical circumstances of his mouth and nasal passages.

"Try to stay as horizontal as possible," Hansen said. "I'll be back."

The doctor nodded and left the room. Pierce looked at Nicole.

"Looks like I'm going to be here awhile. You don't have to stay."

"I don't mind."

He smiled and it hurt, but he smiled anyway. He was very happy with her response.

"Why did you call me in the middle of the night, Henry?"

He'd forgotten and the reminder brought the searing embarrassment again. He carefully composed an answer before speaking.

"I don't know. It's a long story. It's been a strange weekend. I wanted to tell you about it. And I wanted to tell you what I had been thinking about."

"What was that?"

It hurt to talk but he had to tell her.

"I don't know exactly. Just that the things that happened to me somehow made me see your point of view a lot clearer. I know it's probably too little too late. But for some reason I wanted you to know I finally saw the light."

She shook her head.

"That's good, Henry. But you're lying here with your head and face split open. It appears somebody dangled you off a twelfth-story balcony and the cops say they want to talk to you. It seems like you went to an awful lot of trouble to get my point of view. So excuse me if I don't jump up and embrace the new man you profess yourself to be."

Pierce knew that if he were up to it, they were heading down the road to familiar territory. But he didn't think he had the stamina for another argument with her.

"Can you try Lucy again?"

Nicole angrily punched the redial button on her cell phone again.

"I ought to just put this on speed dial."

He watched her eyes and could read that she had reached the voice mail again.

She snapped the phone closed and looked at him.

"Henry, what's going on with you?"

He tried to shake his head but it hurt to do so.

"I got a wrong number," he said.

22

Pierce came out of a murky dream about free-falling while blind-folded and not knowing how far it was he was falling. When he finally hit the ground he opened his eyes and Detective Renner was there with a lopsided smile on his face.

"You."

"Yeah, me again. How are you feeling, Mr. Pierce?"

"I'm fine."

"Looked like a bad dream you were having. You were thrashing around there quite a bit."

"Maybe I was dreaming about you."

"Who are the Wickershams?"

"What?"

"You said the name in your sleep. Wickershams."

"They're monkeys. From the jungle. The non-believers."

"I don't get it."

"I know. So never mind. Why are you here? What do you want? It happened — whatever happened — in Santa Monica and I already talked to them. I don't remember what happened. I have a concussion, you know."

Renner nodded.

"Oh, I know all about your injuries. The nurse told me the plastic surgeon put a hundred and sixty microstitches across your nose and around that eye yesterday morning. Anyway, I'm here on Los Angeles police business. Though it's looking more and more like maybe L.A. and Santa Monica should get together on this one."

Pierce raised his hand and gently touched the bridge of his nose. There was no gauze. He could feel the zipper of stitches and the puffiness. He tried to remember things. The last thing he could clearly recall was the plastic surgeon hovering over him with a bright light. After that he had been in and out, floating through the darkness.

"What time is it?"

"Three-fifteen."

There was bright light coming through the window shades. He knew it wasn't the middle of the night. He also realized he was in a private room.

"It's Monday? No, it's Tuesday?"

"That's what it said in the paper today, if you believe what you read in the paper."

Pierce felt physically strong — he had probably been asleep for more than fifteen straight hours — but was disturbed by the lingering feeling of the dream. And by Renner's presence.

"What do you want?"

"Well, first of all, let me get something out of the way. I'm going to read you your rights real quick here. That way you're protected and so am I."

The detective pulled the mobile food tray over the bed and placed a microrecorder down on it.

"What do you mean, you're protected? What do you need protection from? That's bullshit, Renner."

"Not at all. I need to do it to protect the integrity of my investigation. Now I'm going to record everything from here on out."

He pressed a button on the recorder and a red light came on. He announced his name, the time and date and the location of the interview. He identified Pierce and read him his constitutionally guaranteed rights from a little card he took from his wallet.

"Now, do you understand these rights as I have read them to you?"

"Heard them enough growing up."

Renner raised an eyebrow.

"In the movies and on TV," Pierce added.

"Please answer the question and hold off on being clever if you can."

"Yes, I understand my rights."

"Good. Now is it all right if I ask you a few questions?"

"Am I a suspect?"

"A suspect in what?"

163

"I don't know. You tell me."

"Well, that's the thing, isn't it? Hard to tell what we've got here."

"But you still think you need to read me my rights. To protect me, of course."

"That's right."

"What are your questions? Have you found Lilly Quinlan?"

"We're working on it. You don't know where she is, do you?"

Pierce shook his head and the movement made his head feel a little sloshy. He waited for it to subside before speaking.

"No. I wish I did."

"Yes, it would kind of clear things up a bit if she just walked through the door, wouldn't it?"

"Yes. Was it her blood on the bed?"

"We're still working on it. Preliminary tests showed that it was human blood. But we have no sample from Lilly Quinlan to compare it with. I think I've got a line on her doctor. We'll see what records and possible samples he has. A woman like that, she probably had her blood checked on a regular basis."

Pierce assumed Renner was talking about Lilly checking herself for sexually transmitted diseases. Still, confirmation of the seemingly obvious — that it was human blood he had found on the bed — made him feel more depressed. As if the last slim hope he had for Lilly Quinlan was slipping away.

"Let me ask the questions now," Renner said. "What about this girl Robin that you mentioned before? Have you seen her?"

"No. I've been here."

"Talked to her?"

"No. Have you?"

"No, we haven't been able to locate her. We got her number off the website like you said. But all we get is a message. We even tried leaving one where I had a guy in the squad who's good on the phone call up and act like he was, you know, a customer."

"Social engineering."

"Yeah, social engineering. But she didn't call back on that one either."

Pierce felt the bottom completely drop out of his stomach now. Last he remembered, Nicole had tried to reach Lucy repeatedly and was also unsuccessful. Wentz might have gotten to her — or maybe even still had her. He realized he had to make a decision. He could dance around with Renner and continue to hold up a veil of lies in order to protect himself. Or he could try to help Lucy.

"Well, did you trace the number?"

"It's a cell."

"What about the billing address?"

"The phone's registered to one of her regular clients. He said he does it as a favor. He takes care of the phone for her and the lease on her fuck pad and she gives him a free pop every Sunday afternoon while his wife does the shopping at the Ralph's in the Marina. It's more like Robin's doing the favor, you ask me. The guy's a fat slob. Anyway, she didn't show up Sunday afternoon at the pad — it's a little place in the Marina. We were there. We went with this guy but she didn't show."

"And he doesn't know where she lives?"

"Nope. She never told him. He just pays for the cell phone and the apartment and shows up every Sunday. He lays the whole thing off on his expense account."

"Shit."

He envisioned Lucy in the hands of Wentz and Six-Eight. He reached up and ran his fingers along the seams in his own face. He hoped she got away. He hoped she was just hiding somewhere.

"Yeah, 'shit' is exactly what we said. And the thing is, we don't even have her full name — we got her picture from the website, if it is her picture, and the name Robin. That's it, and I get the funny feeling neither one is legit."

"What about going to the website?"

"I told you, we went —"

"No, the real place. The site office in Hollywood?"

"We did and we caught a lawyer. No cooperation. We need a court order before they'll share client information. And as far as Robin goes, we don't have enough to go talk to a judge about court orders."

One more time Pierce thought about his choices. Protect himself or help Renner and possibly help Lucy. If it wasn't already too late.

"Turn that off."

"What, this tape? I can't. This is a formal interview. I told you, I'm taping it."

"Then it's over. But if you turn that off, I think I can tell you some things that will help you."

Renner appeared to hesitate while he thought about it but Pierce had the feeling that so far everything had been scripted and was moving in the exact direction the detective had wanted it to go.

The detective clicked a button on the tape recorder and the red record light went off. He slid the device into the right pocket of his jacket.

"Okay, whaddaya got?"

"Her name isn't Robin. She told me her name is Lucy LaPorte. She's from New Orleans. You've got to find her. She's in danger. It might already be too late."

"In danger from who?"

Pierce didn't answer. He thought about Wentz's threat not to talk to the police. He thought about the warnings from the private investigator, Glass.

"Billy Wentz," he finally said.

"Wentz again," Renner said. "He's the bogeyman in all of this, huh?"

"Look, man, you can believe what I say or not. But just find Robin — I mean, Lucy — and make sure she's okay."

"That's it? That's all you've got for me?"

"Her website photo is legitimate. I saw her."

Renner nodded as though he had assumed so the whole time.

"The picture's getting a little clearer here," he said. "What else can you tell me about her? When did you see her?"

"Saturday night. She took me to Lilly's apartment. But she left before I went in. She didn't see anything, so I tried to keep her out of it. It was part of the deal I made with her. She was afraid Wentz would find out."

"That was brilliant. You pay her?"

"Yes, but what does it matter?"

"It matters because money affects motives. How much?"

"About seven hundred dollars."

"A lot of bread for just a ride through Venice. You get the other kind of ride, too, did you?"

"No, Detective, I didn't."

"And so if this tale you told me before about Wentz being this big bad digital pimp is right, then her showing you the way to Lilly's apartment sort of puts her in harm's way, doesn't it?"

Pierce nodded. His head didn't go through the fishbowl effect this time. Vertical movement was okay. It was the horizontal moves that caused the problem.

"What else?" Renner said, still pushing.

"She shares that apartment in the Marina with a woman named Cleo. She's supposedly on the same site, though I never checked. Maybe you talk to Cleo and get a line on her."

"Maybe, maybe not. That it?"

"Last thing, I saw her get into a green and yellow taxi on Speedway on Saturday night. Maybe you can trace it to her place."

Renner shook his head slightly.

"Works in movies. Not too often in real life. Besides, she probably went back to the fuck pad. Saturdays are busy nights."

The door to the room opened and Monica Purl stepped in. She saw Renner and stopped in the threshold.

"Oh, sorry. Am I —"

"Yes, you are," Renner said. "Police business. Could you wait outside, please?"

"I'll just come back."

Monica looked at Pierce, her face reacting in horror to what she saw. Pierce tried to smile and raised his left hand and waved.

"I'll call you," Monica said, and then she went back through the door and was gone.

"Who was that? Another girlfriend?"

"No, my assistant."

"So you want to talk about what happened on that balcony Sunday? Was it Wentz?"

Pierce didn't say anything for a long time as he thought about the consequences of answering the question. A large part of him wanted to name Wentz and file charges against him. Pierce felt deeply humiliated by what Wentz and his giant had done to him. Even if the surgery on his face was successful and no physical scars were left behind, he knew without a doubt that the attack was going to be hard to live with, always to have in his memory. There would be scars nonetheless.

But still, the threat Wentz had made lodged in his mind as something very real — to himself, to Robin, even to Nicole. If Wentz was able to find him and invade his home so easily, then he would be able to find Nicole.

He finally spoke.

"It's a Santa Monica case, what do you care?"

"It's all one case and you know it."

"I don't want to talk about it. I don't even remember what happened. I remember I was carrying groceries up to my apartment and then I woke up when the paramedics were working on me."

"The mind is a tricky thing, isn't it? The way it blocks out the bad things."

The tone was sarcastic and Pierce could tell by the look on Renner's face that he did not believe his memory loss. The two men stared at each other for a long moment, then the detective reached into his jacket.

"How about this, jog anything loose?"

He pulled out a folded 8 × 10 photo and showed it to Pierce. It was a grainy blowup of the Sands apartment tower taken from a long distance. From the beach. He pulled the photo closer and saw the small images of people on one of the upper balconies. He knew it was the twelfth floor. He knew it was him and Wentz and his muscle man, Six-Eight. Pierce was being held off the balcony by his ankles. The figures in the photo were too small to be recognizable. He handed it back.

"No. Nothing."

"Right now it's the best we got. But once they put it on the news that we're looking for photos, videos, whatever, we might come up with something decent. A lot of people were out there. Somebody probably got a good shot."

"Good luck."

Renner was silent, studying Pierce for a long while before he spoke again.

"Look, if he threatened you, we can protect you."

"I told you, I don't remember what happened. I don't remember anything at all."

Renner nodded.

"Sure, sure. Okay, then let's forget the balcony. Let me ask you something else. Tell me, where did you hide Lilly's body?"

Pierce's eyes widened. Renner had used misdirection to hit him with the sucker punch.

"What? Are you —"

"Where is it, Pierce? What did you do with her? And what did you do with Lucy LaPorte?"

A cold feeling of fear began to rise in Pierce's chest. He looked at Renner and knew the detective was deadly serious. And he knew suddenly that he wasn't *a* suspect. He was *the* suspect.

"Are you fucking kidding me? You wouldn't even know about this if I hadn't called you people. I was the only one who cared about it."

"Yeah, and maybe by calling us and traipsing all over that scene and the house, what you were setting up was a nice little defense. And maybe the job you had Wentz or one of your other pals do on your face was part of the defense. Poor guy gets his nose smashed for sticking it in the wrong place. It doesn't get my sympathy vote, Mr. Pierce."

Pierce stared at him, speechless. Everything that he had done or that had been done to him was being perceived by Renner from a completely opposite angle.

"Let me tell you a quick little story," Renner said. "I used to work up in the Valley and one time we had a missing girl. She was twelve years old, from a good home, and we knew she wasn't a runaway. Sometimes you just know. So we organized the neighbors and volunteers into a search party in the Encino Hills. And lo and behold, one of the neighbor boys finds her. Raped and strangled and stuffed into a culvert. It was a bad one. And you know what, turned out that the boy who found her was the one who did the deed. Took us a while to circle back around to him but we did and he confessed. Being the one who found her like that? That's called the Good Samaritan complex. He who smelt it dealt it. Happens all the time. The doer likes getting close to the cops, likes helping out, makes him feel better than them and better about what he did."

Pierce was having difficulty even fathoming how everything had turned on him.

"You're wrong," he said quietly, his voice shaking. "I didn't do it."

"Yeah? Am I wrong? Well, let me tell you what I've got. I've got a missing woman and blood on the bed. I've got a bunch of your lies and a bunch of your fingerprints all over the woman's house and fuck pad."

Pierce closed his eyes. He thought about the apartment off Speedway and the seagull house on Altair. He knew he had touched everything. He'd put his hands on everything. Her perfume, her closets, her mail.

"No . . ."

It was all he could think to say.

"No, what?"

"This is all a mistake. All I did . . . I mean . . . I got her number. I just wanted to see . . . I wanted to help her . . . You see, it was my fault . . . and I thought if I . . ."

He didn't finish. The past and present were too close together. They were morphing together, one confusing the other. One moving in front of the other like an eclipse. He opened his eyes and looked at Renner.

"You thought what?" the detective asked.

"What?"

"Finish the line. You thought what?"

"I don't know. I don't want to talk about it."

"Come on, kid. You started down the road. Finish the ride. It's good to unburden. Good for the soul. It's your fault Lilly's dead. What did you mean by that? It was an accident? Tell me how it happened. Maybe I can live with that and we can go tell the DA together, work something out."

Pierce felt fear and danger flooding his mind now. He could almost smell it coming off his skin. As if they were chemicals — compound elements sharing common molecules — rising to the surface to escape.

"What are you talking about? Lilly? It's not my fault. I didn't even know her. I tried to help her."

"By strangling her? Cutting her throat? Or did you do the Jack the Ripper number on her? I think they say the Ripper was a scientist. A doctor or something. You the new Ripper, Pierce? Is that your bag?"

"Get out of here. You're crazy."

"I don't think I'm the crazy one. Why was it your fault?"

"What?"

"You said she was all your fault. Why? What did she do? Insult your manhood? You got a little pecker, Pierce? Is that it?"

Pierce shook his head emphatically, touching off a bout of dizziness. He closed his eyes.

"I didn't say that. It's not my fault."

"You said it. I heard it."

"No. You're putting words into my mouth. It's not my fault. I had nothing to do with it."

He opened his eyes to see Renner reach into his coat pocket and pull out a tape recorder. The red light was on. Pierce realized that it was a different recorder from the one that had been placed earlier on the food tray and then turned off. The detective had taped the whole conversation.

Renner clicked the rewind button for a few seconds and then jockeyed around with the recording until he found what he wanted and replayed what Pierce had said moments before.

"This is all a mistake. All I did . . . I mean . . . I got her number. I just wanted to see . . . I wanted to help her . . . You see, it was my fault . . . and I thought if I . . ."

The detective clicked off the recorder and looked at Pierce with a smug smile on his face. Renner had him cornered. He had been tricked. All his legal instincts, as limited as they were, told him to not speak another word. But Pierce couldn't stop.

"No," he said. "I wasn't talking about her. About Lilly Quinlan. I was talking about my sister. I was —"

"We were talking about Lilly Quinlan and you said, 'It was my fault.' That is an admission, my friend."

"No, I told you, I —"

"I know what you told me. It was a nice story."

"It's no story."

"Well, you know what? Story, no story, I figure as soon as I find the body I'll have the real story to tell. I'll have you in the bag and be home free."

Renner leaned over the bed until his face was only inches from Pierce's.

"Where is she, Pierce? You know this is inevitable. We're going to find her. So let's get this over with now. Tell me what you did with her."

171

Their eyes were locked. Pierce heard the click of the tape recorder being turned back on.

"Get out."

"You'd better talk to me. You're running out of time. Once I take this in and it gets to the lawyers, I can't help you anymore. Talk to me, Henry. Come on. Unburden yourself."

"I said get out. I want a lawyer."

Renner straightened up and smiled in a knowing way. In an exaggerated fashion he held the tape recorder up and clicked it off.

"Of course you want a lawyer," he said. "And you're going to need one. I'm going to the DA, Pierce. I know I've already got you on obstruction and breaking and entering, for starters. Got you there cold. But all of that's bullshit. I want the big one."

He proffered the tape recorder as though the words he had captured with it were the Holy Grail.

"As soon as that body turns up, it's game over."

Pierce wasn't really listening anymore. He turned away from Renner and began staring into space, thinking about what was going to happen. All at once he realized he would lose everything. The company — everything. In a split second all the dominoes fell in his imagination, the last one being Goddard pulling out and taking his investment dollars somewhere else, to Bronson Tech or Midas Molecular or one of the other competitors. Goddard would pull out and nobody would be willing to pull in. Not under the glare of a criminal investigation and possible trial. It would be over. He would be out of the race for good.

He looked back at Renner.

"I said I'm not talking to you anymore. I want you to leave. I want a lawyer."

Renner nodded.

"My advice to you is, make it a good one."

He reached over to a counter where medical supplies were displayed and picked up a hat Pierce hadn't seen before. It was a brown porkpie hat with the brim cocked down. Pierce thought nobody wore hats like that in L.A. anymore. Nobody. Renner left the room without another word.

23

Pierce sat still for a moment, thinking about his predicament. He wondered how much of what Renner had said about going to the DA had been threat and how much of it was reality. He shook free of the thoughts and looked around to see if the room had a phone. There was nothing on the side table but the bed had side railings with all manner of electronic buttons for positioning the mattress and controlling the television mounted on the opposite wall. He found a phone that snapped out of the right railing. In a plastic pocket next to it he also found a small hand mirror. He held it up and looked at his face for the first time.

He was expecting worse. When he had felt the wound with his fingers in the moments after the assault, it had seemed to him that his face had been split open wide and that wide scarring would be unavoidable. At the time this didn't bother him, because he was happy just to be left alive. Now he was a little more concerned. Looking at his face, he saw the swelling was way down. He was a little puffy around the corners of his eyes and the lower part of his nose. Both nostrils were packed with cotton gauze. Both eyes had dark swatches of purple beneath them. The cornea of his left eye was flooded with blood on one side of the iris. And across his nose were the very fine trails of microstitching.

The stitching formed a K pattern with one line going up the bridge of his nose, and the arms of the K curving below his left eye and above it into his eyebrow. Half of his left eyebrow had been shaved to accommodate the surgery and Pierce thought that might be the oddest thing about the whole face he saw in the mirror.

He put the mirror down and he realized he was smiling. His face was almost destroyed. He had an LAPD cop who was trying to put him in jail for a crime he had uncovered but did not commit. He

173

had a digital pimp with a pet monster out there who was a live and real threat to him and others close to him. Yet he was sitting in bed, smiling.

He didn't understand it but knew it had something to do with what he had seen in the mirror. He had survived and his face showed how close he had come to not making it. In that there was relief and the inappropriate smile.

He picked up the phone and put in a call to Jacob Kaz, the company's patent attorney. His call was put through to the lawyer immediately.

"Henry, are you okay? I heard you were attacked or something. What —"

"It's a long story, Jacob. I'll have to tell you later. What I need from you right now is a name. I need an attorney. A criminal defense attorney. Somebody good but who doesn't like getting his face on TV or his name in the papers."

Pierce knew that what he was asking for was a rarity in Los Angeles. But containing the situation was going to be as urgent as possibly defending himself against a bogus murder charge. It had to be handled quickly and discreetly, or the falling dominoes Pierce had imagined moments earlier would become the crushing blocks of reality that toppled both him and the company.

Kaz cleared his throat before responding. He gave no indication that Pierce's request was out of the ordinary or anything other than normal in their professional relationship.

"I think I have a name for you," he said. "You'll like her."

24

On Wednesday morning Pierce was on the phone with Charlie Condon when a woman in a gray suit walked into his hospital room. She handed him a card that said JANIS LANGWISER, ATTORNEY AT LAW on it. He cupped his hand over the phone and told her he was wrapping up the call.

"Charlie, I've got to go. My doctor just came in. Just tell him we have to do it over the weekend or next week."

"Henry, I can't. He wants to see Proteus before we send in the patent. I don't want to delay that and you don't, either. Besides, you've met Maurice. He won't be put off."

"Just call him again and try to delay it."

"I will. I'll try. I'll call you back."

Charlie hung up and Pierce clipped the phone back into the bed's side guard. He tried to smile at Langwiser but his face was sorer than it had been the day before and it hurt to smile. She put out her hand and he shook it.

"Janis Langwiser. Pleased to meet you."

"Henry Pierce. I can't say the circumstances make it a pleasure to meet you."

"That's usually the way it is with criminal defense work."

He had already gotten her pedigree from Jacob Kaz. Langwiser handled the criminal defense work for the small but influential downtown firm of Smith, Levin, Colvin & Enriquez. The firm was so exclusive, according to Kaz, that it wasn't listed in any phone book. Its clients were A-list, but even people on that list still needed criminal defense from time to time. That's where Langwiser came in. She'd been hired away from the district attorney's office a year earlier, after a career that included prosecuting some of Los Angeles's higher-profile cases of recent years. Kaz told Pierce that the firm was taking him as a client as a means of establishing a relationship with him, a relationship that would be mutually beneficial as Amedeo Technologies moved toward going public in years to come. Pierce didn't tell Kaz that there would be no eventual public offering or even an Amedeo Technologies if this situation wasn't handled properly.

After polite inquiries about Pierce's injuries and prognosis, Langwiser asked him why he thought he needed a criminal defense attorney.

"Because there is a police detective out there who believes I'm a killer. He told me he was going to the DA's office to try to charge me with a number of crimes, including murder."

"An L.A. cop? What's his name?"

"Renner. I don't think he ever told me his first name. Or I don't remember it. I have his card but I never looked at —"

"Robert. I know him. He works out of Pacific Division. He's been around a long time."

"You know him from a case?"

"Early in my career at the DA I filed cases. I filed a few that he brought in. He seemed like a good cop. I think *thorough* is the word I would use."

"It's actually the word he uses."

"He's going to the DA for a murder charge?"

"I'm not sure. There's no body. But he said he was going to charge me with other stuff first. Breaking and entering, he says. Obstruction of justice. I guess he'll try to make a case for the murder after that. I don't know how much is bullshit threats and how much he can do. But I didn't kill anybody, so I need a lawyer."

She frowned and nodded thoughtfully. She gestured to his face.

"Is this thing with Renner in any way related to your injuries?"

Pierce nodded.

"Why don't we start at the beginning."

"Do we have an attorney-client relationship at this point?"

"Yes, we do. You can speak freely."

Pierce nodded. He spent the next thirty minutes telling her the story in as much detail as he could remember. He freely told her about everything he had done, including the crimes he had committed. He left nothing out.

As he talked Langwiser leaned against the equipment counter. She took notes with an expensive-looking pen on a yellow legal pad she took from a black leather bag that was either an oversized purse or an undersized briefcase. Her whole manner exuded expensive confidence. When Pierce was finished telling the story, she went back to the part about what Renner had called an admission from him. She asked several questions, first about the tone of the conversation at that point, what medications Pierce was on at the time and what ill effect from the attack and surgery he was feeling. She then asked specifically what he had meant by saying it was his fault.

"I meant my sister, Isabelle."

"I don't understand."

"She died. A long time ago."

"Come on, Henry, don't make me guess about this. I want to know."

He shrugged now, and this hurt his shoulder and ribs.

"She ran away from home when we were kids. Then she got killed . . . by some guy who had killed a lot of people. Girls he picked up in Hollywood. Then he got killed by the police and that . . . was it."

"A serial killer . . . when was this?"

"The eighties. He was called the Dollmaker. They all get names from newspapers, you know? Back then, at least."

He could see Langwiser reviewing her contemporary history.

"I remember the Dollmaker. I was at UCLA law school back then. I later knew the detective who was the one who shot him. He just retired this year."

Her thoughts seemed to drift with the memory, then she came back.

"Okay. So how did that get confused with Lilly Quinlan in your conversation with Detective Renner?"

"Well, I've been thinking about my sister a lot lately. Since this thing with Lilly came up. I think it's the reason I did what I did."

"You mean you think you are responsible for your sister? How can that be, Henry?"

Pierce waited a moment before speaking. He carefully put the story together in his mind. Not the whole story. Just the part he wanted to tell her. He left out the part that he could never tell a stranger.

"My stepfather and I, we used to go down there. We lived in the Valley and we'd go down to Hollywood and look for her. At night. Sometimes during the day, but mostly at night."

Pierce stared at the blank screen of the television mounted on the wall across the room. He spoke as though he were seeing the story on the screen and repeating it to her.

"I would dress up in old clothes so I would look like them — one of the street kids. My stepfather would send me into the places where the kids hid and slept, where they would have sex for money or do drugs. Whatever . . ."

"Why you? Why didn't your stepfather go in?"

"At the time, he told me that it was because I was a kid and I could fit in and be allowed in. If a man walked into one of those places by himself, everybody might run. Then we'd lose her."

He stopped talking and Langwiser waited but then had to prompt him.

"You said at the time he told you that was the reason. What did he tell you later?"

Pierce shook his head. She was good. She had picked up the subtleties of his telling of the story.

"Nothing. It's just that . . . I think . . . I mean, she ran away for a reason. The police said she was on drugs but I think that came after. After she was on the street."

"You think your stepfather was the reason she ran away."

She said it as a statement and he gave an almost imperceptible nod. He thought about what Lilly Quinlan's mother had said about what her daughter and the woman she knew as Robin had in common.

"What did he do to her?"

"I don't know and it doesn't matter now."

"Then why would you say to Renner that it was your fault? Why do you think what happened to your sister was your fault?"

"Because I didn't find her. All those nights looking and I never found her. If only . . ."

He said it without conviction or emphasis. It was a lie. The truth he would not tell this woman he had known for only an hour.

Langwiser looked like she wanted to go further with it but also seemed to know she was already stretching a personal boundary with him.

178

"Okay, Henry. I think it helps explain things — both your actions in regard to Lilly Quinlan's disappearance and your statement to Renner."

He nodded.

"I am sorry about your sister. In my old job dealing with the families of the victims was the most difficult part. At least you got some closure. The man who did this certainly got what he deserved."

Pierce tried a sarcastic smile but it hurt too much.

"Yeah, closure. Makes everything better."

"Is your stepfather alive? Your parents?"

"My stepfather is. Last I heard. I don't talk to him, not in a long time. My mother is not with him anymore. She still lives in the Valley. I haven't talked to her in a long time, either."

"Where's your father?"

"Oregon. He's got a second family. But we stay in touch. Of all of them, he's the only one I talk to."

She nodded. She studied her notes for a long period, flipping back the pages on the pad as she reviewed everything he had said from the start of the conversation. She then finally looked up at him.

"Well, I think it's all bullshit."

Pierce shook his head.

"No, I'm telling you exactly how it hap—"

"No, I mean Renner. I think he's bullshitting. There's nothing there. He's not going to charge you with these lesser crimes. He'd get laughed right out of the DA's office on the B and E. What was your intent? To steal? No, it was to make sure she was okay. They don't know about the mail you took and they can't prove it anyway, because it's gone. As far as the obstruction goes, that's just an idle threat. People lie and hold back with the police all the time. It's expected. To try to charge somebody for it is another matter. I can't even remember the last obstruction case that went to court. At least there were none I remember when I was in the office."

"What about the tape? I was confused. He said what I said was an admission."

"He was playing you. Trying to rattle you and see how you'd react, maybe get a more damaging admission out of you. I would have to listen to the statement to get a full take on it, but it sounds as

179

though it is marginal, that your explanation in regard to your sister is certainly legitimate and would be perceived that way by a jury. Add in that I am sure that you were under the influence of a variety of medications and you —"

"This can never go to a jury. If it does, I'm finished. I'm ruined."

"I understand that. But a jury's view is still the way to look at this because that is how the DA will look at it when considering potential charges. The last thing they will do is go into a case knowing a jury isn't going to buy it."

"There is nothing to buy. I didn't do it. I just tried to find out if she was all right. That's all."

Langwiser nodded but didn't seem particularly interested in his protestations of innocence. Pierce had always heard that good defense attorneys were never as interested in the ultimate question of their clients' guilt or innocence as they were in the strategy of defense. They practiced law, not justice. Pierce found this frustrating because he wanted Langwiser to acknowledge his innocence and then go out and fight to defend it.

"First of all," she said, "with no body, it is very difficult to make a case against anybody. It is doable but very difficult — especially in this case, when you consider the victim's lifestyle and source of income. I mean, she could be anywhere. And if she is dead, then the suspect list is going to be very long.

"Second, his tying your break-in at one scene to a possible homicide at another scene is not going to work. That's a stretch that I cannot see the DA's office being willing to make. Remember, I worked there and bringing cops down to reality was half the work. I think that unless things change in a big way, you'll be okay, Henry. On all of it."

"What big way?"

"Like they find the body. Like they find the body and somehow link it to you."

Pierce shook his head.

"Nothing will link it to me. I never met her."

"Then good. Then you should be in the clear."

"Should be?"

"Nothing is ever a hundred percent. Especially in the law. We'll still have to wait and see."

Langwiser reviewed her notes for a few more moments before speaking again.

"Okay," she finally said. "Now, let's call Detective Renner."

Pierce raised his eyebrows — what was left of them — and it hurt. He winced and said, "Call him? Why?"

"To put him on notice that you have representation and to see what he has to say for himself."

She took a cell phone out of her case and opened it.

"I think I have his card in my wallet," Pierce said. "It should be in the table drawer."

"It's all right, I remember the number."

Her call to the Pacific Division was answered quickly and she asked for Renner. It took a few minutes but she finally got him on the line. While she waited she turned up the volume on the phone and angled it from her ear so Pierce could hear both ends of the conversation. She pointed at him and then put her fingers to her lips, telling him not to enter the conversation.

"Hey, Bob, Janis Langwiser. Remember me?"

After a pause Renner said, "Sure. I heard you went over to the dark side, though."

"Very funny. Listen, I'm over here at St. John's. I was visiting with Henry Pierce."

Another pause.

"Henry Pierce, the Good Samaritan. Longtime rescuer of missing whores and lost pets."

Pierce felt his face redden.

"You are just full of good humor today, Bob," Langwiser said dryly. "That's a new wrinkle with you, isn't it?"

"Henry Pierce is the joker, the stories he tells."

"Well, that's why I'm calling. No more stories from Henry, Bob. I am representing him and he's no longer talking to you. You blew the chance you had."

Pierce looked up at Langwiser and she winked at him.

"I didn't blow anything," Renner protested. "Anytime he wants to start telling me the complete and true story, I'm here. Otherwise —"

"Look, Detective, you're more interested in busting my guy's chops than figuring out what really happened. That's got to stop.

Henry Pierce is now out of your loop. And another thing, you try to take this to court and I'm going to shove that two-tape-recorders trick up your ass."

"I told him I was recording," Renner protested. "I read him his rights and he said he understood them. That is all I'm required to do. I did nothing illegal during his voluntary interview."

"Maybe not per se, Bob. But judges and juries don't like the cops tricking people. They like a clean game."

Now there was a long pause from Renner, and Pierce was beginning to think that Langwiser was going too far, that she might push the detective into seeking a charge against him out of pure anger or resentment.

"You really did cross over, didn't you?" Renner finally said. "I hope you'll be happy over there."

"Well, if I only get clients like Henry Pierce, people who were just trying to do a good thing, then I will be."

"A good thing? I wonder if Lucy LaPorte thinks what he did was a good thing."

"Did he find her?" Pierce blurted out.

Langwiser immediately held her hand up to quiet him.

"Is that Mr. Pierce there? I didn't know we had him listening in, Janis. Speaking of tricks, that was nice of you to tell me."

"I didn't have to."

"And I didn't have to tell him about the second recorder once I told him the conversation was being recorded. So shove that up your ass. I gotta go."

"Wait. Did you find Lucy LaPorte?"

"That's official police business, ma'am. You stay in your loop and I'll stay in mine. Good-bye now."

Renner hung up and Langwiser closed her phone.

"I told you not to say anything."

"Sorry. It's just that I've been trying to reach her since Sunday. I wish I could just find out where she is and whether she's okay or needs help. If anything's happened, it's my fault."

There I go again, he thought. *Finding my own fault in things, offering public admissions of guilt.*

Langwiser didn't seem to notice. She was putting away her phone and notebook.

"I'll make some calls on it. I know some people in Pacific that are a little bit more cooperative than Detective Renner. Like his boss, for example."

"Will you call me as soon as you find out something?"

"I have your numbers. Meantime, you stay away from all of this. With any luck, that call will scare Renner away for the time being, maybe make him second-guess his moves. You're not out of the woods on this yet, Henry. I think you're almost in the clear but other things could still happen. Keep your head down and stay away from it."

"Okay, I will."

"And next time the doctor comes in, get a list of the specific drugs that would have been in your system when Renner recorded you."

"Okay."

"Do you know when you are getting out of here yet?"

"Supposed to be anytime now."

Pierce looked at his watch. He'd been waiting almost two hours for Dr. Hansen to sign him out.

He looked back at Langwiser. She looked ready to go. But she was looking at him like she wanted to ask something but wasn't sure how to ask it.

"What?"

"I don't know. I was just thinking that it was a long jump in your thinking. When you were just a boy, I mean, and you thought your stepfather was the reason your sister left."

Pierce didn't say anything.

"Anything else you want to tell me about that?"

Pierce looked up at the blank television screen again and saw nothing there. He shook his head.

"No, that's about it."

He doubted he had gotten the line by her. He assumed that criminal defense lawyers dealt with liars as a matter of course and were as expert at picking up the subtleties of eye movement and body inflection as machines designed for it. But Langwiser simply nodded and let it slide.

"Well, I need to go. I have an arraignment downtown."

"Okay. Thanks for coming to see me here. That was nice."

"Part of the service. I'll make some calls while I'm driving in and let you know what I hear about Lucy LaPorte or anything else. But meantime, you really need to stay away from this. Okay? Go back to work."

Pierce held his hands up in surrender.

"I'm done with it."

She smiled professionally and left the room.

Pierce detached the phone from the bed's side guard and was punching in Cody Zeller's number when Nicole James stepped into the room. He put the phone back in its place.

Nicole had agreed to come by to drive Pierce home after he was checked out by Dr. Hansen and released. She silently registered pain as she studied Pierce's damaged face. She had visited him often during his hospital stay but it seemed as though she could not get used to seeing the stitch zippers.

Pierce had actually taken her frowns and sympathetic murmurings as a good sign. He would consider it to have been worth all the trouble if it got them back together.

"Poor baby," she said, lightly patting his cheek. "How do you feel?"

"Pretty good," he told her. "But I'm still waiting on the doctor to sign me out. Almost two hours now."

"I'll go out and check on things."

She went back to the door but looked back at Pierce.

"Who was that woman?"

"What woman?"

"Who just left your room."

"Oh, she's my lawyer. Kaz got her for me."

"Why do you need her if you have Kaz?"

"She's a criminal defense lawyer."

She stepped away from the door and went back closer to the bed.

"Criminal defense lawyer? Henry, people who get wrong numbers usually don't need lawyers. What is going on?"

Pierce shrugged his shoulders.

"I don't really know anymore. I got into something and now I'm just trying to get out in one piece. Let me ask you something."

He got off the bed and walked up to her. His balance was off at first but then he was okay. He lightly touched her forearms with his hands. A suspicious look came across her face.

"What?"

"When we leave here, where are you taking me?"

"Henry, I told you, I'm taking you home. Your home."

Even with the puffiness and the road map of stitches, his disappointment was visibly evident.

"Henry, we agreed to at least try this. So let's try."

"I just thought . . ."

He didn't finish. He didn't know exactly what he thought or how to put it into words.

"You seem to think that what happened with us all happened so quickly," she said. "And that it can be fixed quickly."

She turned and headed back toward the door.

"And I'm wrong."

She looked back at him.

"Months, Henry, and you know it. Maybe longer. We hadn't been good together in a long, long time."

She went through the door to look for the doctor. Pierce sat on the bed and tried to remember the time they were on the Ferris wheel and everything seemed so perfect in the world.

25

Blood was everywhere. A trail of it across the beige rug, on the brand-new bed, on two of the walls and all over the telephone. Pierce stood in the doorway of his bedroom and looked at the mess. He could remember almost none of what had happened after Wentz and his sidekick monster had left.

He stepped into the room and bent down next to the phone. He gingerly lifted the receiver with two fingers and held it a good three inches from his head, just enough to hear the tone and determine if he had any messages.

There were none. He reached over and unplugged the phone and then carried it into the bathroom to attempt to clean it.

Dried blood was splashed across the sink. There were bloody fingerprints on the medicine cabinet door. Pierce had no memory of going into the bathroom after the attack. But the place was a mess. The blood had dried hard and brown and it reminded him of the mattress he had seen the police remove from Lilly Quinlan's apartment.

As he used wet tissues to wipe off the phone as best he could, he had a memory of going to a movie called *Curdled* a few years earlier with Cody Zeller. It was about a woman whose job was to clean up bloody crime scenes after the police were finished with the on-site investigation. He now wondered if there was really such a job and a service he could call. The prospect of cleaning up the bedroom was not attractive to him in the least.

After the phone was reasonably clean he plugged it back into the wall in the bedroom and sat down with it on an unstained edge of the mattress. He checked for messages and again there were none. He thought it unusual. He had not been home for nearly seventy-two hours, yet there were no messages. He thought maybe Lilly

Quinlan's page had finally been taken off the L.A. Darlings website. Then he remembered something else. He punched in his number at Amedeo Technologies and waited for the call to ring through to Monica Purl's desk.

"Monica, it's me. Did you change my phone number?"

"Henry? What are —"

"Did you change the number at my apartment?"

"Yes, you told me to. It was supposed to start yesterday."

"I think it did."

He knew that when he had been talking Monica into making the call to All American Mail on Saturday that he had told her to change the number on Monday. At the time he guessed he meant it. But now he felt strangely unsettled about losing the number. It was a connection to another world, to Lilly and Lucy.

"Henry? Are you still there?"

"Yes. What's my new number?"

"I have to look it up. Are you out of the hospital?"

"Yes, I'm out. Just look it up, please."

"I am, I am. I was going to give it to you yesterday but when I went in your room you had that visitor."

"I understand."

"Okay, here it is."

She gave him the number and he grabbed a pen off the bed table and wrote it on his wrist because he didn't have a notebook handy.

"Is there a forwarding on the last number?"

"No, because then I thought all of those guys would be still calling you."

"Exactly. Good work."

"Um, Henry, are you coming in today? Charlie was asking about your schedule."

He thought about this before answering. The day was already half shot. Charlie probably wanted to talk and then overtalk about the Proteus demonstration still scheduled for the next day with Maurice Goddard despite Pierce's urging to delay it.

"I don't know if I'm going to make it in," Pierce told Monica. "The doctor wants me to take it easy. If Charlie wants to talk, tell him I'm at home and give him the new number."

"Okay, Henry."

"Thank you, Monica. I'll see you later."

He waited for her to say good-bye but she didn't. He was about to hang up when she spoke.

"Henry, are you all right?"

"I'm fine. I just don't want to come in and scare everybody with this face. Like I scared you yesterday."

"I wasn't —"

"Yes, you were but that's okay. And thanks for asking how I'm doing, Monica. That was nice. I've gotta go now. Oh, listen, the man who was in my room when you came by?"

"Yes?"

"He's a detective named Renner. From the LAPD. He will probably be calling you to ask about me."

"About what?"

"About what I had you do for me. You know, making that call as Lilly Quinlan. Things like that."

There was a short silence and then Monica's voice sounded different, nervous.

"Henry, am I in trouble?"

"Not at all, Monica. He's investigating her disappearance. And he's investigating me. Not you. He's just backtracking on what I did. So if he calls you, just tell him the truth and everything will be fine."

"Are you sure?"

"Yes, I'm sure. Don't worry about it. I should go now."

They hung up. Pierce got a fresh dial tone and called Lucy LaPorte's number, knowing it now by heart. Once again he got her voice mail but the greeting was now different. It was her voice but the message was that she was taking a vacation and would not be accepting clients until mid-November.

More than a month, Pierce thought. He felt his insides constrict as he thought about what Renner had intimated and about Wentz and his goon and what they could've done to her. He left a message regardless of what she had said in her greeting.

"Lucy, it's Henry Pierce. It's important. Call me back. I don't care what happened or what they did to you, call me. I can help you. I've got a new number now, so write it down."

He read the number off his wrist and then hung up. He held the

188

phone on his lap for a few moments, half expecting, half hoping she would immediately call back. She didn't. After a while he got up and left the bedroom.

In the kitchen Pierce found the empty laundry basket on the counter. He remembered he had been using it to carry grocery bags up from the car when he first encountered Wentz and Six-Eight by the elevator. He remembered dropping the laundry basket when he was pushed out of the elevator. Now the basket was here. He opened the refrigerator and looked inside. Everything he had been carrying up — except the eggs, which had probably broken — had been placed inside. He wondered who had done this. Nicole? The police? A neighbor he did not even know?

The question made him think of Detective Renner's statement about the Good Samaritan complex. If such a theory and complex were true, then Pierce felt sorry for all the true do-gooders and volunteers out there in the world. The idea that their efforts might be viewed cynically by members of law enforcement depressed him.

Pierce remembered that he still had several bags of groceries in the trunk of his BMW. He picked up the laundry basket and decided to go get them because he was hungry and the pretzels and sodas and other snacks he had bought were in the trunk.

Still feeling weak from the assault and surgery, he did not overload the basket once he went down to the garage. He decided on two trips and after he got back into the apartment with the second basketful he checked the phone again and learned he had missed a call. He had a message.

Pierce cursed himself for missing the call and then quickly went through the process of setting up a voice mail access code again. Soon he was listening to the message. It was from Lucy LaPorte.

"Help me? You already helped me enough, Henry. They hurt me. I'm all black and blue and nobody can see me like this. I want you to stop calling me and wanting to help me. I'm not talking to you again after this. *Stop* calling here, you understand?"

The message clicked off. Pierce continued to hold the phone to his ear, his mind repeating parts of the message like a scratched old record. *They hurt me. I'm all black and blue.* He felt himself getting light-headed and reached out to the wall for balance. He then

189

turned his back into the wall and slid down until he was sitting on the floor, the phone on his lap again.

He did not move for several seconds and then raised the receiver and started calling her number. Halfway through, he stopped and hung up.

"Okay," he said out loud.

He closed his eyes. He thought about calling Janis Langwiser to tell her that he had received a message from Lucy, that at the very least she was alive. He could then ask her if she had learned anything new since their meeting at the hospital that morning.

Before he could act on the idea, the phone rang while he was still holding it. He answered immediately. He thought it might be Lucy again — who else had the new number? — and his hello was tinged with a tone of hurried desperation.

But it wasn't Lucy. It was Monica.

"I forgot to tell you, between Monday and Tuesday your friend Cody Zeller left three messages for you on your private line. I guess he really wants you to call him."

"Thank you, Monica."

Pierce could not call Zeller back directly. His friend accepted no direct calls. To contact him, Pierce had to call his pager and put in a return number. If Zeller was familiar with the number, he would return the call. Because Pierce had a new number that Zeller would not recognize, he added a prefix of three sevens, which was a code that let Zeller know it was a friend or associate who was attempting to contact him from an unfamiliar number. It was a sometimes cumbersome and always annoying way to conduct life and business but Zeller was a paranoid's paranoid and Pierce had to play it his way.

He settled in to wait for the callback but his page was promptly returned. Unusual for Zeller.

"Jesus, man, when are you going to get a cell phone? I've been trying to reach you for three days."

"I don't like cell phones. What's up?"

"You can get them with a scramble chip, you know."

"I know. What's up?"

"What's up is that on Saturday you sure wanted this stuff in a goddamn hurry. Then you don't call me back for three days. I was starting to think you —"

"Code, I've been in the hospital. I just got out."

"The hospital?"

"I had a little trouble with some guys."

"Not guys from Entrepreneurial Concepts?"

"I don't know. Did you find out about them?"

"Full scan as requested. These are bad dudes you're dancing with, Hank."

"I'm getting that idea. You want to tell me about them now?"

"Actually, I'm in the middle of something right now and don't like doing this by phone anyway. But I did drop it all in a FedEx yesterday — when I didn't hear from you. Should've gotten there by this morning. You didn't get it?"

Pierce checked his watch. It was two o'clock. The FedEx run came at about ten every morning. He didn't like the idea of the envelope from Zeller sitting on his desk all this time.

"I haven't been to the office. But I'll go get it now. You have anything else for me?"

"Can't think of anything that's not in the package."

"Okay, man. I'll call you after I look at everything. Meantime, let me ask you something. I need to track somebody to a location, an address, and all I have is her name and her cell number. But the bill for the cell doesn't go to where she lives and that's what I want."

"Then it's worthless."

"Anything else I can do?"

"That's a tough one but it can be done. Is she registered to vote?"

"I kind of doubt it."

"Well, there are utility hookups and credit cards. How common's her name?"

"Lucy LaPorte of Louisiana."

Pierce reminded himself that she had told him to stop calling her. She hadn't said anything about not finding her.

"Got that alliteration thing going, huh?" Zeller said. "Well, I can try some things, see what pops."

"Thanks, Code."

"And I suppose you want it yesterday."

"That's right."

"Of course."

"I gotta go."

Pierce went into the kitchen and looked through the bags he had dumped on the counter for the bread and peanut butter. He quickly made a sandwich and left the apartment, being sure to put on the Moles hat and pull the brim down low on his forehead. He ate the sandwich while waiting for the elevator. The bread tasted stale. It had been in the car trunk since Sunday.

On the ride down to the garage the elevator stopped on six and a woman got on. As was the custom with elevator riders, she avoided looking at Pierce. After they started descending she surreptitiously checked out his reflection in the polished chrome trim on the door. Pierce saw her do a frightened double take.

"Oh my God!" she cried out. "You're the one everybody's talking about."

"Excuse me?"

"You're the one who got hung off the balcony, right?"

Pierce looked at her for a long moment. And in that moment he knew that no matter what happened with Nicole, he wouldn't be able to stay in the apartment building. He was moving.

"I don't know what you're talking about."

"Are you all right? What did they do to you?"

"They didn't do anything. I don't know what you are talking about."

"You're not the guy who just moved in up on twelve?"

"No. I'm on eight. I'm staying with a friend on eight while I heal."

"Then what happened?"

"Deviated septum."

She looked at him suspiciously. The door finally opened on the garage level. Pierce didn't wait for her to get out first. He moved quickly out of the elevator and around the corner toward the door to the building's garage. He glanced back to see the woman staring at him as she came out of the elevator.

Just as he looked forward again he almost walked into the door to the storage area, which had come open as a man and woman were walking their bikes out. Pierce lowered his chin, pulled the

192

brim of his hat down further and held the door and waited until they were out of the way. They both said thank you but didn't mention anything about his being the guy who was hung off the balcony.

The first thing Pierce did when he got inside his car was put on the pair of sunglasses he carried in the glove box.

26

The FedEx envelope was on his desk when Pierce walked into his office. It had been a battle to get there. Almost every step of the way he'd had to fend off looks and inquiries about his face. By the time he got to the office section of the third floor, he was giving one-word answers to all questions — "Accident."

"Lights," he said as he swung around behind his desk.

But the lights didn't come on and Pierce realized that his voice was different because of the swelling of his nasal passages. He got up and turned on the lights manually and then went back to the desk. He took off his sunglasses and put them on top of his computer monitor.

He picked up the envelope and checked the return address. Cody Zeller pulled a painful smile out of him. In the return address Zeller had put the name Eugene Briggs, the Stanford department head the Doomsters had targeted many years before. The prank that had changed their lives.

The smile dropped off his face when Pierce turned over the envelope to open it. The pull tab had already been torn — the envelope was open. He looked inside it and saw a white business envelope. He took this out and found that it had been opened as well. The outside of the envelope said *Henry Pierce, personal and confidential.* There was a folded sheaf of documents inside. He couldn't tell if they had been pulled out or not.

He got up and went out his door to the corral where the assistants had their pods. He went to Monica's desk. He held up the FedEx envelope and the torn envelope that had been inside it.

"Monica, who opened this?"

She looked up at him.

"I did. Why?"

194

"How come you opened it?"

"I open all your mail. You don't like to deal with it. Remember? I open it so I can tell you what is important and what isn't. If you don't want me to do it that way anymore, just tell me. I won't mind, just less work."

Pierce calmed. She was right.

"No, that's all right. Did you read this stuff?"

"Not really. I saw the picture of the girl who had your phone number and decided I did *not* want to look at that stuff. Remember what we agreed to on Saturday?"

Pierce nodded.

"Yes, that's good. Thanks."

He turned to go back to his office.

"Do you want me to tell Charlie you are here?"

"No, I'm only staying a few minutes."

When he got to the door he looked back at Monica and saw her staring at him with that look of hers. Like she was judging him guilty of something, some crime he knew nothing about.

He closed the door and went behind the desk. He opened the envelope and pulled out the sheaf of printouts from Zeller.

The photo Monica mentioned was not the same photo of Lilly Quinlan from her web page. It was a mug shot taken in Las Vegas three years before, when she had been arrested in a prostitution sting. In the photo she did not look nearly as breathtaking as she did in the website photo. She looked tired and angry and a bit scared all at once.

Zeller's report on Lilly Quinlan was short. He had traced her from Tampa to Dallas to Vegas and then L.A. She was actually twenty-eight years old, not the twenty-three she promised in her web page ad copy. She had a record of two arrests for solicitation in Dallas and the one arrest in Vegas. After each arrest she had spent a few days in jail and was then released for time served. She had come to L.A. three years earlier, according to utilities records. She had avoided arrest and notice of the police until now.

That was it. Pierce looked at the photo again and felt depressed. The mug shot was the reality. The photo he had downloaded from the website and looked at so often over the weekend was the fantasy. Her trail from Tampa to Dallas to Las Vegas to Los Angeles had ended on that bed in the Venice townhouse. There was a killer out there somewhere. And meantime, the cops were focusing on him.

He put the sheaf of printouts down on the desk and picked up the phone. After digging her card out of his wallet, he called Janis Langwiser to check in. He was on hold a good five minutes before she picked up.

"Sorry, I was on the phone with another client. What is happening with you?"

"Me? Nothing. I'm at work. I just wanted to check in and see if you've heard anything new from anybody."

Meaning, *Is Renner still after me?*

"No, nothing really new. I think we're playing a waiting game here. Renner knows he is on notice and that he's not going to be able to bully you. We have to just see what turns up and go from there."

Pierce looked at the mug shot on his desk. It could just as well have been a morgue shot for all the harsh lighting and shadows on her face.

"You mean like a body turning up?"

"Not necessarily."

"Well, I got a call from Lucy LaPorte today."

"Really? What did she say?"

"It was a message, actually. She said she'd been hurt and she didn't want me to ever contact her again."

"Well, at least we know she's around. We may need her."

"Why?"

"If this goes further we could possibly use her as a witness. To your motives and actions."

"Yeah, well, Renner thinks everything I did with her was part of my plan. You know, being the Good Samaritan and all."

"That's just his view of it. In a court of law there are always two sides."

"A court of law? This can't go to —"

"Relax, Henry. I'm just saying that Renner knows that for every piece of supposed evidence that he puts forward, we will have the same opportunity to put forward our side and our view of that evidence. The DA will know that, too."

"All right. Did you find out from anybody over there what Lucy told him?"

196

"I know a supervisor in the squad. He told me they haven't found her. They've talked by phone but she hasn't come in. She won't come in."

Pierce was about to tell her that he had Cody Zeller looking for Lucy when there was a sharp knock on his door and it opened before he could react. Charlie Condon stuck his head in. He was smiling, until he saw Pierce's face.

"Jesus Christ!"

"Who is that?" Langwiser asked.

"My partner. I have to go. Let me know what you hear."

"When I hear it. Good-bye, Henry."

Pierce hung up and looked up at Condon's stricken face. He smiled.

"Actually, Jesus Christ is down the hall and to the left. I'm Henry Pierce."

Condon smiled uneasily and Pierce casually turned over the printouts from the Zeller package. Condon came in and closed the door.

"Man, how do you feel? Are you all right?"

"I'll live."

"You want to talk about it?"

"No."

"Henry, I am really sorry I didn't get over to the hospital. But it's been crazy around here getting ready for Maurice."

"Don't worry about it. So I take it we're still presenting tomorrow."

Condon nodded.

"He's already in town and waiting on us. No delays. We go tomorrow or he goes — and takes his money with him. I talked to Larraby and Grooms and they said we're —"

"— ready to go. I know. I called them from the hospital. It's not Proteus that's the problem. That's not why I wanted to delay. It's my face. I look like I'm Frankenstein's cousin. And I'm not going to look much better tomorrow."

"I told him you had a car accident. It's not going to matter what you look like. What matters is Proteus. He wants to see the project and we promised him a first look. Before we send in the patents. Look, Goddard's the type of guy who can write the check on the

197

spot. We need to do this, Henry. Let's get it over with."

Pierce raised his hands in surrender. Money was always the trump card.

"He's still going to ask a lot of questions when he sees my face."

"Look," Condon said. "It's a dog and pony show. No big deal. You'll be done with him by lunch. If he asks questions, just tell him you went through the windshield and leave it at that. I mean, you haven't even told me what happened. Why should he be any different?"

Pierce saw the momentary look of hurt in his partner's eyes.

"Charlie, I'll tell you when the time is right. I just can't right now."

"Yes, that's what partners are for, to tell things at the right time."

"Look, I know I can't win this argument with you, all right? I admit I'm wrong. So let's just leave it alone for now."

"Sure, Henry, whatever you want. What are you working on now?"

"Nothing. Just some bullshit paperwork."

"Then you're ready for tomorrow?"

"I'm ready."

Condon nodded.

"Either way we win," he said. "Either we take his money or we put in the patents, go to the press with Proteus and come January there will be a line like fucking *Star Wars* at ETS to talk to us."

Pierce nodded. But he hated going to Las Vegas for the annual emerging-technologies symposium. It was the most crass clash between science and finance in the world. Full of charlatans and DARPA spies. But a necessary evil just the same. It was where they had first courted one of Maurice Goddard's front men ten months before.

"If we last until January," Pierce said. "We need money now."

"Don't worry about that. My job's finding the money. I think I can come up with a few intermediary fish to hold us until we land another whale."

Pierce nodded, feeling reassured by his partner. With the situation he was in, thinking forward even a month seemed ridiculous.

"Okay, Charlie."

"But, hey, it's not going to matter. We're going to land Maurice, right?"

"Right."

"Good. Then I'll let you get back to work. Tomorrow at nine?"

Pierce leaned back in his chair and groaned. His last protest on the timing.

"I'll be here."

"Our fearless leader."

"Yeah, right."

Charlie knocked sharply on the inside of the door, perhaps some sort of signal of solidarity, and left. Pierce waited a moment and then got up and locked the door. He wanted no more interruptions.

He went back to the printouts. After the short report on Lilly Quinlan came a voluminous report on William Wentz, owner-operator of Entrepreneurial Concepts Unlimited. The report stated that Wentz sat at the top of a burgeoning empire of Internet sleaze, from escort services to porno sites. These sites, though directed from Los Angeles, were operating in twenty cities in fourteen states, and of course reachable by the Internet from around the world.

While the Internet companies Wentz operated might be viewed as sleazy by most, they were still legal. The Internet was a world of largely regulation-free commerce. As long as Wentz did not provide photos of underage models engaged in sex and slapped the proper disclaimers on his escort sites, he operated largely in the clear. If one of his escorts happened to be taken down in a prostitution sting, he could easily distance himself. His site clearly said in a prominent disclaimer that it did not promote prostitution or any sort of trade of sex for money or property. If an escort agreed to take money for sex, then that was her decision and her web page would immediately be eliminated from the site.

Pierce had already gotten a general rundown on Wentz's operations from Philip Glass, the private detective. But Zeller's report was far more detailed and a testimonial to the power and reach of the Internet. Zeller had uncovered Wentz's criminal past in the states of Florida and New York. Contained in the printout package were several more mug shots, these depicting Wentz and another man named Grady Allison, who was listed in California corporate records as the comptroller of ECU. Pierce remembered that Lucy LaPorte had mentioned him. He skipped past the photos and read Zeller's opening summary.

Wentz and Allison appear to be a team. They arrived from Florida within a month of each other six years ago. This after multiple arrests in Orlando probably made things tough for them there. According to intelligence files with the Florida Department of Law Enforcement (FDLE), these men operated a chain of strip joints on the Orange Blossom Trail in Orlando. This was before the Internet made selling sex, real or imagined, so much easier than putting naked chicks on a stage and selling blow jobs on the side. Allison was known as Grade A Allison in Florida because of his skill in recruiting top talent to the stages of the Orange Blossom Trail. Wentz and Allison's clubs were called "No Strings Attached," as in full nudity.

IMPORTANT NOTE: The FDLE box connects these guys to one Dominic Silva, 71, Winter Park, FL, who in turn is connected to traditional organized crime in New York and northern New Jersey. BE CAREFUL!

Their pedigree as mobsters didn't surprise Pierce. Not with the way Wentz had been so calculatingly cold and violent when he encountered him in person. What he did find to be an odd fit was the idea that Wentz, the man who could calmly wield a phone as a weapon and wore pointed boots for better bone crunching, could be the man behind a sophisticated Internet empire.

Pierce had seen Wentz in action. His first and lasting impression was that Wentz was muscle first and brains second. He seemed more the caretaker of the operation than the brains behind it.

Pierce thought of the aging mobster mentioned in Zeller's report. Dominic Silva of Winter Park, Florida. Was he the man? The intellect behind the muscle? Pierce intended to find out.

He went to the next page and found a summary listing Wentz's criminal record. Over a five-year period in Florida he had a variety of arrests for pandering and two arrests for something listed as felony GBI. There was also an arrest for manslaughter.

The summaries did not include final disposition of these cases. But reading them — arrest after arrest in five years — Pierce was puzzled as to why Wentz was not in prison.

More of the same questions came up when he went to the next page and reviewed the arrest summaries of Grady "Grade A" Allison. He, too, seemed to have a recurring pandering pattern. He also topped Wentz in the GBI category with four arrests. He also had an arrest labeled "sexbat-minor," which Pierce interpreted to be a charge of having sex with a minor.

Pierce looked at the mug shots of Allison. According to the attendant information, he was forty-six years old, though the photos showed a man who might be older. He had gray-black hair greased back on his head. His ghostly pale face was accented by a nose that looked like it had been broken more than once.

He picked up the phone and called Janis Langwiser again. This time he did not have to wait as long for her to take the call.

"Couple quick questions," he said. "Do you know what pandering is, in the legal sense of the word?"

"It's a pimp charge. It means providing a woman for sex in exchange for money or goods. Why?"

"Wait a minute. What about felony GBI? What is GBI?"

"That doesn't sound like anything from the California penal code but usually GBI means 'great bodily injury.' It would be part of an assault charge."

Pierce considered this. GBI, as in hitting someone in the face with a phone and then hanging him off a twelfth-story balcony.

"Why, Henry? Have you been talking to Renner?"

He hesitated. He realized he shouldn't have called her, because it might reveal that he was still pursuing the very thing she had told him to stay away from.

"No, nothing like that. I'm just looking at a background check on an employment application. Hard to figure out what all of this means sometimes."

"Well, it doesn't sound like anybody you would want to have working for you."

"I think you're right about that. Okay, thanks. Just go ahead and put this on my bill."

"Don't worry about it."

After hanging up, he looked at the last page in the report from Zeller. It listed all of the websites that he had been able to link Wentz and ECU to. The single-space listing took up the entire page. The sexual permutations and double entendres contained in the site names and addresses were almost laughable but somehow the sheer volume of it all made it more sickening. This was just one man's operations. It was staggering.

As his eyes scanned down the list they held on one entry — FetishCastle.net — and he realized he knew it. He had heard of it. It took him a few moments and then he remembered Lucy LaPorte telling him that she had first met Lilly Quinlan at a photo shoot for the FetishCastle site.

Swiveling his chair to face the computer, Pierce booted up and went online. In a few minutes he arrived at the FetishCastle home page. The primary image was of an Asian woman wearing black thigh-high boots and little else. She had her hands on her naked hips and had adopted a stern schoolteacher pose. The page promised subscribers that herein were thousands of downloadable fetish photos, streaming videos and links to other sites. All free — with a paid subscription, of course. The coded but easily decipherable list of subject matter contained within included dominants, submissives, switches, water sports, smothering and so on.

Pierce clicked on the JOIN button and jumped to a page with a menu offering several different subscription plans and the promise of immediate approval and access. The going rate was $29.95 a month, chargeable each month to a credit card of your choice. The menu was careful to note in large letters that the billing record would appear on all credit card statements as ECU Enterprises, which would of course be easier than FetishCastle to run by the wife or boss when the bill came in.

There was an introductory offer for $5.95, which allowed access to the site for five days. At the end of that period your credit card would not be charged further if you did not sign up for one of the monthly or yearly plans. This was a one-time offer per credit card.

Pierce pulled out his wallet and used his American Express card to sign up for the introductory offer. Within minutes he had a pass code and user name and he entered the site, coming to a subject tab page with a search window. He went to the window and typed in

"Robin" and hit ENTER. His search returned no hits. He got the same result with a search for "Lilly" but then had success with "girl-girl" after remembering that it was how Lucy had described the modeling session with Lilly.

He was connected to a page of thumbnail photos, six rows of six. At the bottom of the page was a prompt that would allow him to go to the next page of thirty-six photos or to skip ahead to any one of forty-eight other pages of girl-girl photos.

Pierce scanned the thumbnails on the first page. They were all photos containing two or more women, no men. The models were engaged in various sex acts and bondage scenes, always a dominant female and her subservient subject. Though the photos were small, he did not want to take the time to click on each and enlarge it. He opened a desk drawer and took out a magnifying glass. He leaned close to the monitor screen and looked for Lucy and Lilly, able to work his way quickly across the grid of photos.

On the fourth screen of thirty-six he came across a series of more than a dozen photos of Lucy and Lilly. In each photo Lilly played the dominant and Lucy the submissive, even though Lucy towered over the diminutive Lilly. Pierce enlarged one of the thumbnails and the photo took over the whole computer screen.

The set had an obviously painted backdrop of a stone castle wall. A dungeon wall, Pierce guessed. There was straw on the floor and candles burning on a nearby table. Lucy was naked and chained to the wall with handcuffs that looked shiny and new rather than medieval. Lilly, dressed in the apparently requisite black leather of a dominatrix, stood in front of her holding a candle, her wrist cocked just enough for the hot wax to drip onto Lucy's breasts. On Lucy's face was a look that Pierce thought was meant to convey agony and ecstasy at the same time. Rapture. On Lilly's face was a look of stern approval and pride.

"Oh, I'm sorry. I thought you were gone."

Pierce turned to see Monica coming through the door. As his assistant she had the combination to his office door lock because Pierce was often in the lab and she might need access. She started to put a stack of mail down on his desk.

"You told me you were only going to be —"

She stopped when she saw the computer screen. Her mouth

opened into a perfect circle. He reached to the screen and killed the monitor. He felt lucky that his face was discolored and scarred. It helped hide his embarrassment.

"Monica, look, I —"

"Is that her? The woman you had me impersonate?"

He nodded.

"I'm just trying to . . ."

He didn't know how to explain what he was doing. He wasn't sure what he was doing. He felt even more stupid holding the magnifying glass.

"Dr. Pierce, I like my job here but I'm not sure I want to work directly for you anymore."

"Monica, don't call me that. And don't start with the job stuff again."

"Can I please transfer back to the pool?"

Pierce reached up to the monitor for his sunglasses and put them on. A few days ago he wanted to get rid of her, now he couldn't bring himself to look at her disapproving eyes.

"Monica, you can do whatever you want to do," he said while staring at the blank computer screen. "But I think you have the wrong idea about me."

"Thank you. I'll talk to Charlie. And there's your mail."

And she left, pulling the door closed behind her.

Pierce continued to turn slowly back and forth in his chair, staring at the empty screen through dark glasses. Soon the burn of humiliation dissipated and he started to feel anger. Anger at Monica for not understanding. At his predicament. And mostly at himself.

He reached over and pushed the button and the screen came alive. And there was the photo, Lucy and Lilly together. He studied the wax hardening on Lucy's skin, a frozen drip hanging off one pointed nipple. It had been a job for them, an appointment. They had never met before this captured moment.

He studied the look on each woman's face, the eye contact they shared, and he saw no hint of the act he knew it to be. It looked real in their faces and that was what stirred his own arousal. The castle and everything else was easily fake but not the faces. No, the faces told the viewer a different story. They told who was in control and who was manipulated, who was on top and who was on the bottom.

Pierce looked at the photo for a long time and then looked at every one of the photos in the series before shutting down the computer.

27

Pierce never made it home Wednesday night. Despite the confidence he had portrayed in his office with Charlie Condon, he still felt his days in the hospital had left him behind the curve in the lab. He was also put off by the idea of returning to his apartment, where he knew a bloody mess and cleanup awaited him. Instead, he spent the night in the basement at Amedeo Tech, reviewing the work conducted in his absence by Larraby and Grooms and running his own Proteus experiments. The success of the experiments temporarily energized him, as they always did. But fatigue finally overcame him in the pre-dawn hours and he went into the laser lab to sleep.

The laser lab, where the most delicate measurements were taken, had one-foot-thick concrete walls and was sheathed in copper on the outside and thick foam padding on the inside to eliminate the intrusion of outside vibrations and radio waves that could skew nanoreadings. It was known among the lab rats as the earthquake room because it was probably the safest spot in the building, maybe in all of Santa Monica. The bed-sized pieces of padding were attached to the walls with Velcro straps. It was a common occurrence for an overworked lab rat to go to the laser lab, pull down a pad and sleep on the floor, as long as the lab wasn't being used. In fact, the higher-ranking members of the lab team had specific pads labeled with their names, and over time the pads had taken on the contours of their users' bodies. When in place on the walls, the dented, misshapen pads gave the lab the appearance of having been the site of a tremendous brawl or wrestling match in which bodies had been hurled from wall to wall.

Pierce slept for two hours and woke up refreshed and ready for Maurice Goddard. The second-floor men's locker room had shower facilities and Pierce always kept spare clothes in his locker. They weren't necessarily laundry-fresh but they were fresher than the clothes he had spent the night in. He showered and dressed in blue jeans and a beige shirt with small drawings of sailfish on it. He knew Goddard and Condon and everyone else would be dressed to impress at the presentation but he didn't care. It was the scientist's option to avoid the trappings of the world outside the lab.

In the mirror he noticed that the stitch trails on his face were redder and more pronounced than the day before. He had rubbed his face repeatedly through the night, as the wounds burned and itched. Dr. Hansen had told him this would happen, that the wounds would itch as the skin mended. Hansen had given him a tube of cream to rub on the wounds to help prevent the irritation. But Pierce had left it behind at the apartment.

He leaned closer to the mirror and checked his eyes. The blood had almost completely cleared from the cornea of his left eye. The purple hemorrhage markings beneath each eye were giving way to yellow. He combed his hair back with his fingers and smiled. He decided the zippers gave his face unique character. He then grew embarrassed by his vanity and decided he was happy no one else had been in the locker room to see his fixation at the mirror.

By 9 A.M. he was back in the lab. Larraby and Grooms were there and the other techs were trickling in. There was an electricity in the lab. Everyone was catching the vibe and was excited about the presentation.

Brandon Larraby was a tall and thin researcher who liked the convention of wearing a white lab coat. He was the only one at Amedeo who did. Pierce thought it was a confidence thing: look like a real scientist and you shall do real science. It didn't matter to Pierce what Larraby or anyone else wore as long as they performed. And with Larraby there was no doubt that the immunologist had done so. Larraby was a few years older than Pierce and had come over from the pharmaceutical industry eighteen months before.

Sterling Grooms had been with Pierce and Amedeo Technologies the longest of any full-time employee. He had been Pierce's lab manager through three separate moves, starting at the old warehouse near the airport where Amedeo was born and Pierce had built the first lab completely by himself. Some nights after a long shift in the lab the two men would talk about those "old days" with a nostalgic reverence. It didn't matter that the old days were less than ten years before. Grooms was just a couple years younger than Pierce. He had signed on after completing his post-doc at UCLA. Twice Grooms was wooed by competitors but Pierce had kept him by giving him points in the company, a seat on the company's board of directors and a piece of the patents.

At 9:20 the word came from Charlie Condon's assistant: Maurice Goddard had arrived. The dog and pony show was about to begin. Pierce hung up the lab phone and looked at Grooms and Larraby.

"Elvis is in the building," he said. "Are we ready?"

Both men nodded to him and he nodded back.

"Then let's smash that fly."

It was a line from a movie that Pierce had liked. He smiled. Cody Zeller would have gotten it but it drew blanks from Grooms and Larraby.

"Never mind. I'll go get them."

Pierce went through the mantrap and took the elevator up to the administration level. They were in the boardroom. Condon, Goddard and Goddard's second, a woman named Justine Bechy, whom Charlie privately referred to as Just Bitchy. She was a lawyer who ran interference for Goddard and protected the gates to his investment riches with a lumbering zeal not unlike a 350-pound football lineman protecting his quarterback. Jacob Kaz, the patent attorney, was also seated at the large, long table. Clyde Vernon stood off to the side, an apparent show of security at the ready if needed.

Goddard was saying something about the patent applications when Pierce walked in, announcing his presence with a loud hello which ended conversation and drew their eyes and then their reactions to his damaged face.

"Oh, my gosh," exclaimed Bechy. "Oh, Henry!"

Goddard said nothing. He just stared and had what Pierce thought was a small, bemused smile on his face.

"Henry Pierce," Condon said. "The man knows how to make an entrance."

Pierce shook hands with Bechy, Goddard and Kaz and pulled

out a chair across the wide, polished table from the visitors. He touched Charlie on the expensively suited arm and looked over at Vernon and nodded. Vernon nodded back but it seemed to cost him something to do so. Pierce just didn't get the guy.

"Thank you so much for seeing us today, Henry," Bechy said in a tone that suggested he had volunteered to keep the meeting set as scheduled. "We had no idea your injuries were so serious."

"Well, it's no problem. And it looks worse than it is. I've been back in the lab and working since yesterday. Though I'm not sure this face and the lab go together too well."

No one seemed to get his awkward Frankenstein reference. Another swing and a miss for Pierce.

"Good," Bechy said.

"It was a car accident, we were told," Goddard said, his first words since Pierce's arrival.

Goddard was in his early fifties with all of his hair and the sharp eyes of a bird that had amassed a quarter billion worms in his day. He wore a crème-colored suit, white shirt and yellow tie and Pierce saw the matching hat on the table next to him. It had been remarked in the office after his first visit that Goddard had adopted the visual persona of the writer Tom Wolfe. The only thing missing was the cane.

"Yes," Pierce said. "I hit a wall."

"When did this happen? Where?"

"Sunday afternoon. Here in Santa Monica."

Pierce needed to change the subject. He was uncomfortable skirting the truth and he knew Goddard's questioning wasn't casual or concerned conversation. The bird was thinking about ponying up 18 million worms. His questions were part of the due diligence process. He was finding out what he was possibly getting into.

"Had you been drinking?" Goddard asked bluntly.

Pierce smiled and shook his head.

"No. I wasn't even driving. But I don't drink and drive anyway, Maurice, if that's what you mean."

"Well, I am glad you are okay. If you get a chance, could you get me a copy of the accident report? For our records, you understand."

There was a short silence.

"I'm not sure I do. It had nothing to do with Amedeo and what we do here."

"I understand that. But let's be frank here, Henry. You *are* Amedeo Technologies. It is your creative genius that drives this company. I've met a lot of creative geniuses in my time. Some I would put my last dollar behind. Some I wouldn't give a buck to if I had a hundred."

He stopped there. And Bechy took over. She was twenty years younger than Goddard, had short dark hair, fair skin and a manner that exuded confidence and one-upsmanship. Even still, Pierce and Condon had agreed previously that she held the position because they believed she had a relationship with the married Goddard that went beyond business.

"What Maurice is saying is that he is considering a sizeable investment in Amedeo Technologies," she said. "To be comfortable doing that, he needs to be comfortable with you. He has to know you. He doesn't want to invest in someone who might be a risk taker, who might be reckless with his investment."

"I thought it was about the science. The project."

"It is, Henry," she said. "But they go hand in hand. The science is no good without the scientist. We want you to be dedicated and obsessed with the science and your projects. But not reckless with your life outside the lab."

Pierce held her eyes for a long moment. He suddenly wondered if she knew the truth about what happened and about his obsessive investigation of Lilly Quinlan's disappearance.

Condon cleared his throat and cut in, trying to move the meeting forward.

"Justine, Maurice, I am sure that Henry would be happy to cooperate with any kind of personal investigation you would like to conduct. I've known him for a long time and I've worked in the ET field for even longer. He is one of the most levelheaded and focused researchers I've ever come across. That is why I am here. I like the science, I like the project and I'm very comfortable with the man."

Bechy broke away from Pierce to look at Condon and nod her approval.

"We may take you up on that offer," she said through a tight smile.

The exchange did little to erode the tension that had quickly enveloped the room. Pierce waited for somebody to say something but there was only silence.

"Um, there's something I should probably tell you then," he finally said. "Because you'll find out anyway."

"Then just tell us," Bechy said. "And save us all the time."

Pierce could almost feel Charlie Condon's muscles seize up under his thousand-dollar suit as he waited for the revelation he knew nothing about.

"Well, the thing is . . . I used to have a ponytail. Is that going to be a problem?"

At first the silence prevailed again but then Goddard's stone face cracked into a smile and then laughter came from his mouth. It was followed by Bechy's smile and then everybody was laughing, including Pierce, even though it hurt to do so. The tension was broken. Charlie balled a fist and knocked on the table in an apparent attempt to accentuate the mirth. The response far exceeded the humor in the comment.

"Okay, then," Condon said. "You people came to see a show. How about we go down to the lab and see the project that is going to win this comedian here a Nobel Prize?"

He put his hands on the front and back of Pierce's neck and acted as though he were strangling him. Pierce lost his smile and felt his face getting red. Not because of Condon's mock strangulation, but because of the quip about the Nobel. Pierce thought it was uncool to trivialize so serious an honor. Besides, he knew it would never happen. It would never be awarded to the operator of a private lab. The politics were against it.

"One thing before we go downstairs," Pierce said. "Jacob, did you bring the nondisclosure forms?"

"Oh, yes, right here," the lawyer said. "I almost forgot."

He pulled his briefcase up from the floor and opened it on the table.

"Is this really necessary?" Condon asked.

It was all part of the choreography. Pierce had insisted that Goddard and Bechy sign nondisclosure forms before entering the lab and viewing the presentation. Condon had disagreed, concerned that it might be insulting to an investor of Goddard's caliber. But

Pierce didn't care and would not step back. His lab, his rules. So they settled on a plan in which it would appear to be an annoying routine.

"It's lab policy," Pierce said. "I don't think we should deviate. Justine was just talking about how important it is to avoid risks. If we don't —"

"I think it is a perfectly good idea," Goddard said, interrupting. "In fact, I would have been concerned if you had not taken such a step."

Kaz slid two copies of the two-page document across the table to Goddard and Bechy. He took a pen out of his inside suit pocket, twisted it and placed it on the table in front of them.

"It's a pretty standard form," he said. "Basically, any and all proprietary processes, procedures and formulas in the lab are protected. Anything you see and hear during your visit must be held in strict confidence."

Goddard didn't bother reading the document. He left that to Bechy, who took a good five minutes to read it twice. They watched in silence and at the end of her review she silently picked up the pen and signed it. She then gave the pen to Goddard, who signed the form in front of him.

Kaz collected the documents and put them in his briefcase. They all got up from the table then and headed toward the door. Pierce let the others go first. In the hallway as they approached the elevator, Jacob Kaz tapped him on the arm and they delayed for a moment behind the others.

"Everything go okay with Janis?" Kaz whispered.

"Who?"

"Janis Langwiser. Did she call you?"

"Oh. Yeah, she called. Everything's fine. Thank you, Jacob, for the introduction. She seems very capable."

"Anything else I can do?"

"No. Everything is fine. Thank you."

The lab elevator opened and they moved toward it.

"Down the rabbit hole, eh, Henry?" Goddard said.

"You got that right," Pierce replied.

Pierce looked back and saw that Vernon had also held back in the hallway and had apparently been standing right behind Pierce and Kaz as they had spoken privately. This annoyed Pierce but he said nothing about it. Vernon was the last one into the elevator. He put his scramble card into the slot on the control panel and pushed the B button.

"B is for basement," Condon told the visitors once the door closed. "If we put L in there for lab, people might think it meant lobby."

He laughed but no one joined him. It was a nice piece of worthless information he had imparted. But it told Pierce how nervous Condon was about the presentation. For some reason this made Henry smile ever so slightly, not enough to hurt. Condon might lack confidence in the presentation but Pierce certainly didn't. As the elevator descended he felt his energy diametrically rise. He felt his posture straighten and even his vision brighten. The lab was his domain. His stage. The outside world might be dark and in shambles. War and waste. A Hieronymus Bosch painting of chaos. Women selling their bodies to strangers who would take them and hide them, hurt and even kill them. But not in the lab. In the lab there was peace. There was order. And Pierce set that order. It was his world.

He had no doubts about the science or himself in the lab. He knew that in the next hour he would change Maurice Goddard's view of the world. And he would make him a believer. He would believe that his money was not going to be invested so much as it was going to be used to change the world. And he would give it gladly. He would take out his pen and say, Where do I sign, please tell me where to sign.

28

They stood in the lab in a tight semicircle in front of Pierce and Larraby. It was close quarters with the five visitors plus the usual lab crew trying to work. Introductions had already been made and the quick tour of the individual labs given. Now it was time for the show and Pierce was ready. He felt at ease. He never considered himself much of a public speaker but it was a lot easier to talk about the project in the comfort of the lab in which it was born than in a theater at an emerging-technologies symposium or on a college campus.

"I think you are familiar with what has been the main emphasis of the lab work here for the last several years," he said. "We talked about that on your first visit. Today we want to talk about a specific offshoot project. Proteus. It is something sort of new in the last year but it is certainly born of the other work. In this world all the research is inter-related, you could say. One idea leads to another. Sort of like dominoes banging into each other. It's a chain reaction. Proteus is part of that chain."

He described his long-running fascination with the potential medical/biological applications of nanotechnology and his decision almost two years earlier to bring Brandon Larraby on board to be Amedeo's point man on the biological issues of this pursuit.

"Every article you read in every magazine and science journal talks about the biological side of this. It's always the hot point topic. From the elimination of chemical imbalances to possible cures for blood-carried diseases. Well, Proteus does not actually do any of these things. Those things and that day are still a long way off. Not science fiction anymore but still in the distance. Instead, what Proteus is, is a delivery system. It is the battery pack that will allow those future designs and devices to work inside the body. What we

214

have done here is create a formula that will allow cells in the bloodstream to produce the electric impulses that will drive those future inventions."

"It's really a chicken-and-egg question," Larraby added. "What comes first? We decided that the energy source must come first. You build from the bottom up. You start with the engine and to it you add the devices, whatever they might be."

He stopped and there was silence. This was always expected when a scientist attempted to build a word bridge to the non-scientist. Condon then jumped in, as he had been choreographed to do. He would be the bridge, the interpreter.

"What you are saying is that this formula, this energy source, is the platform which all of this other research and invention will rely upon. Correct?"

"Correct," Pierce said. "Once this is established in the science journals and through symposiums and so forth, it will act to foster further research and invention. It will excite the research field. Scientists will now be more attracted to this field because this gateway problem has been solved. We are going to show the way. On Monday morning we will be seeking patent protection for this formula. We will publish our findings soon after. And we will then license it to those who are pursuing this branch of research."

"To the people who invent and build these bloodstream devices."

It was Goddard and he had said it as a statement, not a question. It was a good sign. He was joining in. He was getting excited himself.

"Exactly," Pierce said. "If you can supply the power, you can do a lot of things. A car without an engine is going nowhere. Well, this is the engine. And it will take a researcher in this field anywhere he wants to go."

"For example," Larraby said, "in this country alone, more than one million people rely on self-administered insulin injections to control diabetes. In fact, I am one of them. It is conceivable in the not too distant future that a cellular device could be built, programmed and placed in the bloodstream and that this device would measure insulin levels and manufacture and release that amount which is needed."

"Tell them about anthrax," Condon said.

215

"Anthrax," Pierce said. "We all know from events of the last year how deadly a form of bacteria this is and how difficult it can be to detect when airborne. What this research field is heading toward is a day when, say, all postal employees or maybe members of our armed forces or maybe just all of us will have an implanted biochip that can detect and attack something like anthrax before it is allowed to cultivate and spread in the body."

"You see," Larraby said, "the possibilities are limitless. As I said, the science will be there soon. But how do you power these devices in the body? That's been the bottleneck to the research. It's been a question that has been out there for a long time."

"And we think the answer is our recipe," Pierce said. "Our formula."

Silence again. He looked at Goddard and knew he had him. The saying is, don't shoot until you see the whites of their eyes. Pierce could see the whites now. Goddard had probably been in the right place at the right time and gotten in on a lot of good things over the years. But nothing like this. Nothing that could make him money down the line — plenty of it — and also make him a hero. Make him feel good about taking that money.

"Can we see the demonstration now?" Bechy asked.

"Absolutely," Pierce said. "We have it set up on the SEM."

He led the group to what they called the imaging lab. It was a room about the size of a bedroom and contained a computerized microscope that was built to the dimensions of an office desk with a twenty-inch viewing monitor on top.

"This is a scanning electron microscope," Pierce said. "The experiments we deal with are too small to be seen with most microscopes. So what we do is set up a predetermined reaction with which we can test our project. We put the experiment in the SEM's vault and the results are magnified and viewed on the screen."

He pointed to the boxlike structure located on a pedestal next to the monitor. He opened a door to the box and removed a tray on which a silicon wafer was displayed.

"I'm not going to get into specifically naming the proteins we are using in the formula but in basic terms what we have on the wafer are human cells and to them we add a combination of certain proteins which bind with the cells. That binding process creates the energy conversion we are talking about. A release of energy that can be harnessed by the molecular devices we were talking about earlier. To test for this conversion, we place the whole experiment in a chemical solution that is sensitive to this electric impulse and responds to it by glowing. Emitting light."

While Pierce put the experiment tray back in the vault and closed it, Larraby continued the explanation of the process.

"The process converts electrical energy into a biomolecule called ATP, which is the body's energy source. Once created, ATP reacts with leucine — the same molecule that makes fireflies glow. This is called a chemiluminescent process."

Pierce thought Larraby was getting too technical. He didn't want to lose the audience. He gestured Larraby to the seat in front of the monitor and the immunologist sat down and began working the keyboard. The monitor's screen was black.

"Brandon is now putting the elements together," Pierce said. "If you watch the monitor, the results should be pretty quick and pretty obvious."

He stepped back and ushered Goddard and Bechy forward so they would be able to look over Larraby's shoulders at the monitor. He moved to the back of the room.

"Lights."

The overheads went off, leaving Pierce happy that his voice had returned enough to normal to fall within the audio receptor's parameters. The blackness was complete in the windowless lab, save for a dull glow from the gray-black screen of the monitor. It was not enough light for Pierce to watch the other faces in the room. He put his hand on the wall and traced it to the hook on which hung a set of heat resonance goggles. He unhooked them and pulled them over his head. He reached to the battery pack on the left side and turned the device on. But then he flipped the lenses up, not ready to use them. He had put the goggles on the hook that morning. They were used in the laser lab but he had wanted them here in imaging because it would allow him to secretly watch Goddard and Bechy and gauge their reactions.

"Okay, here we go," Larraby said. "Watch the monitor."

The screen remained gray-black for almost thirty seconds and then a few pinpoints of light appeared like stars through a cloudy night sky. Then more, and then more, and then the screen looked like the Milky Way.

Everyone was silent. They just watched.

"Go to thermal, Brandon," Pierce finally said.

Part of the choreography. End with a crescendo. Larraby worked the keyboard, so adept that he did not need any light to see the commands he was typing.

"Going thermal means we'll see colors," Larraby said. "Gradations in impulse intensity, from blue on the low end to green, yellow, red and then purple on the high end."

The monitor screen came alive with waves of color. Yellows and reds mostly, but enough purple to be impressive. The color rippled in a chain reaction across the screen. It undulated like the surface of the ocean at night. It was the Las Vegas strip from thirty thousand feet.

"Aurora borealis," someone whispered.

Pierce thought it might have been Goddard's voice. He flipped down the lenses and now he was seeing colors, too. Everyone in the room glowed red and yellow in the vision field of the goggles. He focused in on Goddard's face. The gradations of color allowed him to see in the dark. Goddard was intently focused on the computer screen. His mouth was open. His forehead and cheeks were deep red — maroon going to purple — as his face heated with excitement.

The goggles were a form of scientific voyeurism, allowing him to see what people thought they were hiding. He saw Goddard's face break into a wide red smile as he viewed the monitor. And in that moment Pierce knew the deal was done. They had the money, they had secured their future. He looked across the darkened room and saw Charlie Condon leaning against the opposite wall. Charlie was looking back at him, though he didn't have on any goggles. He looked out into the darkness toward where he knew Pierce would be standing. He nodded once, knowing the same thing without needing the goggles.

It was a moment to savor. They were on their way to becoming rich and possibly even famous men. But that wasn't the thing for Pierce. It was something else, something better than money. Something he couldn't put in his pocket but he could put in his head and his heart and it would earn interest measured in pride at staggering rates.

That's what the science gave him. Pride that overcame everything, that took back redemption for everything that had ever gone bad, for every wrong turn he had ever made.

Most of all, for Isabelle.

He slipped off the goggles and hung them back on the hook.

"Aurora borealis," Pierce whispered quietly to himself.

29

They ran two more experiments on the SEM using new wafers. Both lit up the screen like Christmas and Goddard was satisfied. Pierce then had Grooms go over the other lab projects with him once more just to finish things off. After all, Goddard would be investing in the whole program, not just Proteus. At 12:30 the presentation ended and they broke for lunch in the boardroom. Condon had arranged for the meal to be catered by Joe's, a restaurant on Abbot Kinney that had the rare combination of being a hot place and also having good food.

The conversation was convivial — even Bechy seemed to be enjoying herself. There was a lot of talk about the possibilities of the science. No talk about the money that could be made from it. And at one point Goddard turned to Pierce, who was sitting next to him, and quietly confided, "I have a daughter with Down's syndrome."

He said nothing else and didn't have to. Pierce knew he was simply thinking about the timing. The bad timing. A future was coming when such maladies might be eliminated before they occurred.

"But I bet you love her very much," Pierce said. "And I bet she knows that."

Goddard held his eyes for a moment before answering.

"Yes. I do and she does. I often think about her when I make my investments."

Pierce nodded.

"You have to make sure she is secure."

"No, not that. She is secure, many times over. What I think about is that no matter how much I make in this world, I won't be able to change her. I won't be able to fix her. . . . I guess what I am saying is that . . . the future is out there. This . . . what you are doing . . ."

He looked away, unable to put his thoughts into words.

"I think I know what you mean," Pierce said.

The quiet moment ended abruptly with a loud outburst of laughter from Bechy, who was sitting across the table and next to Condon. Goddard smiled and nodded as though he had heard whatever it was that had been so funny.

Later, during a dessert of key lime pie, Goddard brought up Nicole.

"You know who I miss?" he said. "Nicole James. Where is she today? I'd like to at least say hello."

Pierce and Condon looked at each other. It had been agreed earlier that Charlie would handle any explanations in regard to Nicole.

"Unfortunately, she is no longer with us," Condon said. "In fact, last Friday was her last day at Amedeo."

"Really now? Where did she go?"

"Nowhere at the moment. I think she's just taking some time to think about her next move. But she signed a no-compete contract with us, so we don't have to worry about her showing up at a competitor."

Goddard frowned and nodded.

"A very sensitive position," he said.

"It is but it isn't," Condon replied. "She was focused outward not inward. She knew just enough about our projects to know what to look for in regard to our competitors. For example, she did not have lab access and she never saw the demonstration you saw this morning."

That was a lie, only Charlie Condon didn't know it. Just like the lie Pierce had fed Clyde Vernon about how much Nicole knew and had seen. The truth was she had seen it all. Pierce had brought her into the lab on a Sunday night to show her, to light up the SEM screen like the aurora borealis. It was when things were falling apart and he was desperately grasping for a way to keep it together, to hold on to her. He had broken his own rules and taken her to the lab to show her what it was that had drawn him away from her so often. But even showing her the discovery had not worked to stop the momentum of destruction that had enveloped them. Less than a month later Nicole ended the relationship.

Like Goddard, Pierce missed Nicole at that moment, but for different reasons. He grew quiet during the remainder of the meal.

Coffee was served and then removed. The plates and utensils were cleared away until all that was left was the polished surface of the table and the reflection of their ghostly images in it.

The caterers cleared out of the room and it was time to get back to business.

"Tell us about the patent," Bechy said, folding her arms and leaning over the table.

Pierce nodded to Kaz and he took the question.

"It's actually a stepped patent. It's in nine parts, covering all processes related to what you saw today. We think we have thoroughly covered everything. We think it will hold up to any kind of challenge, now or in the future."

"And when do you go with it?"

"Monday morning. I'll be flying out to Washington tomorrow or Saturday. The plan is to personally deliver the application to the U.S. Patents and Trademark Office at nine A.M. Monday."

Since Goddard was sitting next to him, Pierce found it easier and more nonchalant to watch Bechy across from him. She seemed surprised by the speed with which they were moving. This was good. Pierce and Condon wanted to force the issue. Force Goddard to make his move now, or risk losing out by waiting.

"As you know, it's a highly competitive science," Pierce said. "We want to make sure we get our formula on the books first. Brandon and I have also completed a paper on this and will be submitting it. We'll send it out tomorrow."

Pierce raised his wrist and checked his watch. It was almost two.

"In fact," he said, "I need to leave you and get back to work now. If anything further comes up that Charlie can't answer, you can reach me in my office or in the lab. If there is no answer down there, that means we have the phone cut off because we're using one of the probes."

He pushed back his chair and was getting up when Goddard raised his hand and grabbed his upper arm to stop him.

"One moment, Henry, if you don't mind."

Pierce sat back down. Goddard looked at him and then deliberately cast his glance into every face at the table. Pierce knew what was coming. He could feel it in the tightness of his chest.

"I just want to tell you while we're all here together that I want to invest in your company. I want to be part of this great thing you are doing."

There was a raucous cheer and a round of clapping. Pierce put out his hand and Goddard shook it vigorously, then took Condon's hand that was stretched across the table.

"Nobody move," Condon said.

He got up and went to a corner of the room where there was a phone on a small table. He punched in three numbers — an in-house call — and murmured something into the receiver. He then returned to his seat and a few minutes later Monica Purl and Condon's personal assistant, a woman named Holly Kannheiser, came into the boardroom carrying two bottles of Dom Pérignon and a tray of champagne glasses.

Condon popped the bottles and poured. The assistants were asked to stay and take a glass. But both also had throwaway cameras and had to take photos in between sips of champagne.

Condon made the first toast.

"To Maurice Goddard. We're happy to have you with us on this magical ride."

Then it was Goddard's turn. He raised his glass and simply said, "To the future!"

He looked at Pierce as he said it. Pierce nodded and raised his almost empty glass. He looked at each face in the room, including Monica's, before speaking. He then said: "Our buildings, to you, would seem terribly small. But to us, who aren't big, they are wonderfully tall."

He finished his glass and looked at the others. Nobody seemed to get it.

"It's from a children's book," he explained. "Dr. Seuss. It's about believing in the possibilities of other worlds. Worlds the size of a speck of dust."

"Hear, hear," Condon said, raising his glass again.

Pierce began moving about the room, shaking hands and sharing words of thanks and encouragement. When he came to Monica she lost her smile and seemed to treat him coldly.

"Thanks for sticking it out, Monica. Did you talk to Charlie yet about your transfer?"

"Not yet. But I will."

"Okay."

"Did Mr. Renner call?"

He purposely didn't use the word *detective* in case someone in the room was listening to their conversation.

"Not yet."

He nodded. He couldn't think of what else to say.

"There are some messages for you on your desk," she told him. "One of them, the lawyer, said it was important but I told her I couldn't interrupt your presentation."

"Okay, thanks."

As calmly as he could, Pierce went back to Goddard and told him he was being left in Condon's hands to work out the investment deal. He shook his hand again and then backed out of the boardroom and headed down the hallway to his office. He wanted to run but he kept a steady pace.

30

Lights."

Pierce slid in behind his desk and picked up the three message slips Monica had left for him. Two were from Janis Langwiser and were marked *urgent*. The message on both was simply "Please call ASAP." The other message was from Cody Zeller.

Pierce put the messages back down on his desk and considered them. He didn't see how Langwiser's call could be anything other than bad news. To come from the high of the boardroom to this was almost staggering. He felt himself getting overheated, even claustrophobic. He went over to the window and cranked it open.

He decided to call Zeller back first, thinking that maybe his friend had come up with something new. His page to Zeller was returned in less than a minute.

"Sorry, dude," Zeller said by way of greeting. "No can do."

"What do you mean?"

"On Lucy LaPorte. I can't find her. I got no trace, man. This chick doesn't even have cable."

"Oh."

"You're sure that's her legal name?"

"That's what she told me."

"Is she one of the girls from the website?"

"Yeah."

"Shit, you should have told me that, dude. They don't use their real names."

"Lilly Quinlan did."

"Well, Lucy LaPorte? That sounds like a name somebody dreamed up after watching *A Streetcar Named Desire*. I mean, look at what she does. The chances of her telling the truth about something, even her own name, are probably one in —"

225

"It was the truth. It was an intimate moment and she told me the truth. I know it."

"An intimate moment. I thought you told me you didn't —"

"I didn't. It was on the phone. When she told me."

"Oh, well, phone sex is a whole other ballgame."

"Never mind, Cody. I have to go."

"Hey, wait a minute. How'd your thing go with the big money man today?"

"It went fine. Charlie's ringing him up right now."

"Cool."

"I have to go, Cody. Thanks for trying on that."

"Don't worry. I'll be billing you."

Pierce clicked off and picked up one of the messages from Langwiser. He punched in the number on the phone. A secretary answered and his call was put right through.

"Where have you been?" she began. "I told your assistant to get the message to you right away."

"She did what she's supposed to do. I don't like to be interrupted in the lab. What's going on?"

"Well, suffice it to say your attorney is pretty well plugged in. I still have my sources in the police department."

"And?"

"What I am telling you is highly confidential. It's information I shouldn't have. If it got out, there would be an investigation just on this alone."

"Okay. What is it?"

"A source told me that Renner spent a good part of his morning at his desk today working on a search warrant application. He then took it to a judge."

After the urgency of her messages and her warning, Pierce was underwhelmed.

"Okay. And what does that mean?"

"It means he wants to search your property. Your apartment, your car, probably the home where you lived before moving because that was likely your domicile when the crime occurred."

"You mean the disappearance and supposed murder of Lilly Quinlan."

"Exactly. But — and this is a big *but* — the application was rejected. The judge told him there wasn't enough. He hadn't presented enough evidence to justify the warrant."

"So that's good then, right? Does that mean it's over?"

"No, he can go back in anytime he wants. Anytime he gets more. My guess is that he was relying on the tape recording — what he called your admission. So it is good to know that a judge saw through that and said it wasn't enough."

Pierce contemplated all of this. He was out of his league, unsure what all of the legal maneuverings meant.

"He might now choose to do a little judge shopping," Langwiser said.

"You mean like taking the application to a different judge?"

"Yes, somebody more accommodating. The thing is, he probably went to the softest sell he knew in the first place. Going somewhere else could cause problems. If a judge finds out a search app has already been rejected by a colleague, it could get testy."

Trying to follow the legal nuances seemed like a waste of time. Pierce wasn't as unnerved about the news as Langwiser seemed to be. He understood that this was because she could never be completely sure he was innocent of the crime. That margin of doubt raised concerns about what the police would find if they searched his property.

"What if we let him search without a warrant?" he asked.

"No."

"He wouldn't find anything. I did not do this, Janis. I never even met Lilly Quinlan."

"It doesn't matter. We don't cooperate. You start cooperating, you start walking into traps."

"I don't understand. If I'm innocent, what trap could there be?"

"Henry, you want me to advise you, right?"

"Yes."

"Then listen and take my advice. We make no overtures to the other side. We have put Renner on notice and that is where we keep it."

"Whatever."

"Thank you."

"Will you know if he goes judge shopping or re-applies to the original judge?"

"I have an ear out. We might get a heads up. Either way, you act surprised if he ever shows up with a warrant. I have to protect my source."

"I will."

Pierce suddenly thought of something and it put a dagger of fear in his chest.

"What about my office? And the lab? Will he want to search here?"

If that happened, it would be too hard to contain. The story would leak out and into the circles where emerging technologies are discussed. It would certainly get back to Goddard and Bechy.

"I don't know for sure but it would seem unlikely. He will be going for locations likely used in the commission of the crime. It would seem like he might have an even more difficult time if he goes in and tries to convince a judge to let him search a place of business where it was highly unlikely for the crime to have occurred."

Pierce thought about the phone book he had hidden in the cabinet in the copy room. A direct connection to Lilly Quinlan he had not already acknowledged having. He had to get rid of it somehow.

He then thought of something else.

"You know," he said, "they already searched my car. I could tell when I got into it that night outside Lilly's place."

There was a moment of silence before Langwiser spoke.

"If they did, then it was illegal. We'll never be able to prove it without a witness, though."

"I didn't see anybody other than cops out there."

"I'm sure it was just a flashlight search. Quick and dirty. If he gets a warrant approved, they'll do it legally and they'll do more than a once-over. They'll go for hair and fiber evidence, things like that. Things too small to have been seen with a flashlight."

Pierce thought of the toast he had given less than a half hour before. He realized that a speck of dust might hold his future either way.

"Well, like I said, let them do it," he said, a note of defiance in his voice. "Maybe they'll start looking for the real killer once I come up clean."

"Any ideas on that?"

"Nope."

"Well, for now, you should worry about yourself. You don't seem to understand the gravity of this situation. With the search warrant, I mean. You think that just because they won't find anything that you're free and clear."

"Look, Janis, I'm a chemist, not a lawyer. And all I know is that I'm in the middle of this thing but I didn't do it. If I don't understand the gravity of the situation, then tell me exactly what it is you want me to understand."

It was the first time he had vented his frustration in her direction and he immediately regretted it.

"The reality is that a cop is on your tail and it is unlikely that he is going to be put off by this setback. To Renner, this is only temporary. He is a patient man and he will continue to work this thing until he finds or gets what he needs to get a search warrant signed. You understand?"

"Yes."

"And then that's only the beginning. Renner is good at what he does. Most of the cops I know that are good are good because they are relentless."

Pierce felt his body heat rising again. He didn't know what else to say, so he didn't say anything. A long moment of silence went by before Langwiser broke it.

"There's something else. On Saturday night you told them about Lilly Quinlan's home and gave them the address. Well, they went over there and checked it out but they did not formally search the place until Sunday afternoon after Renner got a search warrant. It wasn't clear whether she was dead or alive and it was obvious she was or had been engaged in a profession that likely involved prostitution and other illegalities."

Pierce nodded. He was beginning to understand how Renner thought.

"So to protect himself, he went and got a warrant," he said. "In case they came across something in regard to these other illegal activities. Or if she turned up alive and said, What the hell are you doing in my place?"

"Exactly. But there was another reason as well."

"To gather evidence against me."

"Right again."

"But how can it be evidence *against* me? I told him I went in there. My fingerprints are all over the place because I was looking for her and for what might have happened."

"That's your story and I believe you. He doesn't. He believes it is a story you made up to cover the fact that you had been in her home."

"I can't believe this."

"You'd better. And under the law he had to file what is called a search warrant return within forty-eight hours. It basically is a receipt for anything that was taken by police in the search."

"Did he?"

"Yes, he filed it and I got a copy. It wasn't sealed — he made a mistake on that. Anyway, it lists personal property that was taken, things like a hairbrush for DNA sampling, on and on. Many items were taken for fingerprint analysis. Pieces of mail, desk drawers, jewelry, perfume bottles, even sexual devices found in drawers."

Pierce was silent. He remembered the perfume bottle he had picked up while in the house. Could such a simple thing now be used to help convict him? He felt his insides churning, his face felt flush.

"You're not saying anything, Henry."

"I know. I'm just thinking."

"Don't tell me you touched these sexual devices."

Pierce shook his head.

"No, I didn't even see them. I did pick up a perfume bottle, though."

He heard her exhale.

"What?"

"Why did you pick up a perfume bottle?"

"I don't know. I just did. It reminded me of something, I guess. Of someone. What is the big deal? How does picking up a bottle of perfume equate with murder?"

"It's part of a circumstantial net. You told the police you went into the house to check on her, to see if she was all right."

"I told them that because that's what I did."

"Well, did you tell them that you also were picking up her perfume bottles and sniffing them? Were you looking through her underwear drawer, too?"

Pierce didn't respond. He felt like he might throw up. He leaned down and pulled the trash can from under the desk and put it on the floor next to his chair.

"Henry, I'm acting like a prosecutor with you because I need you to see the perilous path you are on. Anything you say or do can be twisted. It can look one way to you and completely different to someone else."

"Okay, okay. How long before they do the fingerprint stuff?"

"Probably a few days. Without a body, this case is probably not a priority to anyone other than Renner. I heard his own partner is working on other things, that they aren't seeing eye to eye on this and Renner's going it alone."

"Is the partner your source?"

"I'm not talking to you about my source."

They were both silent for a while. Pierce had nothing more to say but felt a sense of hope as long as he was connected to Langwiser.

"I'm putting together a list of people we can talk to," she finally said.

"What do you mean?"

"A list of people associated in some way with the case and questions to ask them. You know, if we need to."

"I get it."

He knew she meant if he was arrested and charged. If he was brought to trial.

"So let me work on things for a little while," Langwiser said. "I'll call you back if anything else comes up."

Pierce finally said good-bye and hung up. He then sat without moving in his chair as he thought about the information he had just been given. Renner was making his move. Even without a body. Pierce knew he had to call Nicole and somehow explain that the police believed he was a murderer and the likelihood was that they would be coming to search the home they had shared.

The thought of it sent another wave of sickness through him. He looked down at the trash can. He was about to get up to go get some water or a can of Coke when there was a knock on his door.

231

31

Charlie Condon poked his head into the office. He was beaming. His smile was as wide and hard as the concrete bed of the L.A. River.

"You did it, man. You fucking did it!"

Pierce swallowed and tried to separate himself from the feelings the phone call had left.

"We all did it," he said. "Where is Goddard?"

Condon stepped all the way in and closed the door. Pierce noticed he had loosened his tie after all the champagne.

"He's in my office, talking to his lawyer on the phone."

"I thought Just Bitchy was his lawyer."

"She's a lawyer but not a lawyer lawyer, if you know what I mean."

Pierce was finding it difficult to listen to Condon because thoughts about the call from Langwiser kept intruding.

"You want to hear his opening offer?"

Pierce looked up at Condon and nodded.

"He wants to buy in for twenty over four years. He wants twelve points and he wants to be chairman of the board."

Pierce forced the image of Renner out of his mind and concentrated on Condon's smiling face. The offer from Goddard was good. Not quite there, but good.

"That's not bad, Charlie."

"Not bad? It's *great!*"

Condon sounded like Tony the Tiger, accenting the last word too loudly. He'd drunk too much champagne.

"Well, it's only an opener. It's got to get better."

"I know. It will. I wanted to check with you on a couple things. First, the chair. Do you care about that?"

232

"Not if you don't."

Condon was currently the chairman of the company's board of directors. But it wasn't a board with any real power, because Pierce still controlled the company. Condon held 10 percent, they had chipped out another 8 percent to prior investors — no one in the Maurice Goddard class — and employee compensation accounted for another 10. The rest — 72 percent of the company — still belonged to Pierce. So giving Goddard the chair of a largely ceremonial advisory board didn't seem to be giving away much of anything.

"I say give it to him, make him happy," Condon said. "Now, what about the points? If I can get him to go to twenty million over *three* years, will you give him the points?"

Pierce shook his head.

"No. The difference between ten and twelve points could end up being a couple hundred million dollars. I'm keeping the points. And if you get the twenty over three years, great. But he's got to give us a minimum of eighteen million over three, or send him back to New York."

"It's a tall order."

"Look, we've been over this. Our burn rate right now as we speak is three million a year. If we want to expand and keep ahead of the pack, we're going to need double that. Six million a year is the threshold. Go work it out."

"You're only giving me the chair to work with."

"No, I only gave you the invention of the decade to work with. Charlie, did you see that guy's eyes after we put the lights back on? He's not only hooked. He's gutted and already in the frying pan. You're only nailing down details now. So go close the deal and get the first check into escrow. No extra points and get the six a year. We need it to do the work. If he wants to ride with us, that's the price of the ticket."

"Okay, I'll get it. But you ought to come do it yourself. You're a better closer than me."

"Not likely."

Condon left the room then and Pierce was alone with his thoughts again. Once more he reviewed everything Langwiser had told him. Renner was going to search his homes and car. Search the car again. Officially and legally this time. Probably to search for small evidence, evidence likely left behind during the transport of a body.

"Jesus," he said out loud.

He decided to analyze his situation in the same way he would analyze an experiment in the lab. From the bottom up. Look at it one way and then turn it and look at it another way. Grind it to powder and then look at it under the glass.

Believe nothing about it at the start.

He got out his notebook and wrote down the key elements of his conversation with Langwiser on a fresh page.

Search: apartment
     Amalfi
     Car — second time — material evidence
     Office/Lab?

Search warrant return: fingerprints
                   Everywhere — perfume

He stared at the page but no answers and no new questions came to him. Finally, he tore the page out, crumpled it and threw it toward the trash can in the corner of the room. He missed.

He leaned back and closed his eyes. He knew he had to call Nicole to prepare her for the inevitable. The police would come and search through everything: hers, his, it didn't matter. Nicole was a very private person. The invasion would be hugely damaging to her and the explanation for it catastrophic to his hopes of reconciliation.

"Oh man," he said as he got up.

He came around the desk and picked up the crumpled ball of paper. Rather than drop it into the trash can, he took it back with him to his seat. He opened the paper and tried to smooth it out on the desk.

"Believe nothing," he said.

The words on the wrinkled page defied him. They meant nothing. In a sweeping move of his arm he grabbed the page and balled it in his hand again. He cocked his elbow, ready to make the basket on the retry, when he realized something. He brought his hand down and unwrapped the page again. He looked at one line he had written.

Car — second time — material evidence

Believe nothing. That meant not believing the police had searched the car the first time. A spark of energy exploded inside. He thought he might have something. What if the police had not searched his car? Then who had?

The next jump became obvious. How did he know the car had been searched at all? The truth was he didn't. He only knew one thing: someone had been inside his car while it had been parked in the alley. The dome light had been switched. But had the car actually been searched?

He realized that he had jumped the gun in assuming that the police — in the form of Renner — had searched his car. He actually had no proof or even any indication of this. He only knew one thing: someone had been in the car. This conclusion could support a variety of secondary assumptions. Police search was only one of them. A search by a second party was another. The idea that someone had entered the car to take something was also another.

And the idea that someone had entered the car to put something in it was yet another.

Pierce got up and quickly left his office. In the hallway he punched the elevator button but immediately decided not to wait. He charged into the stairwell and quickly took the steps to the first floor. He went through the lobby without acknowledging the security man and into the adjoining parking garage.

He started with the trunk of the BMW. He pulled up the lining, looked under the spare, opened the disc changer and the tool pouch. He noticed nothing added, nothing taken. He moved to the passenger compartment, spending nearly ten minutes conducting the same kind of search and inventory. Nothing added, nothing taken.

The engine compartment was last and quickest. Nothing added, nothing taken.

That left his backpack. He relocked the car and returned to the Amedeo building, choosing the stairs again over a wait for an elevator. As he passed by Monica's desk on his way back to his office he noticed her looking at him strangely.

"What?"

"Nothing. You're just acting . . . weird."

"It's not an act."

He closed and locked his office door. The backpack was on his desk. Still standing, he grabbed it and started unzipping and looking through its many compartments. It had a cushioned storage section for a laptop computer, a divided section for paperwork and files, and three different zippered compartments for carrying smaller items such as pens and notebooks and cell phone or PDA.

Pierce found nothing out of order until he reached the front section, which contained a compartment within a compartment. It was a small zippered pouch big enough to hold a passport and possibly a fold of currency. It wasn't a secret compartment but it could easily be hidden behind a book or a folded newspaper while traveling. He opened the zipper and reached in.

His fingers touched what felt like a credit card. He thought maybe it was an old one, a card he had put in the pocket while traveling and then forgotten about. But when he pulled it out he was looking at a black plastic scramble card. There was a magnetic strip on one side. On the other side it had a company logo that said U-STORE-IT. Pierce was sure he had never seen it before. It was not his.

He put the card down on his desk and stared at it for a long moment. He knew that U-Store-It was a nationwide company that rented trucks and storage spaces in warehouses normally siding freeways. He could think of two U-Store-It locations visible from the 405 Freeway in L.A. alone.

A foreboding sense of dread fell over him. Whoever had been in his car on Saturday night had planted the scramble card in his backpack. Pierce knew he was in the middle of something he was not controlling. He was being used, set up for something he knew nothing about.

He tried to shake it off. He knew fear bred inertia and he could not afford to be standing still. He had to move. He had to do something.

He reached down to the cabinet beneath the computer monitor and pulled up the heavy Yellow Pages. He opened it and quickly found the pages offering listings and advertisements for self-storage facilities. U-Store-It had a half-page ad that listed eight different facilities in the Los Angeles area. Pierce started with the location closest to Santa Monica. He picked up the phone and called the U-Store-It location in Culver City. The call was answered by a young man's voice. Pierce envisioned Curt, the acne-scarred kid from All American Mail.

"This is going to sound strange," Pierce said. "But I think I rented a storage unit there but I can't remember. I know it was U-Store-It but now I can't remember which place it was I rented it at."

"Name?"

The kid acted like it was a routine call and request.

"Henry Pierce."

He heard the information tapped onto a keyboard.

"Nope, not here."

"Does that connect with your other locations? Can you tell where —"

"No, just here. We're not connected. It's a franchise."

Pierce did not see why that would disqualify a centrally connected computer network but didn't bother asking. He thanked the voice, hung up and called the next geographically closest franchise listed in the Yellow Pages.

He got a computer hit on his third call. The U-Store-It franchise in Van Nuys. The woman who answered his call told him he had rented a twelve-by-ten storage room at the Victory Boulevard facility six weeks earlier. She told him the room was climate-controlled, had electric power and was alarm-protected. He had twenty-four-hour-a-day access to it.

"What address do you have for me on your records?"

"I can't give that out, sir. If you want to give me your address, I can check it against the computer."

Six weeks earlier Pierce had not even begun the apartment search that would eventually put him into the Sands. So he gave the Amalfi Drive address.

"That's it."

Pierce said nothing. He stared at the black plastic card on the desk.

"What is the unit number?" he finally asked.

"I can only give you that if I see a photo ID, sir. Come in before six and show me your driver's license and I can remind you what space you have."

"I don't understand. I thought you said I had twenty-four-hour service."

"You do. But the office is only open nine till six."

"Oh, okay."

He tried to think of what else he should ask but he drew a blank. He thanked the woman and hung up.

He sat still, then slowly he picked up the scramble card and slid it into his shirt pocket. He put his hand on the phone again but didn't lift it.

Pierce knew he could call Langwiser but he didn't need her cool and calm professional manner, and he didn't want to hear her tell him to leave it alone. He knew he could call Nicole but that would only lead to raised voices and an argument. He knew he would get that anyway when he told her about the impending police search.

And he knew he could call Cody Zeller but didn't think he could take the sarcasm.

For a fleeting moment the thought of calling Lucy LaPorte entered his mind. He quickly dismissed the idea but not the thought of what it said about him. Here he was, in the most desperate situation of his life, and who could he call for help and advice?

The answer was no one. And the answer made him feel cold from the inside out.

32

With his sunglasses and hat on, Pierce entered the office at the U-Store-It in Van Nuys and went to the counter, his driver's license in his hand. A young woman in a green golf shirt and tan pants was sitting there reading a book called *Hell to Pay*. It seemed to be a struggle for her to take her eyes from it and bring them up to Pierce. When she did her chin dropped, as she was startled by the ugly stitch zipper that wandered down Pierce's nose from beneath his sunglasses.

She tried to quickly cover up like she hadn't noticed anything unusual.

"That's okay," Pierce said. "I'm getting that a lot."

He slid his license across the counter.

"I called a little while ago about the storage space I rented. I can't remember the number."

She picked up the license and looked at it and then back up at his face, studying it. Pierce took off his hat but not the sunglasses.

"It's me."

"Sorry, I just had to be sure."

She used her legs to kick backwards, rolling and spinning on her chair until she came to the computer that was on a table on the other side of the office.

The screen was too far away for Pierce to read. He watched her type in his name. In a few moments a data screen appeared and she started checking information from his driver's license against the screen. He knew his license still had the Amalfi Drive address, which she had earlier informed him was on the rental record for the storage unit.

Satisfied, she scrolled down and read something. Running her finger across the screen.

"Three three one," she said.

She kicked off the opposite wall and came rolling and spinning back to the counter. She slapped the driver's license down on the surface and Pierce took it back.

"Just take the elevator up, right?"

"You remember the code?"

"No. Sorry. I guess I'm pretty useless today."

"Four five four plus the last four digits of your license number."

He nodded his thanks and started to turn from the counter. He looked back at her.

"Do I owe you any money?"

"Excuse me?"

"I can't remember how I paid for the unit. I was wondering if I have a bill coming."

"Oh."

She kicked her chair back across the floor to the computer. Pierce liked the way she did it. One smooth, turning move.

His information was still on the screen. She scrolled down and then said without looking back at him, "No, you're fine. You paid six months up front in cash. You still have a while."

"Okay. Great. Thank you."

He stepped out of the office and over to the elevator area. After punching in the call code, he rode up to the third floor and stepped out into a deserted hallway as long as a football field with roll-down doors running along both sides. The walls were gray and the floor a matching linoleum that had been scuffed a million times by the black wheels of movers' dollies. He walked down the hall until he came to a roll-down door marked 331.

The door was a rusty brown color. There were no other markings on it but the numbers, painted in yellow with a stencil. To the right of the door was a scramble card reader with a glowing red light next to the reader. But at the bottom of the door was a hasp with a padlock holding the door secure. Pierce realized that the scramble card he had found in his backpack was only an alarm card. It would not open the door.

He pulled the U-Store-It card from his pocket and slid it through the reader. The light turned green — the unit's alarm was off. He then squatted down and took hold of the lock. He pulled it but it was secure. He couldn't open the door.

After a long moment of weighing his next move, he stood up and headed back toward the elevator. He decided he would go to the car and check the backpack again. The key to the padlock must be there. Why plant the scramble card and not the key? If it was not there, then he would return to the U-Store-It office. The woman behind the counter would surely have a lock cutter he could borrow after explaining he had forgotten his key.

In the parking lot Pierce raised his electronic key and unlocked his car. The moment he heard the snap of the locks disengaging he stopped in his tracks and looked down at his raised hand. A memory vision played through his mind. Wentz walking in front of him, moving down the hallway to his apartment door. Pierce reheard the sound of his keys in the little man's hands, the comment on the craftsmanship of the BMW.

One by one Pierce turned the keys on the ring, identifying them and the locks they corresponded to: apartment, garage, gym, Amalfi Drive front and back, office backup, desk, lab backup, computer room. He also had a key to the house he had grown up in, though it had long ago been passed from his family. He'd always kept it. It was a last connection to that time and place, to his sister. He realized he had a habit of keeping keys to places where he no longer lived.

He identified all keys on the ring but two. The strangers were stainless steel and small, not door locks. One was slightly larger than the other. Stamped on both along the circumference of the tab was the word MASTER.

His scalp seemed to draw tight on his skull as he looked at it. Instinctively he knew that one of the keys would open the lock on the storage room door.

Wentz. The little man was the one. He had slipped the keys on the ring as they had moved down the hall. Or maybe afterward, while Pierce had been dangled off the balcony. When he had returned from the hospital he had to be let into his apartment by building security. He found his keys on the living room floor. He knew Wentz had had plenty of time to slip the keys on the ring.

Pierce couldn't fathom it. Why? What was going on? Though he had no answers, he did know where he would find them — or begin to find them. He turned and headed back to the elevator.

Three minutes later Pierce slid the larger of the two stranger keys into the padlock at the bottom of the door to storage unit 331. He turned it and the lock snapped open with tooled precision. He pulled it out of the hasp and dropped it on the floor. He then gripped the door handle and began to raise it.

As the door rolled up it made a loud metallic screech that echoed right through Pierce and all the way down the hallway. The door banged loudly when it reached the top. Pierce stood with his arm raised, his hand still attached to the handle.

The space was twelve by ten and dark. But the corridor threw light in over his shoulder. Standing at center in the room was a large white box. There was a low humming sound coming from the room. Pierce stepped in and his eyes registered the white string of a pull cord for the overhead light. He pulled it and the room filled with light.

The white box was a freezer. A chest freezer with a top door that was held closed with a small padlock that Pierce knew he would be able to open with the second stranger key.

He didn't have to open the freezer to know what was in it but he opened it anyway. He felt compelled, possibly by a dream that it might be empty and that this was all part of an elaborate hoax. More likely it was simply because he knew he had to see with his own eyes, so that there would be no doubts and no going back.

He raised the second stranger key, the smaller one, and opened the padlock. He removed it and flipped up the latch. He then lifted the top of the freezer, the air lock breaking and the rubber seal making a *snik* sound as he raised it. He felt cold air puff out of the box and a damp, fetid smell invaded his nose.

With one arm he held the lid open. He looked down through the mist that was rising up out of the box like a ghost. And he saw the form of a body at the bottom of the freezer. A woman naked and crumpled in the fetal position, her neck a terrible mess of blood and damage. She lay on her right side. Blood was pooled and frozen black at the bottom of the freezer. White frost had crusted on her dark hair and upturned hip. Hair had fallen across her face but did not totally obscure it. He readily recognized the face. He had seen it only in photos but he recognized it.

242

It was Lilly Quinlan.

"Ah, Jesus . . ."

He said it quietly. Not in surprise but in horrible confirmation. He let go of the lid and it slammed closed with a heavy thump that was louder than he had expected. It scared him, but not enough to obscure the complete sense of dread that had engulfed him. He turned and slid down the front of the freezer until he was sitting on the floor, elbows on his knees, hands gathering the hair at the back of his head.

He closed his eyes and heard a rising pounding sound like someone running toward him down the hallway. He then realized it was internal, blood pounding in his ears as he grew light-headed. He thought he might pass out but realized he had to hold on and stay alert. *What if I pass out? What if I am found here?*

Pierce shook it off, reached for the top of the freezer and pulled himself up. He fought for his balance and to hold back the nausea creeping into his stomach. He pulled himself across the freezer and hugged it, putting his cheek down on the cold white top. He breathed in deeply and after a few moments it all passed and his mind was clear. He stood up straight and stepped back from the freezer. He studied it, listened to its quiet hum. He knew it was time for more AE work. Analyze and evaluate. When the unknown or unexpected came up in the lab you stopped and went into AE mode. What do you see? What do you know? What does it mean?

Pierce was standing there, looking at a freezer sitting in the middle of a storage room that he — according to the office records — had rented. The freezer contained the body of a woman he had never met before but for whose death he would certainly now be blamed.

What Pierce knew was that he had been carefully and convincingly set up. Wentz was behind it, or at least part of it. What he didn't know was why.

He decided not to be distracted by the why. Not yet. He needed more information to get to that. Instead, he decided on more AE. If he could disassemble the setup and study all the moving parts, then it might give him a chance at figuring out what–and who–was behind it.

Pacing in the small space in front of the freezer, he began with the things that had led him to discover the setup. The scramble card and the padlock keys. They had been hidden, or at least camouflaged. Had it been meant for him to find them? After stopping his pacing and contemplating this for a long moment, he decided no. It had been luck that he had noticed that his car had been entered. A plan of this magnitude and complication could not rely on such luck.

So he now concluded that he had an edge. He knew what he was not supposed to know. He knew about the body and the freezer and the storage unit. He knew the location of the trap before it had been sprung.

Next question. What if he had not found the scramble card and had not been led to the body? He considered this. Langwiser had warned him of an impending police search. Surely, Renner and his fellow searchers would leave no stone unturned. They would find the scramble card and be led to the storage space. They would check his key ring for keys to the padlocks and they would find the body. End of story. Pierce would be left to defend himself against a seemingly perfect frame.

He felt his scalp grow warm as he realized how narrowly he had escaped that — if only for the time being. And in the same moment he felt a full understanding of how complete and careful the setup had been. It was reliant on the police investigation. It relied on Renner making the moves he was making.

It also relied on Pierce. And as he came to understand this he felt the sweat start to bead in his hair. He grew hot beneath his shirt. He needed air-conditioning. The confusion and sorrow that had gripped him — maybe even the awe in which he viewed the careful plan — were now turning to anger, being forged into steel-point rage.

He now understood that the setup — his setup — had counted on his own moves. Every one of them. The setup was reliant on his own history and the likelihood of his moves based on that history. Like chemicals on a silicon wafer, elements that could be relied upon to act in a predictable manner, to bond in expected patterns.

He stepped forward and opened the freezer again. He had to. He needed to look again so the shock of it all would hit him in the face like cold water. He had to move. He had to act in an unpredictable pattern. He needed a plan and needed a clear head to come up with it.

The body obviously hadn't moved. Pierce held the top of the freezer open with one hand and clasped the other over his mouth. In her final repose Lilly Quinlan seemed tiny. Like a child. He tried to remember the height and weight dimensions she so dutifully advertised on her web page but it seemed so long since the day he first read it that he couldn't remember.

He shifted his own weight on his feet and the movement changed the light from overhead into the freezer. A glint from her hair caught his eye and he bent down into the box.

With his free hand Pierce attempted to pull back the hair from her face. It was frozen and individual strands broke as he moved them. He uncovered her upturned ear and there attached to the lobe was an earring. A silver cup holding a drop of amber with a silver feather below. He turned his hand so that the amber caught more of the light leaking into the box. It was then that he could see it. A tiny bug of some kind frozen in the amber, long ago drawn to sweetness and sustenance but caught in one of nature's deadly traps.

Pierce thought about that bug's fate and knew what he had to do. He, too, had to hide her. Hide Lilly. Move her. Keep her from discovery. From Renner. From everyone.

A sigh escaped through his mouth as he considered this. The moment was surreal, even bizarre. He was contemplating how to hide a frozen body, how to hide it in such a way as to hold no immediate connection to him. It was a task fraught with impossibility.

He quickly closed and relocked the freezer, as if it were a measure that would stop its contents from ever coming out and haunting him.

But the simple action broke the inertia in his mind. He started thinking.

He knew he had to move the freezer. No choice. Renner was coming. It was possible that he would find the storage unit even without the clues of keys and scramble card. Whoever had set this up could just make an anonymous call. He could count on nothing. He had to move her. If Renner found the freezer, then everything

245

ended. Amedeo Tech, Proteus, his life, everything. He would be a bug in amber after that.

Pierce leaned down and placed his hands on the front corners of the freezer. He applied pressure to see if it was movable. The freezer slid the last remaining six inches to the rear wall of the storage unit without much resistance. It had rollers. It was movable. The question now was, movable to where?

A quick fix was needed, something that at a minimum would work safely in the short run while he figured out a plan for the long run. He left the storage unit and moved quickly down the corridor, his eyes sweeping back and forth from door to door as he searched for an unlocked, unrented unit.

He passed by the elevator and was halfway down the other wing before he found a door with no lock through the hasp. The door was marked 307. The light on the card reader to the right of the door glowed neither green nor red. The alarm appeared to be inactive, probably left so until the unit was rented. Pierce reached down, flipped the hasp and pulled up the door. The space was dark. No alarm sounded. He found and flipped on the light switch and saw that the space was identical to the unit rented under his own name. He checked the rear wall and saw the electric socket.

He ran down the corridor back to unit 331. He moved behind the freezer and yanked out the plug. He heard the hum of the freezer's electric heart go silent. He threw the cord over the top of the appliance and then leaned his weight into it. The freezer rolled toward the hallway with relative ease. In a few seconds he had it out of the storage room and into the corridor.

The freezer's rollers were set in line, designed to make it convenient to move the appliance backwards and forward in tight spaces, and to provide access for service. Pierce had to bend down and put his full strength into pushing it into the turn into the hallway. The rollers scraped loudly on the floor. Once he had it pointed in the right direction, he pushed harder and got the heavy box moving with momentum. He wasn't quite halfway to unit 307 when he heard the sound of the elevator moving. He dropped into a crouch to put more power into his pushing. But it seemed that no matter how much strength he expended, he could not pick up speed. The rollers were small and not built for speed.

Pierce crossed in front of the elevator just as the humming from the shaft silenced. He turned his face away and kept pushing, listening for the door of one of the cars to open.

It didn't happen. The elevator had apparently stopped on another floor. He blew out his breath in relief and exhaustion. And just as he got to the open door of unit 307 the stairwell door at the end of the hallway nearest him banged open and a man stepped into the hallway. Pierce jumped and nearly cursed out loud.

The man, wearing painter's whites, his hair and skin flecked with white paint, approached. He seemed winded by his climb up the stairs.

"You the one holding up the elevator?" he asked good-naturedly.

"No," Pierce said, too defensively. "I've been up here."

"Just asking. You need a hand with that?"

"No, I'm fine. I'm just . . ."

The painter ignored his response and came up next to Pierce. He put his hands on the back of the freezer and nodded toward the open door of the storage room.

"In there?"

"Yeah. Thanks."

Together they pushed and the freezer moved quickly into the turn and then into the storage room.

"There," the painter said, seemingly winded again. He then stuck out his right hand. "Frank Aiello."

Pierce shook his hand. Aiello's left hand went into the pocket of his shirt and came out with a business card. He handed it to Pierce.

"You need any work, give me a call."

"Okay."

The painter looked down at the freezer, seemingly noticing for the first time what it was he had helped move into the storage area.

"That thing's a bear. What do you have in there, a frozen body?"

Pierce faked a small guffaw and shook his head, keeping his chin down the whole time.

"Actually, it's empty. I'm just storing it."

Aiello reached over and flicked the padlock on the freezer.

"Making sure nobody steals the air in there, huh?"

"No, I . . . it's just that with the way kids get into things, I've always kept it locked."

"Probably a good idea."

Pierce had turned and the light was on his face. The painter noticed the stitch zipper running down his nose.

"That looks like it hurt."

Pierce nodded.

"It's a long story."

"Not the kind I want to hear. Remember what I said."

"What do you mean?"

"You need a painter, you call."

"Oh. Yeah. I've got your card."

He nodded and watched as Aiello walked out of the room, his footsteps moving down the hallway. Pierce thought about the comment about a body being in the freezer. Was it a lucky guess, or was Aiello not what he appeared to be?

Pierce heard a set of keys jangling out in the hallway and then the metallic snap of a lock. It was followed by the screeching of an overhead door being lifted. He guessed that Aiello might be getting equipment from his storage space. He waited and after a few minutes he heard the door being pulled down and closed. Soon the hum of the elevator followed. Aiello was going to take it down instead of the stairs.

As soon as he was sure he was alone on the floor again he plugged the freezer in and waited until he heard the compressor begin working.

He then pulled his shirt out of his pants and used the tail to wipe every surface on the freezer and electrical cord that he could have conceivably touched. When he was sure he had covered his tracks he backed out of the space and pulled the door down. He locked it with the padlock from the other unit and wiped the lock and door with his shirttail.

As he moved away from the unit and toward the elevator alcove a terrible guilt and fear swept over him. He knew that this was because he had been operating for the last half hour on instincts and adrenaline. He hadn't been thinking out his moves as much as just making them. Now the adrenaline tank's needle was on empty and there was nothing left but his thoughts to contend with.

He knew he was far from harm's way. Moving the freezer was

like putting a Band-Aid on a bullet hole. He needed to know what was happening to him and why. He needed to come up with a plan that would save his life.

33

The immediate urge was to curl up on the floor in the same position as the body in the freezer, but Pierce knew that to collapse under the pressure of the moment would be to ensure his demise. He unlocked the door and went into his apartment, shaking with fear and anger and the true knowledge that he was the only one he could rely on to find his way out of this dark tunnel. He promised himself that he would rise up off the floor. And he would get up fighting.

As if to underscore this avowal, he balled a fist and took a swing at the five-day-old standing lamp Monica Purl had ordered and then positioned next to the couch. His punch sent it crashing into the wall, where its delicate beige shade collapsed and the bulb shattered. The lamp slid down the wall to the floor like a punch-drunk boxer.

"There, goddamnit!"

He sat down on the couch but then immediately stood up. All his pistons were firing. He had just moved and hidden a body — a murder victim. Somehow sitting down seemed like the least wise thing to do.

Yet he knew he had to. He had to sit down and look at this. He had to think like a scientist, not a detective. Detectives move on a linear plane. They move from clue to clue and then put together the picture. But sometimes the clues added up to the wrong picture.

Pierce was a scientist. He knew he had to go with what had always worked for him. He had to approach this the way he had approached and solved the question of the car search. From the bottom. Find the logic gateways, the places where the wires crossed. Take apart the frame and study the design, the architecture. Throw out linear thinking and approach the subject from all new angles.

Look at the subject matter and then turn it and look at it again. Grind it down to a powder and look at it under the glass. Life was an experiment conducted under uncontrolled conditions. It was one long chemical reaction that was as unpredictable as it was vibrant. But this setup was different. It had occurred under controlled circumstances. The reactions were predicted and expected. In that he knew was the key. That meant it was something that could be taken apart.

He sat back down and from his backpack he pulled his notebook. He was ready to write, ready to attack. The first object of his scrutiny was Wentz. A man he did not know and had never met before the day he was assaulted. A man that in the initial view was the linchpin of the frame. The question was, Why would Wentz choose Pierce to hang a murder on?

After a few minutes of turning it and grinding it and looking at it from opposite angles, Pierce came to some basic case logic.

Conclusion 1: Wentz had not chosen Pierce. There was no logical connection or link that would allow for this. While animosities existed now, the two men had never met before the setup was already in play. Pierce was sure of it. And so this conclusion led in turn to the supposition that Pierce therefore had to have been chosen for Wentz by someone other than Wentz.

Conclusion 2: There was a third party in the setup. Wentz and the muscle man he called Six-Eight were only tools. They were cogs in the wheels of the setup. Someone else's hand was behind this.

The third party.

Now Pierce considered this. What did the third party need to build the frame? The setup was complex and relied on Pierce's predictable movements in a fluid environment. He knew that under controlled circumstances the movement of molecules could be relied upon. What about himself? He turned the question and looked at it again. He then came to a basic realization about himself and the third party.

Conclusion 3: Isabelle. His sister. The setup was orchestrated by a third party with knowledge of his personal history, which led to an understanding of how he would most likely react under certain controlled circumstances. The customer phone calls to Lilly were the inciting element of the experiment. The third party understood how Pierce would likely react, that he would investigate and pursue. That he would chase his sister's ghost. Therefore, the third party knew about his ghosts. The third party knew about Isabelle.

Conclusion 4: The wrong number was the right number. He had not been randomly assigned Lilly Quinlan's old number. It was intentional. It was part of the setup.

Conclusion 5: Monica Purl. She was part of it. She had set up his phone service. She had to have specifically requested the phone number that would trip the chase.

Pierce got up and started pacing. This last conclusion changed everything. If the setup was tied to Monica, then it was tied to Amedeo. It meant the frame was part of a conspiracy of a higher order. It wasn't about hanging a murder on Pierce. It was about something else. In this respect Lilly Quinlan was like Wentz. A tool in the setup, a cog in the wheel. Her murder was simply a way to get to Pierce.

Putting the horror of this aside for the moment, he sat back down and considered the most basic question. The one for which the answer would explain all. Why?

Why was Pierce the target of the frame? What did they want?

He turned it and looked at it from another angle. What would happen if the setup succeeded? In the long run he would be arrested, tried and possibly — likely — convicted. He would be imprisoned, possibly even put to death. In the short run there would be media focus and scandal, disgrace. Maurice Goddard and his money would go away. Amedeo Technologies would crash and burn.

He turned it again and the question became one of means to an end. Why go to the trouble? Why the elaborate plot? Why kill Lilly Quinlan and set up a vast scheme that could fall apart at any step along the way? Why not simply target Pierce? Kill Pierce instead of Lilly and achieve the same end with much simpler means. He would be out of the picture again, Goddard still walks and Amedeo still crashes and burns.

Conclusion 6: The target is different. It is not Pierce and it is not Amedeo. It is something else.

As a scientist Pierce enjoyed most the moments of clarity in the vision field of a microscope, the moment things came together, when molecules combined in a natural order, in a way he knew they would. It was the magic he found in his daily life.

A moment of similar clarity struck him then as he stared out at the ocean. It was a moment in which he glimpsed the big picture and knew the natural order of things.

"Proteus," he whispered.

They wanted Proteus.

Conclusion 7: The setup was designed to push Pierce so hard into a corner that he would have no choice but to give up what they wanted. The Proteus project. He would trade Proteus for his freedom, for the return of his life.

Pierce backed up. He had to be sure. He ran it all through his mind again and once more came up with Proteus. He leaned forward and ran his fingers through his hair. He felt sick to his stomach. Not because of his conclusion that Proteus was the ultimate target. But because he had jumped quickly ahead of that. He had ridden the wave of clarity all the way into shore. He had put it together. He finally had the big picture and in the middle of it stood the third party. She was smiling at him, her eyes bright and beautiful.

Conclusion 8: Nicole.

She was the link. She was the one who connected all the dots. She had secret knowledge of the Proteus project because he had given it to her — he had goddamn demonstrated it to her! And she knew his most secret history, the true and full story about Isabelle he had never told anyone but her.

Pierce shook his head. He couldn't believe it, yet he did. He knew it worked. He figured she had gone to Elliot Bronson or maybe Gil Franks, head man at Midas Molecular. Maybe she had gone to DARPA. It didn't matter. What was clear was that she had sold him out, told of the project, agreed to steal it or maybe just delay it enough until it could be replicated and taken to the patent office by a competitor first.

He folded his arms tightly across his chest and the moment of nausea passed.

He knew he needed a plan. He needed to test his conclusions somehow and then react to the findings. It was time for some AE, time to experiment.

There was only one way to do that, he decided. He would go see her, confront her, get the truth.

He remembered his vow to fight. He decided to take his first shot. He picked up the phone and called Jacob Kaz's office. It was late in the day but the patent lawyer was still there and picked up the transfer quickly.

"Henry, you were fantastic today," he said by way of greeting.

"You were pretty good yourself, Jacob."

"Thank you. What can I do for you?"

"Is the package ready to go?"

"Yep. It has been. I finished with it last night. Only thing left to do is file it. I'm going to fly out Saturday, visit my brother in southern Maryland, maybe some friends I have in Baileys Crossroads in Virginia, and then be there first thing Monday morning to file. Like I told Maurice today. That's still the plan."

Pierce cleared his throat.

"We have to change the plan."

"Really? How so?"

"Jacob, I want you to take a red-eye tonight. I want you to file it first thing tomorrow morning. As soon as they open."

"Henry, I really think . . . that's going to be a bit expensive to get a flight tonight on such short notice. I usually fly business class and that's —"

"I don't care what it costs. I don't care where you sit. I want you on a plane tonight. In the morning call me as soon as it's filed."

"Is something wrong, Henry? You seem a bit —"

"Yes, something's wrong, Jacob, that's why I'm sending you tonight."

"Well, do you want to talk about it? Maybe I can help."

"You can help by getting on that plane and getting it filed first thing tomorrow. Other than that, I can't talk about it yet. But just get over there and get the thing filed and then call me. I don't care how early it is out here. Call me."

"Okay, Henry, I will. I'll make the arrangements right now."

"When does the filing office open?"

"Nine."

"Okay, then I will talk to you shortly after six my time. And Jacob?"

"Yes, Henry?"

"Don't tell anyone other than your wife and kids that you're going tonight. Okay?"

"Uh . . . what about Charlie? He said today that he might call me tonight to go over last-minute —"

"If Charlie calls you, don't tell him you're going tonight. If he calls after you leave, tell your wife to tell him you had to go out with another client. An emergency or something."

Kaz was silent for a long moment.

"Are you all right with this, Jacob? I'm not saying anything about Charlie. It's just that at the moment I can't trust anybody. You understand?"

"Yes, I understand."

"Okay, I'll let you go so you can call the airline. Thank you, Jacob. Call me from D.C."

Pierce clicked off. He felt bad about possibly impugning Charlie Condon in Kaz's eyes. But Pierce knew he could take no chances. He opened a fresh line and called Condon's direct line. He was still there.

"It's Henry."

"I just went down to your office to look for you."

"I'm at home. What's up?"

"I thought maybe you'd want to say good-bye to Maurice. But you missed him. He left. He heads back to New York tomorrow but said he wants to talk to you before he leaves. He'll call in the morning."

"Fine. Did you make the deal?"

"We came to an agreement in principle. We'll have contracts the end of next week."

"How did it come out?"

"I got the twenty, but over three years. The breakdown is a two-million bump on the front end and then one million bimonthly. He becomes the chairman of the board and gets his ten points. The points will vest on a schedule. He gets a point for the up-front payment and then a point every four months. If something happens and he bails early, he leaves with the points he's accumulated only. We retain the option to buy them back within one year at eighty percent."

"Okay."

"Just okay? Aren't you happy?"

"It's a good deal, Charlie. For us and him."

"I'm very happy. So is he."

"When do we get the up-front money?"

"The escrow period is thirty days. One month, then everybody gets a raise, right?"

"Yeah, right."

Pierce knew Condon was looking for excitement if not jocularity over the deal. But he couldn't give it. He wondered if he'd even be around at the end of a month.

"So where did you disappear to?" Condon asked.

"Uh, home."

"Home? Why? I thought we'd —"

"I had things to do. Listen, did Maurice or Justine ask you anything about me? Anything more about the accident?"

There was a silence while Condon evidently thought about this. "No. In fact, I thought they might bring up that thing about wanting the accident report again but they didn't. I think they were so blown away by what they saw in the lab that they don't care anymore about what happened to your face."

Pierce remembered the blood red color of Goddard's face in the vision field of the heat resonance goggles.

"I hope so."

"You ever going to tell me what happened to you?"

Pierce hesitated. He was feeling guilty over hiding things from Condon. But he had to remain cautious.

"Not right now, Charlie. The time's not right."

This put a pause in Condon's reply, and in the silence Pierce could feel the injury he was inflicting on their relationship. If there was only a way for him to be sure about Condon. If there was a question he could ask. His social engineering skills had deserted him and that left only silence.

"Well," Condon said. "I'm going to go. Congratulations, Henry. Today was a good day."

"Congratulations, Charlie."

After hanging up, Pierce pulled out his key ring to check for something. Not the padlock keys. He had left them behind at the storage facility, hidden on the top of an exit sign on the third floor. He checked the ring once more to make sure he still had the key to the house on Amalfi Drive. If Nicole wasn't home, he was going to go in anyway. And he would wait for her.

34

Pierce took the California Incline down to the Coast Highway and then north to the mouth of Santa Monica Canyon. He turned right on Channel and parked at the first meter he found open. He then got out of the BMW and walked back toward the beach, looking over his shoulder and about him every ten yards for followers. When he got to the corner he looked around once more and then quickly went down the stairs into the pedestrian tunnel that went under the highway to the beach.

The walls of the tunnel were a collage of graffiti, some of it recognized by Pierce even though it had been at least a year since he had walked through the tunnel. During happier times with Nicole it had been their routine to get the paper and coffee on Sunday mornings and take it all down to the beach. But over the last year Pierce had been working on Proteus most Sundays and didn't have time for the beach.

On the other side the tunnel branched into two separate staircases leading up. He knew the further staircase came up on the sand right next to the drainage channel that emptied surface water runoff from the canyon into the ocean. He chose this stairway and came up into the sunlight to find the beach deserted. He saw the yellow lifeguard stand where he and Nicole would have their coffee and read the paper. It looked as abandoned as their Sunday ritual had become. He just wanted to see it, to remember it, before he went up the hill to her. After a while he turned back to the mouth of the tunnel and went back down the stairs.

A quarter of the way back through the sixty-yard tunnel Pierce saw a man coming down the opposite staircase. Because of the light from above him, the man was in silhouette. Pierce was suddenly stricken with the thought of a confrontation with Renner in the tunnel. The cop had followed him and was here to arrest him.

The man approached, moving swiftly and still unidentifiable. He now seemed big. Or at least bulky. Pierce slowed his step but knew that their meeting was inevitable. To turn and run would be a ridiculous show of guilt.

When they were twenty feet apart the approaching man cleared his throat. A few feet later he came into view and Pierce saw that it wasn't Renner. It was no one that he knew. The man was in his early twenties and looked like a burned-out surfer. He incongruously wore a heavy ski jacket that was unzipped and open to reveal he had no shirt on underneath. His chest was smooth and tan and hairless.

"Hey, you looking for some— what happened to your face, man?"

Pierce kept moving past him, picking up his stride, not answering. On prior occasions he had been solicited in the tunnel. There were two gay bars on Channel and it came with the territory.

Pulling away from the curb a few minutes later, Pierce checked the mirrors of the BMW and saw no followers. The tightness in his chest began to relax. Just a little. He knew he still had Nicole to confront.

At the intersection where the canyon elementary school was located, he turned left on Entrada and took it down to Amalfi Drive. He turned left and Amalfi climbed up the north bank of the canyon, winding in a hairpin pattern. As he went by his old home he glanced down the driveway and saw Nicole's old Speedster in the carport. It appeared she was home. He yanked the wheel and came to a stop next to the curb. He sat still for a moment, pulling his thoughts and courage together. Ahead of him he saw a beat-up old Volkswagen idling in a driveway, blue smoke pumping out of the twin exhaust pipes, a Domino's Pizza sign on the roof. It reminded him that he was hungry. He had only picked at his catered lunch because he had been too keyed up from the presentation and the anticipation of making a deal with Goddard.

But food right now had to wait. He got out of the car.

Pierce stepped into the entry alcove and knocked on the door. It was a single-light French door, so Nicole would know it was him the moment she stepped into the hallway. But the glass worked both ways. He saw her the moment she saw him. She hesitated but knew she couldn't get away with acting like she wasn't home. She stepped forward and unlocked and opened the door.

But then she stood in the opening, not giving him passage. She was wearing washed-out jeans and a lightweight navy blue sweater. The sweater was cut to show off her flat and tanned stomach and the gold ring that pierced her navel. She was barefoot and Pierce imagined that her favorite clogs were somewhere nearby.

"Henry. What are you doing here?"

"I need to talk to you. Can I come in?"

"Well, I'm expecting some calls. Can you —"

"From who, Billy Wentz?"

This gave her pause. A puzzled look entered her eyes.

"Who?"

"You know who. How about Elliot Bronson or Gil Franks?"

She shook her head like she felt sorry for him.

"Look, Henry, if this is some kind of jealous ex-boyfriend scene, you can save it. I don't know any Billy Wentz and I am not trying to get a job with Elliot Bronson or with Gil Franks. I signed a no-compete clause, remember?"

That put a chink in his armor. She had deftly deflected his first attack so smoothly and naturally that Pierce felt a tremor in his resolve. All his turning and grinding and looking of an hour before was suddenly becoming suspect.

"Look, can I come in or not? I don't want to do this out here."

She hesitated again but then moved back and motioned him in. They walked into the living room, which was to the right off the hallway. It was a large dark room with cherrywood floors and sixteen-foot ceilings. There was an empty spot where his leather couch had been — the only piece of furniture he had taken. Otherwise, the room was still the same. One wall was a vast floor-to-ceiling bookcase with double-depth shelves. Most of the shelves were filled with her books, two layers on each. She put only books she had read on these shelves, and she had read a lot. One of the things Pierce had loved most about her was that she would rather spend an evening on the couch reading a book and eating peanut butter and jelly sandwiches than go to a movie and Chinois for dinner. It was also one of the things he knew he had taken advantage of. She didn't need him to read a book, which made it easier to stay in the lab that extra hour. Or those extra hours, as it more often was.

"Are you feeling all right?" she said, trying for a level of cordiality. "You look a lot better."

"I'm fine."

"How did it go with Maurice Goddard today?"

"It went fine. How did you know about it?"

Her face adopted a put-out expression.

"Because I was working there until Friday and the presentation was already scheduled. Remember?"

He nodded. She was right. Nothing suspicious there.

"I forgot."

"Is he coming on board?"

"It looks like it."

She didn't sit down. She stood in the middle of the living room and faced him. The shelves of books rose fortress-like behind her, dwarfing her, all of them silent condemnations of him, each one a night he didn't come home to her. They intimidated him and yet he knew he had to keep his anger sharp for this confrontation.

"Okay, Henry, you're here. I'm here. What is it?"

He nodded. Now was the time. It dawned on him that he really had no plan at this point. He was improvising.

"Well, what it is, is that it probably doesn't matter anymore in the scheme of things but I want to know for myself so maybe I can live with it a little easier. Just tell me, Nicki, did somebody get to you, did they pressure you, threaten you? Or did you just flat-out sell me out?"

Her mouth formed a perfect circle. Pierce had lived with her for three years and believed he knew all her facial expressions. He doubted she could put a look on her face that he hadn't seen before. And that perfect circle of a mouth he had seen before. But it was not the shock of being found out. It was confusion.

"Henry, what are you talking about?"

It was too late. He had to go with it.

"You know what I'm talking about. You set me up. And I want to know why and I want to know for who. Bronson? Midas? Who? And did you know they were going to kill her, Nicole? Don't tell me you knew that."

261

Her eyes started to get the violet sparks that he knew signaled her anger. Or her tears. Or both.

"I have no idea what you are talking about. Set you up for what? Kill who?"

"Come on, Nicole. Are they here? Hey, is Elliot hiding in the house? When do I get the presentation from them? When do we make the trade? My life back for Proteus."

"Henry, I think something's happened to you. When they held you over the balcony and you hit the wall. I think —"

"Bullshit! You were the only one who knew the story about Isabelle. You were the only one I ever told. And then you used it to do this. How could you do that? For money? Or was it just to get back at me for messing things up so bad?"

He could see her starting to tremble, to weaken. Maybe he was cracking through. She raised her hands, fingers splayed, and backed away. She was moving back toward the hallway.

"Get out of here, Henry. You're crazy. If it wasn't hitting that wall, then it was too many hours in the lab. It finally made you snap. You better go check into a —"

"You're not getting it," he said calmly. "You're not getting Proteus. Before you even wake up tomorrow it will be registered. You understand that?"

"No, Henry, I don't."

"What I'd like to know is, who killed her? Was it you, or did you have Wentz do it for you? He took care of all the dirty work, didn't he?"

That stopped her. She turned and almost shrieked at him.

"*What?* What are you saying? Killed who? Can you even listen to yourself?"

He paused, hoping she would calm down. This wasn't going the way he had thought or hoped it would. He needed an admission from her. Instead, she was starting to cry.

"Nicole, I loved you. I don't know what is wrong with me, because, fuck it, I still do."

She composed herself, wiped her cheeks and folded her arms across her chest.

"Okay, will you do me one favor, Henry?" she asked quietly.

"Haven't you gotten enough from me? What more do you want?"

"Would you please sit down on that chair there and I'll sit over here."

She directed him to the chair and then she moved behind the one where she would sit.

"Just sit down and do me this favor. Tell me what has happened. Tell me as though I didn't know anything about it. I know you don't believe that but I want you to tell me like you do. Tell me it like a story. You can say whatever you want to say about me in the story, any bad thing, but just tell it. From the start. Okay, Henry?"

Pierce slowly sat down on the chair she had pointed him to. He stared at her the whole time, watched her eyes. When she stepped over and sat down across from him he began to tell the story.

"I guess you could say this started twenty years ago. On the night I found my sister in Hollywood. And I didn't tell my stepfather about it."

35

An hour later Pierce stood in the bedroom and saw that nothing had changed. Right down to the stack of books on the floor next to her side of the bed, nothing seemed different. He stepped over to look at the book that was opened and left on the pillow where he used to sleep. It was called *Iguana Love* and he wondered what it was about.

She came up behind him and lightly touched his shoulders with her fingers. He turned into her and she brought up her hands to hold his face while she studied the scars running across his nose to his eye.

"I'm sorry, baby," she said.

"I'm sorry for that downstairs. That I doubted you. I'm sorry for everything about this past year. I thought I could keep you and still work like —"

Her hands went behind his neck and she pulled him down into a kiss. He turned her and gently pushed her down onto the edge of the bed in a sitting position. He then slid down to his knees on the floor in front of her. With his hands he gently spread her knees and moved forward between them. He then leaned further into her and they kissed again. This time longer and harder. It seemed so long since he had felt the contours of her lips with his own.

He reached down to her hips and pulled her toward him. He didn't do it gently. Soon he felt one of her hands on the back of his neck and the other working the buttons of his shirt. They struggled with each other's clothing until finally they broke apart to work on their own clothes. Both knew without saying anything that it would be faster.

They worked with gathering momentum. When he pulled his shirt off she grimaced at the sight of the bruising on his chest and side. But then she leaned forward and kissed him there. And when they were finally naked they moved onto the bed and pulled each other together in an embrace that was fueled by equal parts carnal lust and tender longing. He realized that all the while he had missed her, missed her sense and the emotional makeup of their relationship, he had also missed her body. He had a flat-out craving for the touch and taste of her body.

He pushed his face down to her breasts and then slowly moved further down, pressing his nose into her skin, holding the gold ring that pierced her skin between his teeth for a moment and tugging it before moving down further. She had her neck back and her throat exposed and vulnerable. Her eyes were closed and the back of one hand was against her mouth, the knuckle of one finger between her teeth.

When she was ready and he was ready he moved up over her body and took her hand and brought it to his center so she could guide him. It had always been their way, their routine. She moved slowly, taking him to her place, her legs coming up his sides and crossing behind him. He opened his eyes to look down on her face. One time he had brought the goggles home and they had taken turns wearing them. He knew at this moment her face would register a wonderfully velvety purple on the vision field.

She stopped and opened her own eyes. He felt her let go of him.

"What?" he said.

She sighed.

"What?" he asked again.

"I can't."

"Can't what?"

"Henry, I am so sorry but I can't do this."

She unhooked her legs and dropped them to the bed. She then brought both her hands up to his chest and started to push him off. He resisted.

"Get off me, please."

"You're kidding, right?"

"No. Get off!"

He rolled onto his side, next to her. She immediately sat up on the edge of the bed, her back to him. She folded her arms and leaned over, as if huddling with herself, the points of her spine creating a beautiful ridge on her naked back. Pierce reached up and lightly touched her neck and then ran his thumb down her spine like he was moving it across the keys of a piano.

"What is it, Nicki? What's the matter?"

"I thought after what we talked about downstairs that this would be good. That it was something we needed. But it's not. We can't do this, Henry. It's not right. We're not together anymore and if we do this — I don't know. I just can't. I'm sorry."

Pierce smiled, though she could not see this with her back to him. He reached over and touched the tattoo on her right hip. It was small enough to go unseen most of the time. He only discovered it the first night they had made love. It intrigued him and turned him on in the same way the belly button ring had. She called it a kanji. It was *fu,* the Chinese character pictogram that meant "happiness." She had told him that it was a reminder that happiness came from within, not material things.

She turned and looked at him.

"Why are you smiling? I would think you'd be upset. Any other man would be."

He shrugged.

"I don't know. I guess I understand."

But slowly it dawned on her. What he had done. She stood up from the bed and turned to him. She reached over for a pillow and held it up in front of her, to cover herself. The message was clear. She no longer wanted to be naked with him.

"What?"

"You bastard."

"What are you talking about?"

He saw the sparks in her eyes but this time she wasn't crying.

"This was a test, wasn't it? Some sort of perverted test. You knew if I fucked you, then everything downstairs was a lie."

"Nicki, I don't think —"

"Get out."

"Nicole . . ."

"You and your goddamned tests and experiments. I said, Get out!"

Embarrassed now by what he had done, he stood up and started putting on his clothes, pulling on his underwear and jeans at the same time.

"Can I say something?"

"No. I don't want to hear you."

She turned and walked to the bathroom. She dropped the pillow and walked casually, showing him the back side of her body as if taunting him with it. Letting him understand that he would never see it again.

"I'm sorry, Nicole. I thought that —"

She closed the bathroom door loudly. She never looked back at him.

"Go," he heard her say from within.

Then he heard the shower come on and he knew she was washing away his touch for the final time.

Pierce finished dressing and went down the stairs. He sat on the bottom step and put on his shoes. He wondered how had he been so desperately wrong about her.

Before leaving, he went back into the living room and stood before her bookcase. The shelves were crowded. Hardcover books only. It was an altar to knowledge and experience and adventure. He remembered one time walking into the living room and finding her on the couch. She wasn't reading. She was just looking up at her books.

One of the shelves was completely dedicated to books about tattoos and graphic design. He stepped over and let his finger tick along the spines of the books until he found the one he knew was there and pulled it out. It was a book about Chinese pictograms, the book from which she had chosen her tattoo. He turned the pages until he found *fu* and read the copy. It quoted Confucius.

With coarse rice to eat, with only water to drink, and my bended arm for a pillow, I am happy.

He should have known. Pierce knew he should have known it wasn't her. The logic was wrong. The science was wrong. It had led him to doubt the one thing he should have been sure of.

He turned the pages of the book until he came to *shu,* the symbol of forgiveness.

" 'Forgiveness is the action of the heart,' " he read out loud.

He took the book to the coffee table and placed it down still open to the page displaying *shu*. He knew she would find it soon.

Locking the door, he pulled it closed behind him and went to his car. He sat behind the wheel thinking about what he had done, about his sins. He knew he got what he deserved. Most people did.

He slid the key in and turned over the engine. The random access memory of his mind produced the image of the pizza delivery car he had seen earlier. A reminder that he was hungry.

And in that moment atoms smashed together to create a new element. He had an idea. A good one. He turned off the engine and got back out.

Nicole was either still in the shower or not answering the door. But he didn't care, because he still had a key. He unlocked the door and walked down the hallway toward the kitchen.

"Nicole," he called. "It's me. I just need to use the phone."

There was no response and he thought he could hear the sound of water running far off in the house. She was still in the shower.

On the kitchen phone he dialed Information for Venice and asked for the number for Domino's Pizza. There were two locations and he took both numbers, writing them down on a pad Nicole kept by the phone. He dialed the first number and while he waited he opened the cabinet above the phone and pulled out the Yellow Pages. He knew if Domino's didn't work, he would have to call every pizza delivery service in Venice to run out the idea.

"Domino's Pizza, can I help you?"

"I want to order a pizza."

"Phone number?"

From memory Pierce gave Lucy LaPorte's cell number. He heard it being typed into a computer. He waited and then the man on the other end said, "What is your address?"

"You mean I'm not on there?"

"No, sir."

"Sorry, I called the wrong one."

He hung up and called the second Domino's and went through the same routine, giving Lucy's number to the woman on the other end of the line.

"Nine oh nine Breeze?"

"Excuse me?"

"Is your address Nine-oh-nine Breeze? Name, LaPorte?"

"Uh, yeah, that's it."

He wrote the address down, feeling the spark of adrenaline dumping into his blood. It made his writing on the pad tight and jagged.

"What would you like?"

"Um, does your computer say what we got last time?"

"Regular size, onion, peppers and mushrooms."

"That's good. Same thing."

"Anything to drink? Garlic bread?"

"No, just the pizza."

"Okay, thirty minutes."

She hung up without saying good-bye or giving him the chance to say it. Pierce hung up the phone and turned to head to the door.

Nicole was standing there. Her hair was wet and she wore a white terrycloth robe. It had been his. She gave it to him as a present on their first Christmas together but he never wore it because he wasn't a bathrobe guy. She appropriated it and it was too big on her, and that made her look very sexy in it. She knew what seeing her in the robe did to him and she used it like a flag she would hang out. When she showered and put on the robe, it meant they were going to make love.

But not this time. No more. The look on her face was anything but provocative or sexy. She glanced down at the Yellow Pages, open to the ads for pizza delivery.

"I can't believe you, Henry. After what just happened and what you did, you just come on down and order a pizza like it's nothing. I used to think you had a conscience."

She walked over to the refrigerator and opened it.

"I asked you to leave."

"I am. But it's not what you think, Nicole. I'm trying to find somebody and this is the only way."

She took a bottle of water from the refrigerator and started unscrewing the cap.

"I asked you to leave," she said again.

"All right, I'm leaving."

He made a move to squeeze between her and the kitchen's center island. But suddenly he changed course and moved into her. He grabbed her by the shoulders and pulled her toward him. He kissed her on the mouth. She quickly pushed him back, spilling water on both of them.

"Good-bye," he said before she could speak. "I still love you."

As he walked toward the door he slid the key to the house off his key ring. He dropped it on the small entry table under the mirror by the door. He turned and looked back at her as he opened the door. And she turned away.

36

Breeze was one of the Venice walk streets, which meant Pierce would have to get out of his car to get close to it. In several neighborhoods near the beach the small bungalows were built facing each other, with only a sidewalk between them. No streets. Narrow alleys ran behind the houses so owners had access to their garages. But the fronts of the homes bordered the shared sidewalk. It was a distinct plan in Venice, a design to promote neighborliness and at the same time put more homes on smaller parcels of land. Walk street houses were highly prized.

Pierce found a parking space at the curb on Ocean near the hand-painted war memorial and walked down to Breeze. It was nearly seven o'clock and the sky was beginning to acquire the burnt-orange color of a smoggy sunset. The address he had gotten from Domino's was halfway down the block. Pierce strolled along the sidewalk like he was on his way to the beach for the sunset. As he passed 909 he nonchalantly took a look. It was a yellow bungalow, smaller than most of the others on the block, with a wide front porch with an old glider seat on it. Like most of the houses on the block, it had a white picket fence out front with a gate.

The curtains behind the front windows were drawn. The light on the ceiling over the porch was on and he took this as a bad sign. It was too early for the light to be on and he guessed that it had to have been on since the night before. He began to worry, now that he had finally found the place that neither Detective Renner nor Cody Zeller had been able to find, that Lucy LaPorte would be gone.

He continued his walk to where Breeze ended at Speedway and there was a beach parking lot. He thought about going back to his car and bringing it over to the lot, but then figured it wasn't worth the time. He loitered in the lot and watched the sun drop toward the horizon for another ten minutes. He then started back down Breeze.

This time he walked even more slowly and his eyes scanned all the homes for signs of activity. It was a quiet night on Breeze. He saw no one. He heard no one, not even a television voice. He passed 909 again and saw no indication that the tiny house was currently inhabited.

As he got to the end of Breeze a blue pickup truck pulled up and stopped at the mouth of the sidewalk. It had the familiar Domino's sign on the top. A small man of Mexican descent jumped out with a red insulated pizza carrier and quickly headed down the sidewalk. Pierce let him get a good lead and then followed. He could smell the pizza despite the insulation. It smelled good. He was hungry. When the man walked across the porch to the front door of 909, Pierce slowed to a stop and used a red bougainvillea tree in the next-door neighbor's yard as a blind.

The pizza man knocked twice — louder the second time — and looked like he was about to give up when the door was opened. Pierce realized he had chosen a poor location to watch from because the angle of view prevented him from seeing into the house. But then he heard a voice and knew it was Lucy LaPorte who had answered the door.

"I didn't order that."

"Are you sure? I have Nine oh nine Breeze."

The pizza man opened the side of his carrier and pulled out a flat box. He read something off the side.

"LaPorte, regular with onion, pepper and mushroom."

She giggled.

"Well, that's me and that's what I usually get but I didn't order that one tonight. Maybe it was like a computer glitch or something and the order came in again."

The man looked down at the pizza and sadly shook his head.

"Well, okay then. I tell them."

He shoved the box back into the carrier and turned from the door. As he came down off the porch the door to the house was closed behind him. Pierce was waiting for him by the bougainvillea tree with a twenty-dollar bill.

"Hey, if she doesn't want it, I'll take it."

The pizza man's face brightened.

"Okay, fine with me."

Pierce exchanged the twenty for the pizza.

"Keep the change."

The pizza man's face brightened further. He had turned a delivery disaster into a large tip.

"Thank you! Have a good night."

"I'll try."

Without hesitation Pierce carried the pizza to 909, went through the front gate and up onto the porch. He knocked on the door and was thankful there was no peephole — at least that he could see. It took only a few seconds for her to answer the door this time. Her eyes were cast down — to the expected level of the small pizza man. When she raised them and saw Pierce and registered the damage to his face, the shock contorted her own unbruised, undamaged face.

"Hey, Lucy. You said next time bring you a pizza. Remember?"

"What are you doing here? You're not supposed to be here. I told you not to bother me."

"You told me not to call you. I didn't."

She tried to close the door but he was expecting it. He shot his hand out and stiff-armed the door. He held it open while she tried to push it closed. But the pressure was weak. She either wasn't really trying or she just didn't have the juice. He was able to keep the door open with one hand and hold the pizza up like a waiter with the other.

"We have to talk."

"Not now. You have to go."

"Now."

She relented and stopped what little pressure she was putting on the door. He kept his hand on it just in case it was a trick.

"Okay, what do you want?"

"First of all, I want to come in. I don't like standing out here."

She backed away from the door and he stepped in. The living room was small, with barely enough room for a couch, a stuffed chair and a coffee table. There was a TV on a stand and it was tuned to one of the Hollywood news and entertainment shows.

There was a small fireplace but it didn't look like it had seen a fire in a few years.

Pierce closed the door. He stepped further into the room and put the pizza box down on the coffee table and picked up the TV remote. He killed the tube and tossed the remote back onto the table, which was crowded with entertainment magazines and gossip rags and an ashtray overburdened with butts.

"I was watching that," Lucy said.

She stood near the fireplace.

"I know," Pierce said. "Why don't you sit down, have a piece of pizza."

"I don't want pizza. If I wanted it, I would have bought it from that guy. Is that how you found me?"

She was wearing cutoff blue jeans and a green sleeveless T-shirt. No shoes. She looked very tired to Pierce and he thought maybe she had been wearing makeup after all on the night they had first met.

"Yeah, they had your address."

"I ought to sue them."

"Forget them, Lucy, and talk to me. You lied to me. You said they hurt you, that you were too black and blue to be seen."

"I didn't lie."

"Well, you sure heal up fast then. I'd like to know the secret to —"

She pulled her shirt up, exposing her stomach and chest. She had deep purple bruising on the left side along the line where her ribs crested beneath her skin. Her right breast was misshapen. There were small and distinctly separate bruises on it that Pierce knew came from fingers.

"Jesus," he whispered.

She dropped her shirt.

"I wasn't lying. I'm hurt. He wrecked my implant, too. It might even be leaking but I can't get into the doctor until tomorrow."

Pierce studied her face. It was clear that she was in pain and that she was scared and alone. He slowly sat down on the couch. Whatever designs he had on the pizza were now long gone. He felt like grabbing it, opening the door and flinging it out onto the sidewalk. His mind was clogged with images of Lucy being held by Six-Eight while Wentz hurt her. He clearly saw the joy on Wentz's face. He had seen it before.

"Lucy, I'm sorry."

"So am I. I am sorry I ever got involved with you. That's why you have to leave. If they know you came here, they'll come back and it will be a lot worse for me."

"Yeah, okay. I'll leave."

But he made no move to get up.

"I don't know," he said. "I'm batting zero tonight. I came here because I thought you were part of it. I came to find out who was setting me up."

"Setting you up for what?"

"For Lilly Quinlan. Her murder."

Lucy slowly lowered herself into the stuffed chair.

"She's dead for sure?"

He looked at her and then down at the pizza box. He thought of what he had seen in the freezer and nodded his head.

"The police think I did it. They're trying to make a case."

"The detective who I talked to?"

"Yeah, Renner."

"I'll tell him that you were just trying to find her, to make sure she was okay."

"Thank you. But it won't matter. He says that was part of my plan. I used you and others, I called the cops, all to cover that I did it. He says the killer often disguises himself as the Good Samaritan."

It was her turn but she didn't speak for a long while. Pierce studied the headlines of an old issue of the *National Enquirer* that was on the table. He realized he was far out of touch with the world. He didn't recognize a single name or photo of a celebrity on the front page.

"I could tell him that I was told to lead you to her place," Lucy said quietly.

Pierce looked up at her.

"Is that true?"

She nodded.

"But I swear to God, I didn't know he was setting you up, Henry."

"Who is 'he'?"

"Billy."

"What did he tell you to do?"

"He just told me that I would be getting a call from you, Henry Pierce, and that I should set up a date and lead you to Lilly's place. He said to make it seem like it was your idea to go there. That was all I was to do and that's all I knew. I didn't know, Henry."

He nodded.

"That's okay. I understand. I am not mad at you, Lucy. You had to do what he told you to do."

He thought about this, turning it and trying to see if this was significant information. It seemed to him that it was definitely evidence of the setup, though at the same time he had to acknowledge that the source of this evidence would not rate highly with cops, lawyers and juries. He then remembered the money he had paid Lucy on the night they had met. He knew little about criminal law but enough to know that the money would be a problem. It might taint or even disqualify Lucy as a witness.

"I could tell the detective that," Lucy said. "Then he would know it was part of a plan."

Pierce shook his head and all at once realized he had been thinking selfishly, contemplating solely how this woman could help or hurt him, not for once considering her situation.

"No, Lucy. That would put you in danger from Wentz. Besides . . ."

He almost said that a prostitute's word would not count for much with the police.

"Besides what?"

"I don't know. I just don't think it would be enough to change the way Renner's looking at this. Plus he knows I paid you money. He'd turn that into something it's not."

He thought of something and changed tack.

"Lucy, if that's all Wentz told you to do with me, and then you did it, why did they come here? Why did they hurt you?"

"To scare me. They knew the cops would want to talk to me. They told me exactly what to say. It was a script I had to follow. Then they just wanted me to drop out of sight for a while. They said in a couple weeks everything will be normal again."

A couple weeks, Pierce thought. *By then the play will be over.*

"So I guess everything you told me about Lilly was part of the script."

"No. There was no script for that. What stuff?"

"Like about the day you went to her apartment but she didn't show up. That was just made up so I'd want to go there, right?"

"No, that part was the truth. Actually, all of it was true. I didn't lie to you, Henry. I just led you. I used the truth to lead you where he wanted you to go. And you wanted to go. The client, the car, all that trouble, it was all true."

"What do you mean, the car?"

"I told you before. The parking space was taken and that was supposed to be left open for the client. My client. It was a pain in the ass because we had to go park and then walk back and he was getting sweaty. I hate sweaty guys. Then we get there and there's no answer. It was fucked up."

It came back to Pierce. He had missed it in the first go-round because he didn't know what to ask. He didn't know what was important. Lilly Quinlan didn't answer the door that day because she was dead inside the apartment. But she might not have been alone. There was a car.

"Was it her car in the space?"

"No, like I said, she always left it for the client."

"Do you remember the car that was there?"

"Yeah, I remember because they left the top down and I wouldn't leave a car like that with the top down in that neighborhood. Too close to all the dregs that hang out at the beach."

"What kind of car was it?"

"It was a black Jag."

"With the top down."

"Yeah. That's what I said."

"A two-seater?"

"Yeah, the sports car."

Pierce stared at her without speaking for a long time. For a moment he felt light-headed and thought he might fall over on the couch, go face first into the pizza box. Everything came rushing into his mind at once. He saw it all, lit up and shining, and everything seemed to fit.

"Aurora borealis."

He whispered it just under his breath.

"What?" Lucy asked.

Pierce pulled himself up from the couch.

"I have to go now."

"Are you all right?"

"I am now."

He walked toward the door but stopped suddenly and turned back to look at Lucy.

"Grady Allison."

"What about him?"

"Could it have been his car?"

"I don't know. I've never seen his car."

"What does he look like?"

Pierce envisioned the mug shot photo of Allison that Zeller had sent him. A pale, broken-nose thug with greased-back hair.

"Um, sort of young, kind of leathery from too much sun."

"Like a surfer?"

"Uh-huh."

"He has a ponytail, right?"

"Sometimes."

Pierce nodded and turned back to the door.

"Do you want to take your pizza?"

Pierce shook his head.

"I don't think I could eat it."

37

It was two hours before Cody Zeller finally showed up at Amedeo Technologies. Because Pierce needed his own time to prepare things, he hadn't even made the call to his friend until midnight. He then told Zeller that he had to come in, that there had been a breach in the computer system. Zeller had protested that he was with someone and couldn't get away until morning. Pierce said that the morning would be too late. He said that he would accept no excuse, that he needed him, that it was an emergency. Pierce made it clear without saying so that attendance was required if Zeller wanted to keep the Amedeo account and their friendship intact. It was hard to keep his voice under control because at that moment the friendship was beyond sundered.

Two hours after that call Pierce was in the lab, waiting and watching the security cameras on the computer station monitor. It was a multiplex system that allowed him to track Zeller as he parked his black Jaguar in the garage and came through the main entrance doors to the security dais, where the lone security man on duty gave him a scramble card and instructions to meet Pierce in the lab. Pierce watched Zeller ride the elevator down and move into the mantrap. At that point he switched off the security cams and started the computer's dictation program. He adjusted the microphone on the top of the monitor and then killed the screen.

"All right," he said. "Here we go. Time to smash that fly."

Zeller could only get into the mantrap with the scramble card. The second door had a keypad lock. Of course, Pierce had no doubt that Zeller knew the entry combination, as it was changed every month and the new number sent to the lab staff by e-mail. But when Zeller came through the trap to the interior stop he simply pounded on the copper-sheathed door.

Pierce got up and let him in. Zeller entered the lab throwing off the demeanor of a man who was seriously put out by the circumstances he was in.

"All right, Hank, I'm here. What's the big crisis? You know, I was right in the middle of knocking off a piece when you called."

Pierce went back to his seat at the computer station and sat down. He swiveled the seat around so he was looking at Zeller.

"Well, it took you long enough to get here. So don't tell me you stopped because of me."

"How wrong you are, my friend. I took so long only because being the perfect gentleman that I am, I had to get her back to the Valley and goddamn if there wasn't a frigging slide again in Malibu Canyon. So then I had to go turn around and go all the way down to Topanga. I still got here as fast as I could. What's that smell anyway?"

Zeller was speaking very fast. Pierce thought he might be drunk or high or both. He didn't know how this would affect the experiment. It was adding a new element to the settings.

"Carbon," he said. "I figured I'd bake a batch of wires while I waited on you."

Pierce nodded toward the closed door of the wire lab. Zeller snapped his fingers repeatedly as he attempted to draw something from memory.

"That smell . . . it reminds me of when I was a kid . . . and I'd set my little plastic cars on fire. Yeah, my model cars. Like you made from a kit with glue."

"That's a nice memory. Go in the lab there. It's worse. Take a deep breath and maybe you'll have the whole flashback."

"No thanks. I think I'll pass on that for the time being. Okay. So I'm here. What's the rumpus?"

Pierce identified the question as a line from the Coen brothers' film *Miller's Crossing,* a Zeller favorite and dialogue bank from which he often made a withdrawal. But Pierce didn't acknowledge knowing the line. He wasn't going to play that game with Zeller this night. He was concentrating on the play, the experiment he was conducting under controlled conditions.

"I told you, we've been breached," he said. "Your supposedly impregnable security system is for shit, Code. Somebody's been stealing all our secrets."

280

The accusation made Zeller immediately become agitated. His hands came together in front of his chest, the fingers seemingly fighting with one another.

"Whoa, whoa, first of all, how do you know somebody's stealing secrets?"

"I just know."

"All right, you just know. I guess I am supposed to accept that. Okay, then how do you know it's through the data system and not just somebody's big mouth leaking it or selling it? What about Charlie Condon? I've had a few drinks with him. He likes to talk, that guy."

"It's his job to talk. But I'm talking about secrets Charlie doesn't even know. That only I and a few others know. People in the lab. And I'm talking about this."

He opened a drawer in the computer station and pulled out a small device that looked like a relay switch box. It had an AC/DC plug and a small wire antenna attached. From one end of it stretched a six-inch cable attached to a computer slot card. He put it down on the top of the desk.

"I got suspicious and went into the maintenance files and looked around but didn't find anything. So I then went and looked at the hardware on the mainframe and found this little slot attachment. It's got a wireless modem. I believe it's what you guys call a sniffer."

Zeller stepped closer to the desk and picked up the device.

"Us guys? Do you mean corporate computer security specialists?"

He turned the device in his hands. It was a data catcher. Programmed and attached to a mainframe, it would intercept and collect all e-mail traffic in the computer system and ship it out over the wireless modem to a predetermined location. In the lingo of the hacking world it was called a sniffer because it collected everything and the thief was then free to sniff through all the data for the gems.

Zeller's face showed a deep concern. It was a very good act, Pierce thought.

"Homemade," Zeller said as he examined the device.

"Aren't they all?" Pierce asked. "It's not like you can bop into a Radio Shack and pick up a sniffer."

Zeller ignored the comment. His voice had a deep quaver in it when he spoke.

"How the hell did that get on there, and why didn't your system maintenance guy see it?"

Pierce leaned back and tried to play it as cool as he could.

"Why don't you quit bullshitting and tell me, Cody?"

Zeller looked from the device in his hands to Pierce. He looked surprised and hurt.

"How would I know? I built your system but I didn't build this."

"Yeah, you built the system. And this was built into the mainframe. Maintenance didn't see it because they were either bought off by you or it was too well hidden. I found it only because I was looking for it."

"Look, anybody with a scramble card has access to that computer room and could've put this on there. I told you when we designed the place you should've put it down here in the lab. For the security."

Pierce shook his head, revisiting the three-year-old debate and confirming his decision.

"Too much interference from the mainframe on the experiments. You know that. But that's beside the point. That's your sniffer. I may have diverted from computer science to chemistry at Stanford but I still know a thing or two. I put the modem card in my laptop and used it on my dial-up. It's programmed. It connected with a data dump site registered as DoomstersInk."

He waited for the reaction and got a barely noticeable eye movement from Zeller.

"One word, *ink* like the stuff in a pen," Pierce said. "But you already know that. It's been a pretty active site, I would imagine. My guess is that you installed the sniffer when we moved in here. For three years you've been watching, listening, stealing. Whatever you want to call it."

Zeller shook his head and placed the device back down on the desk. He kept his eyes down as Pierce continued.

"A year or so ago — after I'd hired Larraby — you started seeing e-mail back and forth between us about a project called Proteus. Then there was e-mail back and forth with Charlie on it and then my patent lawyer. I checked, man. I keep all my e-mail. Paranoid that way. I checked and you could've put together what was happening from the e-mail. Not the formula itself, we weren't that stupid. But enough for you to know we had it and what we were going to do with it."

"All right, so what if I did? So I listened in, big deal."

"The big deal is you sold us out. You used what you got to cut a deal with somebody."

Zeller shook his head sadly.

"Tell you what, Henry, I'm gonna go. I think you've been spending too much time in here. You know, when I used to melt those plastic cars I'd get a really bad headache from that smell. I mean, it can't be good for you. And here you are . . ."

He gestured toward the wire lab door.

Pierce stood up. His anger felt like a rock the size of a fist stuck in his throat.

"You set me up. I don't know what the play is, but you set me up."

"You're fucked up, man. I don't know anything about a setup. Yeah, sure, I've been sniffing around. It was the hacker instinct in me. Once in the blood, you know about that. Yes, I put it on there when I set up the system. Tell you the truth, I mostly forgot about it, the stuff I was seeing at first was so boring. I quit checking that site a couple years ago at least. So that's it, man. I don't know anything about a setup."

Pierce was undaunted.

"I can guess the connection to Wentz. You probably set up the security on his systems. I mean, I doubt the subject matter would have bothered you. Business is business, right?"

Zeller didn't answer and Pierce wasn't expecting him to. He forged ahead.

"You're Grady Allison."

Zeller's face showed slight surprise but then he covered it.

"Yeah, I got the mug shots and mob connections. It was all phony, all part of the play."

Again Zeller was silent and not even looking at Pierce. But Pierce could tell he had his complete attention.

"And the phone number. The number was the key. At first I thought it had to be my assistant, that she had to have requested the number for the scheme to begin. But then I realized it was the other way around. You got my number in the e-mail I sent out. You then turned around and put it on the site. On Lilly's web page. And then it all began. Some of the calls were probably from people you put up to it. The rest were probably legit — just icing on the cake. But that was why I found no phone records at her house. And no phone. Because she never *had* the number. She operated like Robin — with just a cell phone."

Again he waited for a response and got none.

"But the part I'm having trouble with is my sister. She was part of this. You had to know about her, about the time I found her and let her go. It had to be part of the planning, part of the profile. You had to know that this time I wouldn't let it go. That I would look for Lilly and walk right into the setup."

Zeller didn't respond. He turned and moved to the door. He turned the knob but the door wouldn't open. The combination had to be entered to come in or go out.

"Open the door, Henry. I want to leave."

"You're not leaving until I know what the play is. Who are you doing this for? How much are they paying you?"

"All right, fine. I'll do it myself."

Zeller punched in the combination and sprang the door lock. He pulled the door open and looked back at Pierce.

"*Vaya con dios,* dude."

"How'd you know the combination?"

That put a pause in Zeller's step and Pierce almost smiled. His knowing and using the combination was an admission. Not a big one, but it counted.

"Come on. How'd you know the combo? We change it every month — your idea, in fact. We put it out on e-mail to all the lab rats but you said you haven't checked the sniffer in two years. So how'd you know the combo?"

Pierce turned and gestured to the sniffer. Zeller's eyes followed and landed on the device. Then the focus of his eyes moved slightly and Pierce saw him register something. He stepped back into the lab and let the mantrap door close behind him with a loud *fump.*

"Henry, why do you have the monitor off? I see you've got the tower on but the monitor's off."

Zeller didn't wait for an answer and Pierce didn't give one anyway. Zeller stepped over to the computer station and reached down and pushed the monitor's on/off button.

The screen activated and Zeller bent down, both hands on the desk, to look at it. On the screen was the transcription of their conversation, the last line reading, "Henry, why do you have the monitor off? I see you've got the tower on but the monitor's off."

It was a good program, a third-generation high resonance voice-recognition system from SacredSoftware. The researchers in the lab used it routinely to dictate notes from experiments or to describe tests as they were conducted.

Pierce watched as Zeller pulled out the keyboard drawer and typed in commands to kill the program. He then erased the file.

"It will still be recoverable," Pierce said. "You know that."

"That's why I'm taking the drive."

He squatted down in front of the computer tower and slid it around so he could get to the screws that held the shell in place. He took a folding knife out of his pocket and snapped open a Phillips bit. He pulled out the power cord and began to work on the top screw on the shell.

But then he stopped. He had noticed the phone line jacked into the back of the computer. He unplugged it and held the line in his hand.

"Now Henry that's unlike you. A paranoid like you. Why would you have the computer jacked?"

"Because I was online. Because I wanted that file you just killed to be sent out as you said the words. It's a SacredSoft program. You recommended it, remember? Each voice receives a recognition code. I set up a file for you. It's as good as a tape recording. If I have to, I'll be able to match your voice to those words."

Zeller reached up from his crouched position and slapped his tool down hard on the desk. His back to Pierce, the angle of his head rose, as if he were looking up at the dime taped to the wall behind the computer station.

Slowly he stood up, going into one of his pockets again. He turned around while opening a silver cell phone.

"Well, I know you don't have a computer at home, Henry," he said. "Too paranoid. So I'm guessing Nicki. I'm going to have somebody go by and pick up her drive too, if you don't mind."

A moment of fear seized Pierce but he calmed himself. The threat to Nicole wasn't counted on but it wasn't totally unexpected, either. But the truth was the phone jack was just part of the play. The dictation file had not been sent anywhere.

Zeller waited for his call to go through, but it didn't. He took his phone away from his ear and looked at it as if it had betrayed him.

"Goddamn phone."

"There's copper in the walls. Remember? Nothing gets in but nothing gets out either."

"Fine, then I'll be right with you."

Zeller punched in the door combination again and moved into the mantrap. As soon as the door closed Pierce went over to the computer station. He picked up Zeller's tool and unfolded a blade. He knelt down by the computer tower and picked up the phone line, looped it in his hand and then sliced through it with the knife.

He stood up and put the tool back on the desk along with the cut piece of phone line just as Zeller came back through the mantrap. Zeller was holding the scramble card in one hand and his phone in the other.

"Sorry about that," Pierce said. "I had them give you a card that would let you in but not out. You can program them that way."

Zeller nodded his head and saw the cut phone line on the desk.

"And that was the only line into the lab," he said.

"That's right."

Zeller flicked the scramble card at Pierce like he was flipping a baseball card against the curb. It bounced off Pierce's chest and fell to the floor.

"Where's your card?"

"I left it in my car. I had to have the guard bring me down here. We're stuck, Code. No phones, no cameras, no one coming. Nobody's coming down here to let us out for at least five or six hours, until the lab rats start rolling in. So you might as well make yourself comfortable. You might as well sit down and tell me the story."

38

Cody Zeller looked around the lab, at the ceiling, at the desks, at the framed Dr. Seuss illustrations on the walls, anywhere but at Pierce. He caught an idea and abruptly started pacing through the lab with a renewed vigor, his head swiveling as he began a search for a specific target.

Pierce knew what he was doing.

"There is a fire alarm. But it's a direct system. You pull it and fire and police come. You want them coming? You want to explain it to them?"

"I don't care. You can explain it."

Zeller saw the red emergency pull on the wall next to the door to the wire lab. He walked over and without hesitation pulled it down. He turned back to Pierce with a clever smile on his face.

But then nothing happened. Zeller's smile broke. His eyes turned into question marks and Pierce nodded as if to say, *Yes, I disconnected the system.*

Dejected by the failure of his efforts, Zeller walked over to the probe station furthest from Pierce in the lab, pulled out the desk chair and dropped heavily into it. He closed his eyes, folded his arms and put his feet up on the table, just inches from a $250,000 scanning tunneling microscope.

Pierce waited. He had all night if he needed it. Zeller had masterfully played him. Now it was time to reverse the field. Pierce would play him. Fifteen years before, when the campus police had rounded up the Doomsters, they had separated them and waited them out. The cops had nothing. Zeller was the one who broke, who told everything. Not out of fear, not out of being worn down. Out of wanting to talk, out of a need to share his genius.

Pierce was counting on that need now.

Almost five minutes went by. When Zeller finally spoke, it was while in the same posture, his eyes still closed.

"It was when you came back after the funeral."

That was all he said and a long moment went by. Pierce waited, unsure how to dislodge the rest. Finally, he went with the direct approach.

"What are you talking about? Whose funeral?"

"Your sister's. When you came back up to Palo Alto you wouldn't talk about it. You kept it in. Then one night it all came out. We got drunk one night and I had some stuff left over from Christmas break in Maui. We smoked that up and, man, then you couldn't stop talking about it."

Pierce didn't remember this. He did, of course, remember drinking heavily and ingesting a variety of drugs in the days and months after Isabelle's death. He just didn't remember talking about it with Zeller or anyone else.

"You said that one time when you were out cruising around with your stepfather that you did actually find her. She was sleeping in this abandoned hotel where all the runaways had taken over the rooms. You found her and you were going to rescue her and bring her out, bring her back home. But she convinced you not to do it and not to tell your stepdad. She told you he had done things to her, raped her or whatever, and that's why she ran away. You said she convinced you she was better off on the street than at home with him."

Now Pierce closed his eyes. Remembering the moment of the story, if not remembering the drunken confession of it to a college roommate.

"So you left her and you lied to the old man. You said she wasn't there. Then for a whole 'nother year you two kept going out at night, looking for her. Only you were really avoiding her and he didn't know it."

Pierce remembered his plan. To get older, get out and then come back for her, to find and rescue her then. But she was dead before he got the chance. And all his life since then he knew she would be alive if he had not listened and believed her.

"You never mentioned it again after that night," Zeller said. "But I remembered it."

288

Pierce was seeing the eventual confrontation with his stepfather. It was years later. He had been handcuffed, unable to tell his mother what he knew because to reveal it would be to reveal his own complicity in Isabelle's death, that one night he had found her but then let her go and lied about it.

But, finally, the burden grew until it outweighed the damage the revelation could cause him. The confrontation was in the kitchen, where the confrontations always were in that house. Denials, threats, recriminations. His mother didn't believe him, and in not believing him, she was denying her lost daughter as well. Pierce had not spoken to her since.

Pierce opened his eyes, relieved to leave the haunting memory for the present nightmare.

"You remembered," he said to Zeller. "You remembered and you held it tight and you kept it for the right time. This time."

"It wasn't like that. Something just came up and what I knew fit in. It helped."

"Nice penetration, Cody. You have a picture of me up on the wall with all the logos now?"

"It's not like that, Hank."

"Don't call me that. That's what my stepfather called me. Don't ever call me that again."

"Whatever you want, Henry."

Zeller pulled his folded arms tighter against his body.

"So what's the setup?" Pierce asked. "My guess is you have to deliver the formula to keep your end of the deal. Who gets it?"

Zeller turned his head and looked at him, challenge or defiance in his eyes. Pierce wasn't sure which way to read it.

"I don't know why we're playing this game. The walls are about to come down on you, man, and you don't even know it."

"What walls? Are you talking about Lilly Quinlan?"

"You know I am. There are people who will be contacting you. Soon. You make the deal with them and everything else goes away. You don't make the deal, then God help you. Everything will come down on you like a ton of bricks. So my advice is, play it cool, make the deal and walk away alive, happy and rich."

"What is the deal?"

"Simple. You give up Proteus. You hand over the patent. You go

289

back to building your molecular memory and computers and make lots of money that way. Stay away from the biologicals."

Pierce nodded. Now he understood. The pharmaceutical industry. One of Zeller's other clients was somehow threatened by Proteus.

"Are you serious?" he said. "A pharmaceutical is behind this? What did you tell them? Don't you know that Proteus will help them? It's a delivery system. What will it deliver? Drug therapy. This could be the biggest development in that industry since it began."

"Exactly. It will change everything and they're not ready for it."

"Doesn't matter. There's time. Proteus is just a start — we're a minimum ten years away from any kind of practical application."

"Yeah, ten years. That's still fifteen years closer than it was before Proteus. The formula will excite the research, to use a phrase from one of your own e-mails. It will kick start it. Maybe you are ten years away and maybe you're five. Maybe you're four. Three. Doesn't matter. You are a threat, man. To a major industrial complex."

Zeller shook his head in disgust.

"You scientists think the fucking world is your oyster and you can make your discoveries and change whatever you want and everybody will be happy about it. Well, there's a world order and if you think the giants of industry are going to let a little worker ant like you cut them down to size, then you are living in a goddamn dream."

He unfolded his arms and gestured toward one of the framed pages from *Horton Hears a Who!* Pierce's eyes followed and he saw it was the page that showed Horton being persecuted by the other jungle animals. He could recite the words in his head. *Through the high jungle tree tops, the news quickly spread. He talks to a dust speck. He's out of his head!*

"I am *helping* you by doing this, Einstein. You understand? This is your dose of reality. Because don't expect the semiconductor people to sit around while you cut them down, either. Consider this a fucking heads up."

Pierce almost laughed but it was too pathetic.

"My heads up? Man, that's great. Thank you, Cody Zeller, for setting me straight in the world."

"Don't mention it."

"And what do you get for this great gesture?"

"Me? I get money. Lots of it."

Pierce nodded. Money. The ultimate motivation. The ultimate way of keeping score.

"So what happens?" he asked quietly. "I make the deal and what happens?"

Zeller sat quietly for a moment while he fashioned an answer.

"Do you remember that urban legend about the garage work-shop inventor who came up with a form of rubber that was so strong, it would never wear out? It was a fluke. He was trying to invent one thing but came up with this rubber instead."

"He sold it to a tire company so the world would have tires that would never wear out."

"Yeah, that's right. That's the story. The name of the tire company was different depending on who told the story. But the story and the end were always the same. The tire company took the formula and put it in a safe."

"They never made the tires."

"They never made the tires because if they did that, they wouldn't make very many tires anymore, would they? Planned obsolescence, Einstein. It's what makes the world go around. Let me ask you this: How do you know that story is urban legend? I mean, how do you really know it didn't happen?"

Pierce nodded before he spoke.

"They'll bury Proteus. They won't license it. It will never see the light of day."

"Do you know that the pharmaceutical industry invents and studies and tests several hundred different new drugs for every one that eventually comes to market after the FDA is through with it? Do you understand the costs involved? It's a big, huge machine, Henry, and it's got energy and momentum and you can't stop it. They won't let you."

Zeller raised a hand and made some kind of gesture and then dropped it to the armrest of the chair. They both sat silently for a long moment.

"They are going to come to me and take away Proteus."

"They're going to pay you for it. Pay you well. The offer's actually already on the table."

Pierce sprang forward in his seat, the pose of calm completely disappearing. He looked over at Zeller, who was not looking back.

"Are you telling me it's Goddard? Goddard is behind this?"

"Goddard is only the emissary. The front. He calls you tomorrow and you make the deal with him. You give him Proteus. You don't need to know who is behind him. You don't ever need to know that."

"He takes Proteus from me, then holds ten percent of the company and sits as chairman of my fucking board."

"I think they want to make sure you steer clear of internal medicine. They also know a good investment when they see it. They know you're the leader in the field."

Zeller smiled, as if he were throwing in a bonus. Pierce thought about Goddard and the things he had said — confided — during the celebration. About his daughter. About the future. He wondered if it was all sham. If it had all been part of the play.

"What if I don't do it?" Pierce asked. "What if I go ahead and file the patent and say fuck you to them?"

"Then you won't get the chance to file it. And you won't get the chance to work another day in this lab."

"What are they going to do, kill me?"

"If they have to, but they don't have to. Come on, man, you know what's going on. The cops are this close behind you."

Zeller held up his right hand, his thumb and forefinger an inch apart.

"Lilly Quinlan," Pierce said.

Zeller nodded.

"Darling Lilly. They're missing only one thing. They find it and you're history. You do as you're told here and that will all go away. I guarantee it will be taken care of."

"I didn't do it and you know it."

"Doesn't matter. They find the body and it points to you, then it doesn't matter."

"So Lilly is dead."

Zeller nodded.

"Oh, yeah. She's dead."

There was a smile in his voice, if not on his face, when he said it.

Pierce looked down. He put his elbows on his knees and put his face in his hands.

"All because of me. Because of Proteus."

He didn't move for a long moment. He knew if Zeller were to make the ultimate mistake, he would do it now.

"Actually . . ."

Nothing. That was it. Pierce looked up from his hands.

"Actually what?"

"I was going to say, Don't beat yourself up too badly about that. Lilly . . . you could say circumstances dictated she be folded into the plan."

"I don't — what do you mean?"

"I mean, look at it this way. Lilly would be dead whether you were involved in this or not. But she's dead. And we used all available resources to make this deal happen."

Pierce stood up and walked to the back of the lab where Zeller sat, his legs still up on the probe station table.

"You son of a bitch. You know all about it. You killed her, didn't you? You killed her and set the frame around me."

Zeller didn't move an inch. But his eyes rose to Pierce's and then a strange look came over his face. The change was subtle but Pierce could see it. It was the incongruous mixture of pride and embarrassment and self-loathing.

"I had known Lilly since she first came to L.A. You could say she was part of my compensation package for L.A. Darlings. And by the way, don't insult me with that thing about me doing the work for Wentz. Wentz works for me, you understand? They all do."

Pierce nodded to himself. He should have expected as much. Zeller continued unbidden.

"Man, she was a choice piece. Darling Lilly. But she got to know too much about me. You don't want anyone to know all your secrets. At least not those kinds of secrets. So I worked her into the assignment I had. The Proteus Plan, I called it."

His eyes were far off now. He was watching a movie inside and liking it. He and Lilly, maybe the final meeting in the townhouse off Speedway. It prompted Pierce to draw another line from *Miller's Crossing*.

"Nobody knows nobody, not that well."

"*Miller's Crossing,*" Zeller said, smiling and nodding. "I guess that means you got my 'what's the rumpus' coming in."

"Yeah, I got it, Cody."

After a pause he continued quietly.

"You killed her, didn't you? You did it and then you were ready, if necessary, to put it on me."

Zeller didn't answer at first. Pierce studied his face and could tell he wanted to talk, wanted to tell him every detail of his ingenious plan. It was in his nature to tell it. But common sense told him not to, told him to be safe.

"Put it this way. Lilly served her purpose for me. And then she served her purpose for me again. I'll never admit more than that."

"It's all right. You just did."

Pierce hadn't said it. It was a new voice. Both men turned at the sound and saw Detective Robert Renner standing in the open doorway of the wire lab. He held a gun loosely down at his side.

"Who the fuck are you?" Zeller asked as he dropped his feet to the floor and came up out of the chair.

"LAPD," Renner said.

He moved from the lab doorway toward Zeller, reaching behind his back as he came.

"You're under arrest for murder. That's for starters. We'll worry about the rest later."

His hand came back around his body, holding a pair of handcuffs. He moved in on Zeller, twirled him around and bent him over the probe station. He holstered his weapon and then pulled Zeller's arms behind his back and started cuffing them. He worked with the professionalism and practice of a man who had done it a thousand times or more. In the process he pushed Zeller's face into the hard steel cowling of the microscope.

"Careful," Pierce said. "That microscope is very sensitive — and expensive. You might damage it."

"Wouldn't want to do that," Renner said. "Not with all these important discoveries you're making in here."

He then glanced over at Pierce with what probably passed for him as a full-fledged smile.

39

Zeller didn't say anything as he was being cuffed. He just turned and stared at Pierce, who threw it right back at him. Once Zeller was secured Renner started searching him. When the detective patted down the right leg he came up with something. He lifted the cuff of Zeller's pants and pulled a small pistol out of an ankle holster. He displayed it to Pierce, then put it down on the table.

"That's for protection," Zeller protested. "This whole thing is bullshit. It will never stand up."

"Is that right?" Renner asked good-naturedly.

He pulled Zeller back off the table and then roughly sat him back down in the seat.

"Stay there."

He stepped over to Pierce and nodded toward his chest.

"Open up."

Pierce started to unbutton his shirt, revealing the battery pack and transmitter taped across his left ribs.

"How did it come through?" he asked.

"Perfect. Got every word."

"You motherfucker," Zeller said with a steel-hard hiss in his voice. Pierce looked at him.

"Oh, so I'm the motherfucker for wearing a wire. You set me up for a murder and *you* get upset that I'm wired. Cody, you can go —"

"All right, all right, break it up," Renner said. "Both of you shut it down."

As if to accentuate the point, he tore the tape securing the audio surveillance equipment off Pierce's body with one hard tug. Pierce almost let out a scream but was able to reduce it to a "goddamn, that hurt!"

"Good. Sit down over there, Mr. Righteous. It will start to feel better in a minute."

He turned back to Zeller.

"Before I take you out of here, I'm going to read you your rights. So shut up and listen."

He reached into one of the inside pockets of his bomber jacket and pulled out a stack of cards. He shuffled through them, finding the scramble card Pierce had given him earlier. He reached over and handed it to Pierce.

"You lead the way. Open the door."

Pierce took the card but didn't get up. His side was still burning. Renner found the rights card he was looking for and started reading it to Zeller.

"You have the right to —"

There was a loud metallic clack as the mantrap door's lock was sprung. The door swung open and Pierce saw the security guard from the front dais standing there. His eyes looked dulled and his hair was uncombed. He had one hand behind his back as though hiding something.

In his peripheral vision Pierce saw Renner tense. He dropped the card he was reading from and his hand started inside his jacket for his holster.

"It's my security guy," Pierce blurted out.

In the same moment he said it he saw the security man suddenly propelled into the lab by an unseen force from behind. The guard, a man named Rudolpho Gonsalves, crashed into the computer station and toppled over it, landing on the floor, with the monitor then falling onto his chest. Then the familiar image of Six-Eight followed through the door, the big man ducking as he crossed the threshold.

Billy Wentz stepped in behind him. He held a large black gun in his right hand and his eyes sharpened when he saw the three men on the other side of the lab.

"What's taking so —"

"Cops!" Zeller yelled. "He's a cop!"

Renner was already pulling his gun from his holster but Wentz had the advantage. With the utmost economy of movement, the little gangster pointed his weapon across the lab and started firing. He stepped forward as he fired, moving the barrel of the gun in a two-inch-wide back and forth arc. The sound was deafening.

Pierce didn't see it but he knew Renner had started returning fire. He heard the sound of gunfire to his right and instinctively dove to his left. He rolled and turned to see the detective going down, a spray of fat drops of blood hitting the wall behind him. He turned the other way to see Wentz still advancing. He was trapped. Wentz was squarely between him and the mantrap door.

"Lights!"

The lab dropped into darkness. Two flashes of light accompanied the last two shots from Wentz and then complete blackness set in. Pierce immediately rolled to his right again so he would not be in the same position Wentz had last remembered him to be. On his hands and knees he held perfectly still, trying to control his breathing. He listened for any sound that was not his own.

There was a low guttural sound to his right and behind him. It was either Renner or Zeller. Hurt. Pierce knew he could not call out to Renner, because it could help Wentz focus his next shot.

"Lights!"

It was Wentz but the voice reader was set to receive and identify only the top tier of the lab team. Wentz's voice would not do it.

"Lights!"

Still nothing.

"Six-Eight? There's gotta be a switch. Find the light switch."

There was no reply or sound of movement.

"Six-Eight?"

Nothing.

"Six-Eight, goddamnit!"

Again, no reply. Then Pierce heard a banging sound ahead of him and to the right. Wentz had walked into something. He judged by the sound that it was at least twenty feet away. Wentz was probably near the mantrap, searching for his backup man or the light switch. He knew it did not give him a lot of time. The light switch was not next to the mantrap door but it was only five or six feet away, by the electric control panel.

Pierce turned and crawled silently but quickly back toward the probe station. He remembered the gun Renner had found on Zeller.

When he got to the table he reached up and ran his hand along the top surface. His fingers dragged through something thick and wet and then they touched what he clearly identified as someone's nose and lips. At first he was repelled, then he reached back and let his fingers follow the face up, over the crown of the head until they found the knot of hair at the back. It was Zeller. And it appeared that he was dead.

After a moment's pause he continued the search, his hand finally clasping around the small pistol. He turned back in the direction of the mantrap entrance. As he made the maneuver his ankle clipped a steel trash can that was under the table and it went over in a loud clatter.

Pierce ducked and rolled as two more shots echoed through the lab and he saw two microsecond flashes of Wentz's face in the darkness. Pierce did not return fire, he was too busy moving out of Wentz's aim. He heard the distinct *thwap thwap* sound of the bullets meant for him hitting the copper sheeting on the outside wall of the laser lab at the end of the room.

Pierce tucked the gun into the pocket of his jeans so he could crawl more quickly and efficiently. He once more concentrated on calming himself and his breathing and then started crawling forward and to his left.

He reached out one hand until he touched the wall and gathered his bearings. He then crawled silently forward, using the wall as a guide. He passed the threshold to the wire room — he could tell by the concentrated smell of burned carbon — and moved to the next room down, the imaging lab.

He slowly stood up, his ears primed for the sound of any close movement. There was only silence and then a metallic snapping sound from the other side of the room. Pierce identified it as the sound of a bullet clip being ejected from a gun. He did not have a lot of experience with guns but the sound seemed to fit with what he was imagining in his head: Wentz reloading or checking the number of bullets he had left in his clip.

"Hey, Bright Boy," Wentz called out then, his voice splitting the darkness like lightning. "It's just you and me now. Better get ready because I'm coming for you. And I'm gonna do more than make you put the lights back on."

Wentz cackled loudly in the darkness.

Pierce slowly turned the handle on the imaging lab door and

opened it without a sound. He stepped in and closed the door. He worked from memory. He took two steps toward the back of the room and then three to his right. He put his hand out and in another step touched the wall. With fingers spread wide on each hand he swept the wall — his hands making figure eight motions — until his left hand hit the hook on which hung the heat resonance goggles he had used during the presentation to Goddard that morning.

Pierce turned on the goggles, pulled the top piece over his head and adjusted the eyepieces. The room came up blue-black except for the yellow and red glow of the electron microscope's computer terminal and monitor. He reached into his pocket and pulled out the gun. He looked down at it. It too showed blue in the vision field. He put a red finger through the guard and pulled it in close to the trigger.

As he quietly pulled the lab door open Pierce saw a variety of colors in the central lab. To his left he saw the large body of Six-Eight sprawled near the mantrap door. His torso was a collage of reds and yellows tapering in his extremities to blue. He was dead and turning cold.

There was a bright red and yellow image of a man huddled against the wall to the right of the main computer station. Pierce raised the gun and aimed but then stopped himself when he remembered Rudolpho Gonsalves. The huddled man was the security guard Wentz had used to gain entrance to the lab.

He swept right and saw two more still figures, one slumped over the probe station and turning blue in the extremities. Cody Zeller. The other body was on the floor. It was red and yellow in the vision field. Renner. Alive. It looked like he had turtled backward into the kneehole of a desk. Pierce noted a high-heat demarcation on the detective's left shoulder. It was a drip pattern. The purple was warm blood leaking from a wound.

He swept left and then right. There were no other readings, save for yellow reactions off the screens of the monitors in the room and the overhead lights.

Wentz was gone.

But that was impossible. Pierce realized that Wentz must have moved into one of the side labs. Perhaps looking for a window or some sort of illumination or a place from which he could attack in ambush.

He took one step through the doorway and then suddenly hands were upon him, grabbing his throat. He was slammed backward into the wall and held there.

The vision field filled with the blaring red forehead and other-worldly eyes of Billy Wentz. The warm barrel of a gun was pressed harshly into the softness under Pierce's chin.

"Okay, Bright Boy, this is it."

Pierce closed his eyes and prepared for the bullet the best he could.

But it didn't come.

"Turn the fucking lights on and open the door."

Pierce didn't move. He realized Wentz needed his help before he could kill him. In that moment he also realized that Wentz proba-bly wasn't expecting that he would have a gun in his hand.

The hand that gripped his shirt and throat shook him violently.

"The lights, I said."

"Okay, okay. Lights."

As he said the words he brought the gun up to Wentz's temple and pulled the trigger twice. There was no other way, no other choice. The blasts were almost simultaneous and came instanta-neously to the lights in the lab suite coming on. The vision field went black and Pierce reached his other hand up and shoved the goggles off. They fell to the ground ahead of Wentz, who somehow maintained his balance for a few seconds, despite his left eye and temple having been torn away by the bullets Pierce had fired. Wentz still held the gun pointed up but it was no longer under Pierce's chin. Pierce reached out and pushed the gun back, until its aim was no longer a danger. The push also sent Wentz on his way. He fell backwards onto the floor and lay still, dead.

Pierce looked down at him for ten seconds before taking his first breath. He then collected himself and looked around. Gonsalves was getting up slowly, using the far wall to hold himself steady.

"Rudolpho, okay?"

"Yes, sir."

Pierce swung his view to the desk beneath which Renner had crawled. He could see the cop's eyes, open and alert. He was breathing heavily, the left shoulder and chest of his shirt soaked in blood.

"Rudolpho, get upstairs to a phone. Call paramedics and tell them we have a cop down. Gunshot wound."

"Yes, sir."

"Then call the police and tell them the same thing. Then call Clyde Vernon and get him in here."

The guard hustled to the mantrap door. He had to lean over Six-Eight's body to reach the combo lock. He then had to step widely over the big man's body to go through the door. Pierce saw a bullet hole in the center of the monster's throat. Renner had hit him squarely and he had gone down right in his tracks. Pierce realized he had never heard the big man speak a single word.

He moved to Renner and helped the injured detective crawl out from beneath the desk. His breathing was raspy but Pierce saw no blood on his lips. This meant his lungs were likely still intact.

"Where are you hit?"

"Shoulder."

He groaned with the movement.

"Don't move. Just wait. Help is coming."

"Hit my shooting arm. And I'm useless at distance with a gun in my right hand. I figured the best I could do was hide."

He pulled himself into a sitting position and leaned back against the desk. He gestured with his right hand toward Cody Zeller, handcuffed and slumped forward over the probe table.

"That's not going to look too good."

Pierce studied his former friend's body for a long moment. He then broke away and looked back at Renner.

"Don't worry. Ballistics will show it came from Wentz."

"Hope so. Help me up. I want to walk."

"No, man, you shouldn't. You're hurt."

"Help me up."

Pierce did as he was instructed. As he lifted Renner by the right arm he could tell the smell of carbon had permeated the man's clothes.

"What are you smiling at?" Renner asked.

"I think our plan ruined your clothes, even before the bullet. I didn't think you'd be stuck in there with the furnace so long."

"I'm not worried about it. Zeller was right, though. It does give you a headache."

"I know."

Renner pushed him away with his right hand and then walked by himself over to where Wentz's body was lying. He looked down silently for a long moment.

"Doesn't look so tough right now, does he?"

"No," Pierce said.

"You did good, Pierce. Real good. Nice trick with the lights."

"I'll have to thank my partner, Charlie. The lights were his idea."

Pierce silently promised never to complain about the gadgetry again. It reminded him of how he had held things back from Charlie, how he had been suspicious. He knew he would have to make up for it in some way.

"Speaking of partners, mine's going to shit himself when he finds out what he missed," Renner said. "And I guess I'll be headed to the shitter myself for doing this on my own."

He sat down on the edge of one of the desks and looked glumly at the bodies. Pierce realized that the detective had possibly jeopardized his career.

"Look," he said. "Nobody could have seen all of this coming. Whatever you need me to do or say, just let me know."

"Yeah, thanks. What I might need is a job."

"Well, then you've got it."

Renner moved from the desk and lowered himself into a chair. His face was screwed up from the pain. Pierce wished he could do something.

"Look, man, stop moving around, stop talking. Just wait for the paramedics."

But Renner ignored him.

"You know that stuff Zeller was talking about? About when you were a kid and you found your sister but didn't tell anybody?"

Pierce nodded.

"Don't beat yourself up on that anymore. People make their own choices. They decide what path to take. You understand?"

Pierce nodded again.

"Okay."

The door to the mantrap snapped loudly, making Pierce but not Renner jump. Gonsalves came through the door.

"They're on the way. Everybody. ETA on the ambulance is about four minutes."

Renner nodded and looked up at Pierce.

"I'll make it."

"I'm glad."

Pierce looked back at Gonsalves.

"You call Vernon?"

"Yes, he's coming."

"Okay. Wait upstairs for everybody and then bring them down."

After the security man was gone Pierce thought about how Clyde Vernon was going to react to what had happened in the laboratory he was charged with protecting. He knew that the former FBI man was going to implode with anger. He would have to deal with it. They both would.

Pierce walked over to the desk where Cody Zeller's body was sprawled. He looked down upon the man he had known for so long but now understood he hadn't really known at all. A sense of grief started to fill him. He wondered when his friend had turned in the wrong direction. Was it back at Palo Alto, when they had both made choices about the future? Or was it more recently? He had said that money was the motivation but Pierce wasn't sure the reason was as complete and definable as that. He knew it would be something that he would think about and consider for a long time to come.

He turned and looked over at Renner, who seemed to be weakening. He was leaning forward, hunched over on himself. His face was very pale.

"Are you okay? Maybe you should lie down on the floor."

The detective ignored the question and the suggestion. His mind was still working the case.

"I guess the shame of it is, they're all dead," he said. "Now we may never find Lilly Quinlan. Her body, I mean."

Pierce stepped over to him and leaned back against a desk.

"Uh, there's a few things I didn't tell you before."

Renner held his gaze for a long moment.

"I figured as much. Give."

"I know where the body is."

Renner looked at him for a long moment and then nodded.

"I should have known. How long?"

"Not long. Just today. I couldn't tell you until I was sure you would help me."

Renner shook his head in annoyance.

"This better be good. Start talking."

40

Pierce was sitting in his office on the third floor, waiting to face the detectives again. It was six-thirty Friday morning. The investigators from the county coroner's office were still down in the lab. The detectives were waiting for the all-clear signal to go down and were spending their time grilling him on the moment-by-moment details of what had happened in the basement of the building.

After an hour of that Pierce said he needed a break. He retreated from the boardroom, where the interviews were being conducted, to his office. He got no more than five minutes by himself before Charlie Condon stuck his head through the door. He had been rousted from sleep by Clyde Vernon, who had of course been rousted from sleep by Rudolpho Gonsalves.

"Henry, can I come in?"

"Sure. Close the door."

Condon came in and looked at him with a slight shake of his head, almost like a tremor.

"Wow!"

"Yeah. It's 'wow' all right."

"Anybody told you what's going on with Goddard?"

"Not really. They wanted to know where he and Bechy were staying and I told them. I think they were going to go over there and arrest them as co-conspirators or something."

"You still don't know who they worked for?"

"No. Cody didn't say. One of his clients, I assume. They'll find out, either from Goddard or when they get into Zeller's place."

Condon sat down on the couch to the side of Pierce's desk. He was not wearing his usual suit and tie and Pierce realized how much younger he looked in knockabout clothes.

"We have to start over," Pierce said. "Find a new investor."

Condon looked incredulous.

"Are you kidding? After this? Who would —"

"We're still in business, Charlie. The science is still the thing. The patent. There will be investors out there who will know this. You have to go out and do the Ahab thing. Find another great white whale."

"Easier said than done."

"Everything in this world is easier said than done. What happened to me last night and in the last week is easier said than done. But it's done. I made it through and it's given me a hotter fire than ever."

Condon nodded.

"Nobody stops us now," he said.

"That's right. We're going to take a media firestorm today and probably over the next few weeks. But we have to figure out the way to turn it to our advantage, to pull investors in, not scare them away. I'm not talking about the daily news. I'm talking about the journals, the industry."

"I'll get on it. But you know where we're going to be totally screwed?"

"Where?"

"Nicki. She was our spokesperson. We need her. She knew these people, the reporters. Who is going to handle the media on this? They'll be all over this for the next few days, at least, or until the next big thing happens to draw them away."

Pierce considered this for a few moments. He looked up at the framed poster showing the *Proteus* submarine moving through a sea of many different colors. The human sea.

"Call her up and hire her back. She can keep the severance. All she has to do is come back."

Condon paused before replying.

"Henry, how is that going to work with you two? I doubt she'll consider it."

Pierce suddenly got excited about the idea. He would tell her that the rehire was strictly professional, that they would have no other relationship outside of work. He then would show her how he had changed. How the dime chased him now, not the other way around.

He thought of the book of Chinese characters he had left open on the coffee table. Forgiveness. He decided that he could make it work. He would win her back and he would make it work.

"If you want, I'll call her. I'll get —"

His direct line rang and he immediately answered it.

"Henry, it's Jacob. It's so early there. I thought I was going to get your voice mail."

"No, I've been here all night. Did you file it?"

"I filed it twenty minutes ago. Proteus is protected. You are protected, Henry."

"Thank you, Jacob. I'm glad you went last night."

"Is everything okay back there?"

"Everything except we lost Goddard."

"Oh my gosh! What happened?"

"It's a long story. When are you coming back?"

"I'm going to go visit my brother and his family down in Owings in southern Maryland. I'll fly back Sunday."

"Do they have cable down in Owings?"

"Yes. I'm pretty sure they do."

"Keep your eye on CNN. I have a feeling we're going to light it up."

"Is there —"

"Jacob, I'm in the middle of something. I have to go. Go see your brother and get some sleep. I hate red-eye flights."

Kaz agreed and then they hung up. Pierce looked at Condon.

"We're in. He filed the package."

Condon's face lit up.

"How?"

"I sent him last night. They can't touch us now, Charlie."

Condon thought about this for a few moments and then nodded his head.

"Why didn't you tell me you were sending him?"

Pierce just looked at him. He could see the realization in Condon's face, that Pierce had not trusted him.

"I didn't know, Charlie. I couldn't talk to anybody until I knew."

Condon nodded but the hurt remained on his face.

"Must be hard. Living with all that suspicion. Must be hard to be so alone."

Now it was Pierce's turn to just nod. Condon said he was going to get some coffee and left him alone in the office.

For a few moments Pierce didn't move. He thought about Condon and what he had said. He knew his partner's words were cutting but true. He knew it was time to change all of that.

It was still early in the day but Pierce didn't want to wait to begin. He picked up the phone and called the house on Amalfi Drive.

ACKNOWLEDGMENTS

This book could not have been written without the help of Dr. James Heath, professor of chemistry, University of California, Los Angeles, and Carolyn Chriss, researcher extraordinaire. This story is fiction. However, the science contained within it is real. The race to build the first molecular computer is real. Any errors or unintended exaggerations within the story are solely the responsibility of the author.

For their help and advice the author is also indebted to Terrill Lee Lankford, Larry Bernard, Jane Davis, Robert Connelly, Paul Connelly, John Houghton, Mary Lavelle, Linda Connelly, Philip Spitzer and Joel Gotler.

Many thanks also go to Michael Pietsch and Jane Wood for going beyond the call of duty as editors with this manuscript, and as well to Stephen Lamont for the excellent copyediting.

ABOUT THE AUTHOR

Michael Connelly is a former journalist and author of the best-selling series of Harry Bosch novels, including, most recently *City of Bones,* and the bestselling novels *The Poet, Blood Work,* and *Void Moon.* Connelly has won numerous awards for his journalism and novels, including an Edgar Award.